LIES LIES LIES

Daisy and Simon's marriage is great, isn't it? After years together, the arrival of longed-for daughter Millie sealed everything in place. So what if Simon drinks a bit too much sometimes? Daisy's used to it: she knows he's just letting off steam. They are a happy little family of three — perhaps soon to be four, if Simon gets his way. But when a visit to the IVF clinic reveals disturbing information, their family life is thrust into a spiral of destruction. Has Daisy been lying all along? Simon embarks upon a steady decline as pieces of his life fall to ruin, until one night at a party things get out of control, and disaster strikes. The happy little family of three will never be the same again . . .

Books by Adele Parks
Published by Ulverscroft:

IF YOU GO AWAY
I INVITED HER IN

SPECIAL MESSAGE TO READERS

Adele Parks worked in advertising until she published the first of her many novels in 2000. Since then, her *Sunday Times* best-sellers have been translated into twenty-six languages. Adele spent her adult life in Italy, Botswana and London until 2005, when she moved to Guildford. She believes reading is a basic human right, so she works closely with The Reading Agency as an Ambassador of the Six Book Challenge, a programme designed to encourage adult literacy. Adele lives in Surrey with her husband, son and cat.

You can discover more about the author at www.adeleparks.com

ADELE PARKS

LIES LIES LIES

Complete and Unabridged

CHARNWOOD
Leicester

First published in Great Britain in 2019 by
HQ
An imprint of HarperCollins*Publishers* Ltd
London

First Charnwood Edition
published 2020
by arrangement with
HarperCollins*Publishers* Ltd
London

A catalogue record for this book is available from the British Library.

ISBN 978–1–4448–4424–5

For my dear friends Marguerite Weatherseed and Louise Gibbons. Two of the kindest people I have the privilege of knowing.

You are both simply lovely.

Prologue

May 1976

Simon was six years old when he first tasted beer.

He was bathed and ready for bed wearing soft pyjamas, even though it was light outside; still early. Other kids were in the street, playing on their bikes, kicking a football. He could hear them through the open window, although he couldn't see them because the blinds were closed. His daddy didn't like the evening light glaring on the TV screen, his mummy didn't like the neighbours looking in; keeping the room dark was something they agreed on.

His mummy didn't like a lot of things: wasted food, messy bedrooms, Daddy driving too fast, his sister throwing a tantrum in public. Mummy liked 'having standards'. He didn't know what that meant, exactly. There was a standard-bearer at Cubs; he was a big boy and got to wave the flag at the front of the parade, but his mummy didn't have a flag, so it was unclear. What was clear was that she didn't like him to be in the street after six o'clock. She thought it was common. He wasn't sure what common was either, something to do with having fun. She bathed him straight after tea and made him put on pyjamas, so that he couldn't sneak outside.

He didn't know what his daddy didn't like,

just what he did like. His daddy was always thirsty and liked a drink. When he was thirsty he was grumpy and when he had a drink, he laughed a lot. His daddy was an accountant and liked to count in lots of different ways: 'a swift one', 'a cold one', and 'one more for the road'. Sometimes Simon thought his daddy was lying when he said he was an accountant; most likely, he was a pirate or a wizard. He said to people, 'Pick your poison', which sounded like something pirates might say, and he liked to drink, 'the hair of a dog' in the morning at the weekends, which was definitely a spell. Simon asked his mummy about it once and she told him to stop being silly and never to say those silly things outside the house.

He had been playing with his Etch A Sketch, which was only two months old and was a birthday present. Having seen it advertised on TV, Simon had begged for it, but it was disappointing. Just two silly knobs making lines that went up and down, side to side. Limited. Boring. He was bored. The furniture in the room was organised so all of it was pointing at the TV which was blaring but not interesting. The news. His parents liked watching the news, but he didn't. His father was nursing a can of the grown ups' pop that Simon was never allowed. The pop that smelt like nothing else, fruity and dark and tempting.

'Can I have a sip?' he asked.

'Don't be silly, Simon,' his mother interjected. 'You're far too young. Beer is for daddies.' He thought she said 'daddies', but she might have said 'baddies'.

His father put the can to his lips, glared at his mother, cold. A look that said, 'Shut up woman, this is man's business.' His mother had blushed, looked away as though she couldn't stand to watch, but she held her tongue. Perhaps she thought the bitterness wouldn't be to his taste, that one sip would put him off. He didn't like the taste. But he enjoyed the collusion. He didn't know that word then, but he instinctively understood the thrill. He and his daddy drinking grown ups' pop! His father had looked satisfied when he swallowed back the first mouthful, then pushed for a second. He looked almost proud. Simon tasted the aluminium can, the snappy biting bitter bubbles and it lit a fuse.

After that, in the mornings, Simon would sometimes get up early, before Mummy or Daddy or his little sister, and he'd dash around the house before school, tidying up. He'd open the curtains, empty the ashtrays, clear away the discarded cans. Invariably his mother went to bed before his father. Perhaps she didn't want to have to watch him drink himself into a stupor every night, perhaps she hoped denying him an audience might take away some of the fun for him, some of the need. She never saw just how bad the place looked by the time his father staggered upstairs to bed. Simon knew it was important that she didn't see that particular brand of chaos.

Occasionally there would be a small amount of beer left in one of the cans. Simon would slurp it back. He found he liked the flat, forbidden, taste just as much as the fizzy hit of fresh beer. He'd throw open a window, so the cigarette smoke and the secrets could drift away. When his mother came downstairs, she would smile at him and thank him for tidying up.

'You're a good boy, Simon,' she'd say with some relief. And no idea.

When there weren't dregs to be slugged, he sometimes opened a new can. Threw half of it down his throat before eating his breakfast. His father never kept count.

Some people say their favourite smell is freshly baked bread, others say coffee or a campfire. From a very young age, few scents could pop Simon's nerve endings like the scent of beer.

The promise of it.

2016

1
Daisy

Thursday, 9th June 2016

I don't think it is a good idea to bring Millie here to the clinic. I've said as much to Simon on about half a dozen occasions. Besides the fact that she's missing her after-school ballet class and she'll be bored out of her mind, it isn't the sort of place children should be. There's the issue of being sensitive to the other patients for a start. It's too easy to imagine that people who are trying for a child adore every kid they encounter; it's not always the case, sometimes they outright dislike them, even adorable ones like Millie. It's too painful. Millie's tinkling chatter in the waiting room might inadvertently irritate, cause upset. It sounds extreme, but infertility is a raw and painful matter. Plus, I'm worried about what to do with her when we go into the consultancy room for a chat with the doctor. This is *only* a chat. That's all I've agreed to. Yet, I can't very well have her sit through a conversation about sperm and ovulation, the possibility (because it's not a probability) of her having a sibling. But nor am I comfortable with the idea of leaving her with the receptionist; she's just six.

We hadn't initially planned to bring her with us but at the last moment our childminding arrangements fell through, as child-minding arrangements are wont to do. We had little choice. I wanted to postpone the meeting. For ever, actually, but Simon was eager to get talking about the options and said postponing was out of the question. She would come with.

'The sooner we know what's wrong, the sooner we can get it fixed,' he said optimistically, his face alive with a big, hopeful grin.

'There's nothing wrong, we're just old,' I pointed out.

'Older. Not old. Not too old. Lots of women give birth at forty-five years of age,' he insisted. 'Some of those are first-time mothers. The fact that we've already had Millie means you're in a better position than those women.'

I think the fact that we already have Millie means we should leave the matter alone. Be content with one child. I think contentment is an extremely underrated life goal. Simon holds no truck with contentment. He likes to be deliriously happy or miserable. He'd never admit as much but we've been together seventeen years and I know him better than he knows himself. It seems to me that we have spent far too much of our married life in clinics such as this one. Places with beige walls and tempered expectations, places that take your cash and hope but can't guarantee anything in return. When we had Millie — our miracle! — I thought all this aggravation, frustration and discontent was behind us for good. One is enough for me. I had thought, hoped, it would be enough for Simon.

Millie is perfect.

We shouldn't push our luck. I've always been a 'count your blessings' sort of person. I don't want an embarrassment of riches, I prefer to scrape under the radar with a sufficiency. Simon and I do not think alike on this. Obviously, he agrees Millie is perfect. For him, it's her very perfection that's driving him to want to make more babies.

For the last couple of years, more or less since Millie started pre-school, Simon has been saying we ought to try again. I've nodded, smiled, acknowledged his suggestion without entering into any sort of real discussion. I mean, in a way we are trying, at least we're not avoiding the possibility — we don't use contraception. However, at our age, with our history, that's not trying hard enough. We'd have to get some help if we want a second child. I know that. Recently, Simon has significantly upped the ante in terms of his persistence with this idea. He can't seem to just enjoy what we have.

Half term is a good example. We took a cottage in Devon because British families have been doing so for generations and, evidently, we lack the necessary imagination to buck the trend. This year we took a chance, selecting a new part of Devon that we hadn't previously visited. The cottage was dated but well-scrubbed, and whilst the water pressure made showering a slow and disappointing process, there was an open fire, an Aga and a shelf of jigsaws and board games, so we thought the place was perfect. The garden fell away to a footpath that led directly to the beach. I'm always surprised by beaches. They're never as restful or ideal for contemplation as I imagine. British beaches are noisy places: waves crash, seagulls squawk, the wind scrapes the sand, and children laugh, cry and shriek. It's best to accept this, embrace it. We're keen to offer Millie every opportunity that might be presented in an Enid Blyton novel so despite the sometimes iffy weather, we took long walks and endured breezy picnics without admitting to the chill. We went crabbing and scoured rock pools for mini creatures that delighted Millie. We were just a short drive away from a petting farm and a small village packed with pastel-coloured buildings, where every second shop sold fish and chips. Yes, perfect.

It was hardly a retreat though. The place was too picturesque to remain a secret. Indeed, we'd discovered it because it was featured in a glossy Sunday newspaper supplement. Yet despite the identikit families dressed in Boden, trailing plastic buckets and spades, we managed to carve out some privacy, some time to ourselves. We ignored the crowds and the queues, and we drew a magic circle around us. Naturally, Millie made friends with other children on the beach. She's confident, open and pretty, just the sort of kid other kids like to befriend, but when the parents of her new acquaintances invited us to join them for a scone at the café or a barbecue in their rental, we declined. We made up excuses, told small lies about already having plans and commitments. I'm not at all like Millie, I'm not confident about making new friends, I never have been. I was never what anyone would have considered a pretty girl. It's not the worst thing in the world, although some people seem to think it is. As a child, I concentrated on being kind and funny, well informed, with aspirations of being thought of as reasonably clever. It was enough. I got by. I have great friends now but I'm not a fan of making casual, transient relationships on holiday. Why bother? Besides, we were so blissful, just the three of us, we didn't want or need anyone else. Three is the perfect number. Fun facts: the Pythagoreans thought that the number three was the first true number. Three is the first number that forms a geometrical figure, the triangle. Three is considered the number of harmony, wisdom and understanding. I've always thought that three is particularly significant as it's the number that is most often associated with time: past, present, future; beginning, middle, end; birth, life, death.

I sigh, glancing around the fertility clinic reception, I really don't think we need to be here, trying for another baby. It's like we're pushing our luck. Being greedy. Asking for trouble. We're happy as we are.

Simon squeezes my hand. I think of the last night in the cottage. Millie was exhausted after a week of fresh air and long walks, she almost nodded off at the kitchen table over supper. We got her to bed by 7 p.m. and she was asleep the moment her head hit the pillow. Simon suggested we have a glass of wine in the back garden, make the most of our last night and the privacy that our cottage offered. There was a gas heater, one of those that's bad for the environment so I demurred, but Simon persuaded me, 'Just once. Go with it.'

Let's just say, the wine (not a glass but two bottles in the end) and the sound of the sea crashing on the beach, the novelty of spending time alone together without other people or even Netflix, had an effect. We made love under the stars and a blanket. It was exciting, daring. The last time we did anything as risky was so long ago I can't remember when it was exactly. Years and years ago. Afterwards, we lay snuggled up under the slightly scratchy picnic blanket, clinging to one another for warmth, and just allowed ourselves to be. Be relaxed. Be satisfied. Be enough. It was blissful. Until Simon kissed the top of my head and said, 'Do you know the one and only thing that could make this moment more perfect?'

'A post-coital cigarette?' I joked. I've never been a smoker and Simon gave up when we first started dating. I know he still misses it, even after all this time he craves the nicotine hit. Simon likes hits and highs. I don't get it at all. I'm not the sort of person who values kicks above health.

'Well, that would be good, but no. I was thinking a baby, asleep in the other room.'

'We have a baby asleep in the other room.'

'We have a little girl,' he said gently, not unkindly.

'Well, they can't stay babies for ever.'

'That's not my point.'

I felt the warmth of his body along the length

of mine and yet I still shivered. 'You're serious?'

'I love Millie so much. And you,' he added swiftly. 'I can't bear to think that we're not giving her everything.'

'We do give her everything we can,' I pointed out.

'Other than a sibling,' he countered.

'Yeah but it's not as though we tried to deny her that, it just hasn't happened. It's unlikely ever to because neither of us are getting any younger.' And conceiving was never something we were good at. I don't add that. We don't talk about the horrors we went through to get Millie. It's generally agreed that the pain of childbirth is forgotten once you hold the baby in your arms. In my case it was also the pain of years of trying to conceive.

'We should make it happen. She's so gregarious and loving. I can't bear the idea of her missing out on having a sibling.'

'Having a sibling isn't always a bonus,' I argued. 'You're not at all close to your sister.'

'No, but you adore yours. I want Millie to have what you and Rose share.' He turned to me and I saw fire in his eyes. I should have understood then that he wasn't going to let the matter drop. He's a very determined man when he wants to be.

Stubborn, my mum says.

2
Simon

The waiting room was chilly. The air-conditioning was a little too vigorous. It was bright outside so people had risked T-shirts and sun dresses, except for Daisy, she always felt the cold so she was sitting in her jacket. It looked like she was ready to make a dash for the door at any moment. It looked like a protest. Simon knew Daisy didn't want to be there. He understood. He remembered the heartache associated with these sorts of places, certainly he did. And she was right, they were perfectly happy as they were, but his point was that maybe they could be happier still. Why not? Why settle?

When bored, or nervous, or stressed, Simon had a habit of repeatedly tapping the heel of his foot on the floor. This had the effect of causing his whole leg to continually jerk in violent shudders. He never noticed he was doing it until Daisy reached out and put her hand on his thigh, calming him, silently asking him to stop. She did exactly that now. He stopped, picked up a newspaper and quickly flicked through it. There was nothing to hold his attention. Just reports of financial crises and politicians caught with their pants down, nothing new there. He put down the paper and started to whistle. He wasn't aware that he was doing so until Millie giggled and began dancing to his tune, probably saving him from a swift reprimand from Daisy. Daisy always forgave his restlessness, his quirkiness, if it entertained Millie. Despite the vicious air-con he felt clammy. He could feel sweat prickle under his arms. God, he could do with a drink.

He had persuaded Daisy here to visit the clinic on the understanding that they were just going to have a chat with Dr Martell, one of the country's best fertility doctors, or reproductive endocrinologists, to give him the proper name. They were simply going to ask about their options, explore possibilities. That's what he'd told her. But he'd lied. He'd already visited Martell ten days ago for a general health check, as well as a specific test of the health and fitness of his sperm. He wanted to get things moving. Many years ago, he had been told that his sperm was slow but in the end that hadn't been a problem. It had been a case of the tortoise and the hare, Millie was proof of that. However, Daisy made a good point, he was aware that he was seven years older now than when they had conceived Millie, they both were, obviously. That didn't necessarily mean they were out of the game though, did it? Simon was keen to know if there had been any scientific advancements since then, something that could give his boys a bit of an advantage, if you got the gist — or at least something that might level the playing field again. He was forever reading articles about the increase in the number of women having babies in later life. He thought that by taking the initiative and putting himself through the tests first, Daisy would be encouraged. He knew it was a lot to ask. The tests and possible subsequent treatments Daisy might require were significantly more arduous than anything he'd have to endure. IVF had been a slog. But it would be worth it.

He stopped whistling, but Millie didn't stop dancing. She was in a world of her own, clearly the music continued in her head. Maybe she was listening to a full orchestra. Maybe she was on stage at the Paris Opera House. She was a marvel! Millie had an incredible, exceptional talent. She danced beautifully. She was the sort of child who naturally bounced, flew and glided through her day. Daisy often commented that she was in awe of her daughter, as she hadn't been the sort of girl that anyone ever suggested ought to take dancing lessons: her nickname as a child — as bestowed on her by her family — was Fairy Elephant. She lolloped and lumbered, rather clumsily. As a boy, Simon had never been taken to dance lessons either, his family were far too conventional to consider that, but he liked to think he had been pretty good at throwing shapes on the dancefloor (a phrase he used self-satirically); certainly, he was good at sport in general. He'd always thought that Millie had inherited her natural ability to dance from his side of the family, his sister had been a great gymnast and was quite good at tap as a child. She was certainly good at doing flits, thought Simon with a sigh. His sister had announced she was emigrating to Canada about a month after their mother was diagnosed with Alzheimer's. He kept telling himself it was a coincidence, but he didn't know for sure. It was certainly an inconvenience, that he was certain of.

Millie adored all things frilly, pretty, floaty and twirling. Daisy had started her at dance classes just before she turned three. It's not that Daisy was a particularly annoying, overly-ambitious mother, it was simply that Millie needed to channel her energy and desire to coil and whirl somewhere. It turned out she was very good, quite extraordinarily so. Her dance tutor said that in all her nineteen years of teaching, she had never seen equivalent talent, focus and drive in a child so young. Daisy was a teacher — not a dance teacher but a Year Six teacher at a state primary school — and she was aware of the value of that observation. She'd excitedly told Simon that teachers had to be very careful about what they said to parents, as parents all tended to get a little carried away. Everyone believed they'd produced a spectacular little miracle, when in fact most kids were within a recognised range.

Although, evidently Millie *was* a spectacular little miracle.

Simon's eyes followed her around the waiting room; she was on her tiptoes scampering, arms aloft, like ribbons, chin jutting at an elegant angle. An adorable mix of childish abandonment and earnest concentration. Everyone in the room stared at her with an intensity almost equal to his, it was impossible not to. The emotions she triggered varied: amusement, delight, longing. Daisy looked torn, somewhere between jubilant and embarrassed. She'd said she thought it was tactless bringing a child to a fertility clinic, as though they were showing off.

'We don't need to rub their noses in it,' she'd warned. Simon thought her turn of phrase was amusing, quaint. He thought Millie's presence in the waiting room had to be inspiring. Other parents would be encouraged. There was no doubt, she was special. For sure, they had to go in for another one. Millie might very well become a prima ballerina at the Royal Ballet, why not? Who knows what else they could produce: an astronaut, the next Steve Jobs, the person who finds the cure for cancer. Or even, simply a pleasant person who was nice to their neighbours, remained faithful to their partner, became an interested parent. It was life. Life! What was more important than that? You had to try, didn't you? You had to.

Millie danced every single day. She was crabby if she missed a class, even on holidays she carved out a couple of hours practice time. She was just six, but was that dedicated. It was astounding. Aspirational. Her existence was wall-to-wall pink tulle. When she started school she'd had meltdowns every day and, at first, Simon and Daisy had been confused and troubled as to why. 'Do you have friends, Millie?', 'Is your teacher kind to you?', 'Do you like the lunches?', 'Can you find your coat peg?' they'd asked, wracking their brains to imagine any possible irritation or upset.

‘Yes, yes, yes, yes,’ she’d spluttered through distressed tears.

‘Then what is the matter?’ Simon had asked, exasperated, tense. He’d taken the morning off work to be with Daisy when they tried to persuade Millie to go into her classroom.

‘The uniform is ugly!’ She’d howled. ‘It’s green. I want it pink.’ Her explanation, hiccupped out indignantly, had only made Simon laugh. Daisy ultimately solved the matter by sewing a pink ribbon all around the inside hem of Millie’s school skirt. An act that Simon always thought was a display of pure brilliance and devotion.

‘I feel very uncomfortable taking Millie into the consultation room,’ Daisy whispered. ‘She’ll understand enough of what we are talking about to be interested. I don’t want to get her hopes up that there’s a sibling on the way.’ Because Simon had just been thinking about the hand sewn pink ribbon, he was more inclined to indulge Daisy.

‘OK, well how about I go in first and hear what he has to say and then you pop in after me.’

‘Won’t that take twice as long?’ Daisy looked anxiously about her. There were two other couples in the waiting room. They may or may not have been waiting to see Dr Martell. ‘I’d feel awful if we overran.’

‘We’re paying for it, so you don’t have to worry.’

‘It’s impolite.’ Daisy had a heightened regard for being polite. Simon sometimes found that charming, other times he found it frustrating.

‘Well what do you suggest? Leaving would also be impolite.’

Daisy nodded. 'I suppose.'

At that moment a smartly-dressed nurse appeared, she had a clipboard and clipped tones; she oozed efficiency. 'Mr and Mrs Barnes?'

Simon stood up, kissed Daisy on the top of the head. 'Don't look so worried. This is the start of a wonderful adventure,' he told her. 'Love you.'

3

Daisy

The moment Simon vacates his seat, Millie bounces into it, although she still doesn't settle. Instead, she holds her legs out in front of her and repeatedly points her toes up to the ceiling, then stretches them out. I love her energy. She's delicate and yet strong, a winning combination. I was a robust child. Hefty. By the time I was fourteen I hit five foot ten, not a lithe beanpole model-in-the-making five foot ten but large, ungainly, always-in-the-way five foot ten. My arms were as wide as other girls' waists, my breasts seemed to loll around my tummy like some old woman's. I hope puberty is kinder to Millie. I worry that she will inherit my height. That wouldn't be ideal for a ballerina unless she dances in Russia, they like them tall there, but I don't want her to go to Russia. I do worry that by encouraging her to dance I'm basically pursuing a fast-track path to body dysmorphia. But Millie is quite unlike me. As a girl I had glasses and spots, orange hair, freckled skin and the wrong clothes. Even when I had the right clothes they looked wrong on me. It's just the way it is for some people. We can't all be born beautiful.

The good thing about being forty-five is that all that angst about how I look is behind me. I've learnt how to accept myself, make the most of myself, that's what women like me must do. However, I live in awe of my child. Sweet, yet certain. I look at her and I know I've done something right. No matter what.

Before Millie came along, we endured a decade of longing for a baby. Most young, happily married couples wait a few years before they turn their attention to baby-making, I was faster off the blocks. By the time I met Simon, my sister Rose was already the mother of two adorable boys — twins! I realised to make any impact at all on my parents, in terms of providing grandchildren, I'd have to get cracking and ideally produce a daughter. I'm joking, I wasn't motivated to procreate by the innate competitiveness that exists between siblings, I simply adore children and I longed to be a mother. As a young girl I played with dolls, nothing else, I wasn't interested in Play-Doh, colouring books or Lego, for me it was all about pretending to be a mummy. I started babysitting my little cousins when I was twelve and then for various neighbours by the time I was fifteen. I'm a primary school teacher. I like children, the cheeky, boisterous or mischievous types, the shy, arty or cuddly types. I'll take any of them.

I threw away my pill packet the morning we got married. It was one of the most exciting things about the day. For the first few months, I didn't allow myself to be at all concerned when I still got my period. I was busy putting our house together. We'd bought a one-bedroom flat in North London, I was occupied with hanging pictures, picking out furniture, getting a washing machine plumbed in. It was all so new and exhilarating. Back then, every dull chore seemed like such a delicious treat. Adulting was a novelty. I found it thrilling that I was allowed to slob around in pyjamas all day on a wet, wintery Sunday, that I was allowed to say the words 'my husband', and I was allowed to go with said husband to Tesco Metro at 9 p.m. to buy a tub of Ben & Jerry's ice cream, if we so desired. We were in charge of our time and finances, we were a couple. Such thrilling freedom. We were just waiting for the next bit to start.

On our first wedding anniversary, I started to feel qualms of unease. I'd held this secret little fantasy that I'd be announcing our pregnancy that day. I was a month off my thirty-first birthday, Simon was just thirty-two, still young. But, even so. We made an appointment with our local GP. The doctor laughed, told us we had plenty of time ahead of us, told us to relax. When I pushed him, 'Is there anything I can do?' he checked I didn't smoke, suggested I cut back on alcohol, 'Start preparing your body if you want to. You don't need to deprive yourself, though. Don't be silly about it. Just get healthy. Exercise, consider yoga. Everything will be fine. You've nothing to worry about.'

I wanted to do anything and everything I could to chivvy along the process. I took folic acid, I started to meditate, I stopped drinking altogether. Simon picked up the slack. Instead of sharing a bottle over a meal, he started to polish one off on his own. I didn't mind, he was funny and relaxed when drunk. I'm not saying he was usually uptight, but he is quite a reserved man in some ways. Most comfortable in a one-to-one situation.

On our second anniversary I suggested he too might like to stop drinking. That maybe we needed to go back to the doctors and get some tests done. He agreed to the tests.

They examined my fertility first. I don't know why, maybe because medically women are more often the cause for concern, or maybe it's just sexist. I wasn't surprised when the tests came back and said I was to blame for our problems. I had fibroids: non-cancerous, oestrogen-dependent benign tumours, growing in my uterus. These tumours cause pelvic pain and heavy menstrual bleeding. They can also cause infertility. It was recommended that I have a myomectomy to remove them. We did that, another two years passed, we still didn't get pregnant, so we saw another doctor. She recommended that they run some tests on Simon too. I couldn't believe it when the results came back. He also had problems. Sluggish and poor-quality sperm. We were both to blame.

It was a very difficult time. It seemed that we looked at one another in a slightly different light. I didn't want to, but I found myself thinking he was a little less perfect, not quite so golden; I realised that he'd probably been thinking as much about me for a while.

My story, our story, is not particular or peculiar. Everyone knows someone who has struggled with infertility. The very regularity of the story is a tragedy. We started IVF shortly after our fifth wedding anniversary. It takes its toll. I think any couple who has been through it would agree. When we'd been trying to conceive naturally we'd still had a bit of fun, we'd tried different positions, we'd had lots of sex. IVF was not fun. There's no sex involved — well, other than the thing Simon had to do into a pot. I don't think jerking off to porn counts as sex after the age of about fourteen.

I can't bear being in this room. True, we have never visited Dr Martell before, but we've been to enough similar clinics that it makes me feel tired and sad. I reach over to Millie and brush her hair out of her eyes with my hand. I want to lean into her, cover her in kisses, but I resist. I have to try very hard not to smother her in love. There's such a thing as too much. She's confident, content, happy practicing her points. I leave her to it.

When we were going through IVF, I started to think of my body as the enemy. As I mentioned, I've never had the sort of body that filled me with pride, but it had, up until the infertility point, been functional. I'm not often sick, I've never broken a bone, but suddenly it was failing me. Even after four financially and emotionally costly bouts of IVF, my body failed me.

People kept telling me that I should think about something else. 'Don't worry, it will happen!' my friend Connie would say cheerfully. She'd then tell me a story about someone she'd known for years who had given up trying altogether when bang, it happened, she conceived. My mum kept telling me to, 'Take up a hobby. Forget about this business for a while.' Rose suggested a holiday. 'Relax!'

They meant well.

Simon and I would smile, nod, agree. We didn't point out that we didn't have any spare cash to spend on a holiday, repeated rounds of IVF had cleaned out or savings. Rather than taking up hobbies, we were giving them up. Simon played less golf, he'd left his club, the fees were expensive. He said he'd go back to it, but it never happened. It was put on hold. Many things were. We were in limbo. Waiting. The advice was hollow, irritating. Alone together, Simon and I didn't bother to pretend to believe in it. Simon knew my cycle as well as I did. On the day my period was due our house was awash with a terrible expectancy and fear. When I came on, which I did with cruel regularity, I'd simply say, 'Not this month', and he'd say, 'Next time.' Neither of us believed him.

At that point I think we were close to giving up, not only on conceiving, but maybe even on our marriage too. Wanting something that much is damaging. Longing nudges so easily into despair. I didn't know what to do. I was prepared to do anything.

But then everything changed. It happened, just when I thought I had no more reserves of hope. Millie was a miracle. Conceived without any medical intervention.

A miracle. She saved us.

4

Simon

Habit meant that Simon glanced around the office with an interior designer's eye. He could see where the exorbitant consultancy fees were going. Dr Martell sat behind a huge mahogany desk with a superb, mellow antique patina. It wasn't his specialist area, but Simon would date the desk at about 1880. French. It was well figured with a brass inlay, brass mouldings and beadings and shallow bun feet. You wouldn't get much change from £3,000. Behind Dr Martell was row after impressive row of expensive-looking shelves that housed fat, daunting leather-bound medical books. Simon would bet money on them being first editions in many cases. The floor was a polished parquet, his trainers landed on a rich, woollen Persian rug. It was of incredible quality; all the natural dyes had held their exquisite jewel colours. The pile was thick and soft; it was like stepping on velvet. It was about the same age as the desk. You didn't step on a Saruk Ferahan rug in the NHS, thought Simon. The doctor stood up, shook hands and then gestured towards one of the two seats that were placed side by side, facing across the desk.

'Your wife joining us?' The consultant's voice tolled like a bell announcing his expensive education at Westminster, then Cambridge.

'She's just out there with our daughter. We didn't want to bring Millie in here.'

The doctor nodded, an efficient bob of the head; he understood and didn't want to spend any more time on the matter. He opened the file on the desk and started talking.

Simon had heard a lot of the words before. They burnt his ears; the heat of the sting hadn't gone away even after all these years. Even after Millie. Asthenospermia, motility, zona pellucida binding. He had been quite good at science at school, but he quickly became lost. He was trying to concentrate, although annoyingly he found he was drifting in and out, hearing the words but not absolutely one hundred per cent making sense of them. Not quite able to string them together. This did happen to him from time to time. Occasionally in client meetings, after a lunchtime jar, or when Daisy was telling him something about his mother. He didn't mean to lose track. It just happened. *Percentage motile concentration, average path velocity, non-progressive motility*. He wanted to get to the bit where the doctor asked if he had any questions, because he did. One. 'Would there be another miracle?' That was all that mattered, that cut through all these big words and small percentages.

Non-progressive motility though? That couldn't be good. It had the damning prefix 'non'. The doctor continued to intone, Simon reminded himself just how much this consultation had cost and redoubled his efforts to concentrate, to take it in.

'It is estimated that one in twenty men has some kind of fertility problem with low numbers of sperm in his ejaculate. However, only about one in every one hundred men has no sperm in his ejaculate.' The doctor used these words without a trace of embarrassment, of course he did. It was exactly like Simon using the words 'colour palette', 'tactile fabrics', or 'commanding wall feature'.

'So, you have non-progressive motility, which is as I mentioned, defined as anything less than five micrometers per second. That combined with your low sperm count presents us with some difficulties, I'm afraid.'

'What is the motility rate of my sperm then?' Simon asked.

'One point five.'

Oh. It sounded bad. 'And the other thing? The sperm count. What's the range there?'

'WHO normal range is 15 to 213 million cells per ml.'

Simon nodded but it meant nothing to him. 15 to 213 *million*. That was quite a range.

'And mine is?'

'Two.' Martell had the decency to meet Simon's eye. Two million. Not hopeless then. You only needed one, didn't you? Were cells the same thing as sperm? He didn't know. He should ask. The expression on the consultant's face was one of stern concentration. Simon searched it for optimism, assurance, there was none. Martell continued, 'I understand that this is not news to you, Mr Barnes. I realise that our tests simply confirmed what you discovered ten or so years ago. The difference being, we can give you more reliable data on the exact numbers now. We can be more precise about the diagnosis.'

'But things can be done, right? There are advancements,' Simon asserted. 'Cooling the testicles, separating out the good guys. I've read about it.'

'There are cases where things can be done. I'm afraid your readings don't place you in that bracket.'

'What are my chances? Put a percentage to it. Go on, don't worry I won't hold you to it. It won't be legally binding.' Simon laughed at the phrase as though the very suggestion was ridiculous. He knew he had to make the consultant feel at ease. He was surprised the man was being so cautious. His previous experience had been that if there was any hope at all the doctors would push ahead. Often, they were always doom and gloom, always presenting the worst-case scenarios but they still took your money. 'What are we talking about? A four per cent chance? Two, one?' Simon watched as the doctor became increasingly awkward. He dropped his gaze, tapped his fingers on the ostentatious desk. He was able to say 'ejaculate' all day long, but he couldn't talk about this percentage. 'We can pay,' Simon added. It wouldn't be easy but they'd find the money, he'd already decided that.

The consultant sighed quietly and leaned forward in his chair. 'Mr Barnes, you cannot impregnate your wife. You are sterile.'

The word was a fucking weapon. He was no longer capable of fathering a child. The thought exploded in Simon's head. Why? What had happened? Had his sperm quality, or quantity, or mobility or *whatever* deteriorated?

Before he could form the words to ask, Martell said brightly, 'There are options. If you want to extend your family, I would recommend you consider sperm donation, as you did before. That worked out splendidly last time, didn't it?'

'I'm sorry I don't understand.'

The consultant reached for the file. 'It says here you had four rounds of in vitro fertilization. I assumed Millie was conceived that way, correct? I assume with a donor.'

'No.' Simon brightened, realising the doctor was missing an essential piece of information. Despite the odds, Millie had been conceived naturally. He was also irritated; he was paying enough, the least Martell could do was get the facts straight. He tried to be patient as he explained, 'You see that's where you're wrong. She was conceived naturally. Against the odds. Which goes to show I *can* do it. We can. We had been doing IVF. Yeah, like you say, four attempts but — '. Simon stopped talking. There was something different in Martell's face. Not just seriousness, now there was a flash of unease, alarm.

'I had thought a donor, but if not a donor then maybe a lab mix-up. These things do happen, I'm afraid. They are rarely acknowledged but they do. That would have been regrettable, an inquiry would have been necessary, but you are telling me that she wasn't conceived by IVF.'

'Yes, that's right. She was conceived months

after a failed attempt. We weren't even sure we were going to try again.'

'I see.'

'What do you see?' Simon demanded.

Dr Martell sighed slightly. It was a breath that offered a level of apology, or regret. 'All I can say, Mr Barnes, is that with the results here in front of me, it is my professional opinion that a donor would be the only way your wife could conceive.'

Simon began to feel the irritation grow into something bigger. Resentment. Anger. 'Well the results are wrong.'

'We can re-run the tests. Certainly.' The doctor said it like a man who was confident that the results were correct. He brought the tips of his fingers together and placed his chin in his hands. He waited a moment until Simon understood.

'No, no you fucking idiot. *I'm* her dad.' Dr Martell didn't say a word. 'Fuck you, you quack. You've got it wrong. Do you hear me? You've got it wrong!'

Simon stood up and stormed out of the office. The violence with which he flung open the door meant it swung back on its hinges and banged against the wall, causing the pictures of ancient frigates to shiver.

5

Daisy

Friday, 17th June 2016

Millie's recital starts in ten minutes, 5.30 p.m. A time that does, I suppose, acknowledge that the vast majority of the performers are under the age of nine, but does not take into account that the vast majority of the performers' parents work, and commuting isn't easy at this hour. Millie and I came straight from school. I'm lucky that my daughter attends the school I teach at. I'll need to do a heap of marking later tonight, and I had to swap my after-school club duties, but we were able to have a quick tea on the high street and still get here in plenty of time. I'm on the front row. There's an empty seat next to me that I've saved for Simon. I've had to guard it quite ferociously. One woman even had the audacity to point out that the dance teacher's rules (sent out prior to the concert) specifically stated that the saving of seats was prohibited. I pointed out that I wasn't saving *seats*, simply *a seat* and therefore didn't feel the spirit of the rule had been broken. I felt the tips of my ears burn as I said this, yet I held my ground. I then called Simon, again, to chivvy him along, but it went straight through to voicemail. I hope that means he's on the tube, on his way.

Before Millie started primary school Simon and I debated whether it was a wise move for her to attend the same school as the one I teach at. We debated the issue for many months. He'd read some report or other about children being either bullied or spoilt if their parents went down this route. He said it might be suffocating for her and tricky for me. True, it can be embarrassing for a child if they bring home a friend for a playdate and that friend is confused to see their teacher out of the classroom and in the home, but I teach Year Six, not reception. By the time she reaches Year Six all her friends will have adjusted to the fact that I'm their teacher *and* Millie's mother. I also understand that there could potentially be a problem if some of her teachers found it uncomfortable knowing I am in such close proximity, but I'd never dream of interfering. I know the boundaries. I told Simon that I'd always put school trip money in an envelope, put forms in her book bag like other parents. I didn't plan on collaring her teacher in the staffroom and asking for a progress report.

For me, the plus factors regarding her attending the same school were overwhelmingly positive and outweighed any potential negatives. Firstly, I love my school. Newfield Primary is friendly, small enough to be manageable but big enough to be inclusive and representative. The staff are dedicated and approachable. It always scores pretty well on the Ofsted report (good rather than outstanding, but that's more than respectable). Millie and I sharing a schedule makes things easier when it comes to drop off, pick up and school holidays. I immediately get to hear if she's sick or hurt and I never miss her school assemblies or sports day. Besides, quite simply, I like having her close by. That's the most important thing. I waited long enough for her. Now I drink up every moment. I promised Simon I'd be vigilant to bullying, alert to any favouritism, and I put Newfield Primary as my first choice on the application form. Then I crossed my fingers. We are in the catchment area. We got lucky.

On days like this I'm so glad I pushed for us to be at the same school. Since Millie has started to dance I've come to understand just how serious her performances are, at least to her, her dance teacher, and a fair amount of the attending parents. I wouldn't miss it for the world. Not that I'm enjoying myself today, at least not yet. I sit, stiff-backed and self-conscious. I wish Simon would get here soon; my handbag looks bolshie on the spare seat. I wonder where the woman who asked me to give it up is sitting. I daren't turn around to locate her. I nervously check my phone every ten seconds, hoping for news from Simon. Once the performance starts I'll have to turn it off, not put it on silent, because if a message flashes up on the screen, the light is incredibly bright and can be distracting to other audience members, possibly even to the dancers on stage. It said so on the rule list. In capitals. The list terrifies me. I read it and memorised it as though it's been brought down the mountain on two tablets of stone. Generally I really am a rule follower. As a teacher I know rules are set for a reason.

I've left Simon's ticket at the box office for collection. We've been informed that the recital is designed to flow seamlessly between performance pieces and so we were firmly instructed not to enter or exit unless it is an emergency. To give some clarity to what constituted an emergency, we were briefed that if there is a 'fussy child' in the audience, said child was to be exited as quickly and quietly as possible. The rules list actually used that phrase, 'fussy child', like something out of a nineteenth-century novel. We were also advised (warned) that the intermission was the opportunity to chat or eat. Considering all this, I can't imagine that Simon will be admitted once the curtain rises. There was an instruction that we aren't to take photos, although there is to be a professional DVD made that can be purchased at a later date. I think he'll have to make do with that.

Despite the rather draconian list of rules, people around me seem genuinely excited. Many parents are clasping bouquets of flowers or single stems of roses. I have a small bouquet made up of six fat, soft pink roses and sprigs of baby's breath. It's a tradition to present your dancer with flowers to recognise the effort and achievement of having performed in front of a large audience. Besides, everyone loves receiving flowers.

The lights dim, and the music starts up. I feel a surge of excitement that the show is about to begin and a sting of disappointment and irritation that Simon is going to miss it. A chain of little girls dressed as daisies scurry onto the stage. They are all about three years old and what they lack in ability, they more than make up in sheer cuteness factor. The audience 'ooh' and 'aah' volubly, the girls can barely hear the music over the audible swooning. This lot are too little to manage anything more than a bit of twirling, even the planned simultaneous raising of their arms ends up looking like a Mexican wave, but that in no way diminishes the pleasure the audience derive from the performance. When the daisies finish and dip into sweet little curtsys or simply wander off the stage because they've had enough, we burst into raucous applause. Some parents even stand up. A few flashes pop, the rapturous delight has emboldened one or two parents to break the rules. I look to the door and will Simon to slip through it. It stays resolutely shut. I wonder whether he's the other side of it. Trapped. Or somewhere else entirely. A pub. Maybe.

The next group runs onto the stage. Most are dressed as icicles; silver and white, they sparkle and shine. The word 'Frozen' shimmies up and down the rows of spectators. Sometimes it's said with a self-satisfied enthusiasm — a treat delivered — sometimes it's said with a hint of boredom. I have to admit to having seen hundreds of performances of *Frozen*, it's a stalwart favourite in most dance teacher's repertoires. The cute factor intensifies. These little children (mostly girls but two boys) are still fairly unskilled but they are trying so hard. Their faces are scrunched in concentration as they point their toes or bend their bodies to one side, it's impossible not to melt. I risk sharing the observation with the woman sat next to me — well, it's tricky attending these things and not having someone to enthuse with. She nods and comments, 'Good pun.'

I hadn't intended a pun and feel a little embarrassed that she thinks of me as the sort of mother who tries that hard.

Millie's group are next up on stage. The girls are wearing pink tutu dresses with ballet tights and ballet shoes, the one and only boy is wearing shorts and T-shirt and ballet shoes. They are only five to six years old, but they are considerably more in control of their bodies than the last groups; all but one seem to be following the choreographed pattern. They manage to alternate hands on waist, hands above the head, they leap (although not all at once) and they twirl (only one girl looks precariously close to falling off the stage). By this age, most have stopped waving to their parents if they spot them in the audience. About two minutes into the dance Millie has a small solo piece. She has rehearsed this endlessly. I know she's my daughter and I'm biased, but once she starts to leap, other parents gasp with admiration. She's simply enchanting. Her arms flutter like streamers in the wind as she executes artful, mesmerising and deliberate moves. Her toes are pointed, she angles her legs, torso and head with precision, and she morphs into something other than a little girl on a stage; she is the butterfly she's portraying. Everyone stares at her: the other dancers on the stage who are kneeling in a circle around her, the parents, grandparents, the pianist, the ballet teacher. She doesn't notice us. She doesn't scan the audience to catch my eye, she doesn't look to the teacher or the pianist for the lead or the beat, she simply allows the performance to run through her. She's everything every little girl wants to be: strong and beautiful. She elegantly extends her legs, points her toes and throws her arms wide as she commits to a leap. She sails through the air as though she has wings and then the hall door slams open. The noise ricochets through the room.

Most people can't help themselves, it's instinctive, they swivel their heads, attention pulls away from Millie and rests on her father. I hear him say, 'I have a fucking ticket.' Swearing is rife in the circles we mix in, holding back is seen as prudish and lower middle class. Still, I'm mortified. I guess I'm prudish and lower middle class. I don't turn. I keep my eyes trained on Millie and watch her as she lands, not quite as gracefully as I've seen her in do in rehearsals. I notice her eyes slip to the doorway for a fraction of a second. She's no longer in a garden, a butterfly flitting from flower to flower, she's a little girl with an embarrassing daddy.

The children scamper across the stage, toes pointed, legs stretched in front of them, a light, elegant pitter-patter. All I am aware of are his heavy footsteps slamming on the wooden floor as he threads his way towards the front of the hall. Why hasn't he slipped into a seat at the back? I can hear him repeatedly say, 'Sorry, 'scuse me, can I get past?' He sounds impatient, a little sarcastic. His words are slurred.

At the interval, we stand in a frosty silence. Simon is swaying slightly. We have nothing to say to one another. Only the kindest of the mothers try to talk to us.

'The costumes are quite something aren't they?' says Ellie's mum.

'The Year Twos looked like hookers,' replies Simon.

I blush and sip my tea. Ellie's mum pretends she's seen someone else she knows that she needs to have a word with.

Delia's mum picks up the mantel. 'I love this troupe.' It's just a ballet class, not a troupe, but it seems rude to correct her. 'It's so inclusive. Rather lovely that all the children have been given roles, even though they don't all have rhythm. You are lucky. Millie is so incredibly talented. If Delia had as much ability in her big toe I'd be thrilled, we just come here for the exercise really.' She smiles at Simon. I think she's trying to say something outrageous to draw attention away from his behaviour. It's lovely of her but it won't work. A modest grumble about your own kid's mediocrity, whilst said kid is out of earshot, is nothing compared to interrupting the recital.

Delia reminds me of myself as a child. She looks uncomfortable in a leotard on stage. She looks uncomfortable full stop. Her mother thinks she's helping her confidence by putting her on stage, but I think Delia would be happier at

Brownies or in the library.

'Which one is Delia?' Simon asks.

'She is in Millie's group. She was on the far right hand side, most of the time. She's very tall.'

Simon snorts, 'Oh yeah. I know her. I think you're wasting your money.' Delia's mum blushes. Simon is acting as though he doesn't know the parent script, or at least if he does, he can't be bothered to follow it. He's supposed to say her performance was charming, that she was enthusiastic and full of character. I'm only glad he didn't call her fat. Delia's mother says she's going to get another cup of tea.

'Simon, what is wrong with you?' I snap.

'Is there only fucking tea?'

'Will you please stop swearing. There are children around.'

'Yeah, the place is full of supportive siblings, isn't it?' He stares at me with a cool intensity that manages to slice through his more obvious state, one of inebriation.

'Have you been drinking already?' I ask.

'No biggie. Mick from work has had a baby — well, his girlfriend has. We went for a drink to wet the baby's head.'

'But you knew this started at five thirty. You didn't have time to go to the pub. Did you leave work early?' He's clearly had more than one.

'I was only ten minutes late. I didn't miss much. Hell, Daisy, if I have to sit through another rendition of 'Let It Go' I might literally beat myself over the head with that bunch of roses.'

I'd happily do as much, and my only regret

would be that I had the thorns removed at the florist because I'm not careless enough to give my child a bouquet with thorns. The bell, announcing the second half is about to begin, rings.

'I'll wait for you outside,' says Simon.

'No, you have to come in.'

'She's done her bit.'

'She'll be on stage again for the encore. That's when the entire assembly dance together.' He looks at his feet. 'Please Simon.'

He shrugs and follows me back into the hall, like a dog following its master; a snarly dog that might turn and bite at any point.

6

Simon

Simon sat through the rest of the recital as required but was unable to muster any enthusiasm. Watching other people's small, clumsy kids prance about on stage was only bearable if you got to see your own kid. He was ashamed that he'd missed Millie's performance and yet also relieved. It pained him to admit, even to himself, but he was finding it difficult to be around her since they'd visited the fertility clinic. He loved her so much. It hurt. The doubt. The uncertainty. It felt like a wound.

He allowed his eyes to slide to the left, he looked at Daisy the way you might look at the sun. Never full on, it was too damaging, only with a side-eye glance. Martell must have got it wrong. He *must* have. No way. No fucking way would Daisy ever be unfaithful. But Martell had thought that they'd had a donor. They hadn't. He'd thought Millie was born through IVF. She wasn't. Blatantly he had only scanned the history which Simon had bothered to provide. The supposed expert had clearly made assumptions, mistakes. He couldn't be trusted. Most likely the results of Simon's tests were wrong. That was it. When they'd first had a similar round of tests he'd been told the chances of conceiving were 'slight', one doctor once used the word 'negligible'. No one ever said his chances were non-existent. No one ever used the word 'sterile'. Surely a mistake. Or maybe there had been a level of deterioration since. That was probable, wasn't it? Everyone knew that women's fertility dramatically decreased post-forty, it was surely the same for men. Right? These explanations were far more likely than the one the consultant had insinuated. Daisy would not be unfaithful. The idea was ludicrous. He *was* Millie's father.

She didn't look at all like him. She had blonde hair, fine and wavy, pale blue eyes. He had thick, brown curly hair and brown eyes, but he'd always thought Millie had got her colouring from her mother's side. She didn't look like her mother, either though, not really. Not at all. Yes, Daisy had blue eyes, but they were a darker blue and a completely different shape. Daisy had thick red hair. Simon looked about him. There were siblings of the performers sat with their parents in the audience. In many cases the children were mini versions of their parents, recognisably genetically connected, almost facsimiles, but in many other cases the kids didn't look especially like their parents. Simon shook his head. This was madness. How had he let this thought take hold? He should just tell Daisy what the doctor had said. Admit he'd had the tests, that he was hurrying things along. That was no biggie. Then he could ask her straight out. She'd laugh. Well, that or punch him for thinking so badly of her, but that would be better than where he was now. She'd clear it up. He was sure of it. Almost.

He thought back to when Daisy had told him she was pregnant with Millie. Well, she didn't tell him exactly. There wasn't a cutsie moment when she announced it to him by wrapping up a couple of knitted booties, one pink, one blue, the way their friend Connie had done when she told her husband Luke that they were expecting their third. Simon had brought the subject to the table in the end. She was late by six weeks when he did so. He hadn't even dared hope she was pregnant, in fact he had feared she was ill. He knew her cycle as well as she did, couples trying for a baby tended to. She'd been moody and tearful for a few weeks. Hormonal. Off her food. He'd even caught her throwing up with what he later came to realise was a brief but intense bout of morning sickness, but at the time he hadn't made the leap. He hadn't dared to hope. They'd given up, you see. So he hadn't been looking for it.

One morning at breakfast, he watched her push her muesli around her bowl but not spoon much of it into her mouth. 'Are you ill? Do you think you need to go to the doctors?'

'No and yes,' she replied. Lifting her eyes to meet his. He could see something glisten inside her. Something wonderful, but there were also shades of concern, fear. It was like looking at a stunning view through smudgy sunglasses.

'What is it, Daisy?' He'd wanted to take her hand, but she seemed so far away.

'I'm not ill, I'm pregnant.'

She said the word tentatively, like a whispered secret. He felt it glow in his head, his heart. 'You're sure?'

She nodded. 'Nine weeks pregnant,' she replied breathily.

He'd started to laugh, it spluttered out of his nose, the emotion was so raw he couldn't control it at all. 'Why didn't you say something sooner?'

'I didn't dare.'

He understood. They hadn't dared to hope. Now he could touch her. He'd pulled his wife into his arms. He'd almost picked her up and spun her round but then he'd panicked, he didn't want to dislodge anything, he didn't want to be too rough. She'd laughed reading his mind.

'I know, it's terrifying, right?'

He'd covered her face with kisses. 'We need to crack open the champagne. Oh wow, no. Not for you. But me. Yes, I need a drink.' It was not terrifying, it was exhilarating, brilliant.

She started to laugh. 'You're pleased?'

'Daisy, are you insane? What a question. Pleased doesn't cover it.' He was grinning from ear to ear. People used that expression all the time, but it wasn't until that moment that he really understood it.

'One in three pregnancies miscarry. Those are the statistics,' she whispered, cautiously.

'Shush, no. Don't think about that.'

Daisy started to look more relaxed. The tension in her brow easing. They both wanted this so much that they could make it happen, they could keep the little foetus safe. 'You took a test, right?' He suddenly, momentarily panicked.

Had she made a mistake?

'I've taken three,' laughed Daisy. 'I still have one left, if you want me to do it again.'

She did, and there it was: positive. A little plus sign. Positive! Never had a word been so utterly true. They told people straight away. Daisy wanted to wait but Simon just couldn't manage the prescribed twelve weeks, besides which their family and friends were so closely involved in the matter of their fertility that not telling them would have involved direct lies. People were jubilant. Champagne was popped on a regular basis which Daisy happily refused and Simon happily quaffed. Daisy's sister, Rose, cried. Her friend Connie jumped up and down on the spot and clapped her hands. Like a child. They'd done it! They'd made a baby.

Hadn't they?

Simon was brought back to the here and now as Daisy elbowed him in the ribs. He jerked as though he'd been asleep. Daisy scowled at him. Had he dozed off? No, he was just remembering. His mouth felt dry, scratchy. Millie was on the stage again. The entire dance school was, yet she was easy to pick out. She presented roses to the dance teacher. She did so on tip toes. Graceful, itty-bitty movements. Simon stood up to cheer, but somehow he lost his balance. The rows of chairs were too tightly packed. He fell back on top of the woman sat next to him. He landed on her lap. It was very funny. Everyone turned to look at him. And laughed.

7

Daisy

I can hardly bring myself to speak to Simon on the walk home. He smells of booze and he ruined our daughter's recital. Millie fills the gaps. She hasn't stopped chatting since she burst through the hall doors and ran into our arms. I presented her with the bouquet, which she was giddy about.

'Did you see me? Did you, Daddy?' She asks, her face shinning with hope and, if you look carefully enough, a tiny bit of concern.

'Yes,' replies Simon.

She looks doubtful. 'Really.'

'Too right.' Simon lies easily. I don't think he should have lied and lies should never come easily. They should be hard and painful. I'd have preferred it if he'd told her he was a little late. She'd have been disappointed, but she'd have known it was the truth. 'You were the star of the show,' he adds. She was, but he sounds glib.

We get home, just in time for the supermarket delivery. I have it delivered without plastic bags as this is kinder on the environment, but it does mean there's a little more waiting around for the delivery guy as I unpack the crates, so it's not especially kind to him. Simon heads straight upstairs. 'Are you going to run her bath?' I ask.

He doesn't reply.

'I can do it,' Millie says, excitedly. She's still dancing on air. Triumphant, having delivered a terrific performance. She's very independent and likes to be as grown up and self-sufficient as possible.

'OK, but be careful with the hot tap. You know it comes out really hot.' She scampers off. I drop my backpack; it's heavy. There are thirty-plus school books in it. I have a lot of marking to do tonight. I need to buy one of those pull-along shopping trolleys that are the domain of old ladies. I know I'll look frumpy, but it'll save my back aching. I ask the delivery guy to hold on one second. He hovers in the kitchen with the plastic crates. They look heavy too. 'Just put them anywhere,' I say.

I yell up the stairs, 'Simon can you oversee Millie's bath? I'm dealing with the shopping.' I wait. I don't get a response. I cast an apologetic glance at the delivery guy. He's still holding the crates. There really isn't an obvious space to put them. 'Erm, just put them down there on the floor. That's fine.' But he can't leave until I've unpacked. 'Just one moment.' I dash up the stairs and call, 'Simon, hey Simon, where are you? Can you watch out while Millie baths?'

I pop my head into the bathroom. She's not there. Probably changing in her room but she's already started to run the bath. I check that the plug is in properly and I turn down the hot tap, add a little more cold water. Better she has a tepid bath than scalds herself. As I do so Millie explodes into the room.

She reaches for the bubble bath and carefully pours a very generous amount into the water. A smell that's manufactured to approximate strawberries immediately fills the air. She squeals excited to see the bubbles multiply. I start to help her undress, but she moves away from me, 'I can do it.' She's growing up far too quickly.

Where is Simon? We don't live in a big house. He must have heard me call him. He can only be on the loo or in our bedroom. I leave Millie to the task of undressing and stride into our bedroom. As I enter the room I sense movement, Simon was perhaps lying down and has sat up suddenly. Or, maybe . . . I stride over to the bed and duck to look under it. I immediately spot a small bottle of whisky. Simon has obviously just stashed it there.

'What the heck is this, Simon?'

'Nothing,' he says sulkily. His tone is defensive and defiant at once. 'Can't a man have a drink after a long day in the office?'

He has had a drink. With Mick from work. That's why he missed the recital. Or so he said, I don't point this out. I haven't got time. I'm conscious that I'm holding up the delivery guy. 'Yes, he can, but usually people drink in their kitchens or sitting rooms, usually with their partners.'

'It was just a sniff. Just a bit of fun.'

Then why did he try to hide it? I can hear the water gushing into the bath. I'll pick up this matter later. 'Can you go and help Millie get bathed? I need to unpack the shopping.' I take the bottle downstairs with me. It's about two thirds empty. I sigh. I hate it when he has a sneaky snifter in the bedroom. There's no need. He can always open a bottle of wine at dinner. We do so whenever he asks. Personally, I try and not drink through the week. A hangover and a classroom of thirty eleven-year-olds is not a great combination. Sometimes I have half a glass just to keep him company. It's different at a weekend. But even then, I rarely drink more than a glass or two. Millie has no idea about the concept of lying-in, so I like to keep a clear head.

I hear the grocery delivery guy cough loudly. It's not subtle but it is fair. I dash into the kitchen and apologise. I throw my groceries onto any available surface in order to be as fast as possible with the unloading, I accept all substitutes and then bundle him out of the door. I start to clear out the food in the fridge that is out of date and past its best. I consider washing the plastic vegetable drawer because a tomato has been squashed in to the back corner and already looks like a science experiment. I pull out the bulky drawer and look around with faint desperation because the sink is full of breakfast pots that should be in the dishwasher, but the pots in the dishwasher are clean, so they should be in the cupboard. Right. I need to set this place straight. I start to move about the kitchen. First I unload the dishwasher, then refill it with the dirty pots that are scattered about. Then I wash the vegetable drawer and only at this point am I ready to find homes for all the new groceries. I am just beginning to enjoy the sense of order I'm restoring to the room when I suddenly hear Millie scream. It's loud and convincing, not a playful shriek but a scream that's full of pain and panic. I launch myself upstairs, dashing two at a time and explode into the bathroom.

My first thought is that she's crying so not drowned, not dead. Relief. Then I notice the blood. There's a lot of it. Panic. It's smeared on the back bathroom wall and all over her hands and face. I pull her out of the bath, she's wet and slippery but I hold her tight. Examine her quickly. 'What happened? Where did you get hurt?'

'I slipped. I banged my head.' She points to the back of her head. My stomach lurches. There's a nasty cut, and she's losing a lot of blood. I grab a towel and put it over the wound, trying to stem the flow of the bleeding. I realise that the blood on her face comes from her hands, where she's touched her own wound. I can smell iron in the air. I want to be sick, but I must stay focused, useful. I wrap another towel around her and pick her up. She sobs into my shoulder. I can feel her entire body hiccup with stress and pain. 'We need to go to A&E,' I tell her. 'The doctor will take a look but don't worry. It's going to be OK.'

I call to Simon, but he doesn't reply. I haven't got time to look for him. I swiftly dress Millie in pants and a long T-shirt then carry her to the car and drive her to the hospital.

* * *

When we get back from the hospital, the house is in darkness. Millie's head is glued, and she has a sticker declaring her bravery. She's fallen asleep in the back of the car. Usually when she sleeps I'm relieved. She has a lot of energy and by the time she is ready for bed I'm begging her to go. However her sleep makes me slightly uneasy now. It's deep and terrifying. I have been given a leaflet that tells me what to look out for: drowsiness, dizziness, forgetfulness, headaches. I feel queasy just reading it. A close call. The friendly young doctor called it a 'nasty bump'. I was asked a lot of questions. 'Who was supervising her when she slipped?' 'Her father,' I lied. I couldn't bring myself to admit she was on her own. We'd failed her. It isn't a concussion, but you can never be too careful with head injuries. I will wake her every couple of hours tonight. She'll be grumpy, but I don't care.

I lift her from the car and carry her into the house. Her feet trail low, down past my knees, she's too big to carry but I want to hold her close and tight. I lower her into bed, she rolls onto her side as her injury is too tender to allow her to sleep on her back. That thought causes a twinge in my belly. I'd take her pain if I could. I kiss her forehead and she murmurs, 'Don't worry, Mummy. It doesn't hurt now.' Then her eyelids drop heavily, like a metal shutter over a shop window.

I wander into the bathroom. The water is still in the bath. It's pink with her blood. I'm shocked again as I see her blood smeared on the tiles. It's obvious where she fell, the blood is most concentrated there. It's dried hard. There are also small bloody hand prints on the bath edge. I pull the plug and use the hand-held shower to sluice it away.

'What's going on here?' Simon is stood in the doorway. He wipes his eyes, clearly he's been asleep for the entire time we have been at the hospital, four hours. He must have been asleep when she fell.

'Millie slipped as she tried to get herself out of the bath,' I snap.

'Daisy!' I hear accusation in his voice. He thinks this is my fault and maybe it is. I can't trust him. I glare at him.

'I asked *you* to bath her, or if that was too much, at least to watch her whilst she bathed. She could have drowned.'

He looks a little shamefaced and then defiant. 'But she didn't.'

'She's badly hurt her head. It's been glued.'

'Glued?'

'They do that instead of stitches now.'

'So she's OK?'

I know what he's asking but I can't give him that glib reassurance yet. I'm too angry. 'No, she's not OK. I've just told you. She cut her head, banged her elbow. She was really upset. There was a lot of blood. A lot of painful bruising.'

'I need a drink.' He leaves the bathroom and goes downstairs. I'm furious. That was not the response I wanted. But then I sigh. What response did I want? What could he say or do now? I finish cleaning the bathroom. I want it to look spotless by the time Millie sees it next. After washing away all evidence of her fall I also put her dirty clothes in the wash basket. I pop my head around her bedroom door just to check on her, before I go downstairs and join Simon in the kitchen. He's stood by the breakfast bar in semi-darkness. He has only bothered to put on the small light above the hob. I don't flick the switch for the overhead lights. I think it would be too garish. The dimness offers us both a cloak which, for reasons I can't explain or even understand, I feel we need.

'Do you want something to eat? I'm hungry,' I say. We missed supper. This offer is as conciliatory as I'm capable of being right now. I feel I can't blame Simon for the fall, at least not entirely. I knew he was less than sober and in a weird mood. I should have unpacked the shopping and then bathed Millie myself. I shouldn't have allowed her to try to manage and I shouldn't have relied on him. I'm telling myself all of this to try to stop feeling angry with him, but I just find I'm angry with him for a different reason. Not for the fall but because I can't rely on him.

Simon reaches for a bottle of red wine from the wine rack. He slides it out. The sound of the glass bottle scraping against the wooden shelf is a familiar one. Like opening the fridge or the sound of the back door closing, the TV jumping to life; a domestic sound, familiar to our home. 'Do you want a glass?'

'No, it's too late for me,' I say pointedly. Then I dare to add. 'Don't you think you've had enough?'

'No, I don't.' He says firmly as he unscrews the cap and reaches for a glass.

Simon *has* had enough to drink. Too much. Why can't he see it? Why can't I say it?

This happens from time to time in our marriage. Simon likes a drink and then there comes a point where he drinks too much. Usually I wait it out. After months, maybe a year, he'll notice he's over-doing it and cut back. No one is perfect. We all have stuff to deal with. He drank heavily when we were trying to conceive. He drinks heavily if things are stressful at work. I wonder what's on his mind now? I fear it's something to do with wanting another child. The visit to the fertility clinic was so peculiar. The way he ran out of the place. Odd. When I asked him what the doctor had said to upset him, he said he never even got the chance to speak to the doctor, that he'd just been left waiting in the consultation room. He said that was what had annoyed him, the lack of manners. The arrogance. 'I knew you didn't want to be there, Daisy, so I just gave up. I thought, forget it.' I don't really believe him. I suspect it had something to do with his drinking, nearly everything does. Maybe he felt woozy or nauseous, maybe the doctor commented that he didn't seem quite sober, maybe he suddenly just wanted a drink more than he wanted a baby; he did bolt straight to a pub.

He's right about one thing, I didn't want to be at the fertility clinic. It was a great relief to me when he charged out of the building and I was left to hurriedly collect up Millie and our belongings. I daren't even ask him if we got a refund. I don't really care. I want to leave the matter alone. I'm glad he's stopped talking about a sibling for Millie. Yet, I can't ignore the fact that Simon is drinking heavily again. It's not social drinking. It's not even overindulgent drinking. It's purposeful, determined drinking. It's as though he's trying to find something at the end of the bottle. Oblivion, maybe.

'Simon, you were drunk and therefore late to the recital and then you came home and drank some more so fell asleep instead of looking out for Millie. How could you let her down like that?'

I steel myself to look at him. I don't want to because he's ugly to me right now, he's in the wrong. Millie got injured, she will still be in pain tomorrow, she's shocked, scared and it could have been a whole lot worse. That doesn't bear thinking about. But when I lay eyes on Simon, my fury crashes, dissipates. He's staring at the counter. He looks sad, confused.

'I didn't mean to let her down,' he says with a sigh. He looks out to our garden. My eyes follow his. I think I see a fox by the bins.

Whoever means to let anyone down? I wonder. 'Have you got something you want to talk about?' I ask his reflection in the kitchen window.

He shakes his head. We stand in silence for a minute. Then he asks my reflection, 'Have you?'

'No.'

He picks up the bottle of red wine and pours a second glass and I put two slices of bread in the toaster. We eat and drink in silence.

8

Simon

Saturday, 18th June 2016

Simon really wanted to make it up to Millie for leaving her alone in the bathroom. When he thought about her battered head, her aching elbow, when he imagined the moment of panic she must have felt when she slipped, the fear, the confusion — he hated himself. He got up early on the Saturday morning and made pancakes with her. The first couple were misshapen, but he told her that they looked like Mickey Mouse's ears and she was kind enough to agree with him. He got into his groove and then made twice as many as they could possibly eat. They took some up to Daisy in bed because Millie wanted to, even though breakfast in bed was usually only something that occurred on birthdays or Mother's Day. As it happened, Daisy was already in the shower. But they persuaded her to put on her robe and climb back into bed to eat them. She said they were delicious. There was a lot of smiling. Simon's smiles were bashful, then hopeful, then rather pleased with himself. Daisy's were tentative, possibly forced, certainly smaller than he'd have hoped. Millie's smiles were the most fabulous and uncomplicated. Her smiles buoyed everyone up. Like a life raft.

Daisy said she had a lot of marking to do. Simon realised that she'd probably intended to do it the night before but had had to abandon it to dash to the hospital. Usually Millie spent Saturday morning at ballet school and Daisy marked her books whilst she sat in the car waiting for the classes to finish, she had to do it this way because the ballet school was a serious one and not the sort that allowed the mothers to sit on chairs along the wall, chatting and distracting. However, Millie wasn't allowed to dance for a week or so because of her injury. Simon offered to take her to the park instead but even that caused Daisy to look aggravated. 'She can't play on the swings or slides. She has a suspected concussion.'

'We'll just have a stroll about,' he replied. Daisy didn't look convinced. Her brow was knitted with concern. Simon decided not to pursue the matter. He wanted to entertain his child, yes, but he also wanted please his wife. He'd woken up ashamed. Of course Millie was his child. Of course Daisy would never be unfaithful and then pass off another man's child as his. That was madness. He was mortified by his own stupidity and only glad that he hadn't shared his fears with anyone else, grateful that no one could read his mind.

'How about we go and buy a tent?' he suggested.

Millie had been begging to go camping for weeks now. She'd seen people camp on the beach during half term and fallen in love with the adventure and freedom that sleeping outside offered. They didn't own any camping equipment, it wasn't Daisy's idea of fun. Simon used to camp as a boy, he'd been a Scout, and as a young man he'd had a few rowdy nights under the stars at festivals. He had a vague idea that one day they could all go on a family camping trip and he'd impress them with his tent pitching skills. Or, if Daisy wasn't up for that, then maybe a father-daughter camping trip. It would be fun. Not now, not while Millie was injured. But the weather was starting to warm up, maybe they could camp in the garden to start with, to see if Millie caught on to it. If so, they could go further afield at a later date. He suggested as much to Daisy, taking care to do so when Millie was not in earshot, because Daisy would appreciate them talking about it as parents first and reaching a consensus before Millie's exuberance railroaded them into a decision. 'It would take her mind off her injury,' Simon pointed out. 'We don't have to buy a tent. We can borrow one off someone.'

'I'm not sure. Not all night, not when we're still monitoring her. But maybe you could put up a tent, make a den, cook supper on a stove in the garden. She could fall to sleep out there and then you could carry her into her bed,' Daisy conceded.

Millie loved the plan. She and Simon travelled by tube to Holland Park to see their friends, Luke and Connie Baker. They had three kids and all the trappings of a middle class west London family life. They owned little fold-out chairs that 'Came in handy on prize-giving day or at the races', they had a picnic basket with glass, silverware and china 'for Glyndebourne', and a roof rack that was useful when collecting the two-metre tall Christmas tree that they bought from a Chelsea garden centre every Christmas. Simon guessed they'd have camping equipment. One phone call to Luke had confirmed that indeed they had. Luke laughed and told Simon that a few years ago they'd tried camping, 'Connie and my girls hated it. We spent a bloody fortune on all the gear. Only ever used it once.' Luke laughed about things like that. He and Connie were loaded, the waste didn't matter as long as it made an amusing anecdote. 'Borrow what you like. It's good to know it's getting used.'

Luke was an architect. He sometimes put interior design work Simon's way, decent work, Simon couldn't complain. Connie was a photographer and was managing to make a good living out of it even though everyone had an iPhone and filters nowadays, and could take decent snaps for themselves. Simon had known Luke for twenty-something years, Daisy and Connie had made friends at university when they were still teenagers. Simon and Daisy met at Luke and Connie's first wedding anniversary party. Somehow, the fact that they'd found each other through the Bakers, and Luke sometimes commissioned Simon, had led to an unarticulated hierarchy in their relationship. Simon always felt Luke was lording it over him. Simon felt stung by a sudden determination that his girl would like camping, and that they'd go on to have lots of memorable trips away together, which they'd record on his iPhone and post on Facebook.

The trip to the Bakers and back took most of the morning. By the time they returned, Daisy had finished marking her books. They had a sandwich lunch and then pitched the tent together. Millie filled it with pink cushions from her bedroom and a huge number of cuddly toys. Simon doubted there would be room for him to lie down. Daisy found some solar fairy lights in the back of the cupboard where they kept their boxes of Christmas decorations. They draped them over the tent and waited until it got dark. For supper they made beans and sausages. The Bakers' camping stove worked a treat. Millie was too excited to fall to sleep in the tent. At 10 p.m. they all gave up and went inside, but it wasn't with an air of defeat, it was a decisive victory. The day had been won. The day had been glorious. Daisy made hot chocolate in the kitchen.

Simon made his that bit tastier by adding a nip of whisky.

9

Daisy

Thursday, 23rd June 2016

Connie has got it into her head that she wants to throw a party. The Bakers throw a lot of parties, they always have. They're party people through to their souls. Over the years, Connie and Luke have thrown lavish Christmas, birthday, Easter and summer dos, any excuse. Connie is known for her incredible attention to detail and her generous hosting. I used to love them, I really did, but I haven't been to one since Millie was born. I hate parties now. I find excuses. Some of Connie's friends take their kids along but I never have. I tell Simon that I worry about drugs. Connie doesn't indulge but a lot of her guests do. It's not something I want Millie to be around. Truthfully, some of the people Connie mixes with leave me cold.

This is the third time she's brought up the topic of us hosting a joint party, a ludicrous idea. The previous occasions were over the phone; I was able to say someone was at the door and cut the conversation short. This time, it's harder to dodge. We're sat face to face in a coffee shop in Covent Garden. I can't even depend on one of the kids interrupting us because her three girls and Millie are all sitting at a different table. Fran, Connie's eldest, is holding court the way only a thirteen-year-old can. Her younger siblings, Flora who is ten, Sophie age seven, and Millie are in her thrall. She's showing them different apps on her phone. There's no way any one of them will tear themselves away from that.

The café is a noisy, overly trendy place. Pricey but fun. It's a novelty, being out in town after school. Normally Millie and I have a class or rehearsal to dash to. Unfortunately, because of her slip in the bath, Millie isn't well enough to go to classes. I'm trying to make sure we enjoy the time that has been freed up, rather than resentfully dwell on Simon's carelessness. Millie is laughing and giggling with the others. For a moment I'm able to forget the inch-long wound at the back of her head, flagged by matted, dirty hair. I can't bring myself to wash it yet so we've been making do with dry shampoo.

'Come on, Daisy,' Connie insists. 'It's our anniversaries, we have to celebrate.'

As coincidence would have it, Simon and I share our anniversary, more or less, with Connie and Luke. We met at their first wedding anniversary party and married a year later. It was fast. Too fast? The thought springs into my head and I push it away, mortified by my subconscious betrayal. Things aren't easy right now but that's a terrible thought to have. I play with a sachet of sugar in the bowl on the table. I now see that when I was planning my big day, I should have given more thought to the fact we'd be forever sharing our anniversary with the Bakers. I didn't because, after Simon proposed, all I was concerned with was securing the first date possible in the venue I wanted. I practically ran down the aisle.

'Don't you think a joint party will be fun?' Connie asks.

I don't. I can't think why she's suggesting it. The Bakers are not short of money, so I know they can't possibly be motivated by splitting the cost. I can't add anyone exciting to the guest list, we share our best friends and I don't have any acquaintances that Connie would be keen to meet; I'm a Year Six school teacher, she's a photographer for glossy magazines, she has the monopoly on glamorous friends. She's not normally shy of being centre of attention. Honestly? I think I can go so far as to say it's unusual for her to want to share the limelight. So why this sudden and ardent interest in us hosting a joint anniversary party?

'It's not really my sort of thing,' I reply carefully. 'People don't make a big fuss of anniversaries unless it's a round number,' I point out. We've been married sixteen years; the Bakers have been married eighteen.

'But why not? That's a crazy rule! Every year is special.' Connie has always had her own way of looking at things. To be fair it's a brighter, more sparkling way than the rest of us and usually I enjoy her *joie de vivre* but sometimes she can be a tiny bit irritating.

'I think Simon might have already booked something for us that weekend,' I mutter. Connie widens her eyes sceptically, but is too polite to say this is very unlikely. I take care of all the social arrangements, I book our holidays, organise flights, car hire, bookings at Airbnb. Truth be known, I also deal with the less exciting admin: insurance, renewing the TV licence and reading the electricity meter to someone in a remote call centre. Simon isn't the sort to surprise me with a mini-break.

'I have to do something!' she says, laughingly. Connie laughs a lot because her life is perfect. I know, I know, no one's life is perfect but I'm up close and personal with hers and believe me, it is as near to perfect as I can imagine.

'Fine maybe *you* do, but why do you need me and Simon to be involved?'

'I don't want to bag the date and make it all about me. Us,' she quickly corrects herself, remembering to include Luke. 'It's your date too. It will look bad.'

'Who to? I don't care.' I really don't.

'I'll feel bad,' she persists.

I might have agreed to a smaller, more intimate gathering. A dinner party for our nearest and dearest could be nice but that's not Connie's way. Connie's wedding anniversary parties always echo the original, triumphant day, which was a glorious, no holds barred affair, full of possibility, romance and big flouncy skirts. Connie loves looking back at her wedding day. She had her old wedding video digitised and they watch it on every anniversary; I don't doubt she has plans to play it at this party, if it goes ahead. I find taking a trip down memory lane more complex. Sometimes it's just what I need, today I can't face the thought of it.

Last night, I barely got any sleep. Simon came back late. He said he'd had to stay at work for an important meeting. If I'd lit a match near his mouth he'd have probably gone up in flames the alcohol fumes were that bad. When I asked him if he'd been to the pub he said yes, just for one beer, but that was a lie, he smelt of spirits and could barely walk in a straight line. I was so angry. It had only been a few days since his drinking and negligence had led to Millie's accident. I'd hoped his remorse might last longer. We rowed. I called him a bloody liar, he said I was a sneaky bitch. We say some awful things to each other sometimes. Then I cried, he hugged me and told me he has it all under control, that I've got nothing to worry about.

You see, he *is* a bloody liar.

'Do you think it's over the top if Luke and I renew our vows?' Connie suddenly asks. She doesn't meet my eye but instead stares intently at her half-finished wheatgrass smoothie.

'Do you need to renew them? Have you broken your vows?' I ask with the flat honesty that a twenty-seven-year friendship allows. She did. Once. A long time ago. It was a drama. I really don't want to hear if she has again.

'No, I have not,' she says quickly, self-consciously. 'But I thought it would be romantic' She pauses and then, oh-so-casually adds, 'I thought you might want to do it too. You and Simon.'

And there it is. Her reason for asking us to

share a party with them. I had wondered. Now I understand.

It is a pity party.

Literally.

Scalding hot embarrassment seeps through my body, drenching me in shame. Connie beams at me but I know her too well, the smile is shadowed with concern. The side of her mouth quivers ever so slightly. 'Simon popped round to ours last night.' She's trying to sound simply chatty, off-the-cuff. She fails. 'He and Luke are working together on something at the moment and it needed discussing, so Luke had asked him to stop by.'

I nod as though I knew this already. I didn't, Simon doesn't often give me much detail about the projects he works on. He used to. My first thought is relief that his explanation for being late home wasn't totally inaccurate. Going to see Luke to discuss work, even in a pub, is almost the same as having to stay behind for a meeting.

My tentative optimism is knocked back when Connie adds, 'Only Simon wasn't really up for talking about the project. He wasn't making much sense at all, in fact. Just kept going on about how much Millie had loved camping in the garden. He was sort of fixated on that, you know.'

She doesn't say it. She wants to say he was rambling and repeating himself, that he was drunk. I know she does because I've seen it often enough myself. There was a time when Connie might have dared called a spade a shovel but we're more careful with each other now. More reserved.

When we were at university together and when

we shared a flat after that, we saw each other every day of our lives, but that intimacy has been neglected. I can no longer open up to her without reserve. We've replaced one another. We're married now and have been for a long time. That draws a curtain around certain things. Things like her explicitly saying my husband is a functioning alcoholic. She can't say it until I do. I have no intention of doing so. We still love each other. I love her boldness, her candour, her volatility. Her panache. I'm also intimidated by all those characteristics too.

As usual, I try to change the subject. 'I should have brought your camping stove back, I forgot all about it.'

Connie looks briefly impatient as she knows I'm dodging her point. 'Simon returned it last night, actually.'

'Oh good.'

'Well, most of it. He'd mislaid the screw-on pan support bit.'

'We'll buy you another,' I say quickly.

'Oh wow, no. No need. I didn't mean that. We never use it.' She glances at her hands and then carefully says, 'Luke put him in an Uber.'

They know. My friends know my marriage is quaking under the strain of Simon's drinking. I'd hoped we'd hidden it well enough, but they know, and this is Connie's clumsy attempt to fix things. She doesn't understand that what she is suggesting — a party, a renewal of our vows — is a pathetic, inadequate Elastoplast put over an amputated limb. Her idea is idealistic, therefore idiotic. How could we stand up in front of our friends and family and say our wedding vows again? For better, for worse, for richer, for poorer, in sickness and in health. It's a crazy idea. For one thing, Simon rarely stands without swaying, he prefers to slump. He rarely speaks, instead he slurs. It would be utterly humiliating. I'm doing my best to hide, why would she think dragging us out, putting us under the microscope would be a good idea?

She clears her throat and carries on. 'It might be fun to do something celebratory. I know you have a lot on your plate. Your mother-in-law being so ill, the pressure Simon's under at work.'

I flash her a look that could freeze breath. 'What do you know about his work?'

'Luke made me go along to some corporate dinner the other week. Simon's name came up amongst the guests there. They just mentioned that . . . ' she loses her confidence and trails off.

'What?' I demand hotly.

'Well, his workload seems to be getting on top of him. They weren't gossiping. Just saying,' she adds hurriedly. Connie blushes. *They*, whoever *they* are, clearly were gossiping.

I need this conversation to stop. I need to put an end to this stupid idea of hers. I shake my head. 'I'll come to your party, we both will, but we can't possibly renew our vows.'

'I just thought it would be — '

'No, Connie, Absolutely not.' I'm rarely this forceful. Usually I don't have it in me to argue with anyone other than Simon. Not the nurses in my mother-in-law's care home, not the whingy parents of my pupils, not even the annoying cold callers that ring to ask if I've been in an accident recently, certainly not Connie who is wily and persuasive. She seems startled by my determination but, to my relief, she nods.

'OK, I understand.' She pauses and glances at Millie. 'But you know if there's anything we can ever do.'

'There isn't,' I state, plainly.

'If you ever need to talk.'

'I don't.' I glare at her. I need her to drop this now.

On the whole, my friends and family seem prepared to look in the other direction when there's evidence that Simon drinks too much. That he's a functioning alcoholic. Oh yes, I know the label, I just don't see what it achieves in bandying it around. Of course, I've asked him to get help; yes, I'd like him to go to a doctor, a counsellor, but he won't. So what is there to discuss? My friends are understandably embarrassed, or at least they know I am, and in a truly British way, they don't want to make a fuss. We've known each other since we were students. There isn't one of us who hasn't seen every other one of us totally plastered at some point or other, so to date they've made excuses for my husband. They laugh when he fails asleep at the dinner table or slips on their front step as we leave their home. As though it's all one big joke. As though he is a big joke. This has suited me. I don't know what to do to get him to stop drinking, this is a problem I can't solve so I've been happy enough to ignore it. I thought, hoped, that one day he'd wake up and announce that the hangovers were no longer worth it, that he was going to buy a Fitbit and a bike and start getting healthy, that's what most middle aged men do. But he hasn't. Few of my friends get seriously drunk anymore, most abstain from drinking through the week and, other than Simon, I don't know anyone who drinks through the day.

Now, I no longer know what I want from my family and friends. Do I really still want them to politely look away, to refuse to acknowledge what they evidently see? I don't know how to ask for help or even accept it when it's being offered up, as it clearly is by Connie, right now. Sometimes it feels like Simon and I are on a boat, an oar-less boat that's drifting further and further out to sea. My sister and my friends are stood on the shore, watching us, aware we are in deep and dangerous waters but doing nothing other than waving at us; friendly but ineffectual. If Connie holds my gaze for a moment more I might just tell her. Simon isn't coping. I'm not coping.

She shrugs, the moment vanishes. Lost. Well she offered. She can tell herself, and Luke too no doubt, that she's done the right thing. She can congratulate herself on being a good friend without having the awkwardness of me telling her just how bad things are. She brightens up, almost instantly, nothing much depresses her for long. 'But you'll come, right? That's great news. You haven't been to one of my parties for ages. I'll absolutely mention that it's your special day in my speech.'

I don't say anything, and she takes that for

agreement. She often does. I'll think of an excuse to get out of the party later. I slurp down my iced latte and say, 'Look, we've got to go.' I stand up, banging my leg into the small table in my haste. It shudders and the glasses rattle on their unnecessary saucers. The women on the table next to ours stare at me. I wonder whether I've spoken too loudly, sometimes I don't judge those things as well as I ought to, not if I'm stressed. I use my school teacher voice, when really that should be limited to the classroom of eleven-year-olds.

Connie looks crestfallen. 'Don't you want to stay and make some plans? Talk about menus and things?'

'It's not really my forte, I'm sure whatever you decide it will be wonderful,' I garble. 'Millie, come along now, Daddy will be wondering where we are.'

This is unlikely, but Simon isn't the only one who is a bloody liar.

10

Simon

Sunday, 26th June 2016

Simon hated visiting his mother. He thought it was a waste of time. She often didn't know who he was and, even if she did seem to temporarily recognise him, she forgets that they'd seen one another within an hour of his visit. But Daisy was adamant. She was religious about it. She visited every Wednesday after school and insisted that they all visit every Sunday. She said it was their duty. It was the right thing to do. She argued that even if Elsie's relief was only temporary, she was cheered while they were there. This wasn't always true, sometimes Simon's mother just cried when they visited. Or swore, cussed at them in a way that would make a sailor blush and made Millie giggle inappropriately. Daisy always took flowers, which Millie liked to present to her grandmother with a little over-the-top flourish. Once Simon's mother tried to eat the flowers. Millie laughed at that too, she thought her grandmother was being deliberately funny. Daisy never took chocolates; chocolate messed with Elsie's digestive system. Daisy said that dealing with the aftermath wasn't pretty.

Simon thought that it was a depressing hell-hole, the care home. He understood that they tried, he wasn't saying otherwise. The staff were friendly enough, and no doubt dedicated, conscientious, blah blah blah. But in the end, all he could see was an over-heated institution, where people went to die. You couldn't polish that turd.

His father had died of a heart attack just a few years after Daisy and Simon married. At the time, his dad being cut down before he'd even retired, seemed like a tragedy. Now, Simon had redefined what tragic was.

'Hey, do you remember that game show on TV?' he asked.

'Which game show?' Daisy did not quite manage to hold in her sigh of frustration. She didn't like his nonesequential thoughts, his musings. She called them ramblings.

'The one where people would carry buckets of water over greasy poles or rolling logs, and others would interfere, try to knock contestants off balance by squirting water or throwing custard pies. What was it called?' Simon was excited by this thought. He really wanted to know the name of the show. It was on the tip of his tongue. 'Knock-about, something like that . . . '

'*It's a Knockout*,' offered Daisy.

'*It's a Knockout*, that's right.'

'What about it?'

'Nothing.' Simon turned and looked out of the window. It was a bright day. He wished he'd brought his sunglasses.

Even with his head turned away he could feel Daisy's frustration. She wouldn't have liked him to elaborate, though. Not really. He was thinking that sometimes life was something akin to a great big game of *It's a Knockout*. The show was designed to emphasise skill or organisation. Brains mattered, strength and endurance too. People always started the game grinning, showing great determination and spirit but everyone ended up looking foolish; wet, exhausted, broken. Yeah, life was like that game except it wasn't pies that were thrown, it was infertility, depression, madness, infidelity, death. No one was immune, no one was safe. You think you're doing OK, drifting along, going to university, getting hired, getting laid, getting married, things are going well and then suddenly, from out of nowhere, a great big blast of icy water knocks you off your greasy pole. Daisy wouldn't want to hear him say that.

If they had to visit his mother every Sunday, Simon would have liked to do so in the mornings. It was not that he was a make-the-most-of-the-day sort of person, far from it. If anything, it was more of a get-it-over-with mindset. There were two main reasons for his preference. Firstly, if they arrived at 11 a.m. they had to leave at 1 p.m. because that was when the carers served the strained mush that they called lunch to the oldies, so the visit could be a maximum of two hours. Secondly, he liked to go out for long pub lunches, the sort that shimmered with the chance of swelling into the afternoon. There was nothing better in the winter than a roast, washed down by a bottle of red, maybe a couple of whiskies, in front of a fire. In the summer he was more of a G&T guy. The long lingering lunches weren't possible if they had to be at the care home by 2 p.m. However, Daisy didn't agree with Simon. She'd decided it was more convenient to visit his mother in the afternoon. That way she could take Millie to the dance studio for a private lesson in the morning and have a big meal in the evening. Millie wasn't even dancing this week, but it seemed there was no room for flexibility. Simon was pretty sure Millie could be dancing again by now, she seemed as bright as a button, fully recovered. She was practically climbing the walls, she had so much energy to spend, but Daisy wouldn't hear of it. Daisy was milking it, making more of the accident than need be. She was punishing him. Still. Even after the success of the garden camping. It didn't matter what he did. How hard he tried. Daisy wasn't the forgiving type.

She was such a hypocrite.

Daisy argued that the long, lazy lunches weren't as much fun for her as she always drove. She did most of the driving when Millie was with them. She never said anything directly, but he knew she didn't quite trust him, didn't think he was quite up to it. It was insulting if you thought about it, so he tried not to think about it. In all honesty, he did have a bit of a thick head, it was probably best that she drove. Simon hated Sundays. They were swamped with a sense of dread and impending doom. He always had a shot of whisky before he visited his mother. It took the edge off. He couldn't quite remember when he'd started this habit, a year ago? Maybe more.

Dr Martell was back in his head today. The fucker. He thought he'd pushed him out but, today, he'd crawled back in.

Daisy was such a hypocrite.

At first, Simon thought they were going to have a good afternoon with his mother. She was dressed appropriately, smartly in fact. His mother used to have standards, she was a consistently beautiful, elegant woman, but that was no longer the case. He hated it when he found her wearing someone else's scruffy tracksuit, maybe because the staff had got the washing mixed up, maybe because she'd stolen it. Today she was wearing a neat blue dress, tights and shoes. Not mismatched socks and grubby slippers. Someone had brushed her thin, white hair; even put on a bit of lipstick for her. There was some on her teeth but that was not necessarily anything to do with dementia, Daisy often had lipstick on her teeth. Simon felt cheered and had a quick slug from his flask by way of celebration. But then Elsie started to talk, and Simon realised the lipstick was just a mask for the chaos.

'Who is this?' Elsie demanded imperiously, pointing at Daisy.

'It's Daisy, Mum. My wife,' Simon explained unenthusiastically.

Unperturbed, Daisy kissed his mum's cheek. 'Hello, Elsie. You're looking lovely today. What a chic dress. Look, we've brought you some flowers.'

Millie sprang forward. Everything was a performance for her. She beamed and held out the yellow roses.

His mum stared at Daisy, Millie and the flowers with a mix of hostility and surprise. Then her face melted. It was like water. One minute frozen, the next liquid. Simon thought that one day she would evaporate. 'Thank you, they are beautiful,' she said graciously. 'So, you are the new wife, are you? I like you far better than the last one. She was podgy and giggly. A horrible combination.'

Daisy sighed. It was a fact that she used to carry a few extra pounds, something Simon's mother — a lifetime borderline anorexic — hated with a level of ferocity that most people reserved for paedophiles. Also, when Simon first met Daisy, her thing was giggling. She would frequently erupt into chortles and even outright laughter, when most people were only moved to wryly grin in amusement. Simon had thought it was a result of being a teacher, always being around kids. She found life fun, entertaining. He liked it about her. Now, he'd say her thing was sighing.

'I'll go and see if the nurse has a vase,' said Daisy.

'Go with your mum,' Simon instructed Millie.

'It's not a two-person job,' commented Daisy. 'Millie, stay with your grandma. Tell her what you've been up to at school this week.'

Millie looked from left to right, eyes swivelling between her parents. She was an obedient child and found it confusing when they issued conflicting sets of instructions. Which they did with increasing frequency. She hovered near the door, unsure what to do. Simon chose to ignore her. The moment Daisy left the room, he started to rummage through his mother's bedside cabinet.

'What are you looking for?' Millie asked.

'Bedsocks,' he lied.

Elsie suddenly engaged. 'Are you looking for this?' She held up a large print book.

'No.'

'Are you looking for this?' She waved a banana.

'No, I said bedsocks,' he muttered impatiently. Simon found the gin at the back of the cabinet, behind the bed socks. His uncle Alan brought his mother a half bottle every week. It was an irresponsible gift to give a dementia sufferer but, no doubt, Alan believed any comfort he could offer the old lady was justified at this stage. Every Thursday when Alan visited, he secreted a bottle in the cupboard and he believed Elsie knocked it back throughout the week. She didn't, but the gift was gratefully received. Simon quickly put it in his laptop bag, which he'd brought for this purpose. Millie looked at her feet.

'Is this what you are looking for?' Elsie pulled out her hearing aid and shoved it under his nose. Simon could see her ear wax on the plastic.

'No, I told you — '

'What are you looking for?' This time, the question came from Daisy. She was stood in the doorway next to Millie, holding the flowers which were now in a vase of water.

'Nothing. She's confused, you know what she's like.' He turned away and looked out of the window. There wasn't much to see. A carer was pushing an old man in a wheelchair around the small garden. It took less than thirty seconds for them to do a lap. The silence in the room was deafening. Simon wished his mother would say something. She could usually be relied upon to talk nonsense to fill a gap.

Daisy carefully placed the vase on the bedside cabinet. She bent and closed the cupboard door. 'What did you put in your bag?'

'Nothing.'

The room wasn't large and, in the same instant, they both reached for his laptop case. Simon was slightly speedier. He hugged it to his chest.

'What are you hiding?' Daisy demanded.

'Nothing, nothing at all,' Simon insisted.

She started to try to prise the bag off him. Simon was taken aback that she was being so openly confrontational — what was wrong with her? — and so he momentarily slackened his grip. It was enough for her to get some purchase, she yanked the bag off him and opened it.

'You brought gin here?' she asked in disbelief.

'No, I was taking it away.'

'You were stealing her gin?' She glanced at Millie who was trying not to look at her parents. Daisy's shock was palpable. Simon felt it calcify, another layer of disappointment settling on their history.

'Not stealing it. Taking it away for her own

good. She shouldn't be drinking. It messes with her meds. Alan brings her it every week.'

'You steal from her every week?' Daisy shook her head. Disgust oozed from her.

Simon didn't answer. What was the point? She didn't want to know. Not really. She'd prefer not to know that when he nipped into the other rooms, ostensibly to say hi to the other oldies, like a decent chap, he checked their bedside cabinets too. There was usually a quarter of whisky, a small bottle of sherry, at the very least. On a quiet week, he'd settle for a box of liqueurs. He told himself that he was doing them a favour. It was irresponsible to give la la old people alcohol. There could be accidents. He wasn't stealing. They'd give it to him if he asked. They liked him. These old dears that smelt of pee. They all thought he was their son or husband. They didn't know their arse from their elbow. Simon knew Daisy wouldn't understand if he explained all of that, so instead he did the only thing he could think of, he lurched forward and grabbed the gin out of her hands. In an instant he'd unscrewed the top and started to down it. Glug, glug, glug. Temporarily, she was frozen. Then she reacted. She tried to knock the bottle out of his hand.

'Stop it, Simon. For God's sake, stop it.'

But if he stopped drinking she'd take it from him. He knew she would. She did succeed in spilling a fair amount down his shirt, which was a waste. He flopped back into the armchair and slung the empty bottle into the wastepaper basket. It landed with a satisfying clunk. He yelled, 'In the back of the net,' and punched the air. Millie giggled, nervously.

Daisy looked like a fish, her mouth was gaping. She was swirling, sort of gauzy. She looked from him, to the waste-paper basket and back again. 'Who are you?' she demanded.

The air between them shuddered.

'Him? Oh, he's my husband. He's always been rather too fond of the bottle, I'm afraid,' said Elsie. She carefully patted the back of her hair with her frail, veiny hand. Then in a whisper, leaning towards Daisy, she added, 'I find it's best to ignore the matter. It doesn't do to bring it up.' She sighed, shook her head. 'I only wish he had a hobby.'

Simon started to snigger. It was hilarious. It was just fucking hilarious.

11
Daisy

Simon's proposal to me was a fairy tale. Textbook. Perfect. It was at my sister Rose's house just before Christmas, on the twins' first birthday. Simon and I had been dating for not quite six months. I wasn't expecting a proposal, I didn't so much as dare dream about it. Honestly, that's true. If I did dream about it, I'd wake myself up because I didn't want to jinx anything. Even the idea of Simon liking me enough to want to date me was mind-blowing, the possibility that he might one day propose was out of this world. So I was not expecting a ring. He was an amazing boyfriend though, I already knew that. I thought I'd be getting maybe a necklace for Christmas or something especially meaningful, like an early edition of *Little Women*, my favourite book. We'd had the conversation about favourite books. We'd had so many conversations, late into the nights. He was easy to talk to.

The setting was very romantic. Rose's house was dressed for Christmas, there were fresh, green garlands and white twinkling lights everywhere. Rose's 'mum friends' naturally all had kids about the twins' age and many of them had other siblings too so there were smallies everywhere. As usual, I spent a lot of time playing with the children that were old enough to understand games like hide and seek. Everyone I cared for most in the world was at that party: my parents, my sister, her husband and children and, as my sister had sort of adopted my gang, many of my closest friends were there too, including Connie and Luke. Whilst I was playing rowdy games with the kids, I was constantly watching the door because Simon was late. His absence was profound. I suddenly realised that *almost* everyone in the world I most cared for was at the party, but not everyone. He'd leap-frogged into that special position in my heart. He was the most important.

I was beginning to imagine all sorts of dreadful scenarios like he'd fallen under a bus or, worse still, he'd gone off me. No doubt he'd ditched the toddler party and the robust redhead and was sipping gin and tonics in a bar somewhere with a leggy brunette. Then suddenly, I spotted him. He was dressed as Santa with padding, a fake beard, a sack, the lot. I was pretty cross with Rose for roping him in for such a job; I couldn't believe he'd really be comfortable with the role. On the other hand, I was totally delighted because he'd agreed to do it. I mean, no matter how shaky my self-esteem may have been, even I understood that a boyfriend dressing as Santa to entertain your baby nephews and their sticky, noisy, tiny friends, was an act of devotion. I intercepted him under the mistletoe. Giggly, blushing, breathless.

The kids that were old enough to have clue about what was going on were rustled into a line and Simon did the whole 'ho ho ho' thing. He followed the traditional script and asked each child what they wanted for Christmas and whether they'd been good that year. They nodded their little heads, wide eyed and expectant. On cue he delved into his huge sack and produced a present; I can't remember what the gifts were, something tacky and plastic. I remember being surprised because I'd thought Rose would opt for chocolate coins and wooden puzzles. I do remember the children's happy, excited faces. Their pink rosebud mouths lisping thank yous, following the prompts of their watchful mothers.

When all the children had received their treats and were beginning to get restless about what would come next in the constant stream of entertainment and goodies, Simon yelled above their noise, 'There is one girl who hasn't told Santa what she wants for Christmas, yet.' He grabbed my hand and pulled me onto his knee. I was this exquisite mix of mortification and total utter joy. I'd never been happier than in that moment. I'm not normally a fan of being in the limelight and I've never been a fan of sitting on men's knees, I feel too hefty and it's uncomfortable. I could feel the colour rising in my cheeks, but still, I was delirious with happiness.

'Now, Daisy, have you been good this year?'

I heard one of my friends make a joke

referencing something lewd I'd told her, and I promised myself to stop over-sharing. I tried not to be distracted as I replied, 'Quite good.'

'Well, as much as I hate to disagree with you, I think you've been more than quite good. You're wonderful and so I have a special present for you. If you'll accept it.'

I didn't guess. I heard my friends whisper that it was probably flights to somewhere exotic, but I couldn't think clearly enough to hazard a guess, I was so in the moment. Overwhelmed. The room was tight with anticipation and excitement, everyone loves a bit of romantic theatre. At least we did then, now I wonder whether we'd all feel a bit embarrassed if one of us put on a similar show. You get too old for such blatant romance. Too weary, I suppose.

He continued, 'In fact, you are unbelievably good. I never thought that I'd meet anyone quite so good, special and amazing.' His voice was thick and heavy with sincerity and intent. 'So, I would be honoured, ecstatic, if you'd accept my gift.' Then he reached into his sack one more time and pulled out a small ring box. Suddenly everyone else disappeared. I mean, I know they were there, the collective intake of breath nearly starved the room of oxygen, but suddenly they didn't matter to me, not my sister, my parents, my nephews, my friends, no one mattered, except him. His shiny eyes, his dark curly hair, his hopeful nervous smile. 'Will you make me a very happy man, in fact, the happiest man alive, and agree to be my wife?'

Apparently, I screamed then repeatedly yelled

'Yes'. I can't remember that, but it seems reasonable. I can imagine it would be something I'd do. The happiness was almost painful, it was so complete and beautiful that, even whilst I was slipping the diamond on my finger, I was thinking *This can't last. This is too good*. So, in that moment I was never happier or more afraid.

Everyone in the room cheered and applauded. People started singing, 'For they are jolly good fellows'. That seems quaint now. It's a lifetime ago. There was hugging and congratulating, lots of kissing and some crying and champagne corks popping; it was a luminous, glistening moment. Later, Simon confirmed that he'd come up with the entire plan on his own, not just the bit about giving me my ring in that way, but dressing as Santa, giving all the gifts to the children, everything. I worked out as much that evening, when we were snuggled up in his bed, post-coital, emotionally and physically elated and exhausted. The gifts were the tell. If Rose had been in charge she would have chosen different presents for the children, something less fun.

It was such a thoughtful, individual, perfect proposal. For a long time, I believed that moment would stay gleaming in my mind for ever, but it's tarnished now. I'm embarrassed for them. That hopeful young woman, that ambitious young man, because we let them down. I have no idea where that man went.

Or that woman, come to think of it.

12

Simon

Wednesday, 13th July 2016

The TV woke him up. He tried to focus, but it was tricky. There were a lot of voices talking across one another. What was he watching? Four middle-aged women, sitting on stools around a breakfast bar. They were wearing bright tops, but the gaiety was cancelled out by their angry faces. They were arguing although not with each other. Simon listened for a moment or two, long enough to gather they were angry with some man, or some male thing, yet there were no men there to shout at so they were shouting at each other and in general. It was almost funny.

He knew what it was, he knew it. Daisy loved this show. It was *Loose Women*. He didn't know how he knew that, he was hardly the target audience, but he did. He felt remembering the name of the show was something. A small victory. Daisy sometimes watched it in the school holidays. A guilty pleasure when she was ironing or doing something with Millie, crafting or whatever. It must be mid-morning. Why was he asleep in an armchair mid-morning? His head was fucking killing him. It was pulsing, pounding. He must be ill. That was it. He was off work because he was ill. He searched about for the remote control and noticed an empty bottle of red wine and an empty bottle of whisky at his feet. He ignored them. They didn't make sense. Finding the remote was all that mattered. He had to mute the angry women. If only life was as easy. Unfortunately, even when he managed to shut them up, the screaming and yelling continued in his head. He didn't know if it was real, or something he remembered, or just something he was imagining. It was sometimes hard to tell.

Simon looked out of the window, it was pitch black, dead of night, not mid-morning. He turned back to the TV confused. Definitely *Loose Women*. It took longer than it should but then he took a stab at sorting it out in his mind — it had to be a late night repeat. He checked his watch; it was tricky to focus, he couldn't quite see the illuminated numbers. He was really ill. Maybe hallucinating, a fever? He'd heard something was going around, something serious. It was 3.15 a.m. Or maybe 5.15 a.m. He didn't know or care. Not really. What was that smell? It was disgusting. Puke and sweat.

He noticed that his shirt and the arm of the chair were covered in vomit. Some of it had solidified, some of it still oozed. Sloppy and shaming. He peeled off his shirt, balled it up, tried not to let the puke slide onto the floor. He walked through to the kitchen and dropped the soiled garment on the floor, in front of the kitchen sink. He realised that he probably should put it in the washing machine, but he couldn't, not right then. Too much effort. He wasn't up to it. He was ill. Daisy would sort it out when she got up. He tried to remember yesterday. Had he come home from work sick? Had he gone into work at all? Maybe this was not a bug, maybe he'd had a few jars, eaten a curry with a bad prawn. He couldn't remember eating. The puke didn't smell of curries or prawns.

He needed a drink. Water maybe? No, a beer. A beer would be best. Hair of the dog. Because yes, he realised now this was most likely a hangover. Off the scale, a different level, but a hangover all the same. His hands were freezing, his vision was blurred. Not a hangover then, he was still drunk. It would be best to keep on drinking.

As he opened the fridge, the light spilt out on to the kitchen and he nearly dropped the bottle in shock.

'What the fuck are you doing, sitting in the dark?' he yelled.

Daisy sighed. She'd been crying. He could tell. Her eyes were bloodshot and her face blotchy. Simon realised, with a slow sense of regret, that it had not just been a late night but an emotional one, too.

Here it was. Off they went.

'I stayed up to check you didn't choke on your own vomit,' she said with another sigh. Like, how was it possible to have that much air and disappointment to expunge? It couldn't be for real, could it. There had to be an element of theatre to it, a sense of drama. She had her hands wrapped around a mug, the very picture of wifely patience. It fucked him off. Her patience — or at least her show of it — her acceptance, her constant understanding, it all fucked him off. Because it wasn't real. It wasn't her. He didn't believe it. Not anymore. It would be more real if she showed she was angry. He wanted her to be angry. Like him.

He was swaying, ever so slightly. He needed to sit down. Just as he was about to do so, his body collapsed below him. He sent a wooden kitchen chair toppling, his head thumped against the corner of a unit. The pain was blunted by his state, but in the morning there would be a bump. His body relaxed into the pain, working through it. He'd learnt this technique now. Sometimes when he was drinking he hurt himself by accident. One evening, he fell down some steps in town, another time he walked into the closed patio doors thinking they were open. It was best to roll with the pain. Not to fight it.

'Oh Simon.' He could hear pity and despair in Daisy's voice.

He felt warm and then cold, his thighs. He could smell something beneath the puke and sweat. It was a dark and acidic smell. It was piss. He'd pissed himself.

* * *

He woke up, he was in bed. He was relieved. Sometimes, he didn't get to bed. He fell to sleep on a chair in the sitting room, on a bench in the street, or on the train home. That was the worst.

He'd be carried to the last stop on the route and then woken up by a ticket inspector. He couldn't always get an Uber. Occasionally he'd slept on stations, caught the first train home in the morning. Waking up in his own bed was a bonus. He put his fingers to the back of his head where it ached, not just the usual hangover ache, something more specific; there was a lump, but he couldn't feel any stickiness, no blood. There weren't any bottles next to his bed. He was naked but smelt clean. It didn't add up.

Daisy was not in bed. As he sat up he noticed she was dozing on the chair in the corner of the bedroom, the one that was normally covered in discarded clothes. She heard him stir and her eyes sprung open. Always a light sleeper. Instantly, her face was awash with anxiety, resentment, disappointment.

'Morning,' Simon said brightly. Best to style this out. Clearly there had been something but as yet he couldn't recall exactly what that something was, so he wasn't worried. He was in his own bed, there wasn't a bucket or any bottles by his side. He was good. 'What time is it? I need to get to work.' As he asked this, he swung his legs out of bed. The movement was too sudden, too energetic. He felt like crap. His body ached and shook but he was good at ignoring that, good at hiding how awful he felt, how awful he was.

Daisy checked her watch. 'It's noon, just after,' she muttered tonelessly.

'Why aren't you at work?'

'I took a personal day.'

Simon snorted. 'Is that a thing now?'

She ignored his sarcasm. It was unusual for Daisy to take time off work, unprecedented actually. Simon was not sure he wanted to know why she'd done so. He asked the more pressing question instead, 'Did you call my boss too?' Simon calling in sick was not unprecedented and although Daisy didn't like doing it for him — made a big fuss about how she hated lying — she had done so in the past. The truth was, she was a better liar than she made out.

'You really can't remember, can you?' she asked.

'Remember what?'

Another sigh, more of a puff. She really was honestly a tornado of regret and dissatisfaction. 'You don't have a job. You were fired yesterday.'

'What the fu — What are you talking about? Fired? No.'

'You turned up late and drunk, again. But this time you were aggressive with the client and it was the straw that broke the camel's back. Your boss has been looking for an excuse for a while. You know he has.'

She was wrong. She was being a bitch. Dramatic. 'How do you know this?' he demanded.

'You didn't tell me. Luke did.'

'Oh, Saint Luke,' Simon snapped, snidely.

'I don't know why you are being like that. He's your best friend. I called him last night when you came home legless and making no sense. He filled me in on the details.'

Simon dropped his head into his hands and

tried, really fucking hard, to remember what she was going on about. But he couldn't. Nothing. Yesterday was nothing. The last thing he remembered was leaving home, catching the tube into Covent Garden. But he did that most days, he wasn't sure if that was a specific memory or just something that he knew happened.

Daisy looked disbelieving. She thought his memory — or lack of it — was convenient, that he blanked out what he wanted. Right now, Simon thought the blackout was inconvenient. He wanted to know how and why he'd lost his job. Or at least, he probably wanted to know.

So, she told him. Her version, or Luke's version, some bloody version but he couldn't imagine it was the truth. He wasn't drunk when he turned up at the office. Maybe, they could smell alcohol on his breath. Occasionally, he had a nip from his flask as he walked to the station. It was no big deal. Not drunk. And a nip in his coffee, too. Sometimes. Some people like maple syrup in their coffee, he liked whisky. It didn't mean anything. It certainly wasn't a dependency. What the hell? No. He was a creative, an interior designer, no one could expect him to work to a rigid schedule, he needed space. He needed freedom. Who puts a meeting in a diary at 10 a.m. anyway? It was uncivilised. And the client was a dick. OK, Simon could see that it wasn't perhaps his wisest move, calling him the c-word for suggesting mushroom for the colour palette. Maybe that was hard to come back from. Simon didn't really know why he had been so against mushroom, except he'd been thinking something brave, something bold. That's what they pay him for, right? His ideas. Why wouldn't they listen to him? He did not believe that he wasn't able to stand up properly. They felt *threatened*. By him? That was just bullshit.

She made a big thing about saying she couldn't account for his afternoon. Apparently, he stormed out of the agency or maybe security threw him out; she wasn't totally clear on this point. Someone who knew that they were mates had called Luke, who had spent his afternoon looking for Simon. And that made him some sort of god in Daisy's eyes. She kept going on about how good it was of him, how inconvenient. 'He has a job of his own, you know, besides being your babysitter,' she snapped bitterly. 'Can you imagine how embarrassing it was for him? Since he's the one that introduced the client to your firm in the first place. He is always putting work your way. If you ask me it's the main reason the agency have kept you on as long as they have.'

'That's just bullshit. I'm good at what I do and they know it.' Simon was sitting naked on the edge of the bed. His penis flaccid, his head is in his hands. What did this woman want from him? She was stripping away his manhood with her tongue. If what she was saying was true, he'd just lost his fucking job, how about some support please? Some sympathy. She told him that he came home at midnight, that he was 'awkward'. He fell over in the kitchen and wouldn't come to bed. He couldn't remember any of this, but he believed her on that last point. He didn't want to go to bed with Daisy. The thought was a hideous one. After what Martell had told him. Besides, sex is nothing compared to booze. Sex was messy and demanding, it came with secrets, never-articulated caveats and demands. It lied. Booze was pure. Generous. Easy.

'You threw up on yourself. I stayed up all night, checking on you every thirty minutes to see you hadn't choked,' added Daisy. Simon tutted. Her martyrdom was boring. What did she want? A medal? 'You peed yourself,' she added, exasperated.

'Then how come I'm clean now?' Simon challenged. He couldn't believe Daisy had dragged him upstairs if he was in the state she said he was.

'I called Luke. He came around at four in the morning. He helped me get you upstairs and into the shower. We hosed you down.'

She was a lying bitch. He knew she was.

13

Daisy

Saturday, 23rd July 2016

I have never been so desperate to get to the end of a term. It breaks my heart to close the door behind me every morning, knowing Simon is most likely going to spend the day in bed drinking, or slouched in front of the TV drinking. Without the pretence that he's going into work, I fear the 'functioning' part of the label 'functioning alcoholic' is null and void. It's desperate. He isn't shaving, or even showering. He's barely speaking. Still, I've kept it together. I have responsibilities. Millie, Elsie and my job. I've told Millie that Daddy is a bit poorly which is why he isn't going to work.

'Has he got a poorly head again or is his tummy upset?' she asks innocently. 'Poor Daddy. He's often ill. He needs to see a doctor.' Out of the mouths of babes. I don't want to leave him alone more than I have to, but I honour my commitment to visit Elsie. Despite what Simon says, I think Elsie does enjoy our visits; maybe she can't anticipate them or even remember them but when she's in the moment, they seem to bring her some ease. Usually. Unfortunately, this week, she's picked up a urinary tract infection which is common in dementia sufferers, and she's had bouts of terrible hallucinations and intense paranoia. She threw things at me when I went into her room, she thought I was an undertaker and had come to measure her up. I've tried to concentrate on my class, who are all excitedly looking forward to their summer holidays and to the idea of going to big school after that. I busy myself writing reports and rehearsing for the end of year assembly. I manage to warmly thank my students and their parents for their thank you gifts of chocolate and cava but all the time I'm at school, my mind and heart are with Simon.

What are we going to do? My first thought is his health but I'm also concerned about money. How will we pay the mortgage with only my salary? Who will give him a job now? No one in their right mind.

Thank goodness it's the holidays and I can have some breathing space. I'm only just holding on and I know I need to do more than that. I need to hold us together.

The last thing I want to do is go to Connie and Luke's anniversary party. I had not expected Simon to so much as remember it, let alone want to attend. I thought shame would keep him away. I can barely stand the idea of facing Luke, but Simon doesn't have the same sensitivities. He wakes up on Saturday morning and is buoyant about the idea of going.

'We're going, Daisy. We promised Connie and Luke,' he says. As though he's a regular guy and keeping his word is important to him. The fact is, parties mean alcohol. Lots of free-flowing alcohol. They also mean dancing, catching up with old friends and eating gorgeous nibbles, but none of that is important to Simon. For him a party *only* means alcohol. Lots of people will be drinking to get drunk. He'll fit right in.

I haven't seen my friends since Simon was sacked. I'm avoiding them. My sister Rose called as soon as she heard but I fobbed her off. 'Connie has exaggerated things wildly,' I told her. 'You know how she is.' In fact, the account of Simon's dismissal that Rose relayed to me, gifted to her from Connie, was less sensational than what really occurred. I guess Luke did us a favour of playing down how dreadful the whole episode was. 'The truth is Simon and his boss came to a mutually agreeable decision to part ways. Simon is looking for new creative challenges,' I insisted.

'Really, Daisy?' my sister asked, concern oozing from her voice.

'Rose, I'd tell you if there was anything seriously wrong.'

'Would you?'

I'd want to. That's almost the same thing. My sister and I used to confide everything in each other. Then that stopped being possible. I no longer believe a problem shared is a problem halved. I know it for what it is, double the trouble. Some secrets must stay just that. I don't want to go to this party. The thought leaves me feeling panicky and breathless. Even before Simon's humiliating dismissal, I'd had no intention of going. Throughout the day I try to persuade Simon that we shouldn't bother.

'Let's just stay in, have a quiet night,' I suggest.

'What's the matter, Daisy? Are you afraid everyone will be gossiping about us?'

'I just don't like parties. You know I don't.'

'The sooner you start to behave as though nothing is wrong, the sooner everyone else will believe that is the case,' he replies smugly, unrepentant, as though it was me who soiled my clothes and had been hosed down by my best friend. I know what he says is true, but it smacks of wallpapering over the cracks, rather than fixing the problem. Something I can do and have done for a long time. I just don't think I want to anymore. I get the feeling that if I carry on that way, the whole house might fall down around me.

'My parents can't babysit. They are going to a concert at the Royal Albert Hall. They already have tickets.' I offer up this problem, but I didn't expect it to matter to Simon.

'Why haven't you sorted out a sitter sooner?' he asks crossly, then adds, 'We can take her along.'

That's not happening. No way. I nip over the road and arrange for Millie to sleep at her friend India's. Millie and India are in the same class, that and the proximity of their homes means they're best friends. The pair of them are always in and out of each other's houses, having meals, watching TV, playing in the garden, but this will be their first official sleepover. Millie is deliriously excited.

Early afternoon, Millie and I nip out and buy popcorn because India tells me her mum has promised sparkly nail varnish and facemasks. I'm not sure that I approve of six-year-olds wearing nail varnish, and they definitely don't need facemasks, but on the other hand, I once read a feminist book that argued grooming rituals are an important part of female bonding. I don't want to pour cold water on the plan. What harm can a single at-home-spa-night do? Whenever I feel a tidal wave of fear or shame, and I consider backing out of the party, just staying at home and using looking after Millie as an excuse, I remind myself that Millie would be upset if her sleepover didn't go ahead.

It's been a hot, sticky day. The air is thick and heavy. I can almost taste it. It climbs down my throat. Choking me. I start to get dressed without any enthusiasm. I know Connie and Rose have both bought something new to wear tonight. If I judge from the excited frenzy of social media of my friends and acquaintances, it seems as though half of London has done so. Connie's parties are something people get excited about. I'd rather be doing anything else.

I stand in front of my open wardrobe. I'm currently wearing black linen trousers and my beige seen-better-days bra. The trousers were once fashionable, they no longer are, and it's always hard to look smart in linen. I half-heartedly flick through the tops that droop unimpressively on hangers, nothing looks especially 'party'. It surprises me how many of my white T-shirts are stained yellow under the arms. Other tops are bobbled with wear or have faded. Mostly, these things are only fit for gardening or housework. The close, uncomfortable, evening means that although I've just showered my skin is already damp and clammy. Still, I'm definitely going to wear trousers. My legs look like they are wearing a mohair jumper. I'm never waxed and ready anymore, I've let myself go. The truth is, I couldn't care less about what I wear tonight, I don't want to stand out. I'd rather not draw attention, although I fear I will, or Simon will. However, I have my pride. If we must attend, then I need to put my best foot forward. No one can know how bad things are.

I dig out a blue, cotton top, it's old but reliable. I blow-dry my hair even though my arms are heavy. Reluctantly I put on makeup. I don't tackle eyeliner because my hands are shaking too much. I think I look OK. I pop across the road with Millie, to drop her off at India's. The girls are giddy and talk excitedly about their impending manicures and 'camping' in India's bedroom. I must admit, Simon has ignited something with his evening under the stars. It's certainly a more wholesome activity than a spa night. As Simon isn't working and we have weeks of holiday stretched out in front of us, I wonder whether there's any chance that we could do a proper camping trip this summer. It's not my natural comfort zone but maybe I should make the effort. Another effort. I know Simon has experience, maybe it would be good for him to be able to take charge of something; showcase his strengths. If the weather holds it might be fun. Importantly, if we're camping, I could ensure there was no booze, or at least limit it.

Would a break like that help clear Simon's head?

I doubt it, but I simultaneously hope for it. Something has to change.

We can't go on as we are.

I could ask Connie if we could borrow all her camping equipment again, so it wouldn't have to cost much. A change in our routine might be just what we need. At least we'd find some time to talk. Because, the thing is, whilst I don't want to talk to Rose or Connie about my troubled marriage, I find I do want to talk to Simon. You see, despite everything, I still love him.

We've been through bad patches before. Awful, terrible times. And it has got better before. Surely it can get better again. It has to.

For a moment, I'm brushed with a sense of determination. I can and must turn things around. What I feel is not the same as optimism but I'm a breath closer to being resolved. I kiss Millie goodbye and tell her to be good for India's mummy, then I cross back over the road to ours. I will drive to the party tonight. I'm certainly not bothered about having a drink and if I have the car with me I can bring back the camping equipment. We could go away somewhere next week. We could press reset. Why not?

14

Simon

So now she wanted to go camping. Years, he had been trying to persuade her, and she'd never shown any interest. He'd finally proven his point. Millie had enjoyed their foray under canvas in the back garden and Daisy was convinced. He should be pleased. It should feel like a victory.

But it didn't. Nothing did.

He couldn't get Martell out of his mind. Fuck it. Fuck her. She had some nerve, stood there all done up — hair, makeup — beaming. She looked pretty. He could see that. But he wouldn't admit it aloud. He wondered who she was dressing for. Not him. Was it still going on? No, that was impossible. But you heard of it, didn't you? Affairs that lasted years. The other halves just bobbing along, ignorant, like fucking idiots. Fucking losers. He should ask her. Now. Just straight out. Straight up. That would take the grin off her face. Instead he took a gulp of his gin and tonic.

Simon knew he hadn't always been a perfect husband. It had been hard sometimes. All marriages were. It couldn't be a bed of roses. Those years when they both longed for a baby were difficult. His mother used to tell him to count their blessings. He found it easier to count his units. Get pissed. Block it out. It was a shame that he'd ignored Elsie when she was still able to tell him things that made sense. 'Look at what you have,' she'd urged. 'A lovely wife, a nice home, a good job.' But he couldn't focus, at least not on anything other than where the next drink was coming from. Even so, he didn't deserve this. He'd been a good husband. Certainly, good enough. He used to do stuff around the house, bring home a decent salary, spend every weekend with her friends. He showered her with attention, care and compliments. He didn't mess around with other women.

So he liked a swift drink. That was it. That was his only — how should he phrase it? — his only drawback. He wouldn't consider that a deal-breaker. Yet, she had. Apparently. She'd decided she had the right to screw another man and then pass off his kid as Simon's. It was disgusting.

It was difficult to look at her. His eyes used to pull up the length of her body; now he chose to stay entirely focused on the gin bottle on the table.

'What do you think?' she asked brightly. 'We could go to the New Forest.'

He didn't know if he wanted to go camping with her. Being cooped up in such a small place might make him want to kill her. He couldn't think about it now. Next week or even tomorrow seemed a long way away. Instead, he clapped his hands together, 'How about you join me with a little pre-party drink? G&T?'

'I think we need to get going,' replied Daisy.

Puritanical, hypocritical bitch.

15
Daisy

Crisp, white bunting marks out Connie and Luke's patch. The white triangles look like small yachts lining up to dock somewhere glamorous, Sydney Harbour or Monte Carlo, and whilst the bunting is not so much fluttering in the breeze — the early evening air is still, flat — the effect is stylish, captivating. The front door is wide open as Connie is the sort of person who doesn't believe bad things will happen to her. She couldn't imagine a scenario where someone might walk in, go upstairs and take whatever they liked. Ruin everything. I suppose the scenario *is* unlikely as lots of her guests are lingering in the hallway, spilling out of the open door, glasses in hands, laughter on lips but, all the same, keeping a vague eye on the comings and goings. I nervously scan these people, looking for a familiar face and at the same time dreading seeing one. I want to run back down the garden path. I want to go home.

Connie and Luke have done very well for themselves. Their stylish home in Notting Hill reflects as much; for a London property it's a decent size. Even so, every room is heaving with guests; people are pushed against walls, some are sitting or standing on the stairways. Simon vigorously pushes his way through the crowds and heads for the kitchen. First thought, a drink. When the evening is beginning and Simon is heading out, he often puts me in mind of an urban fox. Feral, wily, determined, solitary. When he returns he's more of a sloth. There's a bar set up in the kitchen and two guys are mixing cocktails. I expected something like this, after all it is a party, but my heart sinks. A small crowd are gathered, enjoying the spectacle. People 'ooh' and 'aah' as the cocktail shakers fly and twirl thorough the air like birds, the bartender twizzles 360 degrees, lemons and limes are sliced at a rate of knots. Simon looks impatient. I see his fingers drum on the counter as he must wait his turn.

I can't watch. I keep moving on, through the patio door and out to the dark wood deck. Connie doesn't have grass or flower beds, she has a number of enormous, antique stone urns, out of which spout what she calls, 'architectural plants'. They are purple or black, rarely anything so ordinary as green. Glistening white fairy lights hang in swathes along all three boundary walls and above our heads. It won't be dark for ages yet, but when it is, they'll look wonderful; whimsical, yet warm and inviting. Connie works hard at ensuring she lives in the sort of tableaus that are Instagram-worthy.

'Daisy!' I hear several familiar voices call out my name in unison. Rose, her husband Craig, and Connie wave enthusiastically. They're clustered, chatting. I pray they haven't been talking about us, but imagine they have. I guess Luke is somewhere nearby. He and Connie are great hosts and therefore you rarely find them together at one of their own parties; they're always attending to the needs of others: making introductions, topping up drinks. I smile, hoping to convince people I'm pleased to see them. I should be, it's not their fault I feel uncomfortable. I quash the sensation that I'm going into battle and give myself over to their welcoming hugs and compliments. I issue reciprocal compliments, commenting on Connie's dress (she immediately tells me she got it in a sale), Rose's necklace (she puts her hand to her enormous bosom, 'Oh this old thing'). I'm talking too quickly, we all are. We hardly manage to answer a question before another one is asked. It seems no one wants any awkward pauses.

'Are Sebastian and Henry here?' I glance about, hoping to spot my nephews.

'No, they're at SuncéBeat Festival,' says Craig.

'I don't know that one.' This is not a surprise. I have never in my life been to a music festival.

'It's in Croatia,' says Craig with a beam. He checks his watch. 'They're probably just applying body oil before they climb into the cages to dance.' We all laugh except for Rose who looks mildly concerned that their step-dad might be spot on.

'They're with a friend of theirs, and his parents,' she says, stiffly. 'I'm sure they are doing no such thing.'

'Right, they're certainly looking at the finest examples of early Byzantine architecture in the

Mediterranean region,' laughs Craig. Then he puts his arm around Rose and squeezes her affectionately, aware she'll be nervous about her boys being away, and probably not up to too much ribbing on the matter.

'And your girls?' I ask Connie.

'They've all invited some friends of their own, so I guess they are somewhere about, up to no good or sneaking sips of the cocktails.' Connie says this confidently because her three daughters are still young, lovely and very well behaved, so she has nothing to worry about. Rather than testing the boundaries, they are much more likely to be handing out vol-au-vents to the guests. Henry and Seb are good guys too, they may get a tiny bit drunk from time to time but we've never had any police visits and their academic records seem solid. We just all play along with the idea that the teenagers are hard work because that's what people expect. I've always thought this strategy is a bit daft. It almost implies the kids are letting us down if they are not taking drugs and falling pregnant, somehow failing to fulfil our expectations of teens.

'Oh, there's Lucy!' Connie beams at her old friend. Lucy was once my friend too. I think it's more accurate to say I consider her a frenemy now. I glance at Rose. She straightens her shoulders. Even after all this time, socialising with Lucy and Peter can't be easy for Rose. Their presence here at the party must change the night for her. She won't be quite as relaxed, quite as open.

Connie, Lucy and I met as undergraduates, I introduced my friends to Rose, who had already graduated and had a job but visited me regularly at weekends. We were an unlikely gang but glued by Connie, the common denominator. We did everything together at university and for quite some time beyond. We went on holidays and we briefly flat-shared. Rose then married Peter and they had Henry and Sebastian, but Lucy had a sneaky, adulterous affair with Peter and now *they* are married and have a daughter, Auriol. It's officially messy.

Connie stayed friends with everyone throughout. She can always see both sides of the story and, anyway, argues that the Rose and Lucy stuff is ancient history. True, Rose and Peter split up sixteen years ago. She's been happily married to Craig for almost a decade. I adore Craig, he is a lovely, lovely man and I'm so pleased that my sister has found such complete and comfortable love, but has Connie forgotten the years when Rose struggled as a single mum of twins? Doesn't she think about those things when she issues party invites? I'm not a prude. I know people have affairs, make mistakes and then make amends. I, more than most, understand that we're all human, we're all weak, vulnerable or silly sometimes. There has to be a place for the second chance — I honestly do believe that. But Lucy ate Christmas lunch at my sister's house whilst she was screwing my sister's husband, and now we are all supposed to pretend none of it matters, that we're all still great friends. I think it would be much more normal if there was a level of resentment or anger. A sense of embarrassment or regret. *Something*. Look, there are goodies and baddies. Rose is my sister, Lucy is a home-wrecking bitch.

Lucy heads towards us, waving majestically, smiling broadly. Peter is trailing behind her.

The only good thing about their arrival is that it means I'm certainly not the centre of attention anymore. Lucy is always that. She's too beautiful — and I must admit, although it kills me — too clever, to be anything other. Lucy announces they are taking the summer off. I guess they must have savings that will allow that sort of thing. Naturally, they are shunning package holidays and instead plan to visit somewhere in Mexico to volunteer their time and work in schools for orphans. It appears that Henry and Seb are going along too; Rose and Craig don't look startled by this news. I wonder when it was agreed and why no one has told me.

I'm asked about our holiday plans, I say that we are going camping. I ask Connie if I can borrow her kit. She agrees, readily, which makes me love her, but then she adds, 'You might need to buy a new stove. Ours has a piece missing.' Which makes me loath her. I know I'm not being fair or consistent. She's just stating a fact. But it's being here, at her party, it's putting me on edge. I'm agitated. Defensive. Anyway, why should I be fair? Life isn't, is it?

Simon appears from nowhere. He greets everyone with huge enthusiasm. The conversation bobs along, Simon affably nods his head at pretty much everything everyone says but I can tell he's not following what's being said. He has no interest in the new Ghostbusters movie, the Conservative party leadership election or the final stage of the Tour de France.

'Hot evening, isn't it?' he comments. He knocks back his cocktail as he makes this remark. 'Thirsty-making. I think I'll get another. Anyone else?' In unison our friends look at their glasses and make demure sounds.

'No thanks, buddy.'

'I'm OK with this, pacing myself, you know.'

'It's going to be a long night, I'm taking it steady.'

I hear what they're saying. They are willing him to be cautious, to be careful. They're trying to lead by example, but it won't work. Simon shrugs. 'Suit yourselves.' He heads back into the kitchen. We all watch his back in silence.

16

Simon

Simon spent most of his evening talking to new people. He needed new friends, his old ones were boring and judgemental. Annoyingly, they were judging the wrong person, weren't they? All he did was enjoy a drink. But Daisy, well *she* . . . He wondered what they knew. More than him, no doubt. They told each other everything, those women. Always whispering and gossiping. They'd be laughing at him. They probably had been for a while. Daisy and her sister and the other women were as thick as thieves. They didn't judge each other. One rule for them, another rule for everyone else. Look at how things were with Lucy and Peter for example. They had an affair, under everyone's noses. OK, there was a fuss at the time, but it quickly died down. They are back in the bosom of the pack now. Everyone was keen to carry on as before.

He sighed and jostled his way through the partying people, inching ever closer to the cocktail bar.

They weren't his friends anyway, not really. They were *her* friends and they were all like her: insistent, hypocritical, clearly pursuing agendas.

It was obvious that they were all itching to ask him about his drinking and losing his job. All that crap. It was blatantly apparent by the way they *avoided* the subject. Normally, Craig would ask, 'How's work?' It was the usual icebreaker with men. That or sport. Simon didn't give a fuck about sport. Or work. Or Craig, come to that. He wanted a drink though. He'd been stood at this poncey cocktail bar for ages. It was all very well making a performance out of making a drink, but a man could die of thirst.

'Well hello, Simon!' Simon turned to see who was speaking to him. He didn't know the bloke, although the bloke clearly knew him, not an unprecedented situation. He grabbed Simon's hand, pumped it up and down. 'It's been a while. How are you keeping?'

The fact he'd asked made Simon feel more secure. This man didn't have a clue because anyone who knew how he was keeping didn't ask. 'Not bad, very well,' Simon replied with a grin. Then added wryly, 'I'll be much happier when I get to the front of the queue.'

The bloke laughed as though Simon had just said something really funny, not really mediocre. Then he endeared himself further to Simon when he added, 'Too damn right. Thing is, not worth the wait, these cocktails. Gone in a gulp. Come with me.'

Simon wracked his brain for a name or a context. Fricking blackouts. Names got lost, nights got lost. He usually didn't mind much. There were things it was best to forget, and his nights out were often that. But not remembering someone's name was a bit frustrating. He followed the man because he was tall, friendly, good looking. The sort of bloke that knew what he wanted out of life, knew where to find a good time. This proved to be the case when suddenly he was holding up a bottle of tequila. 'Shots?' he asked.

Simon would have preferred wine or whisky, but shots were fine by him too. Even though they were certainly gone in a gulp, like the cocktails. That was the point of them. He followed his new friend outside to the bit of space that passed as a front garden in London. Simon was relieved that his new friend hadn't headed towards the back garden. Since his name was still eluding Simon, it'd be impossible to introduce him to the gang, and besides, Simon didn't want to talk to the gang. He wished he could remember something about this fella though. He was vaguely familiar. He looked like any one of a number of Connie's guests. Tall, fit, strong, good looking. Simon was enough of a man to be able to say when another man was good looking.

They sat on the wall, facing the house, allowing the evening warmth to envelope them. The party was happening all around them, the place was messy with bowls of tortilla chips and upended beer bottles. His new friend laughed, 'Bugger, I forgot to bring glasses.' He scouted about. There were a few discarded wine glasses scattered on the ground or stood on the wall next to ashtrays full of cigarette stubs. Ants crawling inside them. Simon knew that his pal was considering picking up a couple, tipping the dregs onto the wood chippings and using the glasses, unconcerned about germs, unconcerned about mixing drinks. Simon felt he'd found a fellow committed drinker, and something loosened inside him, unknotted. He felt comfortable. He made friends this way, often enough. In bars and pubs throughout London. The company was easy and transient. He'd probably drunk with this man before. The man seemingly recalled it, Simon didn't. No biggie. Eventually, his friend rejected the idea of retrieving the scattered glasses, perhaps he thought it was too much effort to stoop down and pick them up. Instead, he took a swig from the bottle and then offered it to Simon. Simon took it. Glug, glug.

They started talking about *The Walking Dead* and *Game of Thrones*. Their reviews were forensic in detail. Time slipped. Slid away.

'How's the lovely Daisy?'

Simon was surprised by the question. His companion apparently did know him better than he'd first imagined. Not just someone he'd passed time with at a bar, perhaps he was one of Daisy and Connie's university friends.

'Yeah, good, fine thanks. She's here. Somewhere about.'

'I haven't seen either of you for years.' Simon felt this useful bit of information was quite comforting. He hadn't necessarily forgotten this bloke because they'd recently drunk themselves into a void; he was just as likely to have slipped Simon's mind because it had been a while. Normal middle age stuff. Although, even if it had been a while, alcohol was most probably involved.

‘Hey, Daryll, do you have a light?’ Another guy interrupted their conversation, but Simon didn’t mind. There, he had it! Daryll. All he had to do was hold on to it.

‘No mate, sorry,’ said Daryll with a shrug. The interruption was brief. Daryll turned back to Simon. The tequila bottle was almost empty. ‘Shit, did we drink all of that?’

‘It only had about a third in when you pilfered it,’ said Simon. He paid close attention to such things.

‘Thank God for that. Shall I get us something else? You stay put.’

Simon nodded, pleased. He didn’t want to move, didn’t want to bump into Daisy or any of the others. Daryll was a decent guy, very interesting. Simon knew he would come back with more drink. It wasn’t just some bullshit excuse to get away. He could just sit tight. ‘Maybe some red?’ he suggested.

‘Good plan. I’ll see what I can find.’

Yes, Simon was going to have a good time. He could tell. It was really good luck that he’d bumped into this Daryll bloke.

17
Daisy

'Daisy!' I hear his voice break through the throng of party chatter and music, insistent and demanding. I freeze. 'Daisy, come over here! Come and say hi.'

Simon is sat on the stairs with Daryll Lainbridge. The sight of him slows my blood. My knees wobble. Inappropriately, I almost laugh when I note that legs giving way, no longer willing or able to hold up my body, is a real thing; I had always thought it was just an expression. What is Simon doing talking to him of all people? I put my hand on the wall. Steady myself. It's important I get a grip. Stay upright. Carry on as normal. More important now than ever.

I went to university with Daryll Lainbridge. Back then, I had a vague, hopeless crush on him. Why wouldn't I? He was handsome, intelligent, wealthy and confident, I was eighteen and romantic. We all agreed he looked like Sebastian Flyte from *Bridesbead Revisited*, at least the Anthony Andrews, 1980s TV version of Sebastian Flyte. Whilst he didn't carry a teddy bear, he did wear three-piece suits and an air of arrogance that I ought to have recognised as pretentious, but I found ridiculously attractive. I was desperate to be his Charles Ryder. I wanted to be caught up in his elegant, refined world. In the absence of a better tactic, I tried to ingratiate myself by loaning him my lecture notes and revision cards, which were excellent: neat, informative, comprehensive. Despite this, he struggled to recall my name. When we were undergraduates, he used to call me Curly, an accurate but impersonal get out. He was undoubtedly out of my league, and anyway — naturally — he was mad about Lucy. Well, everyone was. He only had eyes for her, but in a sort of complex *A Midsummer Night's Dream* parody, she didn't notice him, she was in love with my sister's boyfriend. Everyone was looking the wrong way.

Lucy certainly didn't bother staying in touch with Daryll Lainbridge after we graduated, none of us did. He was reintroduced into our social circle after a hiatus of about ten years, when Connie bumped him at Portobello market one Saturday. By then he'd stopped wearing the three-piece suits and I finally recognised them for what they were: not a show of confidence but a desperate bid for attention, a pretention. Much to my mortification, on his reintroduction to our group I realised Daryll had been aware of undergraduate me; he might not have known my name, but he knew me as someone who had always fancied him. He made much of it, even though I had married Simon by then and things had moved on. It was awkward. For a while he did this terrible thing of trying to flirt with me but at the same time making it clear that he was doing me a favour by doing so, a sort of pity flirt. Connie said that I was being too sensitive. That she didn't think he treated me any differently to anyone else. She'd never heard of a pity flirt. She told me to enjoy the attention, if there was indeed any there, because married life could be boring. Connie knows less than she thinks she does.

I'd heard that Daryll has been living overseas for the past few years, Hong Kong, I think, and I was glad. Not far enough. But Connie's friends are the sort that pop backwards and forwards across oceans and continents in club class; there was always a chance he would be here. I'd feared it, hoped against hope that he wouldn't be, but here he is. And, my worst nightmare, he's talking to Simon. I think of all the things that might be said and I pray none of them are. They both look drunk. Is their level of inebriation a calamity waiting to happen or a reprieve? Simon rarely manages to pursue a proper conversation when he's drunk, he hasn't got the necessary attention. On the other hand, he occasionally becomes belligerent, quarrelsome. I shudder. Sometimes, and this doesn't make me proud, I wish I could just peel him off, like skin off a satsuma. That I could slip away from the responsibility of him. And Daryll? What is he up to? Why has he made a friend of Simon? Fear shimmies throughout my body. It's hard to breathe.

I don't know what to do to stop them talking. I quickly realise there isn't anything I can rationally do. I swiftly walk in the opposite direction to their pleas and demands that I join them. I just want to get away from both of them, as far away as possible. I'd like to walk right out of the party, down the street, just keep going. I don't. I stay, even though I know by now that sometimes running *is* the answer.

With determination, I bury myself in the comfort of strangers. People who are happy to talk about what they do with their days: what restaurants they've recently visited or whether their shoes are pinching their toes. Most people appreciate a good listener and I'm not required to say much, which is a relief because I'm not sure I'm up to speaking coherently even about something as straightforward as menus. I feel dazed, not exactly with it. Dizzy. I'd like to say that the dizziness is the feathery and unburdened sort, but it isn't. It's the anxious, slightly queasy sort.

Some women have carved out a space on the wooden floor of the kitchen-diner, plugged in an iPhone and thrown themselves into dancing. I can't pluck up the courage to join them, but seeing others let themselves go on a makeshift dancefloor brings me a sense of happiness. I stand near the action, tapping my toe, hoping the beat can soothe me but knowing it will take more than that. I suppose I want to be persuaded on to the floor, beckoned. Rose is dancing like a dervish. She's flushed and happy. Clearly, tonight, her agenda is to dance until she aches. That's all she has to think about. I wish I could dance until I was sweaty and that the tunes could somehow transport me, protect me.

Someone taps me on the shoulder. My entire

body shivers. Quivers. 'Not dancing?' It's not really a question as it's obvious that I'm not dancing. I shake my head at Daryll Lainbridge and look over his shoulder for Simon. 'I lost your husband, I'm afraid. Very careless of me.'

He grins, and I find myself making a noise that approximates a chortle. I have no idea why. I suppose it's a polite compulsion to humour him, appear amused by him, even though I'm not. I'm the opposite. I have to tread carefully. I should just excuse myself, walk away. That would still be polite enough. It wouldn't draw unnecessary attention. But I don't. I feel trapped by his size and his smile. I'm too hot. He's too close. I could join Rose on the dancefloor but there's always the risk he'll follow me. I don't want to have to dance with him.

'It's been ages, Curly,' he says with a grin. I can feel his breath against my neck. Warm. Fuggy with tequila. What will people think when they see him leaning close to me, whispering in my ear?

'Please call me Daisy,' I comment.

'But everyone calls you Daisy.' I want to point out that they do so because it's my name, but I don't because he adds, 'I've always liked to give my friends nicknames, you know that.' I don't consider myself one of his friends anymore. Far from it, but I stay silent. 'It was good to catch up with Simon. He filled me in on all your news.'

'Right.' I mutter. There's a knot in my stomach.

'I understand you're a mum now.'

'Yes.'

'Just the one?'
'That's right.'
'A girl?'
I nod, a small tight movement. Thinking about Millie helps. I feel braver, more determined. 'Will you excuse me? I promised Connie's youngest daughter I'd pop upstairs and say hello. The older two are staying up but the little one has been packed off to bed and she's feeling a bit resentful.' Before he can object, I turn and quickly head upstairs.
I knock on Sophie's bedroom door. It opens a cautious couple of centimetres, when Sophie sees it's me she flings the door wide, 'Aunty Daisy, come in, come in, come in!' She hurls herself at my body and wraps her arms around me, like a clam. I'm known as Aunty Daisy, not just to Sebastian and Henry, but to Connie's children as well. They gave me the title Aunty Daisy when it looked like no one would ever call me Mummy. It was a compensation and a kindness. Sophie hugs me with uninhibited enthusiasm and obvious joy. I kiss the top of her head and relax into her affection. No sooner do I step into her room, when she demands, 'Where is Millie? Why didn't you bring her?'
'Millie's your daughter, I take it?' chips in Daryll. I jump, startled that he's right behind me. I hadn't realised he'd followed me upstairs. He walks into the little girl's bedroom and sits on her desk chair. It's pink and he's far too big for it. He looks incongruous, like a giant in a fairy glen; unwanted. I move as far away from him as the small room will allow and stand with

my back to the window. Normally, I'd fling myself on the bed, stretch out amongst a thousand cuddly toys, but his presence restrains me.

Sophie declares, 'Yes, that's right. Millie is her daughter *and* she's *my* little friend!' She says every word at a volume that would be appropriate if we were in the next room. She's clearly high on the atmosphere and the e-numbers from the party food. It's amusing that Sophie always calls Millie, her 'little friend'. Millie is a year younger than Sophie, but she's taller.

'Millie is at India's house,' I reply. Sophie scowls. They're so close that Sophie tends towards being a bit bossy and possessive with Millie. Whilst she accepts that Millie has to have neighbourhood and school friends, she doesn't relish the fact. She always feels that she has the greatest claim. 'And you have Jamila here to keep you company,' I remind Sophie, gently. 'Hi, Jamila.' Jamila, a friend of Sophie's who I have met many times, is sat on the floor, bent over several semi-clad plastic dolls; her attention is focused on selecting outfits.

She throws out a small wave in my general direction, doesn't look up but does ask, 'How's the party?'

'Oh yes,' squeals Sophie. 'Is there dancing yet? Has anyone got drunk?' She starts to roll her eyes and stagger about the room, doing quite a good impression of a drunk.

'Oh gross. I hate it when adults get drunk and silly,' comments Jamila sharply.

'Oh no, it's funny,' insists Sophie. 'Who are you?' Sophie demands of Daryll. 'Are you a friend of my mummy's or my daddy's?' Sophie has a remarkable amount of confidence and readily engages with adults. Her conversation always seems way more sophisticated than Millie's. I put it down to her being the youngest of three. I'm grateful she's talking to Daryll, it means I don't have to.

'Both,' replies Daryll with a smile. 'But I've known your mummy the longest. We met at university.'

'Oh, with Aunty Daisy and Lucy?'

'That's right.'

Sophie studies him. 'I don't think I know you.'

'I've been living in Hong Kong for a long time,' he explains. 'I'm here in England for a short time and then I'm going to live in New York next.'

'Why do you move around so much?' Sophie asks.

'Because of my job.' He is a trader or a banker. I'm not exactly sure what he is. Something impressive.

'Doesn't your wife mind, always having to pack up boxes and move house?'

'I don't have a wife,'

'Oh. Why not?'

Daryll looks at me, with something that could be mistaken for longing or sadness, 'It's a long story,' he murmurs. I look at my feet. My face is flushed. I don't want the girls to notice.

'Daddy is looking for you, Aunty Daisy,' comments Sophie.

Luke. The thought of him usually calms me. But right now, the thought of seeing him just fills me with shame. We haven't seen or really even spoken to one another since he helped me hose down Simon and put him to bed. It's awkward. I don't imagine Luke would be tactless enough to bring it up at a party, but what if he did want to talk about it? I think I'd die of embarrassment. I like Luke. I always have. Everyone does. Connie says it's a blight that all her friends are a tiny bit in love with him. He is a wonderful man. Fair, a good judge of right and wrong, and very practical when it comes to problem solving. He is a rare sort of person, who is so completely OK with himself that he can absorb anyone else's abnormalities; secrets sink into him but don't change him, he digests them but doesn't become damaged. Way back when, before I met Simon, Luke was the person I'd often turn to for advice on all matters romantic. I liked the insight he offered into the male mind. Connie always used to scoff at that, she insisted that male minds didn't require much dissecting because they're one track. When Simon and I were trying for a baby, I often used to pop by his office for a cup of coffee, a chat; just if things were getting a bit much.

All that said, Luke isn't the person I can turn to at the moment.

It's tricky, he's Simon's friend as well as mine. I wouldn't be asking him to take sides, but it might appear that way. I don't want to put him in a difficult position. Again. Our last interaction was excruciating. After Simon was finally clean and tucked up in bed, I should have offered Luke a cup of tea or something, but I practically threw him out of the house. I simply wanted to slam the door on the entire episode. My thank you came across as cool, stiff.

Even so, as I ushered him out, he said kindly, 'I'm just at the end of the phone, Daisy.'

'Yes. I'll let you know if I need anything, but we'll be fine. Just fine.'

Sophie is now twirling on the spot. 'My daddy has been going around and around the party asking if anyone's seen you.'

'Always in demand with the men,' comments Daryll, inappropriately and inaccurately. I ignore him.

'Daddy came up to my room because he thought you must be hiding,' adds Sophie.

I blush and bluff, 'Why would I do that?'

Sophie shrugs. 'I don't know, I said most likely you were with Simon, like usual. You look after him as he's always drunk, isn't he? It doesn't mean he's a bad man, that's what Mummy said. Just lacking in . . . ' she pauses and screws her face up in concentration, clearly trying to recall some specific phrase. I'm aware of Daryll listening intently and I want to cut her off, but I'm caught in some sort of morbid fascination. I too need to know what Connie thinks Simon lacks. 'Lacking self-control,' exclaims Sophie with a grin, proud she's recalled the phrase. 'Right?'

She turns her sweet face to mine and waits for my confirmation. I can no longer kid myself. I'm certainly the subject of gossip and speculation amongst my friends, or at least Simon is. I feel embarrassment roar through me. It's all too much.

Simon.

Daryll.

The room seems tight. Airless. The window is open a fraction. I struggle for a moment with the safety catch. I want to fling it wide. I need space and air. I need to get out of here.

Suddenly, Daryll stands up, he takes hold of my arm and pulls me through the bedroom door, out onto the landing. I weakly smile back at Sophie and Jamila, but can't think what to say to them, Daryll marching me out of the room has only made an embarrassing situation worse. I don't know what to do, so I do nothing. Daryll pulls me into the next room. It's Fran's. The walls are covered in posters of The 1975. She has a crush on the little one with floppy hair. I'm not thinking clearly because for a moment I think there's an orgy of bodies writhing on the bed, but no one is in here. It's just a few jackets belonging to guests who don't trust the English summer to provide evening warmth. My head is swimming. I'm shaking.

'Are you OK?' Daryll asks as he closes the door behind us. The room feels miniscule. He sounds concerned but this isn't any of his business. I rub my wrist which he grabbed when he led me out of Sophie's room. He held me too tightly.

'Of course I am,' I snap, reaching for the door handle. He's standing in front of it. Blocking it. I feel woozy. I can't stay in here with him. I know what might happen.

'Everyone is talking about Simon,' he states flatly, sympathy shinning from his eyes. I don't want to see it. I don't want *his* sympathy.

'Are they now?'

'If there's anything I can do.' He smiles, holds his arms out in front of him, wide, welcoming. Almost — I think — offering me a hug. I step away from him, my thigh bangs into the corner of Fran's desk.

'There isn't.' I want this to be a firm statement, but my voice betrays me. It cracks.

Suddenly, the bedroom door is pushed open with some speed and force. Daryll is startled and stumbles forwards. His hands automatically splay out in front of him, landing awkwardly on my body as I break his fall.

'Oh, there you are.' Luke says. He is peering into the room. He looks stern, irritated. His eyes quickly take in the scene. Me, secreted upstairs in a small bedroom with Daryll. Daryll is what my mother would call a ladies' man, what Rose would call a Casanova. What I call a bastard.

Daryll slowly pulls away from me, straightens up. I blush, although he wasn't holding me, he'd just fallen on to me. But as bad as this looks, trying to explain would probably make things worse. For a moment, no one says anything at all. We listen to the noise of the party throbbing through the floor, up the stairs, through the open door. There's loud music, bursts of laughter and a general hum of buoyant chatter. Good party sounds. But then there's something else. Shouting. The music has been silenced. 'You should probably come downstairs,' says Luke. 'It's Simon.'

18
Simon

That first sip, the drink in the kitchen before he set off to the party, there was nothing like it. Simon was still respectful of it, so he did try to sip rather than gulp. Or at least, he mostly did. That sip, it was a potent, amorous purr. It was go time. Time to go.

A gulp? When he arrived at the party, well that was more of a mild erotic shock. Time to let go. To relax, to embrace, to forget. It was all that and more.

The alcohol caressed his tongue, played with his mouth, his mind and body. Like a lover. Better than a lover because it didn't leave him, bore him or betray him. Alcohol didn't ever start talking about bills or care home visits or getting some fresh air. Not ever. Alcohol is as close to time travel as we have, that was a fact, right? Science hadn't come up with anything better. He got to go back. Back to a more carefree place.

What comes next? The high. That had lots of different forms, always good. It depended where he was. Who he was with. It might be that his body felt sort of chill, like he was having a conversation with an old mate, a mate who thought he was funny. Fuck it, he *was* funny. Or maybe sometimes he wanted to feel like he was alone, slipping into a warm bath or a cosy bed. Somewhere comfortable and private where no arsehole was going to disturb him with demands and deadlines or disappointment and dullness. Or if he was *really* feeling it, if he was out, like tonight, at a party say — the high? Well, it was like jumping off a cliff.

And flying.

He was one huge, important, effervescent being. Everything was at least ten times as exciting as it had been half an hour ago, twenty times. Listen to that music, man. It's sweet, right? And look at these people, they're hot, yeah? Hot and clever. Every single word that dropped from their lips was so compelling, so significant. He could listen to them all night. Even though they were all talking at the same time. Wow, it was loud in there. Really loud. He couldn't hear himself think. That was funny, right? Because that was not a bad thing. Shut it out. Thoughts and stuff, who needed them? You make a good point, my man. You are very wise. Really, we should stay in touch. I feel you get me. Yeah, you feel it too? We're like soulmates or something. Yeah, do you hear me? I'll tell you where I'm coming from. Exactly! Exactly that! You have hit the nail on the head, my friend. Here, put your number in my phone. We need to talk more. We really do. We'll go out. Have a beer. But right now, I need to go and pee. We'll catch up. Yeah.

There was always a sodding queue. Good job he had brought a drink with him. What? The bottle was empty. Well then, he'd use that. No point in queueing when he had a handy receptacle. He just needed to find a bedroom because Daisy would go apeshit if he got his cock out and pissed in the bottle whilst he queued outside the bathroom. So uptight. Who the hell had he been talking to downstairs? He didn't know. Darren? Darragh? Nice bloke though. He should have got his number. They could have gone out. Had a few jars.

Oops sorry, sorry Sophie, sorry Sophie's friend. You carry on. Didn't mean to interrupt. Hey, what you watching? Is that Selena Gomez? She's really hot, right? Sorry, sorry probably shouldn't say that in front of you. The girls giggled as he walked into the door frame, trying to exit. I'm going now. Just pretend you never saw me. Fuck what are they playing downstairs? This is my all-time favourite song EVER. I know all the words. Well, like most of them.

It had started to smudge, time had. Or at least falter and jerk. Out of my way. I need to dance. Careful. Watch it buddy. You should dance to this too. Everyone should. Shouldn't they? This song is *awesome*. I promise you. Like the lyrics really *mean* something, don't they? Like they mean everything. Are you hearing that? Do you get that? I am actually a super good dancer. Whoops. Sorry. That will wash out. Don't worry about it. You are cute. You really are. Can I get you a drink? What? You're with him? Don't worry about it. I'm married too, right, who cares? Not my wife, apparently.

Piss off, Luke, don't touch me. You fucking

hypocrite. I was just talking to the woman. No harm done. Right, no harm. No, I am not ready to go home. No, I don't want to call it a night. This might be your idea of late, mate, but it's not mine. I am nowhere near ready to stop the party. We should do shots. PARTY, PARTY, PARTY.

Oh fuck, I'm sorry. Was that valuable? It just fell off the fucking shelf.

19

Daisy

I dash down the stairs, one foot in front of another, apologising to the people who are queueing for the bathroom or simply chatting, as they have to swiftly move out of my path. I take stock of the scene and instantly surmise that Simon, shamefully drunk, has smashed Connie's French porcelain table lamp. I'm overwhelmed by a simultaneous sense of protectiveness and powerlessness and for a moment I can't move, so I watch the scene from the elevated position, two or three steps up the staircase.

Then fury seizes me. Why can't he just behave like everyone else?

The lamp was on the hall console, pride of place. It's eye-catching and Connie likes to tell the story of her great-grandfather living in Paris as a young man. He worked backstage at a theatre but apparently had access to all the artists, writers and philosophers of the time; he used to drink with them in cafes and bars on the Left Bank. An actress had gifted the lamp to him in 1920, the year it was made. It held sentimental value then, now it has that in spades, plus a substantial price tag attached. Not that Connie would ever sell it; she just had it valued for insurance purposes. The lamp was the only thing her great-grandfather brought home and Connie had worked quite hard to ensure that it was passed to her and not any of her cousins or three sisters. I'm not into antiques but I've always admired the lamp. It was designed in the Egyptian taste that was popular during the roaring twenties. It was decorated with fluting and had gilded panther heads on either side. Now, it lies in four big pieces, at first count I can see that there are about ten smaller pieces scattered about. It's irreparable.

I don't imagine Simon caused this chaos deliberately, but it was careless in the extreme. He's apologising loudly although in an aggressive, unconvincing way that really means he thinks Connie is to blame for putting her precious, sentimentally valuable heirloom on a console where people are partying. Guests are crowding around, ghouls. Luke is thoughtfully trying to smooth things over, he takes Simon's arm and tries to guide him somewhere private, but Simon pushes him away. Simon is pale, his temple is pulsing, as though something is beating at him from the inside. 'I don't need your help. This is your fault. If you hadn't stuck your nose in. I was just trying to get away from you,' he sneers. There's an edge to his voice, a layer of meaning that isn't lost on Luke, who keeps his jaw clenched shut, he's determined that nothing he'll regret will escape. He looks away hurt, beat. Simon looks furious, hostile. Something is going to happen, something already has.

Connie pushes through the onlookers. Seeing

the smashed lamp, her face crumples like a used tissue, she turns grey. I feel so sad for her. I'm sorry but powerless. It's done. Ever the perfect hostess, in a loud, calm voice she tells everyone to step back. 'I don't want any cut feet. The important thing is no one is hurt.'

'Connie, I am so sorry, I — ' I break off. She's holding her hand up to silence me. I don't think she can bear to hear a word from anyone right now, least of all me. She smiles up at me. It's forced and as fragile as the gorgeous lamp.

'This isn't your fault Daisy, is it?'

Suddenly I feel exhausted. Bone weary. Exhaustion has pressed its weight on me all day, for many days, for weeks. A choking wad of fatigue is layered upon my sense of responsibility. Layers and layers of dreadful things threaten to bury me. Disappointment, cluelessness, frustration. I open my mouth, but nothing comes out. The space in my mouth swells to stupid proportions. My sister Rose silently passes me my handbag. I head to the door, pulling on Simon's sleeve so he has to follow me.

Once we are outside and at the end of the path I hear the music start up again. I glare at Simon. He shrugs and mutters, 'Sorry.' But he's only as sorry as a little boy caught with his hand in a biscuit tin. Not very, and confident that the misdemeanour will be forgiven because I always forgive him. I'm stunned when he reveals a bottle of wine that he's lifted.

'How did you manage that? Oh, never mind . . . ' It infuriates me that while he sometimes seems incapable of putting on matching socks, he's always astute and wily enough to keep his alcohol flow constant.

'Do you want some?' He offers me the bottle.

'No.' Then, 'Oh give it here.' I need to take a swig. I take a couple of glugs but hand it back to him because I remember we have the car with us, I have to drive. I wish I had the courage to throw the bottle away, but I don't. For one thing I don't want to be responsible for broken glass outside Connie's house and secondly, I can't face the scene that would inevitably occur if I did. 'Come on, let's go home.'

We are parked two or three streets away. We walk in silence. Simon continues to drink from the bottle but not with as much gusto as I expected. He looks pensive, borderline repentant. I once read that family and friends of functioning alcoholics are advised to try to talk to them when they are hungover. I've read a lot on the subject, some of it is contradictory. Damned internet. I understand that there's no point in talking to him if he's drunk, even if I do extract promises from him to change, he won't remember them in the morning. I know this is true, through experience, so I stay silent.

As we walk to the car we pass a pub. People are spilt out onto the pavement. The night is almost unbearably hot. The sort of heat that makes people wild. Everyone looks flushed, sweaty. Simon sways and stumbles next to me but there are plenty of other people outside the pub who are drunk too, so we go unnoticed. This disgusts me and, simultaneously, is a source of relief. It disgusts me because I wonder how in this society — where binge drinking is normalised and being inebriated is seen as funny, friendly, the social norm, and abstaining is seen as dull, pious and a bit odd — how I will ever get him to stop drinking. And it's a source of relief because I simply don't know how much more shame I can shoulder tonight. It's better for me that he blends in.

'Do you remember that we met at a party exactly like that, Connie and Luke's first wedding anniversary party?' I ask him.

'Of course I do,' he mutters sulkily.

I don't know what else to say. Was it there then? This problem. Was it hibernating? Lurking? How would I have been able to tell? We all drank so much back then, too much. You have to be ballsy to not drink. Confident, assured, so certain, and few of us are that. A lot of people pressure each other into drinking because they worry that the sober member of the gang will remember just how crazy the night before was. Drink is marketed as something fun, sexy, magical. The very word intoxicated is such a beautiful word and yet —

'I feel sick.' Simon turns his head and a train of hot vomit pours from him. He straightens, wipes his mouth and then takes another swig from the wine bottle. It's far from beautiful.

The sky darkens, becomes more solid, as though someone had dropped a blind. The clouds ooze and billow, morphing into a single homogenous mass. The evening is cast in a shadowy, deep, deep greyness. A storm is threatening, there is imminent thunder in the air.

When I first met him, he was like a green stalk pushing up through the dull earth. Or maybe a firework exploding in the black sky. He was promise, cleanliness, excitement. He was everything. I search my mind but conclude that honestly, I had no idea that Simon would take this path. He did not drink any more or less than the rest of us, he just carried on while the rest of us eased off. Some people make snap judgements about others, I don't. It's not that I'm wise or considered. It's more that I've never had the self-assurance to trust my gut. The thing about people is that it takes years, and years, and years to know them. Really know them. Because we hide things, all of us, all the time. We're ashamed, cautious or secretive. Sometimes, we just have trust issues and feel people need to earn the right to knowledge about our true selves. We don't gift it generously. And even when you finally think you know someone, something changes. We can't know each other. It's a fool's game trying to.

20

Simon

'Are we nearly home?' Simon's head hurt. It was like someone was smashing it from the inside with a hammer, a great big hammer.

'Almost.' Her tone was cold. He didn't know what he'd done wrong, but something. He couldn't remember.

'I need some water.'

'Can't you wait?'

Something bad then, because otherwise she'd stop straight-away and get the water. Normally she was keen to get him to drink as much of that stuff as possible. He felt suddenly swollen with resentment. Why should he be on the backfoot? He went in for the attack. 'Are you having an affair with Luke?' he demanded.

'What?' She turned to him. Fury in her face. 'What did you just ask me?'

'Are you fucking Luke?'

'Oh wow, Simon. You are something else,' She pulled into a service station forecourt. Slammed the car door behind her and walked quickly to the shop. She hadn't answered the question though, had she?

Thick, fat drops of rain slapped down on the windscreen. He felt a surge of unbridled excitement. He liked a storm. It was different. It was exciting. Bring it on. There was something about the drama and scale that stirred and appealed to him. He reached about for the button to wind down the window, couldn't find it so opened the door and fell out onto the forecourt. That made him laugh. He stood up and breathed in deeply but there was no oxygen in the air, just a horrible closeness that never helped people to think straight. He was just about to close the door, whoops. The keys. He stretched and grabbed them out of the ignition. Didn't want to lock them in the car by mistake, did he? Didn't want to give her another reason to go mad. Tut tut.

There was no one around. The temperature had fallen, as it did just before the downpour. How late was it, he wondered? He could just about make out that Daisy was at the till now. The youth that was serving her looked bored. He had served her without bothering to take out his earbuds, white threads trailing from his ears. Simon sniggered. Pleased. That would have annoyed Daisy. She was always going on about poor manners, service not being what it was. He liked the thought of her being irritated, annoyed. She deserved that and more. Bitch.

'Get back in the car, Simon,' she instructed. She was clutching two bottles of water and something else. An energy drink, probably. That was Daisy's idea of going wild, a Red Bull Sugarfree. Whoop, whoop, that woman sure knew how to party. Not. Although she did, didn't she? Just not with him. With someone else. He glared at her. She cracked open the can and drank it back quickly. Tossing the empty onto the back seat.

'I'll drive,' he said, dangling the keys.

'Don't be ridiculous. You're drunk. Get back in the car and give me the keys.'

'I'm not drunk. You just don't judge sobriety like a normal person.' He slurred the word sobriety. Reducing the potency of his point. 'All you do is criticise, find fault.'

'You are way over the limit. Give me the keys,' she demanded. She really could be so haughty.

'Look, I can walk in a straight line,' he replied. Simon spread his arms out wide as though he was walking a tightrope and then, with exaggerated care, he walked along the white line painted on the ground that indicated a car park space. 'I can drive,' he insisted. 'It's only a couple more miles.' He knew he was annoying her. He was glad. 'I can recite a tongue-twister. Peter Piper picked a peck of pickled peppers. Peter Picker pipped a peck of pickered peppers.' He enunciated with the sort of care an actor might muster, just before he was going out on the stage at the National.

It was raining hard by now. His shirt clung to his body, he noticed that her dress caressed her curves. She looked beautiful and he was furious with himself for noticing. The thick, fat droplets splashed down heavily. She looked sad and tired. Mostly tired. She didn't have the energy to fight him.

21

Daisy

He reaches forward and puts on the radio. He turns up the volume to a level that I think will make my ears bleed. The car is practically shaking. I lean forward to turn it off or at least down, but he lunges at me and pushes my hands out of the way. I realise it's safest not to struggle with him. At least then, two hands are on the wheel. But the music is so loud it pushes the air out of the car. It's a mindless, pointless, clubbing tune. My head hurts. 'So are you then?' he yells, above the music.

'What?' I don't want to speak to him. I'm furious with him. Ashamed of him, burdened by him and scared of him. Being scared is new. I keep my eyes on the road. I don't want to look his way.

'Are you fucking Luke?'

'What has brought such a ludicrous idea into your head?' I snap.

'He's blonde,' he states flatly.

'What?' I can't follow this conversation. He's talking nonsense and we shouldn't be talking anyway. It's important to just concentrate on the driving. The weather is hideous now. The windscreen wipers can't keep up with the rainfall. Backwards and forwards, backwards and forwards. Clearing over and over again. The light from streetlamps shatters on the wet roads. Like shards of glass. Like the lamp in Connie's hallway.

'You hang off his every fucking word,' added Simon.

'You really do swear too much, you know, Simon. I remember when you had a vocabulary.' I sound prim, even to my own ears.

He turns to me. 'OH FUCK YOU!' It's screamed, from the depths of his lungs. From the depth of his soul. His words are full of pain, frustration, anger. The vileness spills, billows like ink. Spreading, blotting our history, staining it. He's not looking ahead, but I am. As we turn the corner, travelling way faster than we should be in a residential street, I see her. I see her but don't understand it. Millie? What's Millie doing out at this time of night? She's dashing across the road from our house back towards India's. She doesn't look both ways as we've taught her. She just steps out.

* * *

It's black. So dark. A deep, terrifying dark. I'm woozy, disorientated. I'm drifting in and out of consciousness. I need to wake up. I was having an awful dream. I want to wake up. I feel my eyelids flutter but still can't see anything. Then someone, Simon presumably, starts flickering the bedroom light on and off. I think so, because the bleak darkness is slapped with shapes, bright flashes. I can hear him groaning, grunting. Not a sex sound. Pain, sadness. His breath is hot. On my neck. I'm in bed, just dreaming. I tell myself this because I want it to be true. I want that more than anything, but it's not The flashes vanish then reappear, vanish again. I can hear the sound of rain on the window. On metal? My eyes stay open long enough for me to see Simon, his head against the steering wheel.

'I've called an ambulance,' he mutters. He's crying. Tears roll down his face.

I scramble for the car door handle. Fling it open and almost fall to my knees in my haste to get out of the car. My head hurts. I can feel something running down my forehead. I lick my lips and taste the iron tang of blood. I've hit my head against the windscreen. The car is scrunched up against the huge oak tree on the pavement outside our house. We've turned, swerved suddenly.

The world stops. It is silent. I can no longer hear the rain splattering against the ground or the car, or the wails of sirens in the distance. I can't hear myself screaming, although my mouth is open and now neighbours are running out of their homes, coming towards us. All I can hear is my heartbeat pounding, so powerful that it is jumping out of my chest. It throbs through my body, it kicks me in the gut, it's cracking open my skull. She is on the ground, flat on her back with her leg twisted under her, an unnatural broken angle. A broken thing. I start to shake, tremble with such violence, as though electricity is flooding through my body, shock after shock after shock. I'm on my knees. My instinct is to scoop her up, cuddle her, but I am being held back. People are telling me not to move her. Her stillness is impossible. She is never this still. Not when she's playing musical statues, not even when she's asleep. My baby is *never* still. I carefully kiss her forehead. Her face is the same. There is blood coming out of the back of her head, more blood than when she slipped in the bath. It runs on to the road, and with the rain, into the gutter.

The dark, the wet, the red lights all slide about me. I turn to look at Simon, He gets out of the car, steps towards us. 'Stay away from her,' I yell, bending over her body. 'Stay away from us.'

But I can't protect her. I'm too late.

22
Simon

They asked him if they could breathalyse him. It wasn't really a question, nor was it a matter of whether he was drunk or not. They knew he was. That was obvious. They were establishing how drunk, exactly. For their files. For his trial. They produced a yellow box from somewhere or other. Simon wasn't sure where. He kept trying to turn around to look at what was happening with Millie and Daisy. No one would tell him how Millie was doing. They wouldn't let him go to her. Was she dead? He couldn't believe that. He wouldn't believe it. But she was motionless. There was a lot of activity around her. Paramedics now. Thank God. They'd fix her. They'd save her. Surely.

The policeman kept saying, 'Hey, over here, mate. Concentrate on what's happening over here?' But he craned his neck. Watched as they loaded his daughter into an ambulance, as Daisy climbed in after her. His wife didn't once glance his way. He asked if he could go in the ambulance too, but he wasn't surprised when he was told a flat no. He had known they wouldn't let him. There were consequences. Please God, let them be taking her to hospital. They'd fix her there, right. She could be fixed. Please God, not the morgue.

'That's my daughter. My wife.' His comment didn't elicit any sympathy. 'How is she doing?' He screamed his question after the ambulance. No one told him anything. The sirens wailed back at him. It was still raining. Not as heavily now but he was wet through. Wet and miserable. To his core. They hated him. He could see that.

Whilst they wouldn't answer him, they asked plenty of questions of their own: his name, address, profession. He tried to concentrate. Tried to cooperate. 'How old are you?' asked the policeman, gruffly.

'What?' He couldn't focus. What had he done? Jesus. Hell. No. What had just happened here?

'How old are you?' He could hear his mother's voice. *Old enough to know better*. But it was in his head because his mother was not there. Nor his wife. Nor his daughter. They had all gone. 'If you can take one long continuous blow into this, please.' The police officer was polite but clearly not to be argued with. Simon blew into the plastic straw attached to the yellow box, until the machine beeped. The officer looked at the reading and was not at all surprised. 'We are arresting you under section five of the road traffic act.'

Handcuffs were snapped on Simon. It was not a violent action, he was not turned around and pushed against the car, like in the TV shows. The officer did his job efficiently, carefully. They both seemed to accept that this was what had to be done.

'My daughter, she just stepped out.' Simon muttered. 'Ran out. Didn't look where she was going. We've told her to *always* look. Why wasn't she in bed?' His head hurt, as did his chest. His neck. But it didn't matter, he didn't care. Millie. His little girl.

They put him in the back of a transit van. He hadn't seen it arrive. Things weren't happening in a smooth, continuous way for him. Time was lurching about. Stuttering. He'd thought it would be a police car. He'd seen it on TV, people like him were put in the back of a car. The van was worse. The van was designed for evil men. It smelt of fear and cruelty. They asked him if he'd been sick.

He hadn't. Or had he? Maybe. He shrugged.

They told him he could have a lawyer. Did he know a lawyer? No. They'd had a solicitor when they'd moved to a new house, some years back. But no. Their area of expertise was doctors. They knew a lot of doctors. He just shook his head. The police officers said they could get him one. After that, they didn't talk to him any more.

He was led into the police station via a back entrance. He was still drunk and felt disorientated. Even after that. Especially because of that. He couldn't sober up instantly, it was science. So, he simply followed instructions, shuffled along next to them, went where they directed him to go, did what they told him to do. He'd been here, to this station once before. A couple of years ago, he'd found an iPhone in the high street and he'd handed it in to the police. At the time, he'd felt really pleased with himself for doing that and then a bit deflated when they'd barely thanked him, barely acknowledged his good Samaritan act that had interrupted his day. He'd never heard whether the phone had been returned to its owner or whether it was still languishing in a lost property lock-up behind the front desk. He had a feeling that things could languish here.

The place they took him to now was very different from the public reception. Significantly more 'back room'. Grubby. One door opened, he waited, it closed behind him before the next one opened and then he was moved forward. They were treating him like a criminal. He was a criminal. This was surreal. How was she? No one would say. The officers that were at the scene handed him over to someone else. They robotically recounted what had happened to a woman behind a desk, keeping it brief, factual. They confirmed the make, model and registration of his car. They confirmed that Daisy was there too but no other witnesses. Everyone looked at Simon, disgust, pity, bewilderment. He could feel the heat of their stares, but he kept his eyes on his trainers.

'We've a brief statement from the wife, but we'll need more. She was injured and distraught. Left in an ambulance.'

'Go and write it up.'

The officers sloped away without throwing him a backward glance. He wasn't worth it. Simon asked about Millie again. No one replied. He wondered whether he'd said the words out loud or just in his head. He was shaking. He was in shock. They asked the questions, they told him. Medical ones now. Did he self-harm?

'No,' he replied, deadpan, not even bothered enough to sound indignant.

'How much have you had to drink?'

'A lot,' he admitted. He wasn't being evasive, it was just that he'd long since given up counting.

'Can you try to be specific?'

'Five maybe six, but over the period of the night.' He thought this sounded reasonable, but it was an underestimate. He was in the habit of lying about that particular question. It didn't matter anyway, they had instruments that gave accurate readings.

'How much do you regularly drink?'

'I like a drink,' he slurred. He'd tried not to slur. He was tired. He wanted to go to sleep. Shut this down. Get out of this nightmare.

'Do you have a drink problem?'

'I have no problem with how much I drink. Other people might have.' He almost sniggered at that. He wasn't himself. He didn't know who that was anyway.

The sooner they let him sleep, the sooner he'd wake up and this would all be different. That's what happened. He drank, he fucked up, he slept and the next day he started again. A fresh day. Things never looked as bad in the morning. That's what Daisy always said to him. Why was he here again? He needed to lie down or he might fall down. He imagined just curling up on the tiled floor, here in front of them. He just needed to sleep.

They got him to breathe into another box. They called it the intoximeter, but he wasn't sure if that was an in-joke, or the real name. They waited a bit and then asked him to breathe into it again. 'His alcohol level is still going up,' said the policewoman with a sigh. 'He's too drunk to be charged. Take him to a cell.'

23
Daisy

Sunday, 24th July 2016

She looks so tiny. My slight sprite has always seemed bigger than she is because of her giddy effervescence. Her demeanour. She's fun, normally: laughing, dancing, skipping. Moving. But now she's still. Silent. No laughing. I can only hear my mother crying. She keeps apologising for it, but I don't mind. She should be crying. She should be wailing. We should be tearing out our hair, beating our chests. How are we just sitting here? How are we going on?

Her skin doesn't look right. It's a sallow yellow. She's usually tanned or rosy with exertion. The sheet is pulled up to her chest. It's white I suppose but it looks grey too. Everything is grey.

My father and sister take turns in patting my mother's arm, pulling her into the occasional embrace. No one touches me. They tried to. When they first arrived, breathless and disbelieving. They hugged me as they fell through the door, but I stiffened, then pushed them away. I don't want their comfort. I don't want anything other than to see her open her eyes.

‘I don’t understand why she was in the street,’ laments my father.

She and India had been camping in our back garden. They had taken India’s younger brother’s tepee out there on Saturday morning and played camp most of the day but that hadn’t been enough for them. They’d wanted to sleep under the stars. They had mentioned as much to me, but I had fobbed them off, said they could play camp in India’s bedroom. I should have known that wouldn’t be enough for Millie’s irrepressible spirit. When she gets an idea in her head, there’s no stopping her. My eyes drop to her now. Stopped. They slipped out, unbeknown to India’s mother. The tepee was totally inadequate for camping, it is just a play tent. The torrential rain had ripped through so they’d chosen that moment to give up and dash back to their beds. They should not have left their beds, but kids do things they shouldn’t. India’s mother told me this while I was kneeling on the street with my baby, waiting for the ambulance. She was sobbing, apologising, saying she should have kept a closer eye on them. Yes, she should have, but this is not her fault, not really.

I don’t answer my father’s question. He and my mother will blame themselves for the accident. They’ll say that she has never slipped out anywhere when under their care. They’ll hate themselves for going to the Royal Albert Hall. I wish I could turn back time. I wish they hadn’t booked tickets and that they had been babysitting because they are vigilant, almost neurotic. It’s true that Millie wouldn’t have been able to slip out of an open patio door under their care. But this is not their fault.

I shouldn't have let him drive. Why did I do that? I should have stood in front of the car if I'd had to. Why didn't I do that? I don't know. I can't remember. I can't remember anything important. I guess I didn't have the energy to fight him. I chose that moment to be weak and pathetic. I allowed him to break me down. I must have got in the car next to him. I suppose I must have told myself that there only a few more minutes left to drive, that he wasn't too bad, that I'd seen him worse. I can't believe I did that now. I'm so ashamed. I probably felt sorry for him. Just for a moment. Less than that. Long enough. Or done with him. Exhausted, I just wanted to get home.

My breath catches in my lungs, this is what drowning feels like.

I should have been more forceful. Did this come about because I wanted to avoid a scene? I gave in to him. I must have. I touch my head. I can't actually remember the journey. I hit my head on the windscreen at the . . . I struggle to let the words drift into my head. Once there, they are real. Immovable. I hit my head on the windscreen at the point of impact. I hit my head on the screen when the car hit Millie and the tree. The doctor who has carefully examined me explained that my patchy memory of last night is likely to be a temporary thing. The result of a concussion, the result of the shock. He says brains are clever things and that most likely my brain has triggered a coping mechanism.

Blanking out the horror. I don't want to cope! It's selfish of me. I should have to remember everything in lurid, excruciating detail, over and over again. It should be seared onto my brain. That's what I deserve.

I try to. I concentrate very hard. My head throbs with the effort. There was shouting. We were arguing. Did I distract him? I wasn't shouting. He was. I need to remember more. I remember the impact, or rather the feeling of it, more than a visual memory. I sunk. Went under. Gave in to the slow pull and drag of blackness.

'I'm so sorry, Millie,' I whisper to my still, ashen daughter. I take hold of her hand and kiss it. It's cold.

This is my fault, and this is Simon's fault.

I hate us both.

24
Simon

Simon didn't have a clue where he was. This happened to him from time to time, so for a moment he allowed that to just be a fact; he didn't try too hard to work out his location. Instead he thought about his body. He was cold. Shivering. The sort of shivering that went deep into his bones, the sort that came with a hangover. His head was splitting. He felt impotent, unable to form thoughts or reason.

He was in a tiled, oblong box. He considered that he probably wasn't awake yet. He was still asleep, just dreaming. He hoped so because this place was grim. His back was stiff and achy. He felt as though he was in the grip of flu. He sat up. Had he slept on a park bench? He had done so once before, and it was not to be recommended. He looked about him. He had in fact slept indoors on a cream plastic bench, just six inches off the floor. There was a thin mattress which seemed a bit like a yoga mat, plastic again, a small apology for a pillow, a thin, scratchy blue blanket. It took him a moment because his head was pounding, ready to explode all over the ugly tiled walls. And then he realised. He was in a cell.

He staggered to the small metal toilet pan that hung on the wall. He could see evidence that he'd tried to use it last night, but his aim had not been so good; it was covered in piss and vomit. He peed now, swaying, he had to place one hand on the wall for balance. He noticed a small sink recessed into the wall. There wasn't a plug and he soon found out that the water flowed out slowly. There wasn't room to put his head under the faucet, so I scooped as much water as I could into his mouth with his hands. It wasn't much. Certainly not enough to assuage his raging thirst. His eyes were too tight for his head. His stomach burnt. He needed a drink. He banged on the door.

'Hey, I need to talk to someone. What the hell is going on here?' No one came. He banged again but then stopped because suddenly he was scared. Banging on the door of a police cell didn't seem like a bright idea. It seemed like he was causing trouble. He didn't want trouble. He couldn't think why he was there. Not precisely. Then someone turned back the pages in the picture book of his memory.

He remembered last night; people kept coming into the room. The cell, he supposed. They would shake him awake, not violently but firmly. 'Where are you? Who are you? Lift your right arm?' they'd demand. He'd answered their questions, lifted his arm, told them to bugger off, he just wanted to sleep.

He had been in a van. He was brought here in a van. That was right. And before that? He was in a car. It was raining. Daisy was furious at him.

Why? He couldn't remember. He'd broken something at Connie's party. That was it. A vase or a plate, a clock? He didn't know. He could see it smash. Pieces bouncing on their hardwood floor. He could hear the gasps of their smug, stinking rich, fertile friends who were standing around passing weed, passing judgement. And he'd been furious with Daisy too because she'd broken so much more than a vase.

Then he remembered glass on the road, the headlights. A thud. More than a thud. The brakes, the car skidding, turning. A crunch.

Millie. He remembered Millie. He saw her bouncing off the bonnet of the car. Like a puppet yanked suddenly upwards by a puppeteer and then the strings were snapped, and she was dropped to the floor, a broken, ruined thing.

Remembering was like pulling a thread on a jumper, a small tug had led to a complete unravelling. He was left with nothing.

He started hammering on the door of the cell. He didn't care how much more trouble he caused now. The damage was done.

2019

25
Daisy

Saturday, 25th May 2019

It was Rose's idea that we all go to the beach. She knows that I prefer being outside, rather than in, that I have always had an aversion to confined spaces. When we grew up this was a mildly amusing quirk, the source of a bit of teasing, but over the past few years it has developed into something close to a phobia. Rose rallied the entire gang: Craig, Sebastian and Henry, Connie, Luke and their three girls. Rose knows I feel it's important that Millie's birthday is marked by a crowd. That I don't feel lonely. Besides, everyone loves the wind to catch in their hair and the sound of the waves endlessly crashing against the shore. No one took much persuading.

Millie has invited along four of her closest school friends as well. She wanted more, she'd have invited her entire class if I'd let her, but I was concerned about being responsible for all of them on the train and at the beach. This way the child to adult ratio is reasonable. I know that Sophie and India will spend the day silently battling for supremacy of Millie's affections;

each trying to out-do the other in a desperate bid to show their loyalty, their protectiveness. That battle has been ever-present but it only intensified given what happened. Sophie once tearfully declared that Millie would have stayed safe if she'd been at the party, and that it was all India's fault for wanting to camp in our garden. Connie was mortified that I heard this emotional outburst, and swiftly hushed up her daughter, sensibly pointing out that it had been Millie's idea to camp, not India's; something she'd heard me say to reassure India. She didn't mention the other bit, but I hold that fact close. Another what if. Another path I could have taken to protect my daughter. Another way I failed her. I shouldn't have taken her to the party with me, but I should have stayed at home when my parents couldn't babysit.

I shouldn't have let a drunk man drive a car.

Once Lucy heard about the plan to picnic on the beach, she asked whether she could come along. Her daughter, Auriol, is best friends with Connie's oldest, Fran. It isn't easy to keep a secret in our gang. I asked Rose what she thought.

'Yes. The more the merrier,' she insisted.

'Are you sure?' I try to avoid Lucy when I can. 'I don't want to put you in an awkward position. I don't want Lucy to spoil your day.'

Rose waved her hand dismissively. 'That hatchet has long since been buried as far as I'm concerned. Surely, anyone who wants to celebrate Millie's birthday is welcome.' I understand her point. Every child's life is so precious, but awareness of that fact is intensified when it comes to

Millie, as her life hung in the balance for so many weeks. Her birthday parties have to be joyful occasions. I can put my personal dislike of Lucy to the side for a day.

Anyway, if there is a crowd of us, then maybe, just maybe we can hide the gap Simon's absence always creates. He is not in a position to feel wind in his hair, hear the waves crash against the shore. He is in prison, serving his jail sentence for nearly killing our daughter.

I don't miss him. I'm too angry with him to miss him and I always will be. When I said this to Connie once she gave me a funny, sad look and said, 'Oh I see, you still love him.'

'Don't be ridiculous,' I'd snapped. She's far too romantic for her own good. I hate him.

I wonder if Millie misses him? We don't talk about it. I've tried but it's difficult. There was so much to talk about at the beginning and she seemed very young to hear it all; the collision, his drinking, the trial, prison. Every conversation we needed to have about him was complicated and painful. All discussions on these matters caused us to fall out, or her to cry or turn moody. It was just easier to stop having the conversations altogether. She hasn't seen him for almost three years and that's a long time for a child. I'm not sure how much she remembers of him. I've left one photo of him in her bedroom; I've taken all of the others down. I can't stand to look at him. Or to think of him. I make an effort to push him out of my head right now. He is not going to ruin today. He has ruined enough of our days.

We have woken up to a rare hot day for May.

The bright sky and decent temperatures are a gift on her birthday. Although, it's England, so it might be gale force winds by lunchtime, it seems we often get four seasons in a day, but it's the optimistic start that matters.

We all travel to Brighton in separate groups, so despite agreeing to meet at the beach, to the right of the pier at 11 a.m., our guests' arrival is staggered. I'm prompt but when we arrive, Rose is already there, settled on the pebbles, facing out towards the sparkling sea. She's set up not too close to the public loos or the noisy amusements, but not too far away from either facility either. Perfect. Rose is good at that sort of thing. My money is on Lucy arriving next and Connie bringing up the rear. She's never been known for her time-keeping.

Craig has already set to work erecting windbreaks, and Henry and Sebastian have been instructed to set up deck-chairs. However, they have abandoned that job in favour of kicking around a football. Since they immediately invite Millie and her gaggle of friends to join in the game, neither Rose nor I complain. We lay out a series of blankets, placing them so that they overlap at the edges, to make sure we stay one big group and don't splinter into factions. Next, we start to blow up orange and green balloons and then tie them around the windbreak to demark the fact that we are a party area. Millie no longer likes the colour pink. I tell myself that every little girl grows out of pink, but the brightly coloured balloons bother me a tiny bit. Millie's rejection of pink wasn't gradual, it was overnight, when she came home from the hospital. By then, she knew that her dreams of being a dancer were over. A girl with screws and pins holding together bone fragments can't expect to ever become a prima ballerina. She threw out all her tutus, leotards and slippers, she demanded that I take down the ballet posters from her walls, she threw out every Angelina Ballerina book, trinket, and toy she owned. She eradicated the colour pink that was so closely associated with her dreams. Six years old is a very young age to have your dreams crushed. Or your pelvis, hip and femur, come to that.

The balloons bob and are lifted when there is a gust of wind, but they don't float constantly upwards as I imagined. I'd have needed helium-filled balloons for that and I couldn't manage those on the train, it was enough carrying the enormous day bag and shepherding the girls. I am very grateful to Rose for transporting the party food. I don't like travelling long distances by car anymore. Not since — I catch myself — I won't think about that today.

My bag is bulging, full of the usual day trip essentials: towels, sun cream, bats and balls and a change of clothes, as well as a few extras because it's Millie's birthday. I've brought candles and matches, in case Rose forgot them (which I admit is unlikely), prizes for the games, party hats, and I've brought along all the cards people have sent Millie, although I left her gifts at home for her to open this evening.

'You should have given more to me, I could have brought all of this in the car,' says Rose when she sees me unpack the towels.

'Oh, these microfibre towels barely weigh anything,' I assure her. In fact, the straps of the bag have dug into my shoulder and I can still feel the weight of it even after offloading it on to the pebbles. I hadn't realised how long it would take to walk from the station to the front. I should have asked for her help, but I don't like to be a burden. Rose does so much already to cushion and comfort, I don't want to exploit her kindness. I call over to Millie and her friends. 'Have you all got sun cream on?' One or two of them reassure me they have; largely I am ignored. They are more interested in scampering to the sea, jumping over waves and squealing with laughter.

We wait until the others arrive before we unpack the food. I am relieved when Lucy and Auriol arrive without Peter. 'He's playing golf,' Lucy explains. I'm not surprised, Peter always plays golf on a Saturday morning and when I say always I mean he's been known to miss weddings because he has an 8 a.m. tee time. 'He's going to try to join us later this afternoon.' My heart sinks a little to hear she's staying for the duration. I had thought she might show her face and then dash off after an hour or so. I say nothing but manage to smile politely.

Even though Rose and I have catered for everyone, Connie and Lucy have brought extra, which is always exciting and welcome. It's clear that Connie has been planning her contribution to the picnic for a while. She's Millie's godmother and takes the role seriously. She has brought along a platter of a delicious-looking tricolore salad, rounds of herbed ciabatta, and she's baked a batch of gooey chocolate cupcakes. Lucy has brought three bottles of champagne and the most enormous punnet of fat, rich raspberries. She tells us she handpicked them from an organic farm. 'Spent all afternoon doing so, yesterday.' I can hardly believe it. 'I know Millie adores raspberries,' she explains simply. From anyone else I'd see this as a notable act of thoughtfulness; Lucy most probably identified an Instagram opportunity. I bet her feed is full of pictures of her picking the raspberries.

I glance up and take a moment to watch my daughter and her friends play in the waves that swish and crash on the shore. The girls continually dash towards the waves, then run away laughing. For now, they are allowing themselves to be little girls. I'm glad I resisted the pleas to have a pop princess party, which is inclusive of a make-up demonstration and a choice of each guest having either false eyelashes or a fake tattoo. Fran, Flora and Auriol are lounging about on towels. The oldest two are chatting, Flora's head is buried in a novel, as usual. All three girls are always keen to get a tan and the pursuit of said tan is taken very seriously. It starts in March and even if it's snowing they insist on being barelegged. Craig, Luke, Sebastian and Henry are playing a paddle and ball game in the shallows. The ball is tapped between them, consistently hitting the mark. The boys and Craig are in swimwear, but Luke didn't get the opportunity to change. He was recruited into the game almost the moment he arrived at the beach. He's in shorts and a T-shirt and he's getting wet and hot but doesn't seem concerned. He's laughing and chatting as usual.

My eyes drift back to Millie, as they always do. I notice that she has fallen over three times in quick succession; the waves don't knock any of the other girls off their feet, she's getting tired. Possibly her leg or hip is hurting, but she'll never admit it. I become aware that Luke's eyes are on her too. He seems to have noticed she's struggling, but he knows better than to make it into a thing. Drawing attention to her struggles makes her embarrassed and angry. Suddenly, he swoops down and hoists her on to his shoulders. She's tall but light. Her legs trail down the front of his T-shirt, towards his hips. She is far too big to be carried anywhere but she squeals with joy all the same as he runs her deeper into the sea and then throws her into the water. Rose, Connie and I look on, vaguely concerned, but she emerges laughing. Lucy comments, 'She loves that he refuses to treat her with kid gloves.' Now Luke picks up the other girls and starts throwing them into the water too, to prove he doesn't treat her any differently at all. The volume of shrieking intensifies as Henry and Sebastian dash up the beach and try to pick up Auriol and Fran, clearly with the intention of dunking them as well.

About fifteen minutes later everyone is sat on the picnic rugs, shivering but wrapped in towels and demanding food. Frolicking in the sea and general mischief-making clearly creates appetites. I notice that Luke is drenched but he holds back and waits until everyone else has a towel before picking one up.

The day passes in a glorious series of happy vignettes. The kids are aged between nine and nineteen but get on all the better for that. They naturally group and regroup throughout the day depending on the activity and energy levels. We play some traditional party games that Millie initially pronounced lame but are in fact fun, something she can't deny when her friends insist they are going to be sick with giggling. We eat candy floss and ice creams, we visit the amusement arcade on the pier and Fran, Flora and Auriol peel off to have a mooch around the Lanes. Sebastian and Henry say they are doing the same, but they are almost certainly going to the pub or to chat up girls. People are shy about saying they are going for a drink in front of me. I swore that once Millie was released from hospital I would give up drinking altogether and for a year I did. But then I started to allow myself the odd glass on special occasions. I realised drink wasn't my enemy just because it is Simon's.

By 5 p.m. Sebastian and Henry return from the pub. We are all starting to feel peckish, which is extraordinary considering how much food we ploughed through at lunch. We laugh and explain away our greed: the sea air creates appetites, we've had a very active day, we ate ages ago, at least three hours since. Craig suggests we pack up and find a fish and chip restaurant. His idea is met with unanimous approval. As I start to push sodden towels and costumes back into my bag, I remember Millie's birthday cards.

'Do you want to open your cards first?' I ask. I know they will get damp if they're next to the towels, or maybe even lost as I cart things back to the station. Thinking about it now, it wasn't the best idea to bring them with us.

'Oh yes!' she cries excitedly, aware that a fair number of them will hold cash or vouchers. She carelessly rips open the envelopes and I scoop up the waste paper, determined not to allow rubbish on the beach. As she hoped, there is quite a haul. She has a sizable cheque from my parents, lots of other people have slipped her a fiver or tenner or vouchers for books, Claire's Accessories and Topshop. She has never bought anything in Topshop and looks fit to burst with the thought of it. Her face is bright with happiness, her smile is stretched across her entire face. I feel something inside me relax a little. It's been a great day, a success. Millie has had the sort of birthday celebrations most nine year olds might hope for. I sigh with relief because it's not always a given. Birthdays and Christmases can be fraught. Most days the two of us rub along very well, on some days we simply aren't enough.

Connie reaches into her bag, 'I have two more. Mine and — '

'Oh, thank you!' screeches Millie, who now seems incapable of managing a normal pitch such is her exhilaration. I can't imagine what she'll be like this evening when she opens the pile of bath bombs, stationery, jewellery and hair clips that are nestled in the numerous small packages in our living room.

'Well there's a story behind this gift,' says

Connie. I try to politely give her my attention but I'm keeping one eye on Millie too, she's already ripped open the envelope and I reach for the discarded paper. Connie's story gets snatched away on the wind, as Millie and her friends continue to laugh and chatter over one another.

'What is it?' India asks, peering over Millie's shoulder.

'Is it a voucher?' asks Sophie, leaning on her friend.

'No,' Millie looks confused. 'It's tickets for Sadler's Wells. A ballet, *Giselle*.' Millie reads the words slowly, all light fading out of her face. 'I don't want to go,' she says stiffly. She won't look at Connie. I quickly snatch the tickets and card out of her hand and put them in my bag.

'No, sweetheart, you don't have to.' I manage to smile at her and glare at Connie almost simultaneously. Quite the feat. 'Come on, let's get packed up. I'm so ready for fish and chips,' I say in my jolliest tone.

Everyone makes a big show of being hungry and we try to drown Millie's pain in chatter about whether we should add pickled eggs or pineapple fritters to our order. As we walk towards the shops and restaurants I collar Connie.

'What were you thinking?' I snap.

'I just never imagined, I should have checked.' Connie looks horrified. 'I want to slap myself in the face,' she adds.

I want to slap her in the face too, but she's my friend and I know she would never deliberately hurt me or Millie. It was a misjudgement that's all. Still, I'm so infuriated I can't quite let it go. I add, 'You know she hates anything to do with ballet. She doesn't want to be reminded of what's no longer possible. Why did you get her tickets to see *Giselle?*'

'That's not *my* gift,' says Connie.

'What do you mean?'

'That was what I was trying to tell you before Millie ripped open the card. It was sent to my house but addressed to Millie.' My heart freezes. 'Do you think it's from Simon?' she asks. 'I'm really sorry, Daisy. I should have checked. I didn't recognise the handwriting and it wasn't like the usual prison post, so I didn't imagine it was from him. But it must be, right?'

'Yes,' I reply firmly, and then start to walk a little faster. 'Come on girls, stay close together,' I yell over my shoulder at Millie and her friends, who it seems are always dawdling or skipping ahead, never simply safely at my side.

Connie looks confused. 'But how? Those tickets cost a fortune and how did Simon get hold of them?'

'I don't know. Someone must have helped him,' I reply stiffly.

'And there were three tickets. Why would he send three? What does it mean? Has a release date been set? He never said.'

I don't answer her. 'Look both ways before crossing over, girls.' We're at a zebra crossing and they are already walking in twos, holding hands, as I've long since instructed them. Everyone follows my road crossing rules to the letter, no one dare do otherwise. The girls wait for the traffic to stop, and then check for bikes a second and third time, before Sebastian and Henry finally beckon them over the road like youthful lollipop men. People understand that I'm extremely fearful of crossing roads and if I exasperate them, no one says so, not even the perky kids.

'Aren't you going to check the card?' Connie pursues. I wish she'd let it go. I don't want to think about the ballet tickets.

'I don't need to.' I reply stiffly. She gives me a strange look, somewhere in between nosy and sympathetic. 'Look, just forget it, can't you.' I snap. Connie flinches, hurt. It's not how I wanted the day to end. Millie, upset. Connie, offended.

Me, terrified.

26

Simon

Inside there was nothing but time.

Simon has been incarcerated for two years, ten months, two days. 1,036 days behind bars. People said he would get used to it, eventually. Get used to the lack of space, the lack of privacy, the lack of choice. He had not. He doubted he ever would.

People were wrong about a lot of things.

First, he had been in the police station, then in a holding prison, then here. He never applied for bail. At the time he was in the grip of going cold turkey and didn't know or care where he would go, even if it was granted. Now, he regretted that. Saw it was a mistake. He should have tried to get home. While there still was one.

It was Millie's birthday today. He wondered what they were doing. No one had told him.

Prison was a scary, brutal place, full of scary, brutal people. He wasn't that. He had to believe he wasn't that. He'd never imagined setting foot in a prison before he landed himself here. Who did?

They parcelled up the day to give the inmates a sense of order and progress, he supposed. It just made him feel as though he was in

Groundhog Day. The same, unvaried routine day after day after day. Nothing could make the time go any faster: not the food, the shitty work, certainly not the conversation.

The best part of the day was when he was asleep. But even sleep was elusive, for many reasons. A lot depended on who he shared his cell with. Due to overcrowding, getting a pad to yourself was a luxury, one Simon had yet to enjoy. He'd had had four cellmates in the past three years. The first two men were serving short sentences. In and then out after some months. The next one was a full-on proper crim. Rick Dale. The two Dale Brothers headed up the most vicious and powerful gang in the prison. They operated several scams and were responsible for the distribution of everything: chocolate, fags, stamps, drugs, mobile phones, booze. Simon quickly came to understand that they were the real internal law and order system with as much, if not more, power than the guards. The punishments they dished out were dreaded far more than a couple of days in the cooler. Rick was the younger brother; on the outside he dealt with drugs and women. He ran dodgy clubs and gangs. He scared the shit out of Simon, who barely slept for the six months they shared a cell.

Dale smoked twenty, thirty fags a day. In theory Simon could have made a complaint about having to pad-up with a smoker, in reality he was unlikely to ever be able to sue the prison service over the long-term health implications of passive smoking. When Rick Dale was first put into his pad, Dale had offered Simon a cigarette.

Simon didn't take it.

'Don't you smoke?' Dale had asked.

'No.'

'You think it's bad for your health, do you?'

Because Simon was still naïve, he'd nodded. Dale punched Simon in the gut, swift, hard. He'd never been punched before he came inside, well at least not since the school playground, and never with any real force. He folded, dropping onto the floor in a heap. Dale kicked him, two, three sharp kicks. It was a swift going over. A warning, a demonstration of the hierarchy and structure, delivered with cold efficiency. Simon understood the lesson. Nothing was as bad for his health as crossing the Dales. The risk the Dales and their gang presented was all-pervasive and imminent. Simon was threatened with words and without them: in the yard, in the canteen, in the shower. Luckily, a better room came up further along the corridor. Quieter. Somehow, Rick Dale managed to wrangle a move. Simon never asked how. This wasn't a place where curiosity was rewarded. Best to keep your head down, your mouth shut.

His latest cellmate, Leon, was better. He was clean enough, decent about privacy and he didn't steal Simon's stuff. They sometimes traded cereal packets or a teabag for a coffee sachet. Simon had long since learnt to supress the impulse to just give someone something, it was viewed with suspicion. Everything had to be traded to keep the equilibrium.

Still, Simon only managed five or six hours of sleep per night. He was never exhausted; the days weren't full enough to help push him towards that longed for unconsciousness. He wished he could still drink until he passed out. Blacked out. Blocked it out. Now more than ever. But that wasn't an option.

At 7.30 a.m. the cells were unlocked. They were given breakfast, served from a hatch. It sounded good, breakfast being served, not having to dash around a kitchen, hunting out cereal, milk, a mug, but not being given any choice as to what you might want to eat was just another punishment. He couldn't sling a couple of rashers of bacon under the grill if he fancied a bacon butty, or wonder how he wanted his eggs that morning: scrambled, fried, poached. They ate what they were given, sitting on benches. No one spoke at breakfast. That, at least, suited him. He needed time each day to adjust. To remember why he was there.

At 8.20 they were moved to work. Simon made hairnets. He sometimes wondered whether there was a genuine market for hairnets anymore, or whether this menial job had been created to humiliate. To keep hands busy, self-esteem low. Working was classed as a Purposeful Activity. They structured the day so that there were as many hours of Purposeful Activity as possible. Library time, exercise, work, the meetings. Not that you got to pick and choose. You couldn't drift from one thing to the other, like an after-school club or an all-inclusive holiday resort. Everything had to be applied for, granted, regimented. Everything was given and could be taken away.

Initially, Simon hadn't applied for anything. He had been occupied dealing with the withdrawal from alcohol. All he could do was curl up on his bunk, tight like a fist and feel glad that the door was shut and locked. He'd screamed, shaken, cried, begged, sworn, kicked. When he got through that, he realised he needed to fill his days or he'd go mad. If he wasn't already gone. He liked to think he chose to work, to apply for a library and a gym pass, but maybe they broke him. Maybe he'd been conditioned, so much so that he was unaware that even choosing to participate wasn't his choice.

There was a period of the day that they called Association Time. This was when the inmates got to chat to one another, play pool or watch television. Some used the rowing machine or exercise bike which sat on the wing. There was also a laundry and a small shower cubicle. Simon loathed Association Time because, perversely, any sort of hint that this was free time only served to highlight that they had no such thing. It was time to kill. To smother. Extinguish. Endure.

Admittedly, it was not a particularly taxing regime, but it was far from stimulating. And it certainly wasn't the holiday camp which some commentators would have the British middle classes believe. The area where Simon 'associated' was desperately cramped, uncomfortably warm. It smelt of testosterone, fear and disappointment. The smell clung to him, forced its way up his nose and into his mouth. Choking him.

The exercise yard was no better. It was a lot

like a school playground but with bigger thugs. It was surrounded by high walls, topped with barbed wire. If a bird ever flew into the yard, the men would stop and stare, sometimes cluster. Grown men captivated! It was horrifying. Then the bird would get startled and fly away. Some of the men would watch it until it was a dot. They radiated longing and fury. They couldn't do what a fucking scrap of a bird could.

Millie's birthday. The date banged around his head. It defied logic. One day was like the next in here, and yet Millie's birthday was remaining stubbornly important to him. He decided to spend a bit of time recalling her past birthdays. The six he had seen. It was something new to think about, at least. There was a clown at one, he remembered spinning plates. But then Simon had dropped them. Daisy had made a fuss. Said he shouldn't have been joining in, he was too drunk, and that the tricks were for the kids anyway. It was an uncomfortable memory. Seared with regret and embarrassment. He thought they'd had a puppet show party once. But he wasn't sure. He couldn't remember.

He could remember her being born though. When Millie was first born Daisy had struggled, not him. She'd said she felt caged. Confined. She'd complained that she couldn't so much as go to the loo on her own anymore. She said she felt she'd lost herself. Simon had called it that. *Struggling*. The doctor had called it postnatal depression. Simon hadn't liked the label, he'd thought it was too fierce, too defining, and he'd tried to protect his wife from it. She'd screamed at him that he didn't understand, that he couldn't protect her from anything. He'd taken time off work and managed all the childcare: nappies, bathing, soothing. Daisy did at least manage to breastfeed Millie, but she'd looked out of the window whilst doing so, seemingly ignoring their rooting, snuffling, gulping child. Rose and Connie visited, ostensibly to help out but they hadn't been much help, not really. Rose had repeatedly tutted and muttered, 'I don't understand. She's wanted a baby for so long. How can she be depressed now?' The world was very black and white to Rose. Connie had mostly stroked a crying Daisy's hair and murmured, 'It's OK, let it all out.'

Millie's care had fallen almost exclusively to him. He hadn't minded. Unquestionably, he would have liked it if his wife had felt well and happy, if she had been as comfortable and delighted with their child as he was, but secretly he had enjoyed how much time he got to spend with his baby daughter. He'd been longing for her too, just like Daisy. Other husbands complained that their wives excluded them when a newborn was brought home. Other wives made their husbands feel clumsy and in the way. At least he didn't have to deal with that.

Babies came out red, wrinkled; they were largely indistinguishable from one another. That's what he'd always thought when he'd visited their friends' countless newborns. He thought they gathered up their looks and personality at about two or three years old. But Millie was perfection from the get-go. When she cried so hard that her back arched and her face turned puce, when she threw up on an outfit that he'd carefully coaxed her wiggling body into (for the third time that day), even when she smelt of urine or worse, she was perfection. The love he felt when he held her close and just inhaled her — all Sudocrem and baby lotion newness — cracked him open, like a nut. Left him exposed. She was so determined and alive. Whilst she was just a scrap, she was a soul, a being, a force to be reckoned with. He couldn't get enough of her. He was the first person she smiled at. It inflated his heart, her smile. Every damn time. Really, he felt his heart swell, grow. He'd happily sit for hours just holding Millie. Breathing her in, running his fingers carefully over her sprouting, golden hair. He even sang to her. He was a tuneless bugger, didn't do any of the songs justice but he didn't care because Millie seemed to like his singing. Mostly he sang hits from the 90s but sometimes old tunes from the 70s that he'd grown up with. Love ballads. He liked to sing Stevie Wonder's, 'You Are the Sunshine of My Life' as he held her close to his chest and jiggled her up and down, dancing around the room. Because she was, without a doubt. Because it was love like he'd never known.

He'd held her tight, until eventually Daisy had stretched out her arms, ready to take their baby.

The next thing he knew Millie was walking, tottering from one piece of furniture to the next. Then running, dancing, leaping. All babies seemed to grow, change and develop so rapidly. You'd blink, and that stage would be over, on to the next thing. He wondered how much he would miss in the time he was away. Would she even recognise him?

Would it matter?

He had time to think, in prison. Lots of it. He couldn't do anything other than think. He understood everything now, it was clear. It hadn't been the baby blues that Daisy had suffered from. It was guilt. Or perhaps grief for the man who had dumped her. He assumed the other man had dumped her or else why would she have stayed? And the beautiful baby he'd sang to? She wasn't his daughter. When he had been drunk, he had been angry. Now he was sober, he hurt.

27
Daisy

It is 7 p.m. by the time we all finish up in the restaurant, milkshakes are slurped, paper napkins are scrunched into balls and the bill is settled. When I come back from the toilets and start to try to round up the girls, get them to make a move to the station, I am met with resistance. They are flagging, exhausted. Peter had arrived for supper as promised, so he and Lucy have two cars between them.

'I know, how about I take Luke, Auriol, Fran and Flora home. That way Connie and Lucy can drive you and your guests back to yours,' Peter suggests, as though the idea has just occurred to him. He's good at dissembling but I'm not fooled, it's clear that this fact has been discussed whilst I was in the loo.

His suggestion is met with loud approval from everyone other than me. 'Oh no, I couldn't possibly ask you to do that,' I say, turning to Connie and Lucy. 'We're far too far out of your way. It will add so much time onto your journey.' They both live in Notting Hill, just minutes away from one another, I'm North London.

'Well, Sophie is staying at yours and I'd have had to pick her up tomorrow anyway,' points out

Connie. 'How about I stay over at yours too. I can borrow some pyjamas, pick up a toothbrush. I can help out with this lot tonight.' She nods towards Millie's guests. 'I'll make hot chocolate.' The six youngest girls are jumping up and down on the spot now, clapping their hands in glee at the idea of more treats to come.

'Oh, an adult sleepover, fun,' chips in Lucy. Her tone leaves me utterly confused as to whether she thinks a sleepover is heaven or hell, and most worryingly, whether she is planning on joining Connie and stopping over too. I throw Rose a desperate look but she just shrugs.

'It will be a struggle with all of them on the train and tube, it's a sensible plan,' she says. Her practicality always overrules any emotional impulse. Sometimes I wonder whether we are related at all.

Connie proposes that she takes Sophie, Millie and India and that I travel with Lucy and the other three little girls. I really could do without having to make small talk with Lucy for the next few hours, but Connie's plan makes sense and I realise that refusing would be beyond rude. Besides, I can't expect the three girls to travel with Cruella de Vil without either me or the birthday girl for company, and I know Millie will refuse to be separated from her two besties. I feel hustled, but I can't stem the tide of these proposed logistics. That's the way it is if you are part of a big gang of friends, sometimes you must go with the flow, even if you'd rather pluck out your own eyes.

The girls climb into the back of Lucy's

incredibly smart Jag. It's a people carrier, even though they are only a family of three and probably don't need a vehicle this size. It's like a tank, a very comfortable one. We're up above the rest of the world, more powerful. More protected. I'm grateful for that at least. I feel nervous. I know Connie is a careful driver, but I wish Millie was travelling with me. Truthfully, I'd like her at my side always. I force myself to fight that instinct on a constant basis because I know it's unhealthy. The girls giggle, impressed at the clean, soft, leather interior. Lucy's car is immaculate, it looks as though it's just been driven out of the showroom. It's quite a contrast to how ours always looks. It's constantly littered with crisp packets, library books, school permission slips, loose coins and banana skins.

Lucy drives carefully, fastidiously keeping within the speed limits. 'There are cameras everywhere on the roads,' she comments. 'I don't want a ticket. It's so inconvenient.' I've never imagined Lucy to be the sort of person to care about limits, she doesn't seem to accept that rules apply to her too. Lucy and I are never alone together. If we see each other, it's in a group, usually Connie glues us together. I'd like to sit in silence, but Lucy has other ideas. Her irrepressible confidence means she's never been one for small talk. She cuts to the chase.

'How's Simon?'

I shift uncomfortably. 'Fine.' I'm too honest for my own good so I find myself adding, 'I imagine.'

Lucy raises an immaculately plucked eyebrow.

Her brow wrinkles just enough for me to realise she is not having Botox, however she is aging beautifully. The woman has always had all the luck. Lucy is tall and slim, with enormous green eyes that are framed by thick lashes. I used to think her long, swooshy hair was her greatest asset but she looks stunning with her new elfin crop. So maybe it's her large breasts or her thin waist that are her best assets.

'You imagine? But you don't know? You're still not visiting him?' she probes.

I glance in the mirror to see if Millie's friends are listening in to our conversation. They're not. One is already asleep, the other two are wearing headphones and listening to their own music, or maybe an audio book, I think hopefully. 'Correct. I'm not visiting him.'

'Wow, you sure can hold a grudge.' There's a smile in her voice. I think that she's referring to the grudge I hold against her as well as my relationship with Simon. I shoot her a look that is designed to silence. It would probably terrify any other person; it certainly quells the kids in my class — and their parents — when necessary. Lucy doesn't take her eyes off the road and doesn't notice it at all. She seems to think my anger is quirky, endearing.

'I would argue that my husband almost murdering our child is grudge-worthy,' I snipe, crossly.

'Almost killing. The charge was never murder. He never intended to hurt Millie,' replies Lucy. All matter of fact. 'The charge was causing grievous bodily injury, wasn't it?'

That's all this is to her, a matter of fact. Causing grievous bodily injury by careless driving under the influence of drink. To me it is the most devastatingly complex emotional nightmare imaginable. We're not on the same page but that's not a surprise, we rarely are.

I lean my head against the window and wonder if I'm a good enough actress to feign sleep. I see that as the only way out of this conversation. I give it a go and I actually do fall asleep because the next thing I realise is I'm being jolted awake by Lucy closing her car door. I watch in the wing mirror as she fills up the car with more petrol. The car is quiet, all the girls are sleeping soundly now. The day's exercise and the comfortable lull of the car have taken effect. I can hear their regular, deep breathing. Besides the fact I find myself travelling home with Lucy, and the blip when Millie opened those ballet tickets, this really has been a good day. I always make a point of noting the good days. It's more than gratitude, it's in the hope that I can somehow store them up. The good days are like bricks and I'm building a protective wall around us so that, when the hard days inevitably arrive, we're shielded.

Lucy opens the car door and asks if I want anything from the garage shop. I shake my head automatically. I'm never keen to ask anything of anyone. I don't like to be a nuisance and I don't like to feel beholden, not even for a packet of wine gums. As she strides inside, men swivel their heads to get a better look. For real. I can see that the shop assistant beams when he claps eyes on her. I sigh. There's an urban myth that the Queen thinks Britain smells of fresh paint because everyone decorates before she visits them. In a similar vein, I think Lucy must believe that all males walk around with permanent grins on their faces, rather than smirks or sneers. Hers is another world.

The sun is setting now, turning the sky a deep purple. It's beautiful. I wind down my window and inhale the smell of early-summer promise. It won't be long before barbecues are being heated up. Times flies in the busy summer term for me. I wonder how Simon feels about time. I don't want to think about Simon. Usually I'm able to push him from my mind but it's harder to do today.

Lucy gets back in the car and hands me a can of Red Bull Sugarfree. 'You're going to need it. If the other three girls are napping like these are, they'll get a second wind when they arrive at yours. You'll have to keep up.'

I'd like to say I never touch the stuff but in fact I resort to Red Bull Sugarfree so often that I think I'd describe it as my favourite tipple. I know it's not good for me, but people do worse things to themselves than drink energy drinks. I mumble my thanks and open the can. The sticky, artificial scent that puts me in mind of sweets we ate in the 1980s and highlighter pens, pings to the back of my head and something flickers like a switch. Is it because Lucy was talking about Simon or because I'm at a service station drinking Red Bull like I was that night?

Suddenly, I see Millie bounce off the bonnet

of the car. I see her sprawled on the pavement, the rain spreading her blood all over the road. I squeeze my eyes shut. Then I shake my head slightly, trying to loosen something else. Was that a *memory?* The bit about her bouncing off the car? I still have nightmares about that night. Of course I do. I often imagine her bouncing off the front of the car, flying upwards and then landing with a sickening crack. Broken. Damaged for ever more. When this happens, I wake up sweating and shaking. I realise that what I dream is not a memory, it's what my imagination has pieced together after reading the police and doctors' reports. But have I just experienced a real memory, rather than an imaging? I don't know for sure, but it was different to how I normally imagine it. The angles seemed wrong, but the thud of her weight striking the car, the way her nightdress fluttered in the air, it seemed so *real*.

I feel a gush of unexpected emotions: terror, horror, and excitement. The thing is, although I think about what happened every day, it is my blessing and curse that I still can't remember the incident in any level of detail. At first, the doctors thought that the effects of my concussion would wear off and things would come back to me. This hasn't happened. I want to remember. I owe Millie that much. She endured it; the least I should do is remember it. Otherwise she was on her own because I've been told Simon can't remember any of it either. I'm not surprised. Blackouts were very usual occurrences for him. I wish he could remember ploughing into our daughter. He deserves to have that pinned into his brain for ever.

This isn't the first time I've remembered a shard of something. Sometimes, when I'm caught in the rain, I get a similar jolt. I remember the pavement digging into my knee, I feel my head ache. I hear shouting. Simon shouting and someone dragging me by the shoulders. Dragging me off Millie, I presume. They didn't want me to touch her in case I caused any complications to her injuries, but all I wanted to do was hold her close. That's a clear memory, wanting to hold her. I make myself think about that now. The feel of hands on my shoulders. I remember being pulled at, quite roughly. That's new. It's not much. It's not important but it's something.

I almost blurt out as much to Lucy. She's not the ideal confidant, but beggars can't be choosers — however, as I turn to her she says, 'So, Connie mentioned that Simon is about to be released. How does that work? I thought he got six years, he's served less than three.'

I'm deflated as the almost-memory flutters away. Frustratingly out of my grasp.

'There's this thing called on-licence. Technically, he'll still be serving his sentence, but he can do it on the outside. There are conditions, naturally,' I tell her.

'What sort of conditions?'

'He'll have to visit a probation officer, his travel will be limited, any job he takes has to be approved.' Although who would offer him a job, I wonder. 'They might make him go to meetings.' I add. 'He'll need a permanent, fixed address agreed beforehand.' This is the tricky one.

'Will he move in with you and Millie?' Lucy asks.

'I don't know. We haven't the money to pay for a separate rental. I thought we might have but when I checked our ISAs it turned out Simon had cashed them in long ago. I suppose he drank our savings away.'

Lucy nods, seemingly unsurprised that he drank away his daughter's uni fund. Since his arrest, plenty has been said about Simon's behaviour. My friends have been shocked and dismayed as I revealed the lows that he sunk to. No one could understand why he didn't ask for bail, so he could be by Millie's bedside when she was in hospital. He should have wanted to be there. Ashamed, penitent, whatever. We didn't know if she was going to make it. He should have wanted to be by her side. She asked for him. I think it was this that crystallised most people's decision not to bother visiting him in prison. His friends and ex-colleagues reasoned that if he didn't care about his own daughter, why should they care about him? After being the focus of gossip, Simon became yesterday's news and was forgotten. Barely spoken of. I see that tide is turning again as we approach his release date. Once again, my family will be shoved to the front of the stage, however much I resist it.

'Do you talk on the phone?' Lucy asks.

'No.'

'Do you write?'

'No.'

'Are you planning on getting divorced?'

I turn away from her, look out of the window and watch the hedgerow and other cars slide by. There's no such thing as a free lunch and I'm certainly paying for this lift. 'I don't know,' I admit.

Lucy nods. I don't want to think about what will happen next. I have taken it a day at a time for years now and that has been enough. Just getting by has taken a Herculean effort, planning, projecting, preparing is beyond me. One foot in front of another, one step at a time, that's what's worked for me. I know enough about the programme that addicts go on to recover, to appreciate that this is the way they tackle their issues. They don't think, 'I'll never have another drink,' because that would be too overwhelming, they'd be more likely to crack, to fail. Instead they think, 'I won't have a drink today,' and they repeat that every day. The hope is that they won't ever have a drink again. Every day I tell myself, 'I won't think about Simon today.' Is it my hope never to think about him again?

'He might not be granted a licenced release,' I point out.

'He didn't send the birthday card and ballet tickets, did he?' comments Lucy. I gasp. How could she possibly know that? 'So, is Daryll Lainbridge back in the UK?' she asks.

'Daryll Lainbridge?' I force my voice to go up at the end of his name, as though I'm asking a question, as though I can't quite place whoever it is she's talking about. It is a hopeless act.

'He was in Boston, wasn't he?'

'New York,' I correct.

Lucy glances at me. I keep my face as still as possible, she's always had quite the skill in reading people. I don't want her to read me. 'Why do you think he sent those tickets to Millie?'

'How do you know he did?' I demand, fractious and startled.

'I recognised his handwriting on the envelope. He has a distinctive, frankly pretentious, cursive handwriting. I remember his essays, at university. Plus, he's sent Christmas cards and even the occasional postcard to me over the years. He always writes in green ink.'

'Oh.' I don't know what to say. I suppose I should have guessed Daryll might have sent cards to Lucy, he was after all infatuated with her for an age. His handwriting is distinctive, and why must he use green ink?

'They must have cost a bit, the tickets,' she adds.

'I suppose.'

'Why do you think he sent them?' she asks again. My cheeks redden. She's like a dog with a bone.

'People do send things to Millie, because of the accident,' I explain.

'Yes, they did, *then*. But it was ages ago.'

To Lucy the accident was ages ago. To me it was yesterday. It is ever present. I see Millie limp out of school after a long day, I see her chase the other kids, following them, no longer leaping ahead, I see her keep her eyes rigidly on the pavement as we pass her old dance school, desperate not to notice the other girls in tutus. The accident is present. Not that it was an accident. It was a crime. People call it an accident to minimise the whole rotten mess. I'm glad the judge and jury saw it for what it was. A crime that had to be punished. Although at the time of sentencing, people commented the judge must have been in a merciless mood. Six years, Millie's entire lifetime at that point. Although, most likely, Simon would only serve half of it inside.

From the police report I know that the car was travelling at thirty-nine miles per hour at the point of impact, too fast to be taking a corner on a residential street. Far too fast. From the doctors' reports I know Millie's bones weren't just broken, they were shattered. She was in hospital for nine weeks and had painful, strenuous physiotherapy for months after that. She was unlucky. Well, obviously, it is unlucky to have an alcoholic father who mows you over in the street, but she was also unlucky because there were complications with resetting the breaks and then she developed sepsis. A life-threatening condition. I stayed by her bedside throughout her slow recuperation, solely focused on her getting better. There were police interviews, Simon's arrest and trial, press interest and scandal. I ignored it all. I let it all flow around me. Nothing mattered to me other than Millie's recovery. I barely ate, slept or even spoke to anyone other than doctors for days. It was agreed that I was in shock. All I could see were the wires that attached her to heart monitors, the intravenous drips and oxygen tanks; it looked as though she was tied to the bed. A prisoner. It appeared that she shrank before my eyes, she looked so tiny and frail.

It was only once she was out of immediate danger, once they said she would live, that I was able to breathe again. Then I was able to notice the people around us. The doctors and nurses were gods to me. Any update or information that dropped from their lips, I licked up like a thirsty dog. They tried to find the time to be kind, to pat my shoulder, to dredge up a hopeful smile even after a fourteen-hour shift. They kept reminding me to breathe. 'It could have been worse,' they said. Which was true, I realised that, but it also could have been better. It should have been. Her father was responsible.

As the weeks passed and she was able to speak, smile, laugh, I was able to take in the detail of our surroundings in a more usual way. I began to appreciate that my friends and family had sat with me throughout the ordeal, nudging their schedules and crafting rotas so that I'd never be alone. They tried to tell me about Simon's trial, his circumstances, but I closed them down. I didn't want to know. I didn't care. My world was inside the hospital walls. Specifically, the paediatric unit. Efforts are made to make the children's ward as cheerful as possible. The cream walls were painted with murals of rainbows and forest animals. The limp nylon curtains that separate the beds had red spots on them, they were not just the insipid green things that hung between the beds of adult patients. There were cards, cuddly toys and chocolate treats on every bedside table. Even so, despite all this, there was the underlying stench of illness and on top of that, a layered hint of bleach. The children were carefully nursed and often spoilt, but everyone just wanted to go home.

'So, what's the story with you and Daryll Lainbridge then?' Lucy asks, roughly pulling me back to the here and now.

'Story?'

Lucy raises an eyebrow and asks, 'Did you have an affair with him?' The question is so out of the blue and yet so long expected that for a moment I don't know how to react. It's as though she's slapped me. 'Daisy, we've known each other since we were eighteen years old and besides that, I'm absolutely unshockable. I won't judge you.' I glare at her. Her face is serene, we could be talking about whether we ought to pick up a pint of milk, not whether I had an affair. Lucy smiles. Her smile is dazzling; a mix between Julia Roberts and Cameron Diaz. 'I'd be the last person to judge.'

I am stunned. I take a long, slow, deep breath in. My therapist, who I saw for some months after the incident, taught me the importance of breathing deeply to combat anger, fear, anxiety. 'But in fact you *are* judging me, Lucy. You are judging me by your own, very low, despicable standards,' I retort. Now it's Lucy's turn to look surprised. Colour floods up her face from her neck. If I wasn't so flustered I'd get some satisfaction out of that. It takes a lot to rile Lucy.

'I think he's an arrogant prick if you want to know the truth.'

I sound defensive. I sound too heated. I should care about him less. I reach into my bag that's at my feet and scramble about for the card and tickets. When I retrieve them, I rip them in half and then quarters. I open the window and throw the pieces out in to the night. The bits dance on the wind for a moment, then vanish. Normally I loathe people who litter but I just needed to get rid of the card. To obliterate it.

We continue the rest of the journey in silence. We're both pleased when the girls wake up and start to chatter about their day at the beach. I notice Ellie has caught a little bit too much sun. I root out some after sun cream. I make quite a fuss. Obviously, I don't like children scorching themselves when they are in my care but mostly I make a fuss to fill the space that Lucy's accusation has created. When we finally arrive at my house I'm relieved to see that the lights are on, Connie has got home before us and let herself in with the key she keeps.

'I won't come in,' says Lucy. 'I better be getting back to Peter.'

'Yes, I think you'd better,' I reply firmly. I slam closed the car door and usher the girls into the house as quickly as I possibly can.

28

Simon

Tuesday, 28th May 2019

In the beginning, Simon thought the group meetings were pointless.

He'd sat in an uncomfortable plastic chair, silent, staring. Well not sat, slouched. None of the prisoners ever sat up straight. They lolled, leaned, or huddled. Defeated, disgraced. There were no ring-fenced resources for helping addicts in prison, so the idea of a therapist coming to run the meetings was impossible. The busy prison chaplain, Billy, stood in. He didn't wear his collar; he wanted to be approachable so he played down his association with God. He knew that it upset as many prisoners as it attracted. There were different denominations and faiths to consider, there were atheists and agnostics to include. Billy welcomed them all. To him, one lost soul was the same as the next.

Simon was told to go to the meetings and he'd done so because he thought it was compulsory, like making hairnets or showering when instructed. His response to attending meetings led by a person of the cloth was complex. He'd assumed the chaplain probably had a low IQ or was simply unbearably naïve. However, over time, Simon found that he grudgingly admired the chaplain, who had something most people didn't. A sense of hope. Or resolve. Peace. Simon had never felt any of those things securely. Billy seemed to understand that men who drank, stuck needles in their arms, or gambled away their homes were all suffering from the same thing; they yearned, they were hungry, incomplete. They lacked something vital. It might simply have been self-discipline or self-esteem. It might have been a god. What did Simon know? The chaplain could at least provide them with a room, twice a week, to talk about the gap, the space, the lack.

Simon had been forced into going cold turkey in custody in the months he'd awaited his trial. It had been agony. A new level of pain that he hadn't believed possible. Every muscle, bone and nerve in his body had screamed out in objection. He felt raw and threatened. The world was hostile. The clang of a door, the turn of a key in a lock, the shove of a shoulder, all intimidated him. He felt perpetually vulnerable; sick and shivering with terror and paranoia. His body folded in on itself. His mind too. It was all he could do to breathe. He concentrated on listening to that sound, the sound of his breathing and the throb of his heart thumping, better to concentrate on that rather than the sound of other men laughing. Were they laughing at him? Other men shouting. Were they coming for him?

By the time he arrived in prison, he was dry. Dry, but still an alcoholic. Always an alcoholic.

Officially, there was no alcohol permitted, obviously, but the ingenious and desperate found a way to home brew. 'Where there's a will there's a way,' his first cellmate had assured him with a sly nod and a wink. Simon had laughed hysterically at that comment because he was scared, because he was excited. He remembered his mother often used that exact expression, along with, 'Necessity is the mother of invention'. Expressions that Elsie had were always positive, full of determination and resolve. When his cellmate used the optimistic little idiom, Simon saw the exhilaration and promise behind it. He'd also recognised the danger and threat, but he didn't care. He knew alcohol abuse ruined stuff — even motivational idioms — but on another level, it solved everything. Or had for a while. On the outside, he'd lived in hope that the answers lay at the bottom of the glass, and then the bottom of the bottle, and then the next bottle and the next. And if they didn't, it didn't matter because he'd drank until he'd forgotten what the questions were. The idea that rules could be broken, even in here, that he'd sniff out alcohol somewhere, appealed to him.

However, despite his initial excitement, the opportunity to home brew had never presented itself to Simon. In all the time he'd been locked up, no one offered him anything. He would have to approach someone if he wanted in on the illegal brewing, the Dales probably. Slowly, it dawned on him that, yes, he wanted a drink, but for the first time in as long as he could remember, he wanted something more. He wanted to stay safe and alive. Hunting out the right people, the people who dared break the rules, and then owing them, would threaten that.

So he stayed sober.

For the first few weeks that he attended the meetings he did not say a word. He wanted to draw as little attention to himself as possible, speaking would confirm attendance, draw notice. Prison was scary as fuck. Group therapy was perilous, possibly suicidal. In prison people didn't often talk about their crimes; confessions were dangerous. He could easily say the wrong thing, something someone could take objection to. Hell, the thought of laying himself bare, exposing himself in a one-on-one private therapy session in North London, with an earnest, bearded, vegetarian liberal had always horrified him. How could this be a good idea? He'd slouched as far back on his chair as he could, looked nowhere other than at his shoes. Countless tales were told about drink and drugs, hate and fear. What it did to a person. What addiction could strip someone down to — our snarling, animal selves. Faces smashed, knuckles bloodied. He'd pretended he wasn't there. And anyway, he wasn't. Not really. He let the meetings happen over his head.

After about a month, Billy had tried to draw him in. He'd asked, 'Simon, do you have anything you want to say?'

They'd been talking about cravings. There was a new guy. He had scratched himself raw. His arms and legs were bleeding. He was jittery, agitated. High on something, coming down, despairing he'd never have a hit again. Despairing about that, more than the fact he was banged up, Simon suspected.

'No,' replied Simon.

At the next meeting there was a guy who was as thin as a reed but could talk for England. 'You wake up with a hangover, but what really ruins the next day is the shame. Even if you were drinking alone, not kicking off, causing no trouble whatsoever, you are still filled with shame because it's starts to become obvious that you're just not able to get your shit together. You're a fucking loser.' Then with more honesty, he added, 'I'm a fucking loser.' No one bothered to contradict him. 'I wonder how much more I might have done with my life had I not spent it drunk,' he mused.

'You'd have robbed a bank, maybe. Not just a couple of poxy corner shops,' replied another con. This got a laugh. They were all glad of the joke, it eased things. Honesty was a downer. Billy mumbled something about change being in everyone's grasp.

Another one of the inmates upped the ante. He'd decided to take this opportunity to shock or maybe scare. Certainly, to be the centre of attention. He described beating an old lady, half to death, for twenty-four pounds. He'd owed his supplier. He'd thought the old bird kept more money in her house. He'd been beaten in turn when he didn't pay up.

The inmate admitted, 'Now, I see I was owed that. You know. Karma or some such fuck. At the time, when they were kicking the shit out of me, I just remember hating the old bitch for not having enough cash for me to rob.'

The man who had scratched himself raw had cried when he heard the story, but Simon didn't know if the response was genuine emotion or simply chemically induced.

Once again, Billy asked, 'Have you anything to add, Simon?'

Simon thought about scrabbling through his mother's bedside cupboard, looking for spirits. He thought about Daisy's face when she caught him. But he'd never beaten up an old woman. He told himself that he wasn't like these people. These criminals, these addicts.

'Nothing to add,' Simon had replied.

He kept going to the meetings, though. He was drawn, with a horrified sense of awe, to these tales about the last gasps. What people did to themselves. What the human body could endure.

The group meetings were . . . endless.

And part of the deal, part of the process. It took him months to work that out. One day Billy was making them talk about loss. Loss of self, loss of dignity and the loss of family support. Big stuff. Everyone watched Jeremy Kyle. Everyone knew the vocabulary of divulgence and revelation. Even cons.

'I lost my way, right.'

'I lost sight of, you know, like what matters.'

'I lost everything, man. Everything.'

The things they said were so familiar that Simon wasn't sure if he believed them and related, or if he'd simply read them in a tabloid. He was trying to decide, when Billy interrupted his thoughts.

'Simon, anything to add?'

'I lost my shoes once. On a bender.'

He hadn't meant to be funny but one or two of the others laughed, then caught Billy's eye and swallowed their laughter. Simon wasn't sure how he'd lost his shoes. Had he kicked them off? Thrown them away? From time to time, throughout his life, he had sometimes seen a lone sneaker in the middle of the road or a shoe stranded in the hedgerow. He'd always assumed these abandoned pieces of footwear were the result of a bunch of blokes messing about; possibly a stag party, stripping a mate, throwing away his shoe, or schoolkids bullying the class swot because he was going places and they were not, maybe throwing his shoes away would slow him down. But when Simon had lost his shoes — not one but both — he'd been alone. He'd taken off his socks too. He couldn't remember doing so but when he got home he was barefoot. His feet were cut, and he'd stood in some dog shit. He walked it right into the house, smearing the crap on the carpet. Daisy had cried whilst she washed his feet. He knew about loss.

'Your shoes?' Billy prompted.

'Yeah, I lost my shoes and my wife's respect.'

Once he'd started talking, he found the meetings were the places he most wanted to be. As his body got used to the fact he could no longer feed his craving, the physical agony began to recede, but it was replaced by mental pain. Regret, anger, depression, self-disgust, universal loathing. All the bad ones. The days were too long, his mind too dark. The yard, the showers, even the library were still full of menace and peril, the small group meetings were as near to safe as he could get in this place. He found that, contrary to his initial fears, the dozen or so cons that attended seemed to abide by the rule of non-disclosure outside the room. Maybe they were equally needy of the space, terrified of being barred, or maybe equally ashamed of their stories, therefore willing to trade silence. It was most likely some sort of self-preservation. Cons were selfish. Addicts were selfish. It stood to reason that the men who fell into both camps saw the advantages of staying silent.

Simon continued to listen to the strangers' stories. The more he heard, the more he recognised. He was shocked, disconcerted, to learn that he wasn't a unique little snowflake, with a private and special relationship with alcohol. He began to understand that addiction was a player, loose. She got around.

'Do you think there's like an alcoholic gene, that you can inherit?' someone once asked. Simon didn't know his name. His hair was long, he wore it in a ponytail. He was overweight by about forty pounds.

'There is evidence that might be the case,' Billy replied carefully.

'My family are always talking about that shit. By the time I was ten or something, they said I had that gene. Like having brown eyes. Something I couldn't change. So why would I even try? They knew I was fucked, even when I was still playing with Lego. My mum, she used to carry around a flask of tea wherever she went.

The supermarket, school pick-up, the park. Except it wasn't tea.'

'My whole clan drink, man. Blacking out is nothing to any of us. It's like a rite of passage. Yeah?' This came from a man who had a Scottish accent. His use of the word clan wasn't entirely ironic.

What was it Simon's mother had said? Not that she could be relied upon for an accurate account, since half the time she didn't know her own name, but she had said his father drank, hadn't she? That it was best to ignore the matter. Thinking about it, Simon realised something he'd always known, but had indeed tried to ignore: his gentle father — who Simon had admired as a boy — was a binger. Sometimes so generous and available and there. Other times absent, closed, even cruel. When it came to booze, his father had always hopped and lolloped along the path between craving and revulsion. Simon had followed after him.

Eventually, Simon had admitted to himself that maybe he should have done this on the outside. Gone to a meeting. Maybe it would have helped. Part of his brain registered that the thought was borderline optimistic. A thought still distilled with a sense of familiar regret, but there was an undeniable hint that things could change, could be improved. That was entirely new.

'Simon, do you have anything to contribute?' Billy had coaxed him.

So, he told them about missing Millie's ballet recital. He told them about the hours she'd practiced, how excited she was to be performing a solo. He admitted that he'd promised her that he wouldn't miss it for the world, that she had in fact elicited this promise three times and got him to seal the deal by clasping pinkie fingers and pinkie promising. Then he explained. 'I was in a bar. One of those really cool ones. Full of young people.' He hoped but doubted the longing stayed out of his voice.

'Young women you mean?' someone interrupted, Simon could hear the snigger.

'I suppose,' Simon shrugged. Other women had never interested him. He knew drunks that needed to fight or fuck once they were legless. He only ever needed another drink. And then another. The longing he was trying to hide was for the bar. 'It was a cocktail bar. I'm not a cocktail man,' he added hastily.

'Is there such a thing?' someone chipped in. There was a smattering of laughter.

'No,' Simon admitted with a small smile. 'I suppose not. But, you know, sometimes cocktails are just the answer.'

'Fast.'

'Exactly. It was dark, with music playing, dozens of bottles were lined up. Overpriced and therefore desirable. The bartenders took pride in what they were doing. They painstakingly poured out each measure into metal shakers, added chunks of ice, and swished.'

Nobody minded that he took his time, set this scene. They were happy to be transported there. There was nowhere they would rather be.

'The bartender shook, poured, garnished. I swallowed, gulped, re-ordered.' Simon sighed. 'I knew I didn't have time to linger but it just seemed like more fun being there than being at a kid's ballet recital.'

No one disagreed. No one said anything for a few moments.

'So, your little girl is a ballet dancer?' asked the guy with a ponytail. Simon didn't like the way his man boobs shuddered as he suddenly, keenly, sat up in his chair to ask the question. Ponytail man licked his lips, coughed. It might have been polite interest, it might have been something much uglier. Simon regretted bringing Millie into the room. She didn't belong here. Even the idea of her didn't belong here. Fuck prison. He'd transported himself for a few moments, but it was hopeless, it was delusional. He was stuck here. Here amongst the depraved and disgusting. This is where he belonged.

'Is she any good?' asked Billy. 'Your daughter? Is she any good at ballet?'

'She was,' Simon replied. 'She used to be.'

No one asked anything more. They all knew his family didn't visit him.

29

Daisy

Tuesday, 11th June 2019

It's been a busy morning at school. During summer term time seems to concertina: a crazy mash of school trips, sports days and report writing. I feel I'm always playing catch-up. I'm on playground duty today which I could do without. I'd like to use the time to write a few more reports but there's a rota and no one is likely to want to swap as it's not a particularly sunny day and we are all under the cosh to write reports.

Being on playground duty requires me to stay alert and focused. The noise is extraordinary: cheers, chants, chatter, laughter and arguments abound. It's a teacher's job to filter, survey, always be on the lookout for the next squabble or scraped knee. I'm vigilant, my eyes constantly scan like searchlights. Millie stands out like a beacon to me, whether she's sitting alone on a bench or huddled in a gossipy group. I'm sure this is true for all mums, our eyes zone in on our own, just checking, keeping them safe. But when I find myself watching Millie as she moves around the playground, I am not reassured; I feel stung with guilt. Her right leg drags just a fraction, pulling behind her, a constant reminder. I try not to be obtrusive when I'm monitoring her, she doesn't like it. More than once she's mentioned how she's really looking forward to moving to big school because she's sick of going to the school her mum teaches at. She used to see it as a perk but now I cramp her style.

I'm happy to report that other children don't find me quite as embarrassing. Today, as usual, various kids are hanging around, desperate for my attention. The little ones pull on my arms, they want to hold my hands, the bigger ones eagerly shout about where they are going to go on holiday this summer; Salou, Disneyland, Whitby. Teachers always attract the extremely shy ones and the biggest show-offs. I don't mind them clamouring for attention, they are fun and make me laugh. I'm doing just that when Keri Thornton, Year Five, charges up to me, yelling.

'Miss, Miss.' I'm not a Miss and haven't been for a long time but the catchall name is used on all female teachers in moments of heightened excitement. 'Oli Jordan and Aafa Khan are smashing each other's brains out near the climbing frame.'

I set off at quite a pace, charging towards the climbing frame, unsure what I'll find. 'Smashing each other's brains out' thankfully turns out to be an exaggeration, they are rolling about scrapping inexpertly and messily. The odd lucky kick does however cause considerable pain, although the moment I use my biggest 'teacher voice' and yell at them to stop, they do so, probably with some relief.

‘What’s going on?’ I demand. Both boys glare at one another and refuse to meet my eye.

Predictably the age-old excuse is spat out. ‘He started it,’ says Oli.

‘No, he did,’ snaps back Aafa.

I swore I’d never trot out the expressions everyone uses. I’ve always wanted to be an enlightened, perceptive and different teacher. But still, I find myself thinking, *I don’t care who started it, I’m finishing it*. That sort of gruff response isn’t good enough nowadays though, there are procedures. This might be a squabble over nothing or it might be part of an insidious bullying campaign. I need to investigate. I also need to get them patched up. I can see that Aafa has a badly scraped knee, Oli has some marks on his cheeks, I can’t yet work out if it is a nip, a bite or a bump. Their breathing is fast and shallow, I don’t know either boy very well, they’re a year below my class, I won’t teach them until next September, but I can tell they are panicked. My plan is to take them to their own form tutor, she’ll know if there’s any historical beef between these two and will be better placed to sort it out.

‘Right, inside now,’ I instruct. The three of us walk at a fast pace towards the school office. It’s then that I see him. He’s standing at the school gate, where parents usually congregate at pick up. I haven’t seen him for three years, but I recognise him instantly, my body registering him at the same time as my mind. My stomach flips, my legs turn to liquid. He realises I’ve noticed him and raises a hand, waves at me, smiles. I don't wave back. He rattles the school gate. It's one of those that has a coded lock. He can't get in, I remind myself. He can't reach me.

'Can you open this thing?' he yells. 'We need to talk.' I put my head down and quickly usher the boys indoors.

I spot a dinner lady. 'Mrs Wilson, will you take this pair to a member of staff? They need first aid and a talking to. They were fighting in the playground.' I garble my instructions.

'Which member of staff?' she asks.

'Any. Tell them the boys need to explain their behaviour.'

She tuts, showing her displeasure at being embroiled in this matter. 'You know we're not supposed to supervise the children.'

'Yes, I'm sorry. I have to go. I have an emergency.' She stares after me, questioning. I'm aware that I am a constant source of gossip at the school.

I dash outside again and head for the gate. He's still there, waiting for me. Smiling. Daryll Lainbridge.

'Daisy, how are you?' He asks the question as though it's the most normal thing in the world that he's suddenly turned up at my school gate, after all this time. His smile broadens, he's hoping to be winning. If I could be dispassionate about this situation, I'd have to admit that he's a handsome man. Charming. Still, even after everything. But I'm not dispassionate about this situation, I'm anything other.

'What are you doing here?' I demand.

'I wanted to know if you received the tickets.

Whether Millie was pleased.'

I have to keep one eye on the playground and I'm glad, it means I have a legitimate excuse for not looking at him. 'Yes, we got the tickets. I didn't know where to find you, so I could return them.' This is a lie, since I ripped them up in a fury.

'Return them?' He looks surprised as though I'm not in my right mind. 'Why would you want to return them?'

'Millie doesn't like the ballet anymore.' This isn't all of it, but I can't bring myself to say the words that need to be said.

He looks crestfallen. 'Oh, well that's a shame.'

'I realise they must have been expensive. I'll pay you back.' We haven't got money to splash, paying Daryll back for a gift that we never wanted, but he is the last person I want to owe anything to.

'It's not about the money, Curly,' he says sadly, I cringe, as I always have done, at the use of the nickname. I realise this is not about the money, but I'm trying to make it so because I don't want it to be about anything else. It can't be. 'She doesn't like ballet anymore, hey?' He shakes his head, he looks distraught, almost as upset as I was when I first realised as much.

'No. How did you hear she ever did?' I ask.

'I can't remember. You pick these things up. I heard she was really something. I thought she had a future there.'

'Yes, she did,' I admit.

'What changed?' When I don't reply, he guesses. 'Her injuries?' I nod. 'Fuck. That fucking bastard.' Daryll kicks the school gate. I look about, alarmed, I don't want to draw any attention.

'Daryll, please, don't. Not here.'

He stares at me, his eyes bright and intense. The sounds of the children in the playground bounce around us. I find myself scanning for Millie. I mustn't, not in front of him. The last thing I want to do is identify her to him. He breathes deeply, then seems to come to his senses. 'Right, sorry.' He pulls his hands through his hair. Not vanity, agitation. 'Well, what would she like for her birthday?'

'Nothing, she doesn't need anything.' I stop myself from adding, *from you*. She doesn't need anything from you. Because that would be inflammatory. Instead I feel compelled to tread carefully, to be as conciliatory as possible. I try to change the subject. 'So, you're back from New York. Are you on holiday?' I'm praying he'll say yes.

'No. It's a permanent transfer. I'm back in London for good, Curly.' He beams at me as though he's delivering great news. 'I would have written to let you know but I didn't know where to find you.'

'We moved,' I mumbled.

'You could have let me know.'

Why would I? But I swallow these words and instead say, 'The thing is we moved in quite a hurry and there was a lot going on at the time. I don't think I was as thorough with my admin as I should have been.' He barks out a sound that is supposed to be near a laugh, but is anything other, shakes his head.

'I'm admin, am I?'

I just want him gone from the school gate. Gone from my life but I daren't create a scene. 'I had to move. I couldn't afford the mortgage on my own,' I explain. I don't know why I tell him this. I don't want him to feel sorry for me. Is he likely to leave me alone if he pities me? No, probably not. He'll see my vulnerability as his advantage. Rallying, trying to sound determined and in control I add, 'I wanted a fresh start.'

I couldn't risk giving up my job, how did I know I would get another one? At least moving to a house that wasn't haunted with memories felt like a step in the right direction. After what happened I felt I was under constant scrutiny. First by the police, press and public, then my friends, my family. I know my friends and family were only looking out for my welfare, watching to see if I was coping on my own but it felt awful to be under constant surveillance. I felt like a child. A naughty child at that.

No one has nets hanging at their windows any more, so nets did not twitch as I walked down our old street, but I felt eyes upon me. The neighbours once waved cheerily from across the road and used to send Christmas cards, but I'd started to feel their collective cold shoulder some years back, when our recycling bins started to overflow with glass bottles.

'Had a party?' my next door neighbour once asked me when he caught me putting some of Simon's empties in the bin.

'Yes,' I lied.

‘I didn’t get the invite,’ he muttered, snidely. Quickly walking away.

By having a drunk for a husband, I brought a dirty cloud into their respectable street. By having a criminal for a husband, I brought a huddle of noisy door-stepping journalists. Even when the journos went away, there was a lingering sense of disrepute. People crossed the street to avoid talking to me. They wouldn’t meet my eyes, but they never stopped watching me.

‘I’m making my mind up about where to settle,’ Daryll says conversationally. ‘I think it’s time for me to buy, put down roots. But, at the moment, I’m renting. Not far from here actually.’

My heart plummets. ‘Oh, I thought you were always a South London man.’

‘Well, I wanted to see what North London has to offer.’ He holds my gaze. It’s awkward. I make myself look away.

I spot the Head coming out of school, she has the bell in her hand. Breaktime is over. The bell will be rung, the children will line up, I’ll be seen with Daryll. I need to get him out of here before people spot him and start to talk.

‘Well, thank you for stopping by,’ I drop out the platitude that’s generally accepted to be a closer. He doesn’t react. More words spill out of my mouth, unchecked and untrue. ‘It’s been nice seeing you, but I need to be getting back to work now.’

‘So, Millie doesn’t like ballet any more.’ It’s as if I haven’t spoken. I hear the bell chime through the playground.

‘No.’

'I'll have a think about what I should get her instead.'

'There's really no need,' I say firmly.

'Oh, I think there is,' he smiles slowly. 'What sort of father doesn't get his daughter a birthday gift?'

I freeze. The world shudders. Falls off its axis. Have I heard him correctly? I don't know what to say.

'Mrs Barnes are you joining us?' The sharp question comes from the Head. The children are now filing past her, back towards the classrooms. I spot Millie. She throws me a quick nod. Daryll notices my eyes trained on her and leaps to the right conclusion. 'Ah, there she is. Right? That's her? She's so pretty.' He waves at her. Out of politeness, Millie gives him a little wave back.

'I have to go,' I mutter.

He smiles, shrugs and turns away. 'I'll see you, Curly. I'll see you soon.'

30

Simon

'Barnes, visitor Connie Baker confirmed for 3 p.m. on Saturday,' barked the guard at roll call.

A blink of something close to eagerness flickered in Simon's belly. He always looked forward to seeing her. A tiny part of him wished he did not; maybe it would be better not to crave hers or anyone's attention. It would be better not to know, or care, about what was going on outside and yet he couldn't help himself.

For weeks, months when he'd first arrived, Simon hadn't cared about visitors, he hadn't even thought about them. After the trial and the sentencing, all he'd thought about was the collapse of the most important relationship in his life. The one he had with drink. How would he survive years in this place without it? Then, eventually, he'd thought about Millie. How was she faring? Sporadically, his lawyer brought news from the hospital, cold factual reports. They didn't get to the heart of how Millie was. And how was Daisy? Was she coping? Did she miss him? Was that an unreasonable hope? He was struck with self-loathing that it had taken him weeks to really care. When he did start to think about visitors, when he yearned for some news from the outside world, he realised no one had attempted to visit him. Not Luke, not Craig, not Rose. None of his colleagues or old college friends.

Not Daisy.

Friendships had been well and truly tested once he was on the inside, and it had turned out that his friends were mostly fair-weathered.

He checked with the guards. Had anyone requested to visit him ? They'd laughed. Which was no sort of answer at all. His sister had written, she'd said she was coming to the UK the following summer. She implied it was his fault that she had to make the momentous and costly journey from Vancouver because she had to check up on their mother. She said she'd stop by then, June or July. Those were the words she used. 'Stop by.' As though it was a matter of rocking up, ringing the bell and being asked in for a cup of tea. It wasn't her fault. Initially, he too had imagined someone visiting him in prison would be a bit like someone visiting a person in hospital. He'd thought there'd be set hours, that people would turn up, maybe not with grapes and chocolates but with something cheering. He'd learnt that wasn't how it worked.

There was no chance of a cheery surprise because the prisoners had to organise their visits in advance. Simon thought that there was a strange sense of justice about that, because on the outside he'd never got involved with admin, Daisy was the only one sober enough to manage their lives. He learnt that he was entitled to three visits a month, but if he wanted someone to visit, he had to apply via a visiting order. At the beginning of each month he was given three visiting order numbers. Then he had to telephone his prospective visitor and give them the VO number, so they could find a convenient time slot. However, even arranging the telephone call was tricky, as the number of anyone he might want to ring had to be cleared by the authorities in advance. When he'd first arrived, he'd been asked to recall those numbers from the top of his head. He didn't have his phone and couldn't remember the mobile numbers of anyone he knew. Eventually he'd remembered their home landline number. After a period of time, that number had been cleared for him to call. Maybe that took a few days, maybe a few weeks. It took time. Everything took time in prison. There were processes for the processes.

He could only make calls to prospective visitors, to relay the VO number, during the brief association periods. He had to wait for a phone to become free, which didn't always happen. Only then could he call his wife's home number. Not his home number. Not any more.

He did call it, over and over again.

He only ever spoke to the answering machine.

He left details of the VO numbers. He left instructions about how the system worked. He wondered whether Daisy was out or whether she was standing by, listening to his pleas, his apologies.

He'd sent his sister a long letter explaining this procedure. She'd replied a month later giving him some news about her children, never again did she mention visiting him.

He told himself that maybe it was a good thing no one came. This world he inhabited was hard and fragile. If someone from his old world crashed into it, he was sure he would shatter. But there were times when he'd wondered what the point of it was. When he'd wondered about what he'd done. Wouldn't it be better just to end it all? Do everyone a favour? They made it hard for a prisoner to do so. Every suicide led to an inquiry and that was never good for the authorities, or ultimately government statistics. Still, some people managed it. They found a way. Simon had started to wonder what those ways might be. Why they didn't just leave the occasional dressing gown cord lying around? No one wanted men like him. It would ease the problem of overcrowding somewhat if they could all just be honest about how fucking hopeless it was.

His sister continued to write. Once a month, then once every six weeks or so. He knew her handwriting, she used tissue-thin airmail envelopes that he thought had gone out of production in the 1980s. Then, when he'd been inside almost a year, he received a very different sort of envelope. It was not from his sister. The envelope was a heavy cream card. Expensive. He'd looked at it for a long while. Turning it over in his hand, considering the possibilities. He'd set it aside for thirty minutes, then — when he could wait no longer — he opened it. Carefully. Slowly. He didn't do anything in a hurry. By that time, he'd learnt the value in eking out any sort of activity. It was from Connie Baker. Daisy's friend. His friend too, yes, but Daisy's friend really. Her letter was full of news of her kids, her work, her latest holiday. She asked him how he was, as though she cared. He was amazed. They lived in a world where most people couldn't be bothered to type out full words in texts and instead resorted to a jumble of acronyms and numbers, yet Connie had sent him a carefully crafted, handwritten letter. It was generous, authentic.

She said she wanted to visit him. She gave him her mobile number, her home and studio numbers, and asked him to have them cleared. Said she'd like to visit soon. He hadn't expected that. And she came. Week after week. Her coming to see him had most probably saved his life. That was not a dramatic exaggeration, it was the truth. On the outside someone might give you change for a tenner, so you can feed the parking meter and you might say, 'Oh, you saved my life', but you are talking bullshit. You have no idea. Simon meant it, he really did. Connie had saved his life.

He remembered her first time. She was late. He had felt panicked. Started to doubt that she would show, when in fact he ought to have recalled that she was always late everywhere. He'd tried to stay calm and distracted by looking around the room, watching the other women visiting other inmates. Some made such an effort. They dressed up, they chattered constantly, tried to appear bright and perky, clearly believing that it was their duty to entertain their wayward husbands. Others sat in silence. Worn down by shame, or betrayal, or fury. Connie came swanning into the visitors' room, full of her usual panache and passion. It had taken her a fraction of a second to recognise him. He was thin and sallow. He must have appeared what he was: closed down. Done. His suspicions had been confirmed when he saw pity and shock swill in her eyes. Emotions she swiftly banished. She beamed widely, over-compensating, and dashed towards him, 'Simon!' Her arms held wide, she'd pulled him into one of her signature enormous hugs. Rocking from side to side in a jolly little dance. The guard had shaken his head at her, firmly asked her to separate. Connie had looked surprised but had followed instructions. Her manoeuvre did look suspicious at worst, incongruous at best. They'd probably thought she was passing drugs. She seemed high.

He had never been sure what had motivated her to visit him. Basic human kindness? Perhaps, but in that case, were all his friends lacking that quality? Did Connie have a bigger capacity to forgive? Was she just a little bit inquisitive, a ghoul? Born in a different era, Connie would most likely have been one of the women knitting by the guillotines during the French revolution, she had the stomach for it. She always put curiosity before sentimentality. She collected experiences. Maybe that's what he was, one of her experiences. Coming here was not dissimilar to signing up for a life drawing class or riding a horse along a beach.

He'd blurted out the question. He phrased it tactlessly. 'Was visiting a prison on your bucket list, Connie?'

'What a macabre bucket list you must imagine I have,' she'd replied, prettily side-stepping the matter.

'Why are you here?' he'd insisted.

'To see you,' she'd replied simply. He must have looked unconvinced because she sighed heavily. 'I'm trying to do a good thing here, Simon. And it's not easy. No one wanted me to come. Everyone is angry about it. Don't you want to see me?'

'Yes, yes I do,' he'd confessed. It was just easier to be honest.

Connie never avoided the fact that he was inside, a prisoner, a criminal. Sometimes he thought she almost relished it. She informed him that she'd travelled by train and then taken a cab from the station. 'It was ghastly, Simon,' she cried, almost excitedly. 'As soon as I said where I wanted to go, the cabbie's attitude was extremely difficult to manage. He kept glancing at me in the mirror. 'Visiting someone are you, love?' he asked, eventually. What a dumb question! The prison is hardly a tourist attraction, it's unlikely that I am just popping by for a selfie at the gate.'

Connie had spoken quickly, loudly and incessantly; she was uncomfortable but desperately trying not to show as much. Simon had looked about him, conscious that she was drawing a lot of eyes. He should have warned her to dress down. She had arrived wearing her usual uniform: skintight black jeans, a clingy black cashmere jumper, her hair swept back into a casual up do. It wasn't that she'd made a particular effort but, even so, she was beautiful.

She was attracting attention. Not the flattering sort, the menacing sort. He wanted to silence her but didn't know how to. She continued, 'The cabbie wanted to know if I was visiting my husband. He was very leery. I said I was.'

'Why did you say that?' Simon queried.

'Oh, I don't know. I think that's what he wanted to hear,' Connie had replied with a grin, waving her hand dismissively. 'Then he wanted to know if he was likely to have heard of you — well — not you, really, my husband. Whether you'd made the papers. It was obvious he was dying to ask. A bank robber? A kidnapper? A serial killer? I just turned and looked out of the window, pretended to be all mysterious. Left him hanging.'

She'd laughed at this. As though his being inside was remotely funny. As if being inside with serial killers could be amusing. He had been offended but simultaneously aware that he no longer had the luxury of showing any offence. Before, on the outside, he'd perhaps have picked a fight, forced a row. Now he knew it was best to keep his own counsel.

'So, how are things? What's your bedroom like?' It was as though she was asking about his holiday accommodation.

'Bedroom?'

'Sorry, what is your cell like?'

'It's about six foot wide by ten foot long.'

'Do you have a window?'

He'd smirked. 'Yes, it's a room with a view, of sorts. A small window covered by a wire mesh, offers the dull view of a wall outside. You can't open it.'

'No, I hadn't expected you could.'

'It was once possible to open them, just a couple of inches, apparently, but the cons kept tipping their waste outside onto the walls and so that privilege was taken away.'

'Waste?'

'Excrement.'

'Oh, I see.' He doubted she did. Simon didn't understand the mentality of someone that would tip piss and crap into a yard where they later had to exercise, especially since doing so led to further deprivation. They were not even allowed the simple relief of fresh air drifting into the cell. He didn't understand these people and he was one of them, of course Connie couldn't 'see'. But he'd admired the way she hadn't blanched. She'd discussed his life with him, as she might chat to an estate agent about the letting market. Gathering facts. 'Do you share?'

He'd nodded. 'Yes, with a guy called Leon.'

'What's he like?'

'Like?'

'Is he . . . ' She'd stumbled then. Her poise faltering. She could hardly ask if he was nice, friendly, good at putting out the bins, as you might ask someone of a neighbour when moving into a new area.

'He's fine,' sighed Simon. 'We get on fine. He likes the top bunk which suits me. By taking occupancy of the bottom bunk, you sort of get control over the floor space.'

'Oh.' She'd then glanced around the room, maybe trying to guess what the cellmate looked like. A shrewd woman, she no doubt guessed that whether he was black, white or brown, tattooed, bald or beaded, he looked hard and sad and angry. They all did. 'What is he in for?'

Simon had shaken his head. 'No one ever asks, and he hasn't volunteered any information. I hope he doesn't.' They'd fallen silent. Simon hadn't wanted the conversation to peter out. He needed Connie to come back. He didn't want to bore her. He'd searched around in his head for something to say. 'The TV is in one corner and there's a metal toilet in the other.'

She blinked slowly. Inwardly gasped. Men peed together all the time, but she was probably wondering about bowel movements. Was she silently speculating whether he held on until he could get access to a more private cubicle? Were they given access to such a thing and even if Simon exercised such modesty, did Leon? If she felt a bit squeamish she managed to bury it.

'So, there's a television?' she said, brightly.

'A tiny one.'

'Oh, well that's nice.'

'Yeah.' He hadn't bothered to tell her about his first cellmate. The one who liked the TV on practically all the time. Droning on and on. He'd watched anything. All the soaps and shows about selling junk found in some granny's attic. It had been a fresh sort of hell. He certainly didn't tell her about Rick Dale.

'So, besides Leon, have you made any friends?' Simon had laughed to himself. It was a laugh that was entirely devoid of humour. He'd have sworn Connie was using the script she'd used on each of her girls when they'd started school.

'You know all that stuff you see on TV, Connie? The stuff about bitches being scared in the shower, the nasty bastards running the show, the screws turning a blind eye?' Connie had nodded. 'They are all true,' he'd confirmed, savagely.

She'd said nothing for a while. Just sat there. Then she'd reached for his hand. 'I'm sorry.'

'Me too,' he'd murmured.

The guard coughed and yelled, 'No touching.'

31

Daisy

Often, on our walk home from school, Millie and I will stop at a coffee shop for a drink or an ice lolly. It's one of my favourite times of the day. That's when she's most likely to tell me about her trials and triumphs at school. Once we are back in the house she switches on the TV and the chances of a cosy mother-daughter chat are reduced. This afternoon I practically frogmarch her home. I feel sick, terrified. When she says she's hot and would like to stop, I tell her there are Cornettos in the freezer. 'But I don't want a Cornetto. I want a milkshake. I've been looking forward to it all day.'

'We can't always be paying cafe prices,' I mutter, by way of an excuse.

'I'll buy my own drink, I have my birthday money,' she replies indignantly. Then with more charm, she adds, 'I'll buy you a coffee too, Mum.' I want to relent, she's hard to resist, and whilst I'd never let her use her birthday money to buy me a drink, it's a very sweet thought. I look back over my shoulder. 'Who are you looking for? You keep looking behind you,' she asks.

Would he follow us home? No, that's madness.

And yet turning up at our school isn't exactly sane. 'No. one.' I reply. 'Come on, I just want to get home. I have a lot of work to do tonight.'

Our new home is a two-bedroomed end of terrace house, just ten minutes away from our old one but also lightyears away. In London, wide, affluent streets are cheek and jowl with tight, poorer ones. Rose and Connie feel sorry that I had to downsize but I'm ok with it. Yes, it's small but our old home with its four bedrooms and long, thin garden just offered Simon more hiding holes for empty bottles and empty promises. It was full of the echoes of arguments and ghosts of secrets and disappointments. Our new home isn't full of anything yet. We've been here almost two years, but I haven't got around to unpacking all our boxes. The ones full of Simon's things are untouched, but most of our things that have a sentimental value are gathering dust: books, photo albums and old toys. I figure that if a thing hasn't been missed by now, we don't really need it. I do plan to hang more pictures on the walls, throw more cushions about, and I will, it's just I'm not sure when. When will I have the energy to turn this house into a home? Before we bought this place, it had been a rental property for many years. As a result, the walls are a non-offensive magnolia colour, the carpets are a neutral beige. It's been well-scrubbed by people who were keen to get their deposits returned. When I bought it, Luke talked enthusiastically about it being a canvas upon which I could stamp my personality. Other than Millie's bedroom, which is a riot of primary colours and chaos, the rooms are still practical, functional, bland. Maybe that's my personality.

The minute we get home, I draw the curtains on the outside world. 'That's better,' I say out loud, with some relief.

'What are you doing, Mummy?'

'You can't see the TV, the sunlight is reflecting on the screen,' I explain.

Millie is amazed. Normally I grumble about the TV being on at teatime and encourage her out into our tiny back garden while I prepare our meal. I'm constantly extolling the virtues of fresh air. It saddens me that not only has Millie been forced to give up ballet but that she hasn't taken up anything else in its place. She could try drama, art or archery. She won't. Now, her only after-school activity is Brownies. It's Brownies tonight. The thought fills me with panic. Usually, I like Tuesdays. The couple of hours to myself are quite useful and, as it is Millie's only extra-curricular activity, I'm very enthusiastic about it with the hope that my gusto will ignite some passion in her. This evening, I'd rather we didn't have to go out. In fact, after what Daryll said, today I'd like us to barricade the doors and never venture outside of these four walls again.

I hand Millie a Cornetto without her having to ask for one, even though eating it at this time is likely to put her off her tea. I don't ask her to wash her hands. Millie takes the treat, even though earlier she'd said she was hankering after a milkshake. She eyes me suspiciously. Living together, alone, we know each other well and she must be aware that this level of indulgence is out of the ordinary. 'Like I said, I have a lot of work to do this evening,' I offer, by way of explanation. It isn't unheard of for me to buy some uninterrupted time in this way. I smile, I hope I'm convincing. I don't feel like smiling. I feel like screaming.

My palms are clammy. I rub them on my skirt. Sweat patches balloon under my arms on my shirt too but I don't want to go upstairs to change. I don't want to leave her alone down here. As I chop tomatoes for the salad, I see the knife rattle in my shaking hand. Daryll's words haunt me. It's impossible. Unbelievable. What a thing for him to say. How outrageous. How dangerous. I never wanted this conversation to happen. He is the reason I avoided Connie's parties for many years. There were one or two occasions, before the accident, when I did bump into him at social gatherings, but he always had a date with him, which was useful. If he had another woman hanging on his arm, hanging on his every word, he had no need for me. No interest in me.

Whilst I'm preparing tea, my eyes are constantly pulled towards Millie who is sat scrunched up in a small ball in the corner of the sofa. She is entirely absorbed in the drama on the screen, she has no idea about the drama unfurling in her life. Another one. My chest is booming with anxiety. What will this do to her? The hair around her face has worked free from her ponytail and the way the light catches it makes it appear as though she's wearing a halo. She's so fair. Not red like me. Or dark like

Simon. Daryll looks like a Viking: tall, broad, blonde, powerful. Millie's school summer dress is a green and white check, it isn't a particularly flattering colour, but she manages to look good in it. Her skin is golden. For someone so blonde, she tans remarkably easy. The summer just gifts me with a rash of freckles, Simon burns in the sun if he's not wearing factor thirty or above. I shake my head. What am I thinking? No. It's impossible.

But it isn't. Not really.

'Mummy, you're bleeding. You've cut yourself.'

'What?'

I don't understand what Millie is saying but her eyes are wide with terror. 'You're bleeding!' she cries.

I look down at my hand. I've sliced my left index finger, badly. The top is practically hanging off. I feel a wave of nausea rush through my body. Now I'm aware of the injury I feel a hit of intense pain that somehow I was shutting out before. I bite back the swear words that I want to launch and reach for a tea towel. 'Millie, quickly get me a plaster from the tin. A big one.' I hold my hand up in the air, away from my clothes and my sight and stumble back into a kitchen chair. The room is swimming. I'm aware of Millie's panic and the smell of blood. My own blood. Millie hands me an Elastoplast. Using my mouth and one hand I manage to plaster up my wound.

'Should you get stitches?' she asks with concern.

'I'll be fine.' I tell her, even though the blood is

already oozing through the plaster. A brown stain. Another one. I wrap the kitchen towel around my throbbing finger. 'It will stop bleeding in a minute or two,' I state, optimistically. My reassurances are cut short when the landline rings. Both Millie and I jump a little, as it's an unfamiliar sound; if anyone wants to get hold of me they call my mobile. 'No doubt that's your granny,' I predict.

'Hello Mum, Look, it's not a good time,' I say as I pick up. My poor mother is sometimes at the wrong end of this easy rudeness.

'Oh, I'm sorry to hear that.' I freeze. I recognise his voice instantly.

I cover the handset and hiss-whisper, 'Millie go and put on your Brownie uniform.'

'But I haven't had tea yet,' she groans.

'Take a banana.'

'Is that Granny? Can I say hello?'

'Just go.' I flap her away with the tea towel that was wrapped around my finger. She reluctantly follows my instructions, slouching out of the room, muttering something about starving to death and her right to call Childline and report me. I'm aware that if I hadn't cut myself, and we were now sitting down to the chicken and salad I had been preparing, she would be picking at her food, insisting she wasn't especially hungry. She's not particularly contrary or difficult, she's just a child. As soon as she's out of the room, I demand, 'How did you get this number, Daryll?'

'Off the internet. You're not ex-directory so it's very easy. I knew you'd be kicking yourself for not giving it to me,' he says confidently. My knuckles are white, I'm grasping the handset so hard. Somehow, him having my home number is even worse than him having my mobile. My home feels invaded. I walk to the back door and check it's locked.

'What do you want?' I ask sharply.

'Wow, Curly, I don't remember you being this biting. What's up?'

'I've just cut my finger,' I tell him although this isn't even a small percentage of the problem. 'It's bleeding quite badly. Like I said, this is not a good time.' There never will be one.

'Oh, I'm so sorry, Curly.'

'And please will you stop calling me that ridiculous nickname.'

'Pet name,' he says.

'Please.' I sound desperate. I *am* desperate. I don't like begging him.

'OK, then. If you don't like it anymore.'

'I've never liked it.'

'That's just not true, *Daisy*.' He lays heavy emphasis on my name. 'Better?'

Am I supposed to be grateful? Weirdly, I sort of am. The fact that he's done this one small thing for me, stopped using that crazy nickname, feels a like a little victory. A step in the right direction. Even though I had to beg for it. I take a deep breath, I don't want him to know he's rattled me.

'And besides cutting myself, I'm very — ' I pause and search for the right word. 'I'm very disconcerted by what you said at the school gate.'

'*You* are disconcerted.' Daryll laughs. 'And how do you think I feel? I didn't even know you were a mother until that party when Simon told me. He didn't mention how old she was though. I don't know why but I just assumed she was just a toddler. I thought it had to be relatively new news, right? The fact that you were a mother. Because we're old friends, aren't we? I'd have heard. People lose touch with one another, a couple of years slip by, we're all busy. I get that. It never crossed my mind that you could have been a mother for *six years* and failed to ever mention it to me. That starts to look like you are keeping her a secret.' He sounds irritated, infuriated. I don't know what to say to refute his assumptions because he's spot on. My throat is dry, I can't swallow, I can't breathe. I doubt I could speak even if I wanted to. 'When I came back to the UK for interviews for this job, I looked up Connie. We went for a coffee. A catch-up chat. Then Connie mentioned you were all going to Brighton to celebrate Millie's birthday. Her ninth birthday. I did the maths, Daisy. I worked it out.'

'She's not yours,' I mutter.

'Certainly she's mine. You and Simon tried for a decade. That's common knowledge and then suddenly, hey presto. I'm not a fool, Daisy. Don't make the mistake of thinking of me as one.'

My mind is working a hundred to the dozen. I'm wondering how to get away from Daryll. Far away. Hanging up the phone won't be enough. He'll call me back and if I don't answer, he'll turn up at school. We have to do something more permanent. We have to run away. Where? Where can we go? To the north of England? Manchester or Leeds, maybe? Those are big cities, he wouldn't find us there. But he would, he *would*. Because he found us here, in London, in amongst eight million inhabitants. That's Connie's fault. If I moved I wouldn't be able to tell Connie where I'd gone because she'd tell him. If I warned her not to, she'd want to know why. I could make something up. But what? The secret would get out eventually. It seems secrets always do. I'd have to cut her off. And that means Rose as well, my sister. And my parents. We'd be alone. He'd still track us down. The UK is tiny, really. He'd find us through a school database or something on the internet. He would find us. Would he have any rights? This thought is horrifying. Could he insist on a DNA test? We must leave immediately, before he can assert any rights. We need to go far away. A foreign country. Canada or Australia. It would be the only way. We need to pack a bag. We must go *now*. Could we leave everyone? Our friends and family? Is that viable? Sensible? Possible? What would that do to Millie? She's been through so much.

I can hear myself panting. I have to slow down. But I can't. I hope he can't hear my shallow breath. I don't want him to know I'm frightened. My head is spinning. I feel faint. The blood from my finger is still flowing. It's on my blouse now. I probably do need a stitch. I should go to the hospital. But there's no time.

'Hey Daisy.' His voice is full of kindness. It punctures my panic. 'I understand you don't even visit Simon.' I want to kill Connie. Why does she always think my business is everyone else's entertainment? 'The little girl hasn't got a dad. I just want to step into my natural place, I just want to get to know her. Would that be such a bad thing?'

I think I'm going to pass out. 'I have to go. I need to get Millie to Brownies.' I bite my tongue the moment the words are out. I shouldn't tell him anything about our life. He can't be part of it.

He can't be part of us.

32

Simon

Friday, 14th June 2019

'So drinking? Why do you do it?' Leon asked.

'What?'

'It's a simple enough question. Why do you drink?'

'Oh man.' Simon couldn't answer him. He lay on his back, staring up at the sagging bunk above him. It was a summer night, it wouldn't get dark for ages. Neither of them had got to the gym today, they weren't tired. They had a lot of energy and Simon had got used to Leon wanting to talk on nights when they couldn't sleep. He saw that it was civilized, normal, but it was still difficult. Leon probed. In another life, with a different set of chances, Leon might have made a good investigative journalist or a detective.

Why did he drink? It was a simple question, but on the other hand it was horrifyingly complex. Simon wanted to find an answer, that's why he kept going to the meetings. There had to be one. He could feel it buzzing around his head like a bluebottle bashing against a closed window, refusing to accept the window was closed, just banging the same spot over and over again, trying to escape. If Simon could find an answer to the question as to why he drank, maybe he could find a solution to help him stop drinking permanently. He worried about that. Inside he couldn't drink. But what would happen on the outside?

Leon was refreshingly unafraid. Simon couldn't work out why. Maybe he knew someone who was protecting him, or maybe he knew nothing and, as yet, didn't realise he needed protecting. Whatever the reason he was refreshingly unafraid. The only problem with that was he asked a lot of questions.

'Like, did you get mucked about with when you were a kid or something?' he asked. 'You know, abused?'

'No.'

'No. Thought not, you're a little posh boy.'

'Posh boys get abused too,' Simon pointed out.

'Yeah but — ' The nuance didn't compute with Leon's world order. Inside, there was a raging need to keep things clear cut. Because nothing was. 'You went to university, right?'

'Yes. Southampton.'

'By the sea. That sounds cool.'

Simon realised that Leon was imagining beaches and sandcastles. Maybe candy floss and funfairs. It hadn't been quite like that, it had been more three-legged pub crawls, subsidised bars and all-night essay crises, but it had been great. Indisputably free. Simon had discovered that most prisoners had a reading age of twelve or under, few had been to university, or even the seaside. Prison wasn't a place that was inhabited by those who had had opportunities. He was an anomaly. Maybe that was why Leon asked him so many questions.

'Did you have a dad?'

'Yes. He died just before my thirty-fourth birthday.'

'Was he like with your mother until then?' Leon sounded incredulous.

'Yes.' Simon knew what Leon wanted to know. 'They were happy; mostly. You know, on the whole.'

'Fuck. That's something, right?' Leon said this in a way that clearly indicated he thought it was everything. A fairy tale.

Simon felt an emotion that was close to protective of Leon. Leon was not much older than Rose's boys. Maybe just two or three years older. It was unbelievable. Sebastian and Henry were out on some rugby pitch somewhere or maybe in a lecture hall or a girl's bed. Leon was here, making hairnets. Sometimes Leon would be reading a newspaper and he'd come across a word he didn't understand; he'd ask Simon what it meant. Simon liked that. It made him feel useful, needed. It demonstrated an element of trust that was notably lacking anywhere else in the prison. Simon was trying to encourage Leon to sign up for some of the educational classes that were made available to prisoners.

Simon didn't want to burst Leon's bubble, so he didn't volunteer any information about the less palatable bits of his life. He didn't add that his father was an alcoholic too, and that not long after his death, his mother had started to show signs of forgetfulness that they'd initially attributed to grief but was later diagnosed as the early onset of Alzheimer's. He didn't mention how much he resented his sister for moving to Canada at around the same time, effectively washing her hands of any further responsibility and aggravating their mother's sense of loss. He didn't mention the years he and Daisy had struggled to conceive, and he certainly didn't mention the other thing. Not ever.

'So why do you drink?' persisted Leon.

'Some people just do, don't they?' Simon wanted to flip the conversation. Move it on. Or close it down. He stayed quiet.

Eventually Leon yawned and admitted, 'I guess everyone has their own shit to deal with.'

Simon tried not to think about what Leon's particular shit might be. What he'd done to land him here. The cell smelt stale. Simon had always had a keen sense of smell. It was one of the least useful senses. He had never been much interested in food, which was a shame because there were several occasions when he would have benefitted from lining his stomach. He wore glasses, his hearing was average, and he couldn't remember anyone ever saying he was a total king in the sack. So, out of smell, taste, sight, hearing and touch, it was his luck to get an A* in smell. Leon had been openly farting all evening. It was the bean curry they'd had for tea. Beside the stench of farts, there was a stew of sweat and male hormones, sour air breathed in and out, in and out. Repeatedly. Simon longed for fresh air and a breeze. Yearned for it. It would be twelve more hours until he could leave this room, and another eight after that until he could go into the exercise yard. He had to try to think of something other than smells and time dragging, otherwise he'd go mad.

Daisy.

He thought of Daisy opening the windows in their house, the mornings after the many nights before, the place stained with regret which she tried to budge with a fresh air breeze. He wished he had happier go-to thoughts but somehow the uncomfortable ones always seemed to bubble to the top of his mind. He remembered she would inch towards him, like a caterpillar. Slowly but purposefully. A bit weird and creepy. In the early years, she used to try to keep it casual, maybe she'd laugh (albeit a bit shrilly). 'Wow, last night was certainly something.' Then, as the years passed, it was the same crawl towards him but different words, 'Do you remember what happened last night, Simon?' And then eventually, no façade, 'Please, please, get your act together.'

During those awkward conversations about what had occurred the night before he would listen with disbelief. She had to be joking, making it up. Lying. She was a liar. The worst was having to admit how little he remembered, how little he knew of his own life. It was easiest to just nod. Pretend he not only remembered but also regretted, as she expected him to. Yes, he remembered telling his boss he was a boring tosser. It was in jest. He'd sort it out. Yeah, yeah, he was sorry that he was caught pissing up against his neighbour's car. He totally remembered getting up on Rose's table and singing.

Yes, *and* the striptease. No, he was never actually going to take off his underpants. Right, agreed, he shouldn't have let it get that far. It wouldn't happen again.

Another lie. His, this time.

She had tried to understand. He supposed. But she was limited. Limited by her own reasonableness. Her own ordinariness and it felt like she was letting him down by not getting it. 'Why can't you just give it up? Just stop. You know. Just say no,' she'd plead.

She might as well have asked him to stop breathing. Drinking was like sending rocket fuel through his body, he could do anything, be anything. He didn't admit, not even to himself, to the fact that in the next moment, the rocket plunged from the sky and crashed. Leaving him drained, desolate. Dead, or as good as. He hadn't connected the two. High and low. Cause and effect didn't run in the same way for him as they did for other people. Normal people. Not until the thing with Millie. Sometimes, when he closed his eyes, he saw her fly off the bonnet of the car, bounce like a ball. He understood then, cause and effect. Taking responsibility for your actions. He didn't tell anyone he had any recollection at all. His history as someone who blacked out served him well. But he did remember. Everything.

Simon breathed in deeply, tried to stay calm. It meant he took in the male mustiness of the cell.

Daisy used to be concerned about his blackouts. He'd laughed at her fears, teased her.

Patronised her, he supposed. For being so pedestrian, for not comprehending. 'Not blackouts Daisy, time travel. I'm like Doctor Who. My Tardis is a whisky bottle. I punch through the mundane rules of time and space that you mere mortals must live with.' He had lost so much time through blackouts. A night gone in the click of his fingers, but inside, time dragged. Crawled. Limped. Sometimes he thought it moved backwards. He could not tolerate living in the moment, an achingly slow moment that lasted an hour, a day, a week, and yet he had no choice.

If only. If only he could time travel.

33
Daisy

I just about manage to drag myself through the week, although I'm barely fit for purpose. For many years now, I've managed on less than six hours of sleep per night. This isn't an Iron Lady thing. I'm not trying to sound hardy and extraordinary, I don't set my alarm clock for an early start, so I can go running, or do some school work or even tackle the ironing pile; I have heard that some weird and wonderful women do this. I'm just someone who doesn't sleep very well. I tell people I don't need much sleep, which makes me sound stronger and more energetic than is the case. It's a lie. Another one. The truth is I can't find sleep. I hunt it like I'm chasing the elixir of eternal youth, but it eludes me. I've tried hot milky drinks, limiting screen time, playing soothing music, putting oxygen-producing pot plants in my room, sleeping with the window open. I've also tried tablets.

They say there's no rest for the wicked.

My relationship with sleep became strained when I was young, before Millie was conceived. I often used to lie awake at night praying, dreaming, imagining, hoping for a family. That particular non-sleeping stage was caused by a mix of anticipation and anxiety, and was characterised by something hungry and possible waiting inside me. And then I was pregnant, and then a new mum. Sleeplessness hit a whole new level. I'm not alone in finding it difficult to sleep whilst you wait to pass the milestone of the twelve-week scan, or when you are towards the end of your pregnancy and you're elephantine, uncomfortable and really terrified about pushing out a cantaloupe melon. I was just like every other mum-to-be. At least, I like to think I was. And then, when she was born, oh, the responsibility, the joy, the demands, the relentlessness of being needed. It's very normal to only snatch two or three hours of sleep in a row, before being woken by the hungry screams of a newborn. When Millie did settle into a regular sleeping pattern and managed to go through the night, I found I still woke every few hours. People with secrets rarely sleep soundly. Fact. I used to wander into her room, watch her sleeping in her cot, transfixed by her small chest rising and lowering rhythmically. I was at once reassured and horrified. She was alive. She existed. I told myself it had all been worth it. That I'd made the right decision. That I didn't have a choice. But there had been a choice. There is always a choice. I would sneak downstairs, express some breast milk, make a hot drink, read a few pages of a book. Try to pretend everything was OK. But it wasn't, not really, because nothing is ever OK in the dead of night. Fears magnify. Sleeplessness has an ever-tightening stranglehold on sense and reasoning.

There were times when I thought I might choke. Suffocate.

When Millie started to toddle around, filling the house and our hearts with her noise and joy, I allowed myself to relax, marginally. I enjoyed a few years of more regular rest. After a day playing with and chasing after an exuberant toddler, I often slept for seven hours on the trot. If I dreamed at all, my dreams were pleasant, interesting, sometimes even sexy. I awoke refreshed and invigorated, ready to start the day. We were happy. All three of us. Or at least I thought so. But then Simon started drinking again, so I guess he wasn't happy. Or at least, he wasn't happy enough. He said he was. He said that drinking was celebratory; just a way to make a Friday and Saturday night buzz, to make a Sunday glide. Then he said drink was his reward too; a beer after a hard, long day at the office. Nothing was as good as the hit of it. Like diving into a lake on a red-hot day, he said. And then, I suppose it became more like drowning in a sludge. I just didn't notice. I wasn't watching him carefully enough.

Since the accident no one can really expect me to find a regular eight hours. It's an unreasonable ask. Recently, my dreams have become increasingly vivid and disturbing. I dream about the collision with new horrifying detail. I dream details such as the light from streetlamps falling on the wet roads. The radio is blasting. Simon screams at me, 'Oh fuck you.' Vile. Millie dashes across the road. She doesn't look. She just steps out. I wake up sweating and crying.

Since Daryll's call, things have only got worse. I don't think I've managed to sleep more than ninety minutes in a row. My eyes sting, my shoulders and back ache with tension, my head feels fluffy. Spongy. Ineffective. I don't know what to do next. I'm lucky that it's summer term and the timetable is disrupted with rehearsals for the Year Six leavers' assembly, music concerts and sports day. I'm not sure I could have stuck to a rigid timetable, if I could have taught anything useful these past few days. I'm in the classroom in body only and it's all I can do to read the class register.

He has not turned up at the school gate since Tuesday, nor has he called, and yet he is all I have thought about. He swims around my head, I feel him over my shoulder, behind each door and around each corner. He is just a breath away. Every afternoon I repeat the pattern of Tuesday; I hurry Millie home, vetoing a stop at the ice cream shop, I put the chain on the door as I shut it behind us, I draw the curtains even though it's light until nine, nearly ten o'clock. Millie has noticed that I'm jittery, so I've allowed her an unprecedented amount of screen time, I find this stops her asking too many questions or being concerned that I'm not my usual self.

It's Friday evening and we're going to Connie and Luke's for supper. Connie invites us over most weeks. This is kind of her. She wants to make sure that our weekends are standout, not afterthoughts. Following everything that happened — the incident, Simon's imprisonment and Millie giving up ballet — it was far too easy for time to become something we filled or even killed, rather than explored and enjoyed. The vast majority of the western world traditionally fill Friday night with excitement, relief and anticipation. Not me. The structure and demands of weekdays are a comfort to me; at weekends I'm aware I could be visiting Simon. That I am not. The two of us feel small on Friday evenings. I don't so much anticipate the weekend, as dread it. Connie's family provides a shield.

Millie loves the Friday suppers at Connie's too. Not only does she get to spend time with Sophie but, for a couple of hours, she basks in the glow that older girls bring to a nine-year-old's existence. Fran and Flora talk to her about music, apps, clothes and TV. They don't care about whether she's eaten her lunch at school or done her homework, questions that inevitably fall from my lips if we're alone together. We've all known each other so long that we don't stand on ceremony, Millie and I are treated like part of the family which is a relief and a compliment. Everyone enjoys whatever food there is — pasta, sometimes a takeaway pizza — and then the girls go about their business. Sometimes I'm asked to help with an English assignment or French plaiting of hair, other times the older girls are moody and uncommunicative and scamper off to their rooms, occasionally they're outright rude and we sit through door-slamming and rows about how late they can stay out. I don't mind. I like it. Friday nights are carefree, noisy, chaotic. I look forward to them just as much as Millie does. This week, more than ever, I'm desperate to pop on the tube and get to Notting Hill, get there as quickly as possible. I realise it is Connie that has brought Daryll back into my life, but she did so inadvertently. Tonight, Connie and her family will put me out of his reach.

Millie and I quickly shower and change. She likes to cast off her school uniform, put on a pretty top and jeans. I also make an effort, if only to stop Connie fretting that I'm letting myself go and therefore must be depressed; a charge she lands at my feet every few months. Tonight, it's important that Connie doesn't notice the bags under my eyes or the concern in them, so I take time with my makeup, I blow-dry my hair and even dig out a pretty necklace. It's like donning a disguise. It's not the first time I've had to do this.

When we arrive at Connie's, Sophie opens the door. As usual, she is giddy with excitement. She's inherited her mother's irrepressible passion for life and so whilst jumping up and down on the spot, she squeals that Millie, 'Must come and see'. I never find out what Millie must see because Sophie is already halfway up the stairs and my daughter is hot on her heels, despite her limp. Their squeals quickly convert to whispers and giggles.

Connie emerges from the kitchen. She looks incredibly glamorous. Sometimes, on a Friday evening I find her in a T-shirt and joggers (admittedly very stylish, high-end ones); tonight, she's wearing a sleek black jumpsuit, heels and silver statement jewellery.

'Been at a client meeting?' I ask. Connie looks vague. 'You're all dressed up,' I prompt.

'Oh, this old thing.' She chuckles as she gestures towards her almost certainly brand-new outfit. 'Well, I know we can be utterly laid back and make literally no effort for one another but tonight I have asked a few guests to come around, so I thought I better, you know, scrub up.'

She shrugs her shoulders endearingly, unaware that her words are the equivalent of dousing me in icy water. Meeting new people is a trial for me. Sooner or later the conversation gets around to whether I have or haven't got a husband. I never know how to answer. Sometimes people realise who I am. Connie doesn't make a secret of the fact that she visits Simon in prison. I think she covertly revels in the fact that her visits show she is at once fearless and compassionate. Since I don't visit him, logic dictates that I have neither quality. People who work out who I am are either embarrassed or morbidly curious and as a result I'm blanked or battered with difficult questions. Neither thing is pleasant. So, I don't ever relish meeting new people, but tonight I'm particularly disinclined. I was longing for a quiet, cosy, comfortable feet-up Friday.

'Come on through, meet Jess and Kyle. You'll love them. Jess works with clay and makes the most wonderful art. Kyle made a fortune developing a very clever app and now dabbles in the stock market. You know, just for fun.' Connie always gives a quick precis of her guests. I suppose the idea is so that we can find common ground. I doubt it. Jess, who 'works with clay' just sounds a bit pretentious. I can't imagine she'll value the fact that I sometimes work with Play-Doh. I have no resources to dabble in the stock market. The closest I come is totting up my nectar points to see if I might have enough to cover entry into a theme park, so that Millie and I can have a free day out.

If I could, I'd just turn around and go home right now, but how would I persuade Millie to leave? I do what is expected of me. I plaster on a smile and push on. In the kitchen I find not only a new, cool-looking couple — presumably Jess and Kyle — but also Lucy and Peter. I glare at Connie, but she studiously avoids my eye and pretends not to notice when I grit my teeth as Lucy and then Peter — my ex brother-in-law! — lean in to kiss the air that floats about my ears. Connie busies herself with preparing smoked salmon blinis.

Jess holds out her hand for me to shake. I am grateful that she's at least sensible enough not to try to air-kiss a stranger. Her partner barely looks my way. He's deep in conversation with Peter, talking with some passion about the latest Netflix show that everyone is watching but I have yet to download. Because he doesn't pause to be introduced to me, I peg him as a sexist dick and wonder how I'll struggle through the evening. Luke is opening wine. He stops, folds me into a hug that somehow conveys a level of sympathy and support. Then he returns to his task, leaving me to Jess.

'Are you another one of Connie's university friends, like Lucy?' Jess asks. She's a petite, well-groomed woman, with glossy hair. She's likely to be in her mid-to-late forties but could pass for early thirties. Connie's media friends all age well. She stares at me as if she's waiting for me to perform a trick or burst into song. I'm clearly the object of some interest and it makes me wonder what perky little edit Connie introduced me with.

'Yes,' I reply but I don't elaborate. There's a certain kudos to having known Connie for ever, I'm aware of that. She's the sort of person people want to claim but I can't be bothered to exploit it right now. I'm too irritated with her for springing a dinner party on me. Connie no doubt senses my awkwardness and feels compelled to ease it. She leaves the blinis and flings an arm around my shoulders.

'Daisy was the first friend I made,' she declares, beaming. I notice her arm is soft and smooth. I can vaguely smell her body lotion. It's Mademoiselle by Coco Chanel. I lean my head back a fraction and inhale, we're comfortable with one another.

It's bizarre to think that I met Connie at university, when we were younger than Henry and Sebastian are now. That seems unbelievable because my twin nephews, whilst over six foot tall, still seem like fledglings to me and yet when I started university I thought of myself as so adult. Grown up. Not that I believed I knew everything, far from it, but I did believe that I had to stand on my own two feet, that I was on my own. Out there. For better or worse. It's something I've always believed, and I've been proven right. Seb and Henry still expect Rose to do their laundry at the end of each term, they expect Craig to pick them up from parties and for Peter to pay their bills.

'Did you take the same course?' demands Jess. I know how this works. She's working towards asking me what I do for a living, but she's trying to be tactful about it. She wants to know if I'm a useful person to know. I'm not especially, unless she has kids doing SATs. If so, then she'll ask for my twitter handle. Connie's arty friends are ruthless.

'We did,' gushes Connie. 'Daisy helped me find my way. She's been one of my best friends for ever.'

'And what do you do?' Jess demands imperiously.

'I'm a teacher.'

'Oh, how very noble. Marvellous profession.' I'm unconvinced that she believes this because at that moment the doorbell rings and she offers to answer it, with the sort of eagerness that indicates she wants to shake me off.

Connie however beats her to it. I busy myself by accepting a glass of wine from Luke and letting Jess turn to chat to Lucy.

I can't believe my eyes. I feel like I've been cattle-prodded. He's standing in their kitchen, all smiles and charm and bonhomie. He hands Luke a bottle of champagne — not prosecco — real champagne, Tattinger no less. He hands Connie an enormous bouquet of peonies. The heavy scent of them makes me feel dizzy, sickly. Connie beams at him, comments that they are beautiful, asks him what he wants to drink and then she launches into the introductions. 'This is Jess and Kyle.' I notice that Kyle breaks off his conversation to shake hands this time. Of course he does. Daryll Lainbridge is the sort of man who commands a room. People want to shake his hand, to be noticed by him, to be his friend. 'And you know everyone else,' says Connie with a beam.

'Absolutely. Old friends. Lucy.' He leans towards her but doesn't actually kiss her. Lucy only allows air kisses. Daryll may be charming and smooth but Lucy is celestial and there is, and always will be, a pecking order. Daryll stretches out his hand towards Peter. They grasp one another firmly. Almost a grip. Quite certainly a competition. They look one another in the eye and pump away. I'm frozen to the spot. I glance at Connie and she's beaming at me. She flings a small, flirty wink my way and grins. I'm dazed. Slow. Daryll is leaning into me now. He kisses first my left cheek, then my right. I don't move. I feel the kisses land, firm. Almost territorial. One of his hands is on my shoulder, the other on my elbow. Practically an embrace. I feel everyone watch us. As he pulls away his hand that was on my shoulder, it grazes the side of my breast. I'm sure it does.

'How's your finger?' Daryll asks.

'My finger?' I look at my hands. I'm still wearing a plaster. It was a nasty cut, I almost certainly should have gone to hospital. I remember that I told him about the cut. 'Fine,' I reply stiffly.

He reaches down and takes hold of my hand.

He draws it to his lips and then gently kisses the plaster. 'There, all better.' He squeezes my hand, which hurts, because of the cut and because of the tightness of his grip. I pull my hand back from him. Alarmed. It is starting again. I look around the room, startled. Has anyone else noticed? They haven't. Or if they have they are politely pretending not to, giving us some space. I don't want space. I'll fall down the void, but no one understands that. People are talking about what to drink, deciding whether to accept a blini, telling one another about the troubles they had finding a parking spot.

And I'm stood alone. Breathless. Blistered. Terrified.

34

Daisy

'Shall we sit down?' Connie nods towards the dining table that is beautifully laid with glassware, napkins, candles and an extravagant vase of white flowers. She's certainly made an effort. 'Everything's ready.' She beams widely.

I follow the others as we trail towards the table, exclamations of delight about the delicious smells coming from the oven and the brilliance of Connie's table-laying make the process tediously slow. I have been in her kitchen, with Daryll, for forty-five minutes now. Every minute has felt like ten. Thankfully, Daryll has mostly chatted to the men and Lucy, although sporadically he's tried to draw me into their conversation. 'Isn't that right, Daisy?' he asked at one point. I had no idea what they were talking about but found myself nodding like a puppet. He smiled, pleased with me, and I wondered what I'd just agreed to or with. I can't concentrate on what's being said because all the conversations, the tasteful background jazz music, and the noise from the street that's drifting in through the open windows, are blurring into one distorted cacophony. All I can hear is the thud of Millie and Sophie's footsteps coming through the ceiling, as they run around upstairs. The sound of their occasional squeals and giggles punctures my consciousness. I want them to be quiet. I want Millie to hide. My little girl is just above us. So close. Daryll also seems to be hyper-aware of that fact. At one point, after a particularly loud burst of girlish laughter, his eyes flick to the ceiling. 'The little girls certainly seem to be having fun,' he comments with a big, friendly grin.

'Oh yes. They adore each other. There's always lots of laughter, until there's tears, that is!' says Connie. I feel as though Daryll is a ticking bomb, a bomb that's right underneath my daughter. What is he going to say next? Is he going to announce to the room that he's Millie's father? That seems like insanity and yet I fear that's exactly what he's planning.

'Don't stand on ceremony, there isn't a seating plan. Sit where you like,' instructs Connie.

I drop into the seat closest to me, reasoning that at least if I'm sitting down, I can't fall down. Daryll immediately pushes past Jess and sits next to me. I knew he would. I can hardly move to another chair, it would draw too much attention and anyway, he would probably follow me. He glances about and seems to notice that the table is only set for eight. 'Oh, aren't the girls going to join us?' he asks, disappointed.

'Fran and Flora are out at friends, and Sophie and Millie were promised pizza in their bedroom as a treat. Luke has already taken it up,' explains Connie. 'You'll thank me later, if they join the table their ears flap. Then they tend to repeat everything that we've said, out of context, and at the most awkward moment,' she laughs. 'There's no such thing as a secret around a nine-year-old.'

'Like what sort of secret might you be trying to keep?' Daryll asks with a grin.

Connie pauses, considers his question. It is an off question, she *must* see that. I can barely breathe. 'Well, nothing really,' she smiles. 'Just the odd indiscrete comment about a teacher or another friend, you know.'

'Ah, they repeat your gossip, I see.' He laughs but it's awkward because his comment seems like a judgement. Connie shrugs and starts to hand around the bowls of salad and rice.

'It's quite a hot chili, be warned,' comments Luke, trying to kickstart the conversation in another direction. He's sat the other side of me and I'm grateful. His proximity is a help.

'Shame that they're not joining us, I'd really liked to have the opportunity of getting to know Millie, and Sophie too,' adds Daryll, obviously Sophie is an afterthought. I pick at my bread but can't bring myself to put it in my mouth.

'How was work this week, Daisy?' asks Luke. 'Wasn't there a music concert or something?' I nod. 'Did it go well?' I nod again. Then I clear my throat and prepare myself to start talking about how Mrs Dubrad dropped the sheet music and didn't seem to notice that she'd gathered the pages up in the wrong order, she just carried on playing regardless. It would be an amusing enough anecdote. I could throw it out there. I could pretend everything is normal, march on with my secret, I've done it before. But —

'Does Millie play an instrument?' asks Daryll.

I shake my head. Silenced.

'Sophie plays the violin,' Connie chips in. Then in a stage whisper, she adds, 'Horribly! Do *not* ask for a demonstration, whatever you do.' Everybody laughs as they are supposed to. Connie can poke gentle fun at Sophie's skill set because she's practically perfect in every way. I never laugh at Millie. She has a scar running from her waist to her knee, she walks with a severe limp and her hips ache if she stands for too long. These things mean she's not as able to be ribbed. Still, she's practically perfect in every way. To me.

I try to eat. The food really does look wonderful and it's not much of a compliment to Luke, the chef, that I just push it around my plate. But I think if I swallow I might throw up, I try to join in with the conversations but find my brain is lagging behind. It's all I can do to laugh when everyone else does, fake it. Like I did before. Act as though nothing is wrong, as though I've nothing to hide. I try to walk the fine line between polite enough and not at all encouraging when Daryll asks me question after question about my life and about Millie. With each detail I give him I feel I am sinking in quicksand. Yes, she's pretty good at sciences. No, we don't have a pet. Yes, she does seem to be quite good at French, but she's very young, it's too early to call her a linguist. They are just learning colours, numbers and the seasons. No, I hadn't realised he was a fluent French speaker.

I can't refuse to answer him because Connie is sat opposite Daryll and she's clearly thrilled by the attention he's showing me. She keeps throwing me meaningful looks, flashing eyes, her demeanour is entirely nudge, nudge, wink, wink. Slowly, because I'm not firing on all cylinders, I start to understand what is happening here. Connie is trying to pair me up with Daryll. For months now she's been saying its time for me to think about my relationship with Simon, reminding me that I haven't seen him for nearly three years. She often suggests I should go and visit him, discuss our future. I've told her I'm not ready to make a decision.

I'm not interested in dating and I thought my friends had gathered as much. I see now that Connie has decided to take the matter into her own hands. To speed things along. When I try to talk to Luke, Connie pulls the conversation in a way that means I have to speak to Daryll again. She asks Luke to top up glasses, to hunt out the sour cream so he has to leave the table. Leave me to Daryll.

Then Daryll slips off his shoe and places his socked foot on top of my foot. I'm only wearing sandals, so no socks or tights. I can feel the warmth of him pulse through me. My stomach lurches. I'm pinned.

At nine fifteen, Millie and Sophie wander into the kitchen. They're looking for pudding.

'So, this is Millie!' Daryll jumps to his feet and moves towards her quickly. I want to spring to my feet and fling myself between them, but I don't. How would I explain that? For one dreadful moment I think he is about to pick her up or hug her, such is his enthusiasm. I'm relieved when he settles for putting out his hand for her to shake. Bewildered, she does so but she looks at me quizzically. I think everyone must notice he doesn't acknowledge Sophie at all. Millie is used to getting more than her fair share of attention; some of it wanted, some of it not. For many months after the accident she received gifts of toys and chocolates from people who had heard she'd been hurt. Sometimes the gifts were from quite distant acquaintances. Everyone felt sad and sorry and wanted to do something to cheer her up. Then, after the trial and Simon's imprisonment, she received invites out of the blue from all and sundry. It quickly became apparent that these were inquisitions dressed up as playdates. People wanted to quiz her: was she planning on visiting her father in prison? Would she make a full recovery? Did she still want to dance? Basically, they wanted to know whether she was scarred: physically or emotionally. Until all of this, I hadn't been aware what a huge draw other people's misery was to some. Millie withdrew for a while, understandably she objected to being made to feel like a circus act. She became timid and preferred to hang out with family friends. Her skin has thickened over time and she's learnt to accept, or rather ignore, curious glances and impertinent questions. However, that was all a long time ago. I see by the way she catches my eye that she is wary of Daryll, his enthusiastic greeting seems a little off to her. He's staring at her with an inappropriate intensity. I hold my breath, utterly terrified he's about to claim her right now, right here. In front of everyone.

'Wow, you are a beauty,' he states. His eyes are sparkling, possibly wet with emotion, he looks every inch the proud father. Millie blushes, she doesn't answer him but skips over to Luke.

'What's for pudding?' she asks.

Daryll turns to me and beams. 'Really, she's a beauty.'

'Like her mother.' This comment comes from Lucy. I snap my eyes towards her. She's staring at me with a steady power and I wonder if she's been watching me all evening. Her comment is quite out of character, she doesn't often fling compliments about.

I check my watch. 'Oh, look at the time. Come on Millie we have to go. We have an early start tomorrow.'

'We do?' Millie looks confused. 'Why?' she asks.

I'm being slow. I should have known she'd ask why. I quickly try to think of an excuse and eventually say, 'It's the school summer fair. I'm helping out.'

'But your summer fair was three weeks ago,' says Connie.

I curse her surprising attention to detail, who knew she listened so closely to me? I rack my brains and, luckily, I remember an invite my sister proffered. 'Not my summer fair. We're heading over to Craig's school.' I turn to Jess and Kyle. 'My brother-in-law is a headmaster at a school that's just around the corner. The one Connie's girls went to. Sophie still goes there actually.'

'You are coming to our school fair?' asks Connie, no doubt surprised I've never mentioned as much to her.

'Yes. It's a family three-line-whip that we show up and support. Rose says it's all hands on deck.' I think that by mentioning Rose I might make Peter and Lucy uncomfortable, and that might hasten my exit. However, I realise I've walked myself into a trap.

'Why don't you stay over?' suggests Luke. 'It seems crazy to trail all the way home only to have to return early tomorrow. Have another drink.'

'Oh no, I couldn't. I don't have anything with me. Nothing to wear,' I'm quite a different body shape to Connie so there is no danger of her offering to lend me clothes. However, just to make sure, I add, 'I said I'd loan them our school's hook-a-duck kit. I need to pick that up.' This isn't true but that's the problem with lying, one leads to another. 'In fact that's why I have to go now. I need to check that is all clean and ready to go. Come on, Millie, get your jacket.'

'Millie could stay here though,' points out Connie. Ever the generous hostess.

'Oh yes, yes!' yells Millie.

'You can pick her up tomorrow on your way to the fair,' adds Sophie happily.

'We could all go to the fair,' chips in Luke. 'Do you fancy that, Sophie?'

If the truth be known, Sophie is a bit too sophisticated for school fairs, but she does adore my daughter, 'OK, if Millie can stay.'

'I'm so staying,' declares Millie, firmly. What can I do now? I look from my daughter to the door. I just want to get us both away from here. Away from Daryll.

'I wouldn't mind an early night, actually,' says Daryll. 'It's been a busy week in the new office. How about we share an Uber back to North London, Daisy?'

I'm snookered. I've walked right into it. I make a quick calculation. I more or less have to leave the dinner party now I've made such a big thing about the darn hook-a-duck, and I won't be able to extract Millie, since there's the offer for her to stay over. I certainly don't want to leave her here with Daryll. I'm not suggesting he'd kidnap her or anything wild. But. Well. I can't absolutely rule it out. I don't know what he's thinking. I don't know what he's capable of. I realise that my best course of action is to accept the lift, get Daryll away from Millie. She's safer here with Luke. And Connie too, of course. It's just I know Luke is very calm and capable. He'd never let any harm come to Millie. I don't want to be alone with Daryll but it's obvious I'm going to have to face this situation. We need to talk.

'OK,' I nod.

Daryll checks his phone. 'There's an Uber just three minutes away. Come on.'

I notice that Connie looks pretty chuffed. I'm sure she thinks her little matchmaking stunt has turned out beautifully. I grab Millie and, much to her embarrassment, pull her into a tight hug and cover her head with kisses.

'Alright, Mum. It's a sleepover, not a trek to Outer Mongolia,' she says impatiently. I recognise her phrase as one my mother uses, and it just makes me want to hold my daughter closer.

‘Go on now, go upstairs,’ I instruct.

She and Sophie grab packets of sweets and dash off. I’ve got her away from Daryll, at least. I’d thought he too might swoop in to kiss her goodbye. I can’t stand the idea of him touching her. Connie and Luke hug me. Jess and Kyle throw casual disinterested goodbyes my way, it’s clear they are indifferent about whether I stay or go and are keen to get on with eating dessert and drinking more wine. Peter waves casually, but doesn’t get up. Lucy, always well mannered, stands up and kisses me goodbye. Air kiss left, right, then left again. She murmurs, ‘Goodbye and take care.’ The usual platitude. Then adds, ‘So we’ll see you here at 9 a.m. sharp. If you are not here we’ll send a search party.’ Everyone laughs.

‘You’re coming to the school fair?’ I ask, surprised.

‘Well, it is Auriol’s old school. I ought to support, and besides, someone has to keep an eye on you.’ Do I imagine it? Did her eyes flick to Daryll? What is she thinking? All these innuendos and hints are mortifying.

Then all too suddenly, I’m outside on the pavement, alone with Daryll.

35

Simon

Saturday, 15th June 2019

Connie had been wide-eyed when she'd first visited. A little shocked, a little high on the strangeness of it all. He'd watched her disorientation and wondered whether she would come back. Would one visit be enough for her? Or too much? He had been impressed that she'd returned, again and again, long after the novelty must have worn off. He had been drunk most of the time when he lived at home, steeped in the stuff, but he remembered enough to know that Saturdays — for any family — were hectic and precious. Connie was a mother of three. The visits to prison cost her.

Now, after two years of visiting, there was no sign of bewilderment or fear or thrill-seeking. When Connie visited, she behaved as though she was in a boardroom, school hall or a pub, just a place, nowhere in particular. It was remarkable what a person could get used to. The visitors' room was a straightforward enough environment. There was a series of small tables that had barriers below the table top, to stop people trying to pass things to one another. One or two plastic chairs were set on the visitors' side of the table, depending on how many people were expected. Always just one, in Simon's case. There was a hatch with a tuck shop that sold tea and snacks to the visitors. A highlight for the prisoners.

Today, Connie sat down and, as usual, immediately started talking about her week. She'd had her hair highlighted but she was unsure about the colour. It disguised the grey that was peeking through, but she thought it was a little too blonde, maybe not quite dignified at her age. What did Simon think? Simon didn't have an opinion on her hair, but he mumbled that she looked lovely. She flashed a fast, appreciative smile his way and then got to the part of the visit he liked best. She gave him some news about Millie. Apparently, she'd been presented with her artist badge at Brownies last week. She was still hoping for a kitten. Talked of little else. She was at a school summer fair today. Not her own school but the one Craig taught at. The whole gang were going along.

'Sorry you're missing out,' he mumbled.

Connie shrugged. 'I did pop by for a short time, but as it happens I'm quite well stocked with jam and poor-quality jewellery made by delusional, bored mothers,' she said with a smile. 'Millie was pretty excited about it though.'

'Still, at her age? Isn't she over such things by now?' Simon asked. He didn't want her to be. He didn't want her to grow up too quickly, but he was realistic.

'Well, there will be cheap sweets and hair

braiding. Both still winners.'

He drank up the news, any snippet. Grateful for Connie's willingness to risk Daisy's wrath by passing these nuggets on. She'd once told him it made her feel like a spy, a traitor. But she'd continued to give him the news regardless. She wasn't choosing his side, she was just doing what she wanted to do, what she thought was right. Connie was more complex, subtle and deep than people imagined. He never considered what she might want to do for Daisy. What she might think was right.

'So, has there been any news about your on-licence release? When will you hear the decision?' Connie asked.

Simon expected to hear by the beginning of next month. If it went well, he might be out of prison within a month. But if it went badly, he had another three years to serve inside. He couldn't bear the burden of Connie's optimism.

'Not sure,' he lied.

'I'm certain it will be through soon,' she said, unperturbed. She always believed if she wanted something enough, it would be granted. That hadn't been Simon's life experience. 'And then have you thought about what's next?' Connie stared at him, but he didn't want to meet her gaze. He faked an interest in the table top.

'Next?'

'Where will you live? What will you do about employment?'

He shook his head. 'There are schemes to get crims back into work,' he reassured her. She looked doubtful, as well she might.

'You can stay with us.' He could tell the offer was impulsive, fuelled by pity and desperation but he grabbed it anyway.

'Really?'

'Yes, for a while, until you find your way.'

'Have you OK'd that with Luke?'

'No, but he'll be fine with it,' she replied dismissively.

Simon doubted it. He had once thought of Luke as his friend, his best friend, but now he knew him for what he was. His biggest enemy. Simon had had time to think about Millie's parentage. Time to reason, soberly, about who Daisy had conceived their child with. He still thought of Millie as their child, he couldn't stop himself from doing that. Even though she wasn't. But, after three years, he hadn't changed his mind. He believed Millie was Luke's, biologically. It all fitted together. He was an idiot not to have seen it until he did. Millie was tall, slim and blonde — like Luke. She looked quite a lot like Connie's three daughters. They all had a similar build. They were all equally pretty. But it wasn't just thinking about Millie's physicality that had convinced him, it was thinking about Daisy, knowing her like he did. He thought about the people they had mixed with around the time of Millie's conception. They were a tight group. Always had been. They never seemed to need anyone, other than each other. It was always Daisy, Connie, Rose and their partners. Sometimes, if Daisy couldn't wiggle out of it, it was Daisy, Connie and Lucy and their partners. Often, it was just the four of them, Daisy, Simon,

Connie and Luke. But Connie worked long hours and wasn't always around, even when there was a plan in place. She blew them out at the last minute, told them she'd catch up, to start without her. Promises she rarely made good on. And Simon? Well, often, he was drunk; passed out in the corner. Leaving Daisy and Luke, alone.

He could imagine how their affair went. A slow build. A tragic, difficult thing. They would both have been sick with guilt. It wouldn't have been easy for them, and yet they had inched closer to one another. Late at night, one glass of wine too many, one accidental brush of the hands, one lingering look. Daisy would have been motivated by what? Loneliness? Desperation? He was kidding himself, Luke was hot, a catch. Daisy had always had a soft spot for him. She probably jumped at the chance. And Luke? Well, Luke must have felt put-upon. Resentful. Those countless occasions when Connie would text, saying she was running late or not able to make the planned date after all. Had he wondered if she was up to her old tricks? Connie had form. That must have bothered her husband. There must have been trust issues. Maybe he just thought, fuck it, he was owed a go. And Daisy was there. All gentle, domestic and understanding. Not Luke's usual type but perhaps a refreshing change to Connie. It killed Simon that he'd handed his wife over on a plate.

It seemed unlikely to him that Daisy had ever gone out and struck up a conversation with a stranger in a bar, embarked on an affair that way.

She was fundamentally shy, and it took her years to trust someone, to call them friends. He just couldn't see her throwing caution and her pants to the wind. There were no opportunities to meet a lover through work for Daisy. As a teacher in a primary school, nearly all her colleagues were female. He knew the few men that had ever worked with Daisy; he'd considered them and dismissed them. One was gay, one was twenty years older than Daisy, the other was fifteen years younger. She conceived when she was in her late thirties, he just couldn't see her cradle snatching at that stage in her life. Any stage really. He had thought back to that time. For hours and hours, he'd crawled around his own head, poking and turning over the patchy memories. Had Daisy behaved strangely? Had she gone out more frequently? Did she attend an evening class or visit the gym regularly around then? Where had she found the opportunity to have an affair? He couldn't identify an opportunity. He was convinced it had happened under his nose. But that was what happened, wasn't it? Nearly every man inside this place had a story about some bitch who had done the dirty on him. Admittedly, he didn't believe all the stories were absolute gospel, but there was certainly an identifiable pattern. Lots of women had affairs with their husband's best friend.

They were brazen. They'd managed to carry on as though nothing had happened. Daisy had insisted that Luke and Connie were godparents to Millie, even though it put Rose's nose out of joint. Thinking about that now killed him. What he couldn't be sure about was, had they continued to see each other? Surely not. They'd have been caught out, at some point, after all this time. But would they? By whom? Connie was a shrewd person but an exceptionally busy and trusting one; would she ever suspect St Luke of having an affair? Unlikely, she thought he was devoted to her. It wasn't vanity as such, just confidence. Misplaced confidence, as it happened. And Simon had mostly been too pissed to notice if his wife was in the room, let alone whether she was sneaking off into someone else's bed. They might have got away with it continuing. Or they might have called it a day. He didn't know. He might never know.

The one thing he felt pretty sure of was that Luke was very unlikely to want to take Simon in as a lodger. Simon would no doubt end up in a bedsit above a shop or a laundrette somewhere. A place where damp crept up the walls instead of art work, and the smell of greasy kebabs and diesel fumes from buses snuck in because the window wouldn't close; jammed open, even in the winter. Without a job he couldn't expect better. And who would employ him? His life was a mess. It wasn't supposed to be like this.

'And what about Daisy?' Connie asked. He jolted at the sound of her voice. He'd drifted inside his own head. He wondered what she'd been saying, what he'd missed.

'Daisy?'

'And Millie,' Connie pursued. 'It's been a long time since you went away, Simon. Things change.'

He shrugged. Connie looked as though she was on the verge of saying more but she didn't because at that moment the bell rang, announcing the fact that visiting time was over.

Connie squeezed his hand. 'Hang in there, buddy.'

He shrugged. 'What else can I do?'

'Nothing,' she admitted.

He'd always admired her honesty.

36

Daisy

When the alarm goes off, I reach to silence it. It didn't wake me because I haven't slept. Not at all. Unrested, I ache. Slowly, I unfold my body and swing my legs out of bed. As soon as I sit up, I drop my head into my hands. How has this happened, again? I'm so ashamed. So weak.

I slowly walk into the bathroom. I notice the mouldy grout, the smudges of toothpaste on the basin unit, the hard water marks on the shower door. The pretty, colourful soaps and body-washes that Millie and I adore can't cut through the chaos and filth. I turn on the shower and nudge up the temperature as high as I can tolerate, and then a degree or two more. I want to wash it all away but the water pools around my feet as Millie's long hair has clogged up the plug hole again. It's a disgusting job clearing it out, but I set about it, because who else will otherwise?

I'm glad that I have Craig's school's summer fair to attend. Something to focus on, something to stop me crawling back into bed, pulling the sheets over my head and hiding from the world. A school summer fair is my sort of thing. I can keep busy and not think about last night, not think about what might be next.

I pull on the first thing that I find in my wardrobe, a summer dress. It's a warm day but I am chilly. I grab my denim jacket and throw it over the dress. This makes me look a bit trendier and, importantly, stops me shivering. I button it up to the neck.

Rose is pleased to see me. Craig is being kept busy at the makeshift stocks, where children pay 30p to throw wet sponges at him. He's a good sport and there's a long queue so I don't suppose we're going to see much of him today. Rose, who thinks of herself as a sort of First Lady of the school, dashes around from one stall to the next, 'Just checking everything is under control'. Once she establishes that it is — that the mums and dads who are manning the stalls are doing a fine job — she grabs a book of raffle tickets and suggests we try to drum up a few last-minute sales. I nod, but my head isn't in the game.

'You OK?' she asks on noticing that I haven't made a single sale.

'Fine,' I force myself to smile. If she was looking at me I think she'd notice it's not a very real smile, but she's scanning the playground, looking for people who might part with a quid for a five hundred to one chance of winning a box of Milk Tray.

'Late night at Connie's?' she asks.

'No, I left early, but I didn't get much sleep.' I blush and turn away from her, just in case that is the moment she decides to catch my eye. I love my sister but there's no way I can tell her what happened last night and certainly not here on the tarmac of a primary school, in the middle of candy floss and face painting stalls.

'Oh look, there's the gang.'

Connie, Luke and Lucy are walking towards us. I'm not surprised Peter isn't with them, he'll be playing golf. Sometimes I've thought his determined pursuit of his hobby was selfish, today I feel oddly sentimental about the consistency of the fact that Peter always plays golf on Saturday. The world should have some certainties; it shouldn't be chaotic and surprising all the time. I really hadn't thought Lucy would make good on her promise to come along, I'd assumed she'd offered after a glass or two of wine and that this morning she'd shun the early start. But here she is.

I scan about for Millie and spot her and Sophie at the stall where you must guess how many sweets are in a jar. They are giggling and self-contained. Usually, I wait until Millie comes to find me, because I don't like to appear over-protective, but today I can't stop myself; I dash over to her and give her a hug. She allows it, but only because this isn't her school and she doesn't know anyone other than Sophie. If I'd attempted the same at our school, she'd stop speaking to me for a month. I inhale deeply, breathing her in, my beautiful girl, my miracle. She smells lemony, an unfamiliar shampoo or body wash that she's used this morning, she's wearing Sophie's clothes, as a result of the impromptu sleepover, and yet she is one hundred percent known to me. She is mine. She is home, and goodness, and all things right in the world. I feel better for seeing her. Being a parent is mind-blowing. The way you love a child is different from any other sort of love. It's more intense and absolute, more demanding. More healing. Friends and lovers come with conditions, parents come with responsibilities, self-love is always butting up against self-loathing — at least that's been my experience — loving Millie is pure and total. Comforting.

I force myself to break away from her, greet the others. Connie is practically bouncing on her toes, effervescent even by her standards. 'So, how did it go last night?' She nudges her elbow into my side. I rub my rib, disgruntled. I should have expected this.

'What are you on about?' asks Rose, aware that Connie is sniffing out gossip and wanting in on it.

'Daisy left mine early last night. With Daryll.'

I hate myself for colouring, but have never had any control over my blushes. My reaction causes Connie to squeal and Rose to smile. Lucy looks on, not bothering to get overly-involved.

'Delicious Daryll?' asks Rose. We only know one Daryll.

'Yes,' confirms Connie. 'He was certainly giving all the signals, wasn't he, Lucy?'

'Very attentive,' Lucy confirms, coolly.

'So, what happened?' demands Rose.

'You're assuming something did,' I reply, stalling.

'You said you didn't get much sleep!' Rose puts her hand to her mouth; her shock and excitement are palpable.

'No!' Connie gasps. 'Did you stay up talking or — '

'All right, children,' Luke interrupts, firmly. He throws significant side-eye glances at Millie and Sophie, who are blatantly listening into the conversation and no longer interested in how many sweets are in the jar. Connie looks frustrated but clamps her mouth shut. She knows the boundaries.

'Well, we'll have to catch up later. I have to go.' I don't ask her where she is going. I can guess it is to visit Simon, she does so most Saturdays. When she first started doing so I was irritated with her, angry. I thought it was disloyal. She never asked me if she could visit him, she just took it upon herself and then informed me of the situation. But, as I know Connie never judges or takes sides, it wasn't a complete surprise to me. Over the years her visits have ignited a raft of emotions: sometimes I've felt jealous or excluded. As time went on, I realised I felt a level of relief, gratitude. At least part of me is glad she visits him. I can't bring myself to do it. I can't forgive him for nearly killing my daughter, but I hate the thought of him being entirely cut-off from the outside world. Who else would visit him besides Connie? His mother isn't capable, his sister lives abroad, he'd fallen out with so many people before he went inside. There's no one on Team Simon. It makes no sense to be jealous that she's doing something I'm certain I don't want to do: see my husband. Yes it does feel odd that she's now closer to him than I am, that she knows more about him than I do. It's not how it should be.

But it is how it is.

Connie leans in to hug me and she whispers in my ear, 'You go girl! I'll ring you tonight. I want all the details.'

I flinch. I don't want to give her details about Daryll. I pull apart from her. She dashes off. I watch her go but everyone else's eyes are on me.

'Erm, anyone fancy a coffee?' I offer by way of changing the subject.

The school fair is only small but, even so, we split up. The girls beg for fivers and then dash off, desperate to spend them. I think of Simon's Mum, Elsie. Her expression for such zeal about spending was that the money was 'burning a hole in the pocket'. I miss Elsie. I still visit her regularly, twice a week, but she's 'there' less and less often. I don't think she knows who either Millie or I are anymore, even when we are stood in front of her. She never asks after Simon, she doesn't reference him at all. I don't think this is through shame or anger, she's simply lost him. He's slipped her mind. When Elsie was first diagnosed with Alzheimer's, I thought it was the cruellest thing that one day she'd forget us all. Now I'm grateful. It would torture her to know her son is in prison. It's hard enough feeding her, changing her, answering the same questions over and over again. How much harder would that be if the questions were about Simon?

Rose says she has to go back to the raffle stall to get some change and so that leaves just Lucy, Luke and me. We wander towards the cutesy sky-blue caravan where coffee can be bought. At our school we had a bunch of parents (let's face it, mostly mothers) serving not-quite-hot instant coffee from a huge urn. Here, there is a choice of 'beautiful artisan coffees' prepared and served by (self-professed) 'skilled baristas' who insist on running through a menu of coffee that they claim they have 'curated'. Any other day, I might have felt a rush of competition and made a mental note to get Rose to find out how much this thing cost to hire. Today, I have no energy. Although I ostensibly listen to the curated choice of beverages, I don't even know what two thirds of the drinks are. I order an Americano. The barista looks disappointed. We all three sip on our coffees and watch others bob from one stall to the next.

'This is nice,' says Luke. I smile weakly and nod.

Lucy makes some comment about the coffee being, 'Surprisingly OK, considering'.

'So, are you going to spill?' Luke blows on the top of his coffee. Not looking me in the eye is a kindness. 'Has Connie got it right? Is there something between you and Daryll?'

I don't know how much I want to say. Saying nothing at all is not an option. Before, it had been in Daryll's interests to keep quiet, so I knew I could keep things to myself. I no longer think that is the case. Something has changed with Daryll, last night he spoke of wanting to be a family man, claim his place. Which terrifies me. We are miles apart. It's bound to get out now. Our tight-knit gang always get to the bottom of things if they try. It's a wonder that I've been able to keep the secret this long. I suppose no one was digging. I wasn't the focus. We were all busy with our young families, everyone accepted what they were told because no one had the time or energy to double-check. How do I start to unpick what they think they know about me?

When the Uber drew up outside my house I had known that Daryll would get out too. I live in a street terrace, there's no path to be walked up, we were immediately at my front door. He took my bag from me and rummaged until he found the keys, I didn't stop him. He unlocked the door and walked into my home as though it was his. I followed him. He closed the door behind me.

'Shall I fix us both a drink?' he asked, taking command.

I shook my head. 'No.' Then I added, 'Thank you.'

'Well, I want one. What do you have in?'

'Not much. There's some white in the fridge.' I generally have an open bottle in my fridge. I can pace myself, go weeks without touching a drop. Sometimes it's a couple of weeks old by the time I think about finishing it off, so it is undrinkable and I have to chuck it. Daryll marched through to the kitchen and flung open the fridge door. The light flooded out on to him, as though he was an actor in the spotlight. Tall, broad, handsome. He took out the bottle and examined the label. He didn't look very impressed. I was not surprised, the wine cost four quid. I felt his judgement. Still, he shrugged and muttered,

'Beggars can't be choosers,' then briskly began opening and closing cupboards until he found where I keep the glasses. He poured himself an enormous one, and downed half of it in a few gulps. He stood leaning against the kitchen counter. He seemed to own the room. He expanded into it, comfortable, in charge. Other than family and Luke, who is practically family, no man has been inside my kitchen.

'So, our friends seem to think we'd make a lovely couple,' he said, smiling. 'Tonight was so obviously a set-up. Nice to think we have their blessing. I know they mean so much to you.' I didn't know what to say so I chose to say nothing at all. 'I think the time is right for me, Daisy. I'm ready to be a family man,' he stated, his smile stretching further across his face. His teeth are straight, white, but it was not a lovely smile. It struck me as a threat. 'Millie is a treat. Pretty and talented. Ideal.'

'You can't just step into her life. You can't just assume — ' I wanted to be forceful and certain but my voice came out in a whisper.

'Indubitably I can.' He cut me off. Imperious. He could do what he liked. He always had.

He glanced around the kitchen, we hadn't put on any lights. I don't know why. He hadn't, so nor had I. I was following his lead, even whilst wanting to grasp control. Somehow, he disabled me. The moonlight and streetlights tumbled through the window, which illuminated the room enough for us to see each other and the outline of the furniture. It was untidy, as usual. I've never prioritised housework but suddenly I wished I was more like Rose; you could eat your lunch off her kitchen floor, if you so desired. My place looked neglected, squalid. It looked like a place that people lived in when they'd given up. I swiftly moved towards the lamp on the side table; putting that on always made the place look cosy. I had tricks to cheer up the rooms. When Millie is at home I always light scented candles, put on the radio and all the sidelamps. I try, and it works. With her, this small house is a home, despite everything. Without her, I admit, the house looks hopeless. Although, I was utterly grateful she wasn't there at that point. The orange light from the lamp flooded into the room.

'Turn it off,' he commanded. And I did. I immediately snapped off the switch. 'Look at this place,' he muttered. 'She deserves better than this.' It's true she does but . . . He continued, 'I could give her better than this. My daughter shouldn't be living in a two-up two-down.'

I didn't dare breathe. What did he mean? He could give her better than this? Might he try to take her from me? Was that possible? No, that would not happen. Mothers had rights, didn't they? I wouldn't allow it. But Daryll was above anything as pedestrian as the law. He wouldn't care what a court said. He did as he pleased. What if he snatched her? Ran away with her? You hear of it. It sounds extreme, but it happens. How furious with me was he? Did he really resent being locked out of her life all these years? Did he have rights? I had to tread carefully. Think this through.

It took everything I had to mumble, 'It's late. I need an early start. You should go.'

He shook his head, almost sympathetically. 'That's not going to happen. Let me tell you how it is, Daisy. I am Millie's father. A DNA test will confirm that. The only sorry excuse for a father she has, is an alcoholic who is currently rotting in jail because of nearly killing her. I want to be a family man now. All my friends are married off. I've somehow been left behind.' He looked momentarily confused, as though it was something he couldn't quite comprehend. 'It's rather wonderful to discover I have a ready-made family and I'm going to be a father to my daughter now.'

I shook my head. 'She's my daughter.'

'True enough,' He looked pleased that I'd brought this up. 'And if you play your cards right, you can be a part of my plan too. You scrub up well, Daisy. You're the sort of woman who has grown into her looks. And whilst this place doesn't showcase your talents,' again he glanced around my home, barely hiding his disdain, 'I know you could make a good partner. You could run a proper home. We could be a proper family.' He started to undo his belt. His flies. He swiftly walked towards me.

'I'm married,' I muttered. Shaking my head.

'That never stopped us before.'

* * *

'Earth calling Daisy, come in Daisy,' Luke teased, bringing me back to the playground, hauling me out of the memories of the night before. Luke is waving his hand in front of my face, laughing. 'Hey, daydreamer.' Lucy looks less amused, she's never been a fan of daydreamers. 'So, come on then, tell your old mate, Luke. Did anything happen between you and dashing Daryll?' I nod. 'Oh wow, it will kill Connie that I know this before she does,' Luke laughs. 'So, what is going on? Are you going to see him again? Are you two a thing?'

'We're something, I suppose,' I say with a shrug. 'I don't know what, exactly.'

Luke flings his arm around me and gives me a squeeze, I flinch. I'm not ready to be congratulated on this news. Or touched. 'Well good luck to you, Daisy. You deserve to be happy. Don't ever forget that. It's early days, right? Hard to define.' I nod again and scan the playground, searching for Millie.

'There she is,' says Lucy. Reading my mind. 'At the ice cream van. Quite safe.'

37
Simon

Tuesday, 25th June 2019

Simon had never been in the governor's office, but he had heard it being spoken of from time to time, with reverence, with fear, and it had acquired a mythical status in his mind. He hadn't expected the grandeur of Dr Martell's office, but he had thought it would have some creature comforts. Things Simon hadn't seen for years, such as framed photographs on a desk, mugs with funny sayings written on them, perhaps some pictures hung on the walls. He found he was excited to see such things, something less sparse, less pedestrian, less mean than he'd got used to. It was sometimes hard to remember that he was once a man who earned his living by making places more beautiful, now he was surrounded by such constant ugliness.

However, the office was a disappointment. There was nothing grand or even comfy about it. Simon was shown in to a cramped, unprepossessing room, where there wasn't much space beyond that for the desk and a few chairs. The chair behind the desk was an ergonomic one, which suggested the governor (a man of some bulk and height) suffered from a bad back, and there were two plastic chairs in front of the desk. Simon and his solicitor silently settled into them. The desk was dwarfed by tidy but towering piles of prison, probation and psychiatric reports. There was a polystyrene cup with dregs of coffee, no sign of mugs with pithy little slogans. What would a prison governor's mug say anyway, Simon wondered? He thought about that for a while and came up with, 'I don't need to worry about identity theft. No one wants to be me.' He laughed at his own joke but didn't share it, even when his solicitor glanced at him with something like concern.

The Governor was not at his desk when they were shown to their seats. Obviously, a powerplay that occurred in every office in the world would certainly play out in a prison. A place rife with hierarchy, pecking orders, ranks. They would be made to wait so there was no uncertainty as to who had the control. A guard took up his post by the door. Simon's solicitor was a different one to the one he'd had at the trial. This woman looked tired, almost bored. She didn't make any conversation, but instead re-read the notes and files pertaining to Simon's case. At least Simon hoped it was a re-read, he didn't want to think his solicitor was winging it and just acquainting herself with the facts for the first time five minutes before the meeting began.

The other cons all had a view on what the on-licence release meeting entailed. Some had told him it was a formality, that he was certain to be let out because the problem of overcrowding was more insistent than the problem of him driving dangerously. Others said that it was part of the system's sick tormenting process and that he didn't have a chance. That on-licence release was dangled like a carrot but rarely given. Simon didn't know what to believe. It felt much like when he'd first been arrested and landed in a strange unfamiliar world where things were done to him, said to him, happened to him but he had no control. The governor came into the room. He shook Simon's solicitor's hand but not Simon's. It stung, that small discourtesy. It did what it was designed to do: reduced him, put him in his place.

The governor sat down heavily and picked up the top file. His eyes skimmed across the report and recommendations. When he'd finished reading, his eyes flicked up at Simon. Simon thought he saw compassion.

'Well this looks straightforward. Have you made your client aware of the conditions?' The question was put to the solicitor.

'As an offender with a determinate sentence, you can be put on-licence which means you can serve the remainder of your sentence in the community. This licence is supervised by the Probation Service and includes conditions that you must meet.'

'Such as?'

The solicitor looked surprised that Simon had interrupted her. She slid a piece of paper across the desk towards him. He read that he had a requirement to, 'be of good behaviour and not to behave in a way which undermines the purpose of the supervision period.' It was a vague, all-encompassing condition. It made him think of the times when, as a boy, his mother used to tell him to 'be good' which was less directional than 'play nicely' or 'be quiet' or 'stop teasing your sister.' He had never liked the instruction to 'be good' because he discovered that he rarely knew what was considered bad until he'd eaten the last biscuit or left his bike in the street, and then he was rounded upon. He considered asking for a tighter definition, but he feared he'd come off as cocky and that in itself might be a breach of the condition. The second condition was easier to understand: he was required not to commit any further offence. He would also need to keep in touch with his supervisor.

The solicitor turned to the governor. Simon wondered whether they needed him here at all. That was the thing about being a convicted criminal: people didn't think you had anything to offer or say, or if you did they didn't want to hear it.

'I'd recommend that Mr Barnes meets his supervisor twice a week, initially. Licence conditions are not designed to be punitive. As you are aware they are designed for risk management and public protection purposes. Mr Barnes, a first-time offender, who pleaded guilty to the charges, has shown remorse and displayed exemplary behaviour during his incarceration, therefore he does not represent any risk to the public'

The governor nodded. 'Yes, fine.'

'We need to confirm an address of permanent residence and that address needs to be approved in advance.' The solicitor turned to Simon this time, and Simon suddenly felt shy, inadequate. He'd wanted to take back control of his life but the first thing they'd asked him he didn't have an answer to. The governor and solicitor waited expectantly.

'You are married, Simon?' the governor asked. Simon nodded. 'So will you be returning to the family home?'

'She moved.' Simon coughed. 'My wife moved. We, she, couldn't afford the mortgage.'

'Will you be residing with your wife?' Simon shrugged. The governor looked disappointed. 'Well you'll need an address before we can progress. A hostel. Something.'

'I'll get one,' Simon assured him. Although he wasn't sure how.

The solicitor was clearly on a deadline and wanted to push on. 'You're required not to undertake work unless it is approved by the supervisor and to notify the supervisor in advance of any proposal to undertake work, even voluntary.' Simon thought this was confusing. Surely, they shouldn't be putting barriers in the way of ex-cons getting work. But again, he stayed silent. 'You are encouraged to disclose your on-licence status to any potential employer. In some cases it will be a legal requirement.' Simon wondered what sort of work he could hope to find. 'There is a requirement not to travel outside the British Islands, except with prior permission of the supervisor. Do you understand?'

Simon nodded. 'Where do I sign?'

Sometimes there were extra conditions.

Offenders were told they could not make contact with certain people or live at the same address as children. Others were required to submit to drug tests. There was nothing in place to address the issue of drinking, because alcohol was a legal substance even if it did lead to amnesia, lies, violence and crime.

Simon didn't have to plead his case, the way he would have if this had been a parole hearing. This was a process. There were conditions and rules that he had to abide by and then he could earn his freedom. That was the deal society made. Yet he found he wanted to explain himself, offer something more. He wanted to be heard.

'I'm going to go to meetings. I'm going to stay sober. And I'll make her see that I'm not useless. Not hopeless. I'm going to make it up to them, for the time I lost, being in here and the time before that. The time I threw away. I'm going to be a better man.'

The governor coughed. Embarrassed for Simon. 'Right. Sign here to say you've read and understood the conditions. Get back to me with that address. And Simon — '

'What?'

'Good luck to you. Be good.'

38

Daisy

Thursday, 4th July 2019

As a rule, Daryll does not text or call, he just turns up. Since the dinner at Connie's, he has knocked at my door twice, late at night, after Millie was fast asleep. Both times I let him in. For a man who professes to want a family, he doesn't seem especially interested in getting to know Millie. But, honestly, I'm grateful for that. I dread the day when he does say he wants to get to know her better. At the moment he seems willing to just have me, as and when. I'm prepared to be a human wall and stand between them, for as long as possible. I haven't mentioned him to her yet, as I don't know how to start the conversation.

Because of this pattern, I'm surprised to receive a text from him today.

> Taking you out for dinner. Have something to discuss. Dress up. Dx

Not an invite, just orders that I have to obey. Some women like their men to dominate them, at least from time to time. It's part of the attraction. I do not. With Daryll, I see it for what it is. He holds all the cards. He is the biological father of my much-loved daughter. If I don't behave as he wants, if I disobey him, I have no idea what the consequences might be.

I ring for an agency babysitter because I don't want to ask my friends or family, it will lead to too many questions and I never feel comfortable with Millie doing sleepovers at friends whilst I'm out, for obvious reasons. I follow instructions and 'dress up'. It's not that I want to make myself more attractive to Daryll, I just don't want to infuriate him. Things are bad enough. I have a long-sleeved black chiffon dress, that's a classic, I decide that it will do. I'm shocked when I try it on because it's loose. It used to be quite snug. I don't really spend much time looking in the mirror but when I check my reflection my weight loss is confirmed. All my life I have longed to be skinny, or if not that then certainly slimmer. I've achieved that. I look fragile, gaunt. I'm disappearing. It goes to show, you have to be careful what you wish for.

Even though the babysitter is sitting downstairs, Millie perches on the side of my bed and watches me get ready. She is curious because other than school dos with other teachers, and my book club, I rarely go out without her. 'Are you going on a date?' she asks. She meets my eye through the mirror as I apply lipstick.

'What would you think if I was?'

She shrugs. 'I wouldn't mind.'

'I'm having dinner with an old university friend.'

'The man I met at Connie's? Daryll?'

'Yes.'

She considers this for a moment and then asks, 'Do you think Daddy will mind?' I don't know how to answer her question. I'm stunned she's asked it. She hardly ever mentions Simon. The doorbell rings and I'm surprisingly grateful that Daryll is prompt.

She follows me down the stairs, limping heavily, which suggests she's tired or maybe upset. I'd have preferred it if she'd stayed out of Daryll's sight, but I didn't know how to suggest it to her without raising her suspicions.

The babysitter has let Daryll in. I find him stood in the kitchen chatting affably to her. The babysitter is known to me, June. June is in her late fifties and I taught her two boys. I spotted that the younger one was dyslexic and got him the proper help. I know she likes me and, the same as most people who live around here, she knows more about my life than is ideal. She beams at me, commenting indiscreetly, 'It's nice to see you getting out.' She stands behind Daryll's back and puts her thumbs up. He's the sort of man who gives a good first impression.

'Ah ha! Here they are. The two ladies I've been waiting for!' says Daryll. I smile politely but Millie looks a bit perplexed. She can't imagine why this stranger might be waiting for her or why he might be calling her a lady. She's a girl and then she'll be a woman. Her generation are aware of the expectations and restrictions that come with being labelled a lady. 'I have something for you, both.' He presents me with an enormous bouquet of flowers. It's pretty, mostly pink. A long time ago, Simon used to buy me yellow, red or orange flowers. He knew they were my favourite colours.

'Oh lovely, I'll find a vase,' I say automatically. The flowers *are* lovely. It's impossible for flowers to be ugly, still I want to throw them in the bin.

'And this is for you, Millie.' Daryll stoops to the floor and picks up an enormous cardboard box. He carefully places it on the breakfast bar. I immediately notice that there are holes in the box and in the moment I think, 'Oh no, he wouldn't.' Millie opens the lid and reveals . . .

'A kitten!' She squeals with delight and scoops a grey ball of fluff out of the box. 'Oh my days! She's the most adorable thing ever!'

'He, I think,' says Daryll, with a laugh.

'He's the most adorable thing!' She starts to plant kisses on the kitten, kiss after kiss. 'Is he for me, really?'

'Yes.'

'Oh, thank you, thank you. He's perfect.' The tiny scrap wiggles in her hands so she carefully places the kitten on the floor and for a moment we all just marvel at the immeasurably cute little thing.

But I'm also fuming. What a stupid, irresponsible gift to give a child. Bringing a pet into a family is a big deal, what makes him think he can make that unilateral decision. He should have discussed it with me.

'How did you know that I've always wanted a kitten?' Millie asks excitedly.

'I just had a feeling that you needed something

to love, and everyone loves kittens, right?'

June puts her hand to her heart, I think she's about to burst with happiness, she evidently thinks Daryll's gesture is generous and romantic. Millie obviously thinks it's just the best idea ever. I think it's a trap. He could have given Millie sweets, that would have been a suitable first meeting gift, but that wouldn't have been as memorable or impactful. Sweets are not permanent. 'I've a few other things in my car. A basket, a litter tray, some toys. I'll just go and get them,' he says, flinging his most charming grin left, right and centre.

'Oh, you've thought of everything,' says June, approvingly.

'Hasn't he,' I mutter more darkly.

Daryll returns with three huge carrier bags of shopping from Pets at Home. He does indeed seem to have thought of everything. He sets up a litter tray in one corner of the kitchen, food and water in another, Millie isn't much interested in anything other than the kitten. I realise that this equipment must have cost a fair amount and that with every fluffy mouse on a ribbon that is unpacked Daryll is marking his territory. There is no way I can ask him to take all this away. Asking Millie to give up the kitten is an impossibility.

'What are you going to call him?' I ask, accepting the inevitable.

'Oh, I don't know. Maybe Cloud. He's so fluffy, and light grey. He's sort of a rain cloud colour, isn't he?'

'Oh no, that's not a very good name,' says Daryll, abruptly.

Millie looks surprised to be brooked, mostly her suggestions are met with approval because there's just the two of us, and other than eating vegetables and bedtimes, I'm usually open to her suggestions and views. 'What do you think, then?' she asks Daryll.

'I'd give him a proper name, like Stanley or Cedric. Eric. We should call him Eric'

Millie doesn't look convinced but is too polite to say so. She looks to me for support. 'What do you think Mum?'

'I like Cloud,' I say bravely.

'We're calling it Eric,' says Daryll. 'End of discussion.'

* * *

We leave the house not long after that. I don't want to go out, I want to stay in and watch Millie play with her kitten, but I don't want Daryll to spend the evening with Millie. I'm still trying to put the brakes on whatever is happening here. I'm still hoping to retain some control. The fact I have very little was highlighted to me when Daryll looked at his watch and said, 'We have to leave now, Daisy. We have a reservation. I'm leaving my car here. We'll take the tube. I want a drink and I certainly don't want to drink and drive.'

We catch the tube into central London. Daryll doesn't seem to want to chat, I get the feeling he is saving it all up until we get to the restaurant and that suits me. I have nothing to say to him. We get off the tube at Temple and he leads me down a narrow passage to a restaurant that tourists would never discover and is almost certainly designed for clever people in the know. I don't consider myself to be one of those types but Daryll does and always has. There's something about how he holds himself, how he dresses and even speaks, that suggests he's out to make an impression; he cares that people notice him. When I was young, I used to think his stiff formality was posh and proper. I was in awe of him. As I got to know him better, and maybe as I got to know myself better too, I thought his aloofness was a cover for either arrogance or insecurity or both. It is possible to be both things at once, and the combination is toxic. Now, I think his rigid reserve is a symptom, a disguise to hide what he really is. A man with utter disregard for anyone else's feelings, desires or concerns. A psychopath.

He's picked the sort of restaurant that is so trendy it's terrifying. The entire place is white. The walls, ceiling and floors, the tablecloths, napkins and chairs. Even though I'm dressed up, I felt like a smudge. We are sat in straight-backed chairs that are as beautiful as they are uncomfortable. Daryll smiles at me. 'Isn't this splendid? Our first date.'

I nod stupidly, because it all seems too bizarre. Who has a first date, nine years after their child is born?

A waitress appears at our table. She is very young. Maybe twenty. She's clearly a model-in-waiting, so beautiful she seems unreal. Daryll turns the full force of his charm and attention on her. I notice that she's impervious. I think he does too, because he looks irritated but won't quit. He just ups the ante. He's all attention and smiles. He says, 'I hope the food is as gorgeous as you are.' She glances at me and I think I see sympathy in her eyes. I blush. Seeing him outside of my bedroom I look at him in a different light. I can see him as others do. When the waitress looks at Daryll she sees a man who is approaching middle age and hasn't accepted it. He is old enough to be her father. He was once so handsome and considered by many to be irresistible. I think for the first time I start to understand why he's chosen to have me in his life. I remember that about him. His chiselled good looks, his allure. I shore up his vanity. Women he meets now will still see a good-looking man, but they might want to add the old qualifier 'for his age'. Older women, like June, will think he's charming, swoon-worthy, but Daryll would never be interested in an older woman and it appears that younger women are no longer interested in him. Women my age come with baggage, it just so happens that my baggage is his.

Daryll orders us both a gin and tonic. 'They serve Hernö gin here. You have to try it.'

'I don't really drink spirits.'

'You'll love it.'

The beautiful, and I like to think ballsy, waitress returns with our drinks and some olives. I leave both untouched but Daryll pitches in enthusiastically. He orders for both of us from the specials board. Just a main course because he comments, 'You don't stay looking this good if you over indulge.' He laughs as he says this, but

I think he does want to draw attention to his lean physique. I imagine he works at it. I don't have the energy to mention that I don't like my steak rare. I like it medium to well done. I know it's not the fashionable way to have it but I just don't like to see all that blood swilling around on my plate. It doesn't matter, I have no appetite anyway, so it doesn't matter what he orders for me. As soon as we are alone, he pitches in.

'I have put an offer in on a house and it's been accepted. I'm a cash buyer so the sale will go through in five to six weeks.'

'Oh. Well, congratulations.' I know it's not a simple case of him giving me his good news.

'Your house needs to go on the market immediately. I imagine it will take a little longer to sell but if we give it a lick of paint, cheer it up a bit, someone will want it.'

I seem to have no control over my body. It turns to stone. Then it turns to sand. I trickle to nothing. 'Why would I put my house on the market?'

'Don't be silly, Daisy. We agreed Millie deserves better than you can give her. You are both coming to live with me. I've also put her name down at a private school, nearby. It's a good one. Does well on the league tables, it's not just a matter of convenience. It's an all-girls school.'

'I don't want Millie to go to a single-sex school.' That's just part of it. I don't want any of this.

'It will be more suitable, going forward, as she gets older.' The wine he ordered is brought to our table. He takes his time to examine the label. I notice he moves his head back a fraction to focus on the label, as though they'd bring the wrong one. He takes his time to swirl the wine around the glass, sniff it, then slowly sip and swill it in his mouth. It's excruciating. The wine waiter and I keep our eyes on the bottle the entire time.

'Oh yes, very fine,' he pronounces and at last two glasses can be poured. I need mine but also feel it's important to keep a clear head. He holds his glass aloft. 'New beginnings.' I tap my glass against his and take the smallest of sips. My hand is shaking as I take the glass to my lips. I hope he hasn't noticed.

'Millie likes her school. She has friends there.'

'She'll make new friends,' he says jovially. 'I don't think it's healthy that you teach at the school she attends. You could give up your job but even so I think private school is the way to go.'

I don't. I take a deep breath. 'This is all happening too fast for me.'

Daryll looks surprised. 'Daisy, your dreams are coming true. We both know you've been in love with me for ever. Way before you even met Simon Barnes. I'm giving you a beautiful home, I'm giving your daughter a father, and instead of getting old alone, you get to be my partner. Maybe my wife.' He winks at me and sips more wine.

Does he honestly believe this plan of his makes sense, that he can railroad me this way? Not just me, but Millie too. He so clearly doesn't understand the first thing about being a parent. I can't just pluck her out of school, take her from her home, tell her she has a new daddy in six weeks!

Yes, he does think he can railroad me this way because I've never been able to show him that he can't. But this is different now, this isn't just about me it's about Millie too. It's all about Millie, everything I've ever done was for her and I'm not going to allow him to bully us.

I take a deep breath and gather my courage.

'Here we have two steaks,' the waiter puts the food on our table. I notice that the beautiful waitress is nowhere to be seen. She's probably asked her colleague to take over. She probably said she didn't want to serve the creepy, controlling man. The waiter fusses for a bit. Offers various condiments that Daryll considers but after some time, rejects. He asks for something they don't offer. A particular sauce, I'm not really concentrating on what he's saying, something about it being served that way in New York. The waiter returns to the kitchen, says he'll see what he can do.

Daryll takes my hand in his, he slowly turns it and then brings my wrist to his lips. Anyone looking on will see the tenderness in the gesture. It sends shivers through me. He leans closer to me and whispers quietly.

'This is what is going to happen, Daisy. You are going to visit Simon and you are going to ask for a divorce. You are going to tell him, Millie and all your friends and family that Millie is my daughter.'

'But,' I gasp.

'You will tell everyone we had a love affair and that we are resuming it. Your friends will forgive you. Even understand. Your life with Simon was not easy and you turned to me for comfort. Everyone forgave Connie. Everyone forgave Lucy. You are the only person who holds grudges. You are the one who judges. Others will see this as the love story it is.' He lets go of my hand and picks up his knife and fork. I watch as he slices through the tender meat. 'What you need to bear in mind, Daisy, is that I'm going to be Millie's father, regardless of how much you like my plan. I've already talked to a lawyer. She will be living at my new home in Muswell Hill for a minimum of one week out of every two. She's mine as much as she's yours.'

'No, she's not. I've been with her since — '

'Yes she is.'

'Don't you see how disruptive this will be for her? We have to take things slowly. We have to put her first.'

He smiles. 'The shared custody thing, that's happening, Daisy. Understood?'

He puts a piece of meat in his mouth and starts to chew. I push my plate away and stare at the serrated steak knife. I've never been a violent person, but I want to plunge it in his heart. The problem is, I'd have to find it.

39

Simon

Saturday, 6th July 2019

Simon sat in the visitors' room, uncertain whether she would show up. He couldn't believe it, after all this time. It was a hard-hitting fact that he had finally been granted on-licence release — and with continued good behaviour he would be out and on the other side within as little as a week or so — before Daisy had finally agreed to come and see him. But he refused to sulk. He wasn't going to resent or regret. That was no way forward. He had to see the timing as an opportunity, a good thing. This was better than him just turning up at her house. They could have the difficult conversations in here, where there were parameters. Here, things could be controlled. It would give him time to show her he'd changed. Give her time to believe it. The conversations ahead of them would inevitably be painful. He realised he had a lot to explain, she had a lot to forgive. But it was the other way round too. She just didn't know what he knew about her. What he was prepared to forgive. If they were to have a future together, he had to talk to her about Millie's parentage. He'd thought about it for hours and hours. The possibility of pushing the whole business under the carpet was not an option for him. The secret would be like a bad stench that would ultimately permeate their relationship. He had to have it out with her. And then they could move onwards. He hoped so, but did they have it in them? Could they leave their misery and wrong-doings in this place?

Go forward, rehabilitated? Restored?

He carefully watched the door as the visitors trailed in. Mostly women, the men visiting their sons, brothers or friends were in the minority. The world's caring, consoling, calming was usually left to women. How did the visitors prepare to enter this block of despair and disgrace, he wondered? He noted that some scanned the room, searching out their men. These women displayed a myriad of emotion: frustrated, hopeful, anxious, exhausted. Others arrived and behaved like well-trained animals or robots, blank-faced, unwilling or unable to betray any emotion, they mechanically moved towards set tables. They knew that their men would be sat at the same table every week, because he was comfortable with a routine or maybe he was staking out ownership, preferring to take the table under the window to benefit most from the natural light, or the one near the kids' play corner so his offspring could be occupied. Any sort of advantage mattered here. Even after all this time, Simon still didn't have a regular table. He was not high up enough on the prison pecking order to be able to mark out any sort of territory. He sat wherever was left and tried not to look like a man who had been beaten up by life.

Well before they reached the main prison, the security checks began for these women. There were forms to be filled in, ID to be handed over, scans, searches, questions, cameras. Once inside they endured a series of holding rooms and queues. Wives, mothers, girlfriends and children patiently queued, enduring constant monitoring and suspicion. He knew this because Connie had told him. She said that the women behaved differently from the way they might have in any other queue; they did not chat, swap pleasantries, pass the time of day. They kept their heads down, avoided conversation. The women with kids hissed and snapped their children into obedience.

They were all ashamed. They'd rather be anywhere else.

Before they were allowed in here the visitors had to remove shoes and belts, put all their belongings through an X-ray machine. Exactly like they were going on holiday, not dissimilar to visiting the top of the Shard, and yet so very far from embarking on a treat. They walked through more metal detectors and then were subjected to a body search. Pretty thorough ones: the lining of clothes, the soles of feet and the inside of mouths were all checked. The frisking was done by a woman, at least.

Then they would put their shoes back on and pass from the reception area, through a corridor and towards another locked door. Passing through this door involved another wait, as it was only unlocked by staff in the control room after they'd re-checked visitors' identity documents. No two doors in the unit were allowed to be opened at the same time. That was the anthem of visiting time: locks scraping, doors banging, locks scraping, doors banging.

What would Daisy make of it all, he wondered? Had Connie warned her?

Then, she walked in. There she was. Daisy. His wife. Still, after all these years. She glanced about. He forced himself to sit up a little straighter. It was an effort. Physically and mentally. She caught his eye but didn't smile a greeting. Her hair was shorter, just skimming her shoulders. When he saw her last it had fallen down her back, and she was thinner than he remembered. He imagined she'd be secretly pleased about that, even though the weight loss might have come through suffering, even though he couldn't say whether it suited her. She looked tired.

He wondered what he looked like to her. He was wearing prison clothes, as was everyone else. An ill-fitting but clean grey tracksuit, that sliced away his identity, that was the point of it. His hair was greasy. He hadn't been able to get to the showers today. There had been some sort of scuffle in there. Someone ended up in the hospital unit. Two broken ribs and a broken nose. Simon had also lost weight since he'd been inside. Obviously, the food was crap and he couldn't drink. Maybe he'd arrived carrying a couple more pounds than he should have had, but he knew he'd gone past looking healthy. Now he looked gaunt. Hungry. He didn't linger in front of a mirror. They weren't allowed real mirrors in prisons, in case anyone broke one and used a shard as a weapon or a way out, but he knew what he looked like from the metal substitute. His eyes were sunken, missing somewhere in the back of his head. His cheeks were burnt by broken veins, his actions were sluggish, inept. He wondered whether he was frightening to look at. Whether he looked brutal or brutalised.

A week or so. Nearly there. Nearly done.

She pulled out the chair opposite him and sat down, silently. The quietness was notable even though there was a lot of noise around them. Maybe because of that fact. Visiting times could be rowdy. People brought their children. He would never have wanted Millie to see inside this place; not that he was given a choice. Millie. What must she be like now? Connie had brought some photos over the years, he would be able to recognise her in the street if he saw her. But that was not the same as knowing her. He looked at his wife. A furtive glance, then away again. Neither of them could stand prolonged eye contact. He'd been excited to see her, or something close. Now he was terrified. What did she want from him ? Why was she suddenly here ? So much time had passed. She was at once a stranger and the person he knew better than anyone else in the world. What did that say about his life?

He hadn't expected the conversation to flow. How could it? After three years of silence and six years before that of Daisy tricking him, deliberately withholding information. What could she say that would throw a rope across that chasm? He thought she might offer him scraps of news, he did not expect a feast. She might tell him about what she had done last week. Whether her pupils were being cooperative, cheerful, determined at the moment. She must be moving towards the end of term now. Would she talk about Millie? The daughter that wasn't his.

The silence stretched. He didn't know what to say. Where to start. He didn't want to talk about his desolation, his sorrow. Suddenly shy, he told himself that how he felt was probably immaterial to her, anyhow. It was indulgent to go there. Talking about his pain was honest, but a downer, and talking about his hopes was a leap. They were long since out of the habit of saying the first thing they thought of. It was easier to avoid anything raw. The thing that sat between them, most defiantly, most dreadfully, was the sense of accusation. His and hers. Mute but brutal. The silence tormented. His scalp itched with irritation.

When they were first married, Daisy used to tell him practically everything that happened to her when they were out of one another's sight, she'd recount every thought that had drifted in to her head whilst they were apart. And he would do the same for her. She'd tell him about the wrangles in the staff room, what she'd had for lunch, how long she'd had to wait for the bus home. And he'd tell her what his clients had said about his proposals, that he had trouble working the complicated coffee machine in the boardroom, that there had been traffic on the M25 so he'd listened to the radio to pass the time. In those days, they'd never stopped chatting, they never ran out of things to say. He remembered that they'd wanted to know everything about one another, they'd resented the times they had to be apart, and so they'd tried to play catch up. They'd sometimes be left hoarse or knackered as they'd talked late into the night, early into the morning. Even at the weekends, when they spent every moment together, they still had things to talk about because they'd discuss the TV dramas they were watching, they'd theorise on what might happen next or mercilessly pick apart characters that they didn't believe in, they'd discuss what they might eat for supper or they'd analyse their friends after seeing them. Who was happy? Who was not. There were never silences.

But then things had changed. Because of his drinking. Because of the shared baby-longing. Because of her infidelity. Just because.

The meetings were making him remember stuff. Live with it. Own it. It was agony because, now he wasn't drinking, he remembered so much, but he wasn't sure she did. It seemed she'd forgotten needing and wanting or having a connection.

She'd lied to him. Betrayed him. He had to live with that too. Own that.

'How's school?' he asked. It was somewhere to start. She stared at him, cold, uncooperative.

'Fine.' She shrugged her shoulders.

He pushed on, bravely. 'Are you still at the same place? Newfield Primary.'

'Yes.' She sighed.

He wasn't sure what the sigh meant. He wondered what it was like there for her now. How long had the mothers whispered about him, about her, as they gathered at the school gate? Did some still put a protective arm around their child and usher them away from Daisy as she walked past? Did they judge her for being married to a man who drank so much he'd nearly killed their child? Three years was a long time to many people working in offices — in advertising or TV it would be a lifetime — but Simon knew that school communities were like elephants, they never forgot. Daisy no doubt sill wore Simon's disgrace. Had the Head of her school gently hinted that it might be better if she considered a fresh start, a new school? He wondered to what extent she had been ostracised. Was she suffering out there? Lonely?

As he was in here.

He hoped not.

The children wouldn't treat her with any level of suspicion. If they were aware that their parents were gossiping, it wouldn't matter to them. All the kids cared about was if their teacher was fair, consistent: if she remembered to dish out sweets at Christmas and Creme Eggs at Easter. He recalled her doing that. They'd both made a few last-minute dashes to the supermarket to buy the treats that said end of term.

He watched his wife and wondered about her life. A life he had once shared and now seemed remote to him. She looked sad. Deeply sad. And there was something else. She was alight with something. On fire. Was there nervousness, fear?

Yes fear, he recognised it. It was something to do with her eyes darkening a shade. Naturally, she was scared. She was sat in a prison visiting room; he couldn't expect her to put out bunting. She glanced around the room, perhaps searching for something to talk about. After a while she alighted on a piece of news she was prepared to share. 'I still visit your mother,' she stated.

'Oh, that's good. Thank you.' His voice was flat, contradicting the words. He wanted to sound enthusiastic. He wanted to show he cared and was grateful, but he couldn't summon up the energy. No doubt he sounded as though he didn't care. Not enough. 'Does she recognise you?' There was no hope in his voice.

'No. I don't think so.'

'Right.'

'She's quite well, though. Otherwise,' continued Daisy, with equal dreariness. 'Considering,' she added.

Simon felt patches of sweat bloom under his arms. His bones felt too big for his flesh, he felt squashed and tense, his skin was tight and uncomfortable. He imagined he was an explosive device, ticking. He concentrated very hard on his breathing. In. Out. In. Out. Slowly. Counting in his head. He sighed, dredged up something from somewhere. A respect for their past? A hope for their future? 'Considering what?' He asked. 'Her condition or mine?'

'It's not all about you, you know,' Daisy snapped.

'I was only trying to make a joke,' he said defensively.

'It's not a laughing matter.'

No. Nowhere near. He knew that. Simon nodded. Chastised. Sad. Hopeless. What could he say that would please her? Nothing. In the meetings, he'd been told to try to communicate. To find words. Not to bottle everything up. That had raised a half-smile. The expression 'bottle everything up'. Choice words when lecturing to a bunch of alcoholics.

'I often find myself thinking about our first date,' he said suddenly. Daisy stared at a spot over his shoulder, but he knew she was listening, even if she didn't want to be. 'What was the name of that Italian restaurant we used to go to? The one where all the customers shared bench seats and tables, just mucked in. Do you remember? You could take your own wine and just pay a couple of quid corkage. Was it Luigi's?'

'No. Carlo's,' she muttered, with obvious reluctance. Her desire to be factually correct temporarily outweighing her fury at him.

'That's it.' He nodded satisfied. Simon knew their first date was at Carlo's not Luigi's, he had deliberately made that mistake, so Daisy would engage. He was clever like that. 'We'd just scoot over, and some stranger would plonk themselves down. Stranger one minute, friend the next, because we always got talking to them, didn't we?'

'Often,' she admitted, because it was true. Simon had been gregarious once and had no problems starting a conversation with anyone.

'We eat at benches here, in the canteen. There isn't much swapping of small talk though,' he informed her. She scowled at him. He wasn't trying to make her pity him. He was just stating a fact. He saw her face close down. Pain, anger? Something. He shouldn't have told her that. She wasn't ready to hear about this place. He thought about Carlo's instead. A noisy, smoky, over-hot dive. They'd loved it! His heart swelled with longing. A saunter down memory lane was a coping strategy. He didn't want to be here. Of course not. Who would? She looked away, stared at the plastic table, refusing to go along with him. Unable, or unwilling, to give him what he needed. He carried on regardless.

'It was a warm night. And afterwards, when we left the restaurant, we walked around the streets. Just wandered, didn't we?' The bliss of that. What careless freedom. Wandering. 'The streets were crammed with tourists and locals, tumbling out of pubs and bars. We walked to a park. Which park was it?' It was Regent's and Daisy most likely knew that, but she didn't reply. 'There had been some sort of show. The actors were just leaving, still in costume.' His face, usually so tight and tense, cleared. 'Shakespeare, right?'

She shrugged. 'I don't remember.' She knew it was *A Midsummer Night's Dream*. He was certain she did.

It could have been the two bottles of white wine that they'd drunk, or the surreal situation of walking through a London park inhabited by imps and fairies, but Daisy had, in the past, confirmed that it was the most perfect and promising first date any woman could ever have hoped for. Romance shimmered in the air, like gossamer. Simon had taken off his socks and trainers and dangled his feet in the park fountain, she'd followed suit and joined him. They hadn't given a thought to how clean, or rather dirty, that water was. Daisy had been wearing linen trousers, he was in chinos, they rolled them up. Their thighs were pressed up against one another's, their bare arms too; hot and sticky. As the crowds had started to thin out, Daisy began to be concerned about when the gates would be locked, whether they'd be trapped in the park all night.

They'd ended up having al fresco sex in, or at least near, the fountain.

Unbelievable. A different life. A different world.

Simon wondered if Daisy was thinking about this too. He hoped so.

'Do you remember when we would spend ages just kissing?'

'Don't.'

'I'd find a curve or a freckle. It was like a wonderous thing. The most wonderous thing.'

'Stop it Simon.'

'I'm trying to say sorry, Daisy.'

'You can't. You can't say sorry for nearly killing a child. For killing our marriage. You don't get to say sorry because it's not enough.'

'I know that. I do know that. But how can I fix this?'

'I don't know. Maybe some things are so badly broken that they can never be fixed.'

'I don't believe that.'

'She was in hospital for weeks. There were complications. She nearly died and she'll never be a dancer.'

'She can be something else. Something else great. Kids want to be things at age six that they don't get to be.'

'How can you be so callous?'

He had sounded frustrated, indifferent. He wasn't that, he was lost. He was trying to be hopeful but he didn't know what she wanted. 'Why are you here, Daisy?'

40

Daisy

The silence stretches from his side of the table to mine. It stretches across the years we have been married — the happy and sad ones — smothering them. We used to have so much to say to one another. You do, at the beginning, don't you?

We would go to restaurants, not trendy loud ones, that's never been my thing. Most often an intimate place that served good pasta, somewhere where the waiters would shave parmesan over the dishes into satisfying mounds, rather than delicate sprinkles. I've always been a woman who appreciates carbs. Sometimes, we would be talking so much — laughing, joking about something or other — that we'd fail to notice that the other customers had dripped away, called it a night. More than once, tired waiters would start to sweep the floor around us, basically pushing us out of the door. We'd apologetically leave an over-generous tip and grab our coats, dash for the door.

'Grab your coat, you've pulled,' he'd say. It was a catch-phrase, a long time ago. Simon used it frequently, whenever we left anywhere, as we left my mum and dad's house after a Sunday tea, or if he picked me up from school. He'd put his head around the staffroom door and say, 'Grab your coat, you've pulled.' Not caring if the headmistress was sat there, sipping her tea, dunking her biscuits. It always made me giggle.

From our very first date we held hands in public. That was the thing that made me trust him. I'd dated enough shady men, who had multiple women on the go and couldn't risk public displays of affection. He used to make me feel safe. I used to believe in him. The ghosts of that happy couple seem to be dancing around our table. Haunting us. In prison they don't let you hold hands, it's in the rule list we were sent. I studied the list, as I used to study the rules for Millie's recitals that were sent from the dance school. I don't like breaking rules. Not that I want to hold Simon's hand. But if I did, I couldn't. I could be passing him something. A blade maybe. Would a wife do that? Pass her husband a blade? I suppose she might. If he was desperate enough. If she was. Although I don't know how such a thing would get past the entry searches. Most likely they are worried about passing drugs. There are certainly wives that would do that. Keen to provide a high, still.

I am not able to cheer him. That's not why I've come, although I think he hopes it might be. I don't know what to say to him anymore, nor does he know what to say to me. Too much has gone unsaid. I hate it here. I hate sitting amongst these violent men: thieves, rapists, murderers. I know there is violence and cruelty everywhere, but they are clustered here and that sickens me. It's squalid, frightening. By extension, I hate him for bringing this place into my life. The visit is painful, punctuated with silences and unvoiced accusations, reprisals, apologies. A swell of conflicting emotions that threaten to drown us both.

'I'm sorry, Daisy. This is hard for me.' He blurts suddenly. Hard for him! I look away from him: blink rapidly, fight back tears. 'Oh God, sorry. Now I've made you angry.' I shake my head. He upweights his comment. 'Furious?'

Maybe, or maybe I'm shocked, sad. I don't know what I feel. My heart is slamming against my ribcage. My breath seems stuck. It's too much. I feel too much. Loss, regret, fear, pain. None of it good. I want to find the words. I want to tell him about Daryll. Everything about Daryll. I never wanted to trick him into being Millie's Daddy. I just didn't know how to tell him the truth. And now we are here and I can't tell him that or anything. We became strangers long ago. We don't know each other anymore.

In a low, almost inaudible voice he leans towards me and confesses, 'I don't like getting visitors.' I snap my gaze towards his. Appalled.

'Don't you? I would have thought you did. Connie gives up her time to come and see you. Don't you appreciate that?' I sound shrill and pious. I wish I didn't. Honestly, her visiting him is between them. The truth is, his confession that he doesn't like visitors offends *me*. I'm *here* and he's telling me he doesn't like visitors. And yet, what right do I have to be offended? After all this time.

He rushes on, lamenting his truthfulness almost the moment it falls between us. 'Well I do, yes but . . . It's, complicated. I look forward to Connie's visits, but I dread them too.' He runs his hands through his hair. A deliberate, forceful move. 'After she's left, the comedown knocks me back for days. They're two very different worlds. The world I was in on the outside and the world I am in now. I'm required to be two entirely different people. A visit is like a collision of those different worlds.'

Simon flinches, instantly regretting his use of the word collision. It had been an innocent word before, now it is full of potency and doom.

He shuffles uncomfortably. 'And *you* visiting, I've longed for it, but I'm terrified of it too.'

I stare at him but say nothing. He thinks I'm judging him. That I believe he has no right to be moaning. After all, he is in here to be punished. Punishments are supposed to be uncomfortable, hard. But I'm not judging. I'm lost. Scared. I didn't come here expecting to learn that he has been longing to see me. We are over. We are finished. We are impossible. But.

'After today, I'll spend days wondering how you feel it went. How *you* are. And I'll worry about it,' he says.

'I'll be fine,' I lie, coldly.

'Will you? Are you?' Simon stares into my eyes, desperate. I don't add anything. Eventually he mutters, 'In here, everything is different. Well, that's bloody obvious.' His voice shudders. It is costing him, articulating this, saying anything at all, probably. 'I've had to build some sort of wall around myself, you know? A barrier to keep me sane and safe.'

I nod slowly. I understand barriers. Walls. But it is impossible to know how far my sympathy should extend. 'There were walls before,' I point out. 'The drink.'

'I'm not drinking, Daisy.'

'Well, you can't. You can't get to any.'

'I'm not going to drink on the outside either.'

I'd heard him say 'never again' at noon when he woke up after a bender and then at 5 p.m. he'd ask, 'Is it too early? The sun has set over the horizon somewhere, right? I just need the hair of the dog.' He probably sees my doubt, he must recall the endless empty promises.

He sighs. He can't want this level of emotional honesty. 'Yes. Yes, I know you've heard it all before.' He snaps impatiently. 'I'm just trying to explain that I struggle to bring down those walls and be the person I was on the outside.'

I don't mean to, it's instinctive, but my face curls into an involuntary sneer of disgust. 'I don't want that person,' I whisper, angrily.

'No, no understandably not. I didn't mean the man I was immediately before the accident.' I glare at him. 'I mean, I'm trying to find the old me. I'm trying to be the old me, Daisy. The person I was before I started drinking. I am apologising for not being *that* person. I'd like to be him again.' Simon stops speaking. His gaze drops from mine to the floor. After an age, he pulls his eyes back to mine. I can see doing so requires a huge effort, like pulling a cartload of bricks up a hill. 'Wouldn't you want to see that person again?'

It's a blow. It feels like someone has kicked me

in the gut and left me doubled in pain because seeing him like this reminds me of when we first met. When we were awash with hope, shyness and possibility. When we struggled to articulate our fleeting, intimate thoughts because we believed we'd be understood and communication mattered. I see now that he is not drinking, he's an entire man again. His mind and heart seem clearer. Beautiful.

I take a deep breath and say, 'I want a divorce, Simon.'

41

Simon

Simon hardly remembered walking back to his cell. He followed the line of slumped-shouldered men, who were battling the gloom of the fact that visiting time was over for another week. He put one foot in front of another. Hot with humiliation and disappointment. Burning with frustration. Sweat trickled down his back, pain shuddered through his being. She wanted a divorce. After all this time. True, Daisy hadn't visited in the three years since he'd been locked up, but he'd chosen to interpret that as a good thing. He'd told himself she didn't want to see him inside, so that they had a chance of continuing on the outside. Not quite an uninterrupted timeline but a pause rather than a full stop. He wasn't an idiot, he knew they were losing time, that he was. But he had thought that when he returned, sober and better, she'd want him back. That's what he'd believed.

Or at least hoped. It was one of the things he told himself to survive.

Maybe he was an idiot.

A spark of anger sizzled inside him. He swallowed hard. Tried to control it. Not allow it to burn through him. He knew pain, regret, fury could cremate a man.

He'd gone through so much here. The withdrawal had been hideous and yet he'd accepted it, welcomed it. The minute he woke up in that police station cell, the night after the horrible accident, he'd known that he'd never ever get sober on the outside. Maybe he had realised as much the moment Millie's body struck against the car and then flew into the sky, landing splat, crack on the road. He felt the thud clatter through his own body and knew he'd hit rock bottom. It hadn't been a logical, thought-out thing. It was instinct. Instinct as a father and a husband. He realised that prison could save him. Save *them*. It was their only chance. The instinct of a survivor, he supposed.

Withdrawal had been a process where he'd accepted and absorbed pain. Physical and mental. He vomited for so long and hard that his stomach retched until finally he was vomiting up blood. He shook and sweated, his heart almost beat out of his chest, his blood pressure soared. The headaches were severe enough to make him cry out. He actually screamed. On the outside he'd have been given an injection of Librium to ease the symptoms. Inside he was given a plastic bowl to vomit in.

A few days without alcohol, and he'd started to experience profound confusion and disorientation. It was terrifying as he struggled to differentiate between what was happening and what was in his head. It was hard enough that he was in a cell, arrested, a criminal. An alien situation, it was impossible to compute without the crutch of drink. Then came the hallucinations. Gruesome. He saw his daughter march into his cell, then a car came through the wall and crashed into her, mowed her down, flattened her. Blood and guts flew about, drenching his clothes, splattering his face. It was horrifying. He'd pulled himself into a tight ball and begged someone, anyone, to make it stop. He'd been unsure what was real, what was a nightmare. Hard to know, as he was living in a nightmare and steeped in paranoia, shame, grief.

Then, prison life. He'd dealt with the day-in, day-out humiliations: crapping in a room with another bloke watching; having to ask for access to a telephone, a visitor, or a bar of soap; making fucking hairnets. And the things he'd seen, heard, had done to him. He'd done his best to go unnoticed, stay beneath the cons' radar. Vanish. Still, he'd seen things, heard things; disturbing, scarring, cruel things that he would never quite be able to forget.

He'd endured the monotony, the waste, and the terrible food. He'd done it all for her but now she wanted a divorce.

He punched the wall. Fuck, that hurt. He'd probably broken his hand, but it felt good too. A relief. He punched it again. And again.

'Stop, stop it man,' Leon was up on his feet and dragging him away from the wall. Leon was skinny but towered above Simon. Normally, he maintained an air of passivity, calmness; he didn't give much away, but seeing Simon's outburst had riled him. 'We don't want any trouble. You can't mess up the cell,' he spat out the words. In fact, Simon hadn't damaged the wall, only his hand. It throbbed. Simon could hardly focus on what Leon was saying. He didn't care if he got into trouble. Or even if he got Leon into trouble. He couldn't care anymore.

'I need a drink,' he yelled.

'What? Man, no, no you don't.'

Since he'd arrived, he'd heard stories of inmates who stockpiled orange juice and sugar, marmite, sometimes a bit of fresh fruit if they could get hold of it. They fermented it into hooch. It sounded OK to him. He'd been warned that these ingredients were the most sanitised version of illegal juice, sometimes ketchup or bread, milk, jelly or cake frosting were used. Whatever they could get their hands on. Plastic bags of gunk would swell, balloon under beds, the stench not quite trapped by dirty towels or laundry bags. Sometimes there were floating colonies of mould. It was squalid and desperate. Everything about addiction was. He didn't care, he'd take some if he could.

'I'm going to talk to the Dale brothers. They brew, and I need a drink.'

'No, no, you're not thinking straight. You don't want to get involved with the Dales. Nasty crew. Dangerous. Sit down, tell me what happened.' Leon practically pushed Simon back into the small plastic desk chair, then he sat down on the bottom bunk bed opposite, the only other place to sit. 'Come on, what happened?' Simon turned his head away. 'You might as well tell me, there isn't exactly a queue of sympathetic ears in this place,' Leon insisted.

Leon and Simon were now friends, or as close as a person got to having a friend in here. Simon had to talk to someone. He couldn't look at Leon but kept his eyes on the dirty floor and muttered, 'Daisy wants a divorce.'

'Oh, sorry man.' Leon didn't sound particularly surprised. Simon found that annoying, offensive. His head shot up, and he glared at his cellmate but his anger was met with a shrug. 'Most of them do. The decent wives. Why would they want to stay with men like us? It's only the skanks and the desperate that stay with cons,' Leon explained.

'No,' said Simon firmly. 'Some very decent women stand by their men.' Even as he said the words he realised they were wholly inadequate. The domain of the wives of faithless politicians, or 1960s country and western singers.

Leon looked thoughtful. On the outside, he would have been recognised as emotionally intelligent. 'But would you really want her to? I mean *really*. If you love her you should let her go. If she's a decent woman, she deserves a decent man, not a con.'

Was that it? Simon wondered. Another man? He supposed it was an option. She'd betrayed him before. But it wasn't how he'd thought things were going to be. He'd imagined a different ending. 'Why would she ask for a divorce now?' he demanded.

'Well, you'll be out soon,' replied Leon. 'Think of it from her point of view. You're an OK bloke. I know that. You've been good to me. But you nearly killed your kid because you like getting pissed, and when you are on the outside, you'll be able to get pissed again. You'll stop being a decent bloke *again*. I mean, right now, yeah, you had a setback and the first thing you want is a drink. What will you be like on the outside?'

Simon gazed at Leon. It was hard to hear him. All he could think about was getting a drink. Getting out of this conversation and drinking until he couldn't remember any of it.

Leon seemed insistent on drawing attention to the harsh realities. 'There will be setbacks out there. You won't be able to get a job. Or someone will say something. Rub you up the wrong way. And you are going to reach for the bottle straightaway. If you love your wife then you should divorce her, let her get on with her life. You owe her that.'

'No, I don't.'

'Yeah, you sort of do.'

'No. I don't,' repeated Simon firmly. Then slowly, with a hint of menace he added, 'She owes me.'

Leon squinted. 'What do you mean?'

'I didn't nearly kill our daughter. She did.'

'What?'

'I just took the blame.' The air crackled with Simon's revelation.

'What the fuck? What are you saying?'

'She was driving. Not me.' Simon's voice quivered under the strain of the disclosure. It was so big. So dreadful. Leon squinted at him. Took a moment to see if he'd heard properly, if he'd understood.

'She was driving? Your wife was?'

‘Yes.’ Simon paused. ‘Look, I’m not blameless. I know that. I mean, we were fighting. I was drunk and distracting. I kept lunging for the radio. I wanted to turn it up louder. I was singing at the top of my lungs and she was worried about the neighbours, so she kept trying to turn it down again. She took her eyes off the road.’

‘Shit.’ Leon wiped his mouth, shook his head but continued to stare at his cellmate. Simon understood. He knew Leon was weighing it up. Judging him, deciding whether to believe him or not. Simon did his best to remain open and readable. It was hard, after years of trying to hide, lie and bury the truth. Tentatively, in his head, he crawled back into the moment, again this was something he’d tried to avoid doing. It was too much. Too pitiless. Remembering was cruel.

‘She wasn’t wearing her seatbelt,’ he muttered. ‘That was so unlike her. She’s normally all, ‘safety first’, but earlier I had tried to get in the driving seat of the car. We stopped at a garage to get some water and stuff. I was still pissed and trying to annoy her. I said I wanted to drive. I’m not even sure I did. I was just being a pain in the arse. You know? She’d had to push me out the way and then she set off driving in a fluster, so she didn’t put on her belt.’

The words swirled around the cell. Trapped, like the two men. Real and raw. Leon looked frightened, concerned. He still didn’t know what to believe. Everyone inside said they were innocent, banged up unjustly. Simon could be bullshitting. Yet there was something about the way he was telling the story — sorrowful, hopeless — that made Leon believe him, or at least made him want to listen to more.

'We were almost home. Just coming around the corner into our street. Music blaring, like I said. Daisy was cross about that, distracted. Millie just ran in front of the car. As quick as a flash. It was done in a second. Daisy swerved but hit a tree.'

'Fuck.'

'The impact was hard. She hit her head on the windscreen. She was out of it. Concussed.' Simon breathed in deeply, slowly. He'd buried these memories for so long, choked back the words a hundred times, they scratched his throat now as he made this confession and gave the truth life. 'I jumped out of the car. Checked on Millie first. Luckily, I wasn't so far gone as I'd drowned that instinct.' Simon shook his head, sad. Weary. 'You know, I've lost nearly every night I ever drank, so it was easy to pretend I'd lost that one too, but I never have. It's been in my head ever since. Banging away at my brain. Every last detail. Torturing me. I called the ambulance. I knew it was bad. I thought she was dead.'

'But I don't understand. Why did the police think you were driving?' asked Leon, sceptically.

'You know that weird clarity that sometimes takes over when you've been drinking? That certainty and focus?' Leon shrugged, he wasn't a big drinker. 'I'd had it before, sometimes it was bullshit. Sometimes I was focused on something trivial like getting a kebab and I would travel ten miles in a cab to find one, but that night the focus was for the good. I just knew. Instinctively, instantly knew.'

'Knew what?'

'That Daisy could never have lived with that. Killing her daughter. I realised she didn't have to. I could save her from that. I *wanted* to save her. I had to. I decided to take the blame. So I dragged her into the passenger seat and as I did so, she started to come around.'

'She can't remember any of this? Because she hit her head? Because she wasn't wearing a seatbelt?'

'Correct. I always thought there was a chance she'd remember what really happened at some point, but it appears she hasn't.'

'You are shitting me. You are making this up.'

'No, no I'm not,' replied Simon calmly.

'Wow. Wow.' Leon's mouth was wide open. He shook his head, trying to clear it. 'You did three years in here, for your Mrs?'

'We were lucky Millie pulled through. I suppose if I'd known for definite that she would I might have made a different call. But I don't think so. As I say, it wasn't something I thought about, it was a reaction. An impulse. I realise that as things turned out, since Millie recovered, it is unlikely Daisy would have got a custodial sentence as she hadn't been drinking, at least not enough to put her over the limit.' Simon sighed. 'But if Millie had died, Daisy couldn't have lived with herself. I'd have lost her anyway. At the time, when it happened, I thought it was our only chance. Me coming in here, instead of her.'

'You were drunk when you made the decision. You could have changed your mind at a later date, when you sobered up. Before it went to trial. Why didn't you?'

'Millie was in hospital for ages. By the time I knew she was safe it was too late to change my story. No one would have believed me if I had.'

Simon wouldn't say it, couldn't say it, even though he'd confessed so much to Leon, it was a step too far. But the truth was, his noble instinct had remained intact. He had never thought of changing his story. Daisy was a respected teacher, she brought out the best in kids doing their SATs, set them on to a path to do who knows what possible greatness. He was an unemployed interior designer, a drunk, who brought nothing but disgrace. Daisy visited his mother, talked to the doctors and care workers to ensure she got the best attention. He stole gin from her bedside cabinet. Daisy was Millie's mother. He didn't know what the hell he was. It had not been a difficult decision. Not really. Daisy did not belong behind bars.

Leon let out a low whistle. 'You must really love your woman,' he observed.

'I do,' Simon replied simply.

That two-word combination, so potent, so important, shimmied around the cell; an echo that temporarily countered the stale despair. He did. He loved her. He'd done the only thing he could. Even though she had betrayed him. Even though he was a drunk. Despite everything. He'd found a way to be the better man.

Simon felt strangely light. He'd held that story

close for three years. Every time he had spoken at meetings, he'd eased some pain, and grief, and guilt but he'd never been able to release that narrative. The only one that would heal him. The only one that would set him free, allow him to transcend the walls, slip through the bars, float above the barbed wire. He hadn't planned to tell anyone ever. He'd only told Leon because he'd suddenly felt a need to be respected again, even momentarily, even by a con.

'But she wants a divorce,' muttered Leon, now understanding Simon's despair.

'Yeah, she does. And I want a drink.'

42

Daisy

I run from the prison gate. Other visitors seem in a hurry too, the prison spits us out of its big mouth, like vomit. It's not a good summer's day; after a hot spell, storms are threatening. It's spotting with rain already, thick, heavy drops. I shiver, pull my jacket around me, but I can't get warm. I spot Daryll across the road, stood outside his car, waiting for me. I see him before he sees me. I watch as his eyes sift through the crowds. I briefly consider turning around and going in the opposite direction. But it's a stupid thought. I move towards his car. Suddenly, the threat of rain is a reality. The heavens open. The rain falls down my face. I'm glad. He can't see my tears.

He notices me and grins, holds his arms wide, waiting for me to fold into them. What a picture that would make, what a touching scene. I see one or two other women sling a smile in our direction. He is every inch the supportive, attentive boyfriend. I don't fall into his arms but dash around to the passenger side of the car and say, 'Let me in, I'm getting soaked.'

'How did it go?' he asks. I nod. It's not really an answer, just an acknowledgement that I've heard his question. I can't afford to ignore him. He unlocks the car. When we get in, he cranks up the heater. 'That rain came from nowhere,' he comments, pleasantly.

'Yes,' I mutter, hoping that he's not going to make me talk about the visit. That would be best. It's possible he assumes I've followed instructions and therefore there is nothing to discuss. I never know with Daryll, what he'll do or say next. What he thinks of as normal. Daryll checks his mirror, indicates and then carefully manoeuvres out into the traffic. He makes a point of being a conspicuously safe driver. I should appreciate that.

'How was he?'

My heart sinks. So, we are going to talk about Simon. I'm not sure I can find the words to describe what we've just been through. I don't know what I was expecting; seeing Simon after all these years was never going to be easy. I should have known there would be strangeness, silences, strain. And yes, there were all of those things in abundance. I had not expected to feel any sympathy. I had not anticipated the strength of the pull of his familiarity. There were mannerisms, the way his nostrils flare, the way his ears move when he raises his eyebrows, gestures that I hadn't realised I remembered but are tattooed on my brain. I slide my eyes towards Daryll. I've known him since being an undergraduate at university, but he is a stranger to me. We've eaten meals together, I've watched him clean his teeth and put his feet on my coffee table as he stretches out in front of the TV. He has slept in my bed, but he is still a stranger.

'So, how was he?' Daryll pursues his point with a little more bite.

'Thin, pale,' I mutter.

Daryll glances in the mirror. It's almost a non-gesture, almost imperceptible, but I guess he was checking his tan. Reassuring himself that he is bronzed, healthy, large. A contrast. 'You asked for a divorce?'

'Yes.'

Daryll nods, satisfied.

'He seemed shocked,' I murmur.

'Really? Well, he shouldn't be.'

'Sad,' I add quietly, as I turn my head and look out of the window. I'm met with a depressing street scene. Rain in the summer time ruins things. People are rushing, holding newspapers over their heads that have long since turned soggy and ineffectual, they slide about in their flipflops, unprepared and irritated because of that. Still, they are outside and free to dash across the road, into the corner shop. They can pick up a magazine, a carton of milk, a Diet Coke whenever they want. Getting wet in a downpour is a coveted privilege that the prisoners I've just encountered must dream about.

I wonder what Simon dreams about. I daren't think that it's me, or Millie.

I wonder if he also has nightmares about the night it happened. About everything that went before. How is he, right at this moment? What an extraordinarily basic thing for him to confess, that the let-down after someone has visited almost wipes out the pleasure of the visit.

Not that he can have gained much pleasure from my visit. Suddenly, I feel ashamed about the way I blurted out my request for a divorce. I hadn't planned to bring it up so sharply. Although I can't imagine a good way of asking for a divorce. I think of the tips of his fingers. They were still. I think of his hands, clasped together, elbows on the table, leaning as close to me as was allowed. His stillness surprised me. He used to constantly fidget. Incessantly drum his fingers. It drove me mad. I guess that was the drink. And now he is still.

'Well, he only has himself to blame,' says Daryll confidently. We are pulled up at a red light. He puts his hand on my knee and squeezes, too tightly. He has huge hands, paws. Like a bear. I am not a small woman, but he makes me feel fragile. Breakable. 'Did you tell him about us?' I shake my head. Daryll sighs, disappointed in me.

'I didn't want to hurt him,' I confess. 'I can't imagine how he will feel when he learns Millie isn't his biological daughter.' How will I ever tell him this? I don't want to. I've never wanted to but Daryll is insistent that I do. That I tell everyone. I've said I will but that I need time. I suggested we have a dinner party and announce it properly. I said it was the right thing to do after all the sneaking around, after all the lies and secrets. He liked that idea but he immediately pointed out that my place is too small to host a dinner party. Actually, I've thrown a number of successful kitchen suppers for my friends and sister, but I knew that cosy approach wouldn't meet Daryll's approval. I suggested we waited until he has the keys to his new home. He corrected me. '*Our* new home, Daisy.'

'Yes, of course.'

Which gives me four weeks.

The lights change and Daryll carefully slips into gear, pulls forward a metre or two. The cars are crawling along. The whole world has ground to a halt because of the rain.

'You know, I've been thinking about Simon and I imagine he already has an idea that Millie isn't his,' comments Daryll.

'You do?' I'm shocked at the suggestion. 'Why do you say that?'

'Oh, I don't know. I just think back to that night, the one of the collision.' Daryll, unlike everyone else, does not speak about 'the accident'. I should be grateful for that. 'He was so weirdly on edge at Connie's party. Aggressive. Angry. Wouldn't you say? Not at all normal. Didn't you notice?'

I can't honestly remember. His moods were turbulent that summer, and before, if I'm brutally honest. 'I'd long since lost sight of what was normal with Simon,' I admit with a sigh.

'He was knocking back the booze.'

'Yes, but it was a party.' I don't know why I'm defending Simon on this particular point, to Daryll of all people. I should shut up.

'I thought he had that bitter air about him, a man stung. A man aware he'd been played for a fool.'

I shoot Daryll a look. I can't stop myself. 'He

hadn't been played.'

'Yes, he had, Daisy,' Daryll affirms smoothly. I flush scarlet but don't know how to respond. Daryll has always had a way of closing things down. Wiping out nuance. 'I've often wondered if he didn't do it on purpose.'

'What? What do you mean?' I demand, shocked.

'Just what I say. If he had worked out she wasn't his, he'd have been furious, humiliated. I'm not suggesting that he'd have tried to kill her if he was stone cold sober, but he wasn't stone cold sober, was he? Something subconscious was going on. Maybe he wanted her gone.'

Daryll shrugs and leaves the horrifying suggestion hanging in the air. No. No. That's impossible. Simon wouldn't have deliberately hurt Millie. *Never*. I can't believe that. I won't. Simon made some careless mistakes, true. The time in the bathroom when he left her unattended and she slipped, and the occasions he forgot to pick her up from a class or a playdate, and I'd get a call from a harassed teacher or a concerned parent, were examples of neglect, true. The result of his drinking, yes. But the thought of him inflicting deliberate hurt is ludicrous.

Yet, something clicks into place in my brain. On that journey home, I remember Simon asked me if I was having an affair with Luke. To be precise, he asked if I was fucking Luke. Suddenly I feel buried in dread and panic. He had worked it out. He knew Millie wasn't his. Daryll is right about that much. But that is all. I do not believe, not for a moment, that Simon might have wanted rid of her.

I turn away from Daryll and notice a father and daughter running along the street, hand in hand. The little girl's toes had come out of one of her sandals, but she continues to run with the sandal flopping around her ankle, held only by the strap. After a step or two, the father notices and stops. He kneels down in the rain and takes off her sandal, puts it back on again, tightening the strap just the correct amount, so she can run securely. His shirt turns dark as the rain splatters onto his back. Drenching him.

I think of Millie sat on the stairs in our old home and Simon bent over, carefully mastering how to correctly tie her ballet slippers. Tender, precise, wishing to do a good job.

Then I think of the fact she'll never dance again.

I think of Simon arranging her food on her plate into a picture, usually a face. Chicken arranged to look like hair, carrot sticks making eyebrows, tomatoes arranged to look like lips and peas grouped in piles for eyes. She used to giggle at his masterpieces and then gobble down food that, if I presented in the regular way, she would reject.

But I think of the months she spent in hospital, with no appetite at all.

I see him blowing bubbles in the back garden, I see him crawling on all fours whilst she rode on his back yelling, 'Giddy up horsedaddy.' I see him talking to her teachers at school about her reading books, her friendship groups, her mislaid pencil case. I see him holding baby Millie and saying, 'She's the most beautiful girl in the world, Daisy.' I'd tried to smile but it was only minutes after the birth. I was confused, in pain, exhausted. Mostly I was afraid. He saw the concern in my face and tried to reassure me. 'I'm going to do everything I can to look after our little girl. To protect her. I'm going to bring up a Daddy's girl, I promise you,' he'd laughed. I'd never been a Daddy's girl. I always thought girls that were had such confidence, such an advantage. I remember him singing 'You Are the Sunshine of My Life', as he held her close to his chest and jiggled her up and down, dancing around the room. I can see him do it.

He would never hurt her.

I slyly try to wipe away the tears that are now falling pretty fast. Daryll tuts, irritated to notice I'm upset. He wants me to move on. Not look back.

'You did the right thing asking for a divorce,' he says firmly. Daryll smiles at me. Reaches over and squeezes my leg again. 'And, now that's done, I think it's time we talked to Millie and set things straight there.'

Panic shoots through my body. 'It's too soon,' I mutter. Poor Millie. She's been through such a lot for one so young. How on earth is she supposed to cope with the news that her daddy is not her daddy? That I am divorcing that man, and this man — this stranger — is going to be her daddy from now. That he has been all along.

'No. Daisy, it's long past due,' replies Daryll sharply.

'Please don't make me. Not yet. Please,' I beg. I shouldn't beg him. I know it never works.

43
Daisy

I am so relieved when Daryll drops me off outside Connie's house and says he's not coming in.

'There's somewhere I need to be,' he says, mysteriously. He likes to make a mystery out of his life. He tells me little about what he does or who he sees when he's not with me. I never ask. I don't care. Should I? It's clear he thinks I should when he adds, 'Aren't you curious about who I'm with when we're not together? Aren't you jealous?' He strokes my cheek, but I move my head away.

'Someone might see.'

'We don't have to creep around anymore, Daisy,' he says with a laugh.

'We don't want to ruin the surprise of the announcement,' I mumble as I scramble for the door handle and clamber out of the car.

'I might come over later. If you play your cards right. Late, when Millie's in bed.'

I don't reply but rush up Connie's path. Her door swings open with the sort of efficiency that suggests she has been watching from the window. 'Was that Daryll?' she asks.

'Yes,' I reply, looking over her shoulder,

desperate to rest my eyes on Millie.

'You should have invited him in.' I know Connie is curious about my new relationship and desperate to get me to open up about it a bit more. She's probably wondering why I haven't indulged her by swapping any gossipy details. I don't know where to start. Anything I say will lead to my lie, so it's best not to say anything at all. Right now, all I need is Millie. I need a fix of her. I need to be fixed *by* her.

Connie clocks me scouring the house and understands. 'Millie and Sophie are upstairs with Fran and Auriol. They are all playing with Eric'

Millie adores her kitten and wouldn't hear of leaving him alone all day. We had to drag the poor thing halfway across London in a travel box.

'They're good kids.'

'They are. Do you want a cup of tea?' I really want to dash upstairs and just check on Millie. Just see her sat with her friends. Safe. Content. But I can't, it would look peculiar. Neurotic. It would embarrass her. Instead I say yes to the offer of tea and yell a cheery, 'Hello girls' up the stairs. I identify Millie's happy 'Hi Mum', in amongst the plethora of greetings. That's enough.

I follow Connie through to the kitchen where I find Lucy, sat on a bar stool, leafing through some specialist architect magazine belonging to Luke. My heart sinks a little when I see her, as it always does. I've accepted that she's likely to always be part of my life, as long as Connie is. It doesn't mean I have to like the fact. I'm grateful to Connie for looking after Millie this afternoon, Rose couldn't do it — she and Craig are on holiday — but I know the price she will be hoping to extract is a low down.

I'm proven right when Connie passes me a towel to dry off my hair and cuts to the chase, asking, 'So, how did it go?' I can't believe she's expecting me to offload when Lucy is here. Although I can, Connie seems oblivious to the fact that I still have an issue with Lucy. I suppose she reasons that as Rose doesn't, I can't possibly have. She thinks we're all old friends. That scars have just thickened our skin.

'Hard,' I admit. 'He's changed.' Connie and Lucy nod. 'Where's Luke?' I ask, trying, but not expecting, to change the subject.

'At some design exhibition. He did tell me which one, but I forget,' replies Connie, dismissively. She immediately returns to what interests her. 'So, what did you talk about? Where did you start?'

I sigh and decide to bite the bullet. 'I asked him for a divorce.'

'What?' Connie nearly scalds herself as she was pouring the boiling water from the kettle into the mugs and is distracted by my declaration. 'But why?'

'Because he almost killed my daughter.'

'But why *now*? You've known that for three years.'

'Because he's about to get out. We need to put things in order. It can't be a total shock to you.' This conversation is between Connie and I. Lucy says nothing, although she doesn't take her eyes off me. She's taking it all in. 'You are the one that's been telling me to move things along,' I add huffily.

'Well, to sort things out.'

'That's exactly what I'm doing.'

'But I thought there would be some discussion. A time to see if you could work things out. Give it a go.'

I stare at her, dumbfounded. 'Isn't this what you wanted? You set me up with Daryll at your dinner party.'

'That's what you think? I've had you over for dinner with a number of spare men over the past three years,' points out Connie. 'I was just evening up the table plan.'

I search her face. She looks entirely honest. It occurs to me that what she's saying is correct. She's introduced me to a dentist, a landscape gardener, a banker and a lesbian trade unionist. I have never left the dinner party with any of them, and there has never been a sense of expectation that I should, or disappointment when I didn't. Why did I think things were different when I discovered Daryll in her kitchen? Did I project? Did I read more into the situation because of my past with him? I try to remember why I was so sure she was setting me up, that she wanted Daryll and I to be a couple. And anyway, why would it make a difference to me what she thought? I rub my temple. I'm tired. There's too much going on. I remember that when Daryll took me home, he suggested that, 'our friends' clearly thought we would make a 'lovely couple'. Was that when the idea took hold? I can't pin this on Connie.

I stare at her. She looks genuinely taken aback. Bemused. 'Honestly, I was quite surprised when you left with him that night. You've never left with anyone before. Not that I'm judging either way,' she adds in a rush. Connie's blue eyes are wide, I know she's desperately trying to say the right thing but unsure of what that is. 'I knew you were seeing him, but I assumed it was some sort of flirtation. You know, an ego boost. I mean it's just been a few weeks. You've never been the sort of person to rush into anything.'

By this, Connie means she's assumed there is no sex involved. She probably thought he was taking me on long edifying walks across Hampstead Heath or maybe we'd had the odd jaunt to an arthouse cinema to watch a foreign film. She has imagined any relationship I might have now would be akin to those I had at uni and in my twenties before I met Simon. She thinks she knows me. It's true, other than Simon — who I had sex with on our first date — I always waited for months before I got intimate. But I was young back then. Everything was different.

'But a divorce? So suddenly?' She seems stumped, sad. She slumps on to a stool.

'Did you think we'd carry on as normal? That he'd move back in with us?'

'I thought there might be a chance. I've been visiting him throughout, Daisy. I believe he has feelings for you. Honestly, I thought you had feelings for him.'

'I don't know what gave you that idea. He's an alcoholic.'

'People have feelings for alcoholics!' she snaps. 'Why are you always so judgy? Didn't you ever do anything wrong?' I can't answer her. We stare at one another, an angry stalemate that is cushioned by years of friendship and rooted in concern. Eventually she adds, 'Besides, he's changed.'

'They don't change.'

'Do you want milk in your tea?' This question comes from Lucy. Connie and I turn and stare at her. Blinking. She pours milk into all three mugs and then slides them across the breakfast bar. If this was anyone else, I would assume they were trying to helpfully break the tension; I realise that most likely Lucy is simply bored of the conversation.

Anyway, Connie is undeterred. She continues, 'I hadn't realised this thing with Daryll was so serious. I mean, you haven't said much about it.'

'We're not still kids. I don't need to give you a blow by blow account,' I snap.

Connie looks a bit offended, I sound sharper than I intended but I have to keep her at bay.

'Would you like to talk about him now?' Lucy asks.

I jolt with surprise, the hot tea splashes over the rim of my mug.

'No, I wouldn't. Since you ask, I don't think my relationship with him or any other man is anyone's business but my own.' Connie stares at me, shocked. I know I'm behaving like a bitch. I'm pushing her away. It's for the best.

Lucy simply says, 'I understand.'

'In fact, I need to go. I've just remembered

that I have something to do.'

'What?' asks Connie. I can't decide if she's being polite and taking a genuine interest, or being impertinent and openly doubting that I could have anything better to do than sit here gossiping with her. The fact is, I have a lot to do and if I stay here I might break. I might say more than I should.

'Things,' I reply vaguely and stand up, bustle to the bottom of the stairs and call up to Millie. 'Come on, Millie. We have to leave *now*.'

'No time to finish your tea?' Connie asks.

'No,' I reply firmly. It takes Millie a Jurassic age to amble down the stairs, gather up her stuff, put Eric into his travel box and finally head for the door. She so obviously does not want to leave, and keeps breaking off to have conversations with Sophie. By contrast, Connie, Lucy and I wait in silence. I glare at the floor, but I can feel their eyes on me. Penetrating, questioning. It's a relief when we are on the step and the door bangs behind me.

44
Simon

All afternoon, Leon begged Simon not to approach the Dales.

'You're so close man. Nearly out of this hell hole. Don't fuck it up.'

But Simon wouldn't listen, couldn't hear. 'There's nothing for me on the outside. It doesn't matter anymore.'

'The Dales, they're bad news. You know that, yeah.'

He did, but he didn't care. The Dale brothers didn't brew hooch themselves, largely because the process was smelly and inconvenient, and they did not want that sort of mess and stench emanating from their own cells. They did, however, decide who could take the risk and then they took a cut of profits made, for granting those cons permission. They also decided who could get access to the drink. The brewers wouldn't sell it to you without the approval of the Dale brothers. Since Rick Dale had moved out of his cell, Simon had avoided the Dales as much as he could. He'd never gone anywhere near their dining table, their cells; he left the gym if he saw the brothers and their gang walk in; he spent most of his time in the library, a place neither man ever set foot. But that very evening during Association Time he knocked on their door, walked into the lion's den. A lamb.

'Hello, Simon,' said Rick, 'Long time no see.'

Simon felt uncomfortable that Rick Dale remembered his name, but he should have expected it. They remembered everything. Knew everything. Because information was power. This was yet another grimy reminder of what his life had become; he was on first-name terms with a violent, ruthless killer. He didn't want to remember that, or anything. He wanted to forget. 'To what do we owe this pleasure?'

'I want a drink.' Simon wondered if they could hear the fear in his voice, whether that or the desperation shouted the most.

'Do you now?'

Simon nodded. 'I need one.' He did. Needed it. Longed for it. Had to have it. Being sober meant that things were sharp and more audible; since Daisy's visit, he needed the roar and the blur. No matter what. He missed the bubbly recklessness, the padded landing that being drunk provided. He'd served three years in prison for that woman and she wanted a divorce. OK, she didn't know he'd served the time for her. Although — and this thought ripped him in half — what if she did know?

What if she had remembered the night and had left him in here to rot anyway?

It was too much to stand. How could he ever be sure? She was a liar. A cheat.

More than once, he had asked Connie what Daisy remembered about the night of the accident, and he'd always been told, 'Absolutely nothing. She wishes she could.' But was she screwing him over? *Again*. What had he done? What had he sacrificed? In the moment he'd made the decision to take the heat there had been some logic to it, some majesty, chivalry even. Seeing Millie's body sprawled out in the rain; blood and hope running into the gutter had made him think he had to get sober. He knew he couldn't do that on the outside.

Now he knew he'd been kidding himself. He needed his old mate, alcohol. It was all he could depend on. He was never going to be sober. Inside or out, he was an alkie. So what?

'Have you got a drink?' Simon demanded. His voice came out more aggressive than he intended but he didn't care. He didn't care about anything. The big man — who accompanied the brothers everywhere — six foot wide and tall, stood up slowly and stepped towards Simon. His stance said he didn't like Simon's tone. It was impossible to back down now. Simon took a step towards the giant and squared up to him as best he could.

'Easy tiger,' murmured Pete Dale, the older brother. Simon wasn't sure who was being asked to step down; he was relieved when the mountain of a man stepped back,

'Have you got a drink that you'd think of sending my way?' Simon clarified, choosing to ignore the silent stand-off. It wasn't that he was fearless, he was careless. Drink, the getting and having, had always made him careless and now more so than ever, apparently.

'It costs,' Pete Dale informed him. Not money. Well, not *just* money. Simon knew that much, after three years inside. He'd be made to pay in a myriad of ways. Favours, covers, lies.

'I'll pay.'

'You're nearly out,'

'I am.'

'You could be useful.'

Simon nodded. 'I'll need a job.'

Pete and Rick exchanged a look. Eventually, Pete the decision-maker nodded. Rick reached under the bottom bunk mattress and pulled out a quarter bottle of whisky. *Whisky*. It was too good to be true. Simon had been expecting access to some poxy hooch. Something that was likely to burn his gut but would at least blunt his pain. Rick held out the small bottle.

'Take it.' Pete urged.

'All of it?' Simon asked, fearful and yet excited. He could imagine the liquid carousing down his throat.

'Yeah.'

Simon hesitated. That was a lot of whisky. If he took it, the debt would be substantial. Debts were always disproportionate in here. He'd seen prisoners become sex slaves because someone had swapped a work rota. But if he didn't take it now, if he just turned around and walked out the cell, he'd owe them anyway because he'd asked for something and they'd agreed to his request. Besides, he wanted the drink. He'd be mad not to. Rick shook the bottle, slightly. The amber liquid shimmied. Simon snatched it.

'Lads, lads, sorry to interrupt.' It was Leon.

He looked flustered, nervous. 'The screws are cell-spinning. I think they're heading your way. I just wanted to let you know.' He threw the comment out, it was directed towards the Dales although Leon was careful to keep his head down.

'There's been no word,' said Rick, suggesting they were usually warned when the screws were planning a shakedown. Everyone cocked their head and sure enough the sounds of irritated yells, heavy boots, sassy comments and sharp put-downs suggested Leon's report was accurate. Cells were being searched. Flustered, Simon threw the as-yet-untouched bottle of whisky on to the bunk and quickly left, bustling Leon out in front of him. He didn't see what Pete and Rick did with their contraband, but he guessed the mountain man took it, hid it in his room, or got someone else to take the rap. Someone who owed a favour.

'Fuck,' swore Simon, once he and Leon were safely ensconced back in their own part of the block. Their cell had been searched and found to be clean. 'That was a once in a lifetime offer. They won't offer me whisky again.'

'It's good news. You didn't drink anything. Another day sober,' said Leon.

'Fuck that,' snapped Simon. He was a man who lived with regrets. When he drank he used to regret whatever had caused Daisy's silent fury or the unexplained bump, then his regrets escalated. He'd lost his job, Millie, Daisy, his freedom. Right now, all he regretted was walking away from the whisky. What could he do?

Suddenly he had an idea, he turned to Leon. 'Hey, you did them a favour today. Saved them getting caught with anything. Maybe you could ask them for the drink?'

'Piss off, Simon,' said Leon wearily. He then climbed on to his bunk, faced the wall and fell silent.

45
Daisy

Millie isn't best pleased about being pulled away from playing with Sophie. No doubt she hoped we'd all spend the evening together. So she's a bit sulky and as soon as she finishes her supper, she scoops up Eric and says she wants an early night. I doubt she means sleep, most likely she'll be dividing her evening between playing with the kitten and sending outraged WhatsApp messages to Sophie, complaining about the unfairness of life, my unreasonableness in particular. Fine by me. It's not great parenting, to allow her to be on social media all night, but it's the path of least resistance and that's all I'm capable of right now. The hardest thing about being a single parent is that when you are exhausted, either physically or mentally, there is no one to pass the baton to. Ever. Tonight, I just don't have it in me to try and talk her round or cheer her up by offering a movie night with popcorn. Besides, I have things I need to be getting on with.

I lock the doors. Put the chains on. Close the curtains. As Millie has gone to bed, I don't switch on any lights or lamps, even when it starts to get dark outside. It's better if the house looks empty. Daryll said he might come here.

Although, he might not; he often says it's a possibility but then doesn't show. He likes to keep me on my toes. On edge. If he does come I want him to think I've stayed late at Connie's. I can't face him tonight. I just can't.

I pour myself a large glass of white wine. I don't often drink alone. For obvious reasons. Tonight, I'm grateful for the past-its-best bottle lingering in the fridge. I want to dash, as speedily as possible, into that state when I can't quite think, feel or remember as sharply. I put on the TV, not that I imagine any of the Saturday night shows will hold my attention. They're all too buoyant, too loud for my mood. I struggle to absorb their relentless upbeat tone so I put on a DVD instead. I'm probably the last person in the UK to still have a DVD collection, but I find it so easy to sling a little disc into a machine, rather than battle with three remote controls and choose between two million TV channels. I select *Roman Holiday*. A romantic classic. It's always been a favourite of mine. I discovered it before I met Simon and that's useful. I find any old movies that have memories of him attached are a bit too hard. Even comedies like *Guardians of the Galaxy* are uncomfortable because I remember him dampening the trip to the cinema as he was agitated, keen for a drink and unwilling to sit for a couple of hours without one. Remembering Simon acting like that hurts me. Then, I remember how when he loved the movie his eyes twinkled and his face creased as he laughed out loud, finally got lost in the comedy. Remembering Simon acting like a regular husband kills me.

I press mute and let the film play silently in the background. On the off-chance Millie is trying to sleep, I don't want to disturb her. Sound travels in our small house; it's cheaply insulated and sound-proofed. That's caused me some concern recently. I wonder what exactly, she's heard. I've tried so hard to ensure she's not disturbed. It's OK doing without the sound. I'm not planning on watching the movie. I have far too much to do. Besides, I know it so well that I can recite most of the lines. It's just something to have in the room, to stop the loneliness creeping in. Although loneliness does usually find a way in anyhow, it curls like smoke underneath the front door. Suffocating.

Right, enough. Those sorts of thoughts won't help. I'm feeling sentimental. Vulnerable. It's the drink. It must be. I need to remember I was lonely when I lived with Simon too, at least some of the time. It was far from perfect.

I need to get busy. We can't take much with us. A suitcase and a backpack each. Any more will be too cumbersome. I don't know where we're going, where we will live. There's a possibility that we'll be moving around for a while, so we can't drag huge amounts of luggage with us. I need to be ruthless. It's impractical to imagine I'll pack anything other than essentials. My first thought was to move to Canada, perhaps somewhere near Simon's sister. I briefly had this idea that Simon could join us. But that's madness. How is my sister-in-law likely to greet me if she ever discovers why I had to run? And besides, Simon is on-licence, he can't leave the country for another three years. He drove our car into our daughter, not something I can forget. We're not a family anymore. It's weak and crazy of me to daydream about a happy ending for us. Then I wondered whether we might go to Australia. I have an old friend living out there, Sam and her husband James and their children. They are somewhere near Melbourne. Sam's Facebook feed it always full of pictures of her kids, playing in swimming pools looking tanned, healthy and happy. It would be nice to go somewhere where I have a contact, a start, not just an absolutely terrifying blank canvas. But I ruled out that possibility too, because Sam is an old work pal of Connie's, that's how we met. How can I explain to Sam that Connie mustn't know where I am? I have to be brave. I have no choice. I must cut everyone completely out of our lives. To keep Millie safe, I have to give up everyone and everything. My friends, my family. I can't bear the idea that it will be for ever. I can't think that now. Maybe after some time I could contact my parents and Rose, ask them to keep the secret. I have to be realistic about which country I'll be allowed to emigrate to. I'll need to sell the house and have my half of it forwarded on, as most countries that I'm considering need proof of financial independence. I have an estate agent booked to come and give a valuation on Monday. Tomorrow, I'm going to have to do a huge clean up. There's a lot to do.

I pour myself a second glass of wine. The first one has gone down surprisingly quickly, considering how cheap and old it is. A flash of concern shimmies through my body. I'm always hyper-aware of the dangers of using alcohol to unwind, to combat stress, to blackout anything awful. But then I remind myself that my consumption of alcohol is within the realms of normal, as is my attitude towards it.

I search through the drawer where I keep passports, certificates and medical records, and other important documentation. I dig out everything I think might be useful but force myself to leave Millie's swimming and 'Kind Behaviour in Class' certificates. My eye flits to the pile of old photo albums, stashed in the same drawer. Millie was born into a digital age and all her baby photos are on my computer or phone; these albums are pre-her. Pictures of me at university and then in my first flat. Ones of Simon and I on early dates. Our wedding album. Photos of our holidays and day trips. I hesitate, knowing that leafing through them brings me as much pain as it does pleasure. There's no way I can carry these with me, it doesn't make sense even wanting to. If I'm going to start again why should I want to look back? Yet, I wonder whether I might have time to scan the images, upload them to The Cloud and access them again somewhere halfway around the world. Scanning takes an age. Maybe I can just take photos of them on my phone. The quality won't be great, but it's something, better than nothing,

I carefully pick up the top album, open it up. The tissue paper, between the pages, flutters, filling the room with the ghost of luxury and promise. There we are. So familiar yet so distant. I pick up my phone and start to take snaps of the photos. I tell myself I'm doing this for Millie. At some point in her life she will ask about her daddy, I know she will, and I haven't yet worked out exactly what I will tell her to explain our flit, but I will at least be able to show her these pictures. Pictures of when her mum and dad were so in love and had a shiny future in front of them. I carry on for quite some time, inevitably pausing, studying photos for longer than necessary. A drop of water splashes on to the photo album. I look up at the ceiling, my first thought a leak. Then, I realise I'm crying. Seeing Simon today has been harder than I imagined. I had expected the environment to be brutal, to feel scared, for him to have changed, for me to feel distant. But I had not expected to *recognise* him. Recognise him in that deep, connected way people do if they've lived with someone for years and years. The smell of him. The way he moves his head. The way he shrugs. I hadn't thought I'd still know him so well. But sober, he is the man I knew a long time ago.

My doorbell rings. I jump, startled but then freeze. I won't answer it. I can't. Not tonight. I just can't face Daryll tonight. He won't start banging on the door, will he? He wouldn't want to wake Millie. To date, he's always been as careful as I have, to be silent, but I don't know if that is consideration specifically or just part of the thrill. Daryll is unpredictable. My phone beeps. Again, I jump. I carefully reach for it, nervous about what the message might say. I let out a sigh of relief. It's from Lucy.

Are you in? I'm stood outside. I think you are in.

I'm so relieved that it's not Daryll, I don't spend any time wondering what Lucy can want with me. I stand up and answer the door. Lucy is on the step, holding an expensive-looking bottle of wine.

'Can I come in?' she asks. Her coming here alone and uninvited is unprecedented and so I'm stunned into simply nodding and waving her through. I lock the door behind her. She stands in the small hallway and watches me draw the chain across the lock. 'Do you want a drink?' She holds up her bottle.

'Yes. OK. Good timing actually, I've just finished off the bottle that I had in the fridge.' If Lucy disapproves of my drinking alone, which is unlikely, she's cool enough not to let it show. I expect her to confidently stride into the kitchen and search out glasses the way Daryll did the first time he visited, but she doesn't. She hangs back and waits until I lead the way. I open the wine in silence and pour us both a large glass. It's too late for moderation, at least for me.

'I've brought snacks too,' she adds, dipping into her large, leather bag, that is oh-so-artfully-artlessly slung over her shoulder. She produces salt and vinegar Pringles, my all-time favourite snack, which has remained my preferred choice despite the invention of Kettle Chips and other temptations. She also produces a large slab of Dairy Milk, the sort with hazelnuts in. I actually gasp. I can't kid myself. These sorts of snacks have never passed Lucy's lips. They are thoughtful gifts, bought to please me.

I eye her warily.

'I thought things were a bit odd between us all, today,' she says, by way of explanation.

'Things are always a bit odd between us,' I comment, daringly. Then I stare accusingly at my wine glass. I'd never have been so blunt without the Dutch courage. To my surprise Lucy laughs.

'I love that about you, Daisy. You refuse to pretend anything is something it's not. You are refreshingly honest.' Then she pauses and stares right at me. 'Usually.'

I blush. Her gaze is so penetrating I almost believe she can read my mind. 'Shall we go through?'

We sit at either end of the sofa. I wait to hear what she has come to say. She so clearly has something on her mind. Lucy glances at the TV and comments, 'Oh, Audrey Hepburn. You've always loved her, haven't you?'

'Yes,' I mumble, surprised she recalls something so trivial about me.

'Do you remember when we went shopping for your wedding dress? You wanted a dress like the one Audrey Hepburn wears for the ball in *My Fair Lady*. Or, more accurately, you wanted your own transformational moment. Not quite guttersnipe to duchess, but Daisy to Audrey.'

I nod. I do remember the occasion very well. Doesn't every woman remember hunting for her wedding dress? No matter how many years pass. I'd initially been quite unrealistic about what might suit my curvy figure. Some might say delusional. Connie, Rose, Lucy and Sam all accompanied me on my wedding dress hunt. I remember emerging from the changing room in a wholly inappropriate gown. It was so tight I could barely move in it. I thought I might cry with disappointment when I looked in the mirror. Not so much elegant as elephant. Humiliated and frustrated I'd waited for Lucy to lash me with her caustic tongue. But she surprised me. She pointed out that Simon loved my curves. She reminded me that he was marrying *me*. A woman he'd seen in thermals and with greasy hair, that whilst everyone wanted to look their best on their wedding day, no one was expected to change into someone altogether different. It was, I have to admit, very kind of her. She saved the day. She was a great friend.

Of course, that was before I knew she was sleeping with my sister's husband.

I can still recall what she said. I was struck by her wisdom. 'This marriage isn't about the wedding day, it's about you and him, not a dress.' She then encouraged me to buy a dress that suited my body shape, rather than squeeze myself into an unrealistic ideal. I would like to dismiss the incident, put it down to Lucy simply being unable to allow a fashion *faux pas* on her watch, but I don't honestly believe that to be the case. She thought I should pick a different style because, I suppose, thinking about it, Lucy has always been keen for people to be true to themselves. She wanted me to buy a dress that flattered an hourglass figure, because I have an hourglass figure.

As though Lucy is following my thoughts she

starts to quote herself. 'How often has he told you that he loves your hips, your bot, he hangs on those massive tits.'

These were the very words she said to me when I stood in the bridal shop, starring hopelessly at my own refection in the far-too-tight, inappropriate dress. Right now, she delivers the punch line with a huge guffaw. I can't help it, I laugh too.

'I was so shocked that you said *tits* in a wedding dress shop.'

'You were!' Lucy laughs again. 'I had to promise not to say anything rude in the church. Not that I actually made it to the church,' she adds ruefully. 'Since you uninvited me.'

'Well, that was your own fault for seducing my sister's husband,' I snap back, the happy moment instantly banished.

Lucy stops laughing and rolls her eyes, 'Are you ever going to let that go?'

'Probably not,' I mumble, although right now, eighteen years later and three huge glasses of wine down, I think it hardly matters. After all, Rose is happy. She called me this evening from Greece. 'Just checking in,' she'd said. She meant just checking up — on me. She told me about the turquoise waters with towering cliffs, the whitewashed villages packed with culinary delights. She said that she and Craig had spent most days lounging on the fine sand beaches, reading books and just chatting. She sounded breathlessly happy, as she has done for a decade. Maybe it is time to let it go — my resentment at Lucy and Peter's infidelity. It's not like I'm short on things to feel indignant about. Things to feel furious about.

Lucy tucks her feet up under her bottom. She leans back, clearly ensconced on the couch for the night. 'So, you asked for a divorce?'

'Yes. Surely *you* haven't got a problem with that.'

'Me? No.' Lucy replies with a shrug. 'If it's what you want.'

'Why wouldn't it be what I want, considering everything?'

She shrugs again, but I'm not fooled. She's only pretending to be disinterested. 'I don't know. I always had you down as someone who was in it for good. You know, someone who would go the distance, no matter what.'

'Well, you were wrong. Everyone has their limits.'

'And you want a divorce to pursue your relationship with Daryll Lainbridge, right?' I nod, briefly. Not quite able to say the words. 'Now, *that* I'm confused about, because last time we talked about him, you described him as an arrogant prick.'

I blanch. Then rally. 'Well, things change.'

Lucy sits silently for a few seconds. It feels longer. Eventually she asks, 'What's going on, Daisy? It doesn't add up.'

I swallow back another slug of wine. I'm at the stage of drunk that feels careless and invincible. I pour some more and make a thing of topping up Lucy's, although she's barely touched hers. The fresh glass gives me permission. I throw caution to the wind. It's going to come out at some point, that point might as well be now. 'Can you keep a secret?'

'It's one of the top skills on my CV.'

'I'm serious, Lucy.'

'OK.' She smiles, but there's caution in her eyes.

'You can't tell anyone what I'm about to tell you. I mean *anyone*. *Ever*. Not Peter, not Connie. No one. Do you understand?'

'Yes.'

'You promise? You swear?'

'On what, a bible?' Lucy looks sceptical.

'On Auriol's life.'

'You think that's necessary?'

'I do. Swear?'

'I swear.'

'On Auriol's life?'

'Yes.'

I know I'm making her uncomfortable. I pause. Hesitate, and then can't hold it back. 'Millie is Daryll's child.'

'What? You had an affair?'

I should just say yes. That's what I'd planned to tell her and everyone. Daryll's right, she would understand that, but I can't. Because it's not true. I have never been unfaithful to Simon.

'It wasn't like that,' I mutter.

'What then? He's your sperm donor?'

'That's how I've always thought about it.'

'What do you mean? You're not being clear.' She stares at me in a way that makes me think she knows before I say it. Somehow, she understands.

'He forced me.'

'You mean he raped you?'

I can't say the words. Even now. All these years later. If I say them, it's true. My beautiful miracle girl was born as a result of brutal violence.

'Daisy?' And if she'd reacted angrily, indignant or shocked, I might have clamped up. I might have found a way to close it down, backtrack, deny everything I'd just confessed. But she doesn't, she sounds concerned.

'He's still forcing me,' I whisper.

'Daisy.' I can't look at her, but I hear the horror in Lucy's voice now. 'Are you saying he is raping you on an ongoing basis?' The words she picks are straightforward. Almost clinical. And they are the ones I need. She's trying to establish fact. I've been wading through a quagmire for years. Alone.

I nod.

'Oh, my poor love.'

I don't recall Lucy ever calling anyone 'Love' before, although I assume she must use endearments when speaking to Peter and Auriol. She doesn't move closer to me. She doesn't try to pull me into a hug, as I'm certain Rose or Connie would have if I'd told them this awful thing. I'm glad. I don't want to feel another person's weight, not so much as a hand on my shoulder, not even a tentative squeeze of my arm. Any physical contact scares me. Repulses me. These past few weeks I haven't even wanted Millie to hug me. If I could peel off my skin I would. If I could stop being a body and just be my mind, I would. Actually, if it wasn't for

Millie, I might stop altogether. Just be done with it. Done with me. I have thought about that. At night, lying on my back, staring at the ceiling. I've wondered whether that's the only way to escape this. But I won't leave her. Never.

I force myself to look at Lucy. It's important I read her face as well as hear her words. I've long since doubted what people say; what they do is all that counts. 'You do believe me, don't you?'

'Of course I believe you,' she replies fiercely, and her face twists into an expression that is one hundred percent authentic.

Oh God, the relief, the relief. Slowly, I roll up my sleeves. I show her the bruises on my upper arms. I unbutton my blouse and let it slip over my shoulders, with shaking legs I stand up and turn around, to show her the marks there and on my back. Bruises, where he's held me down or tied me up and I've silently struggled.

'We have to go to the police.'

'No. No, I can't, and you promised you wouldn't tell anyone,' I say forcefully. I pull up my blouse quickly, as though I can rub out what she's just seen.

'But I didn't know you were going to tell me this.'

'No buts. You swore on Auriol's life,' I insist. I *can't* do that. Doesn't she see? Telling people won't help. 'I don't want Millie to know she's a product of rape. Not ever. You can't tell anyone. You promised.'

I know she is sweeping her mind to think of the right thing to say. I wish she'd leave. I should never have said anything to her. I've kept the secret this long. I should have just kept my mouth shut for a few more weeks. I had a plan. She didn't need to know. No one did. What is wrong with me? It's too late for anyone to help me, so why have I opened my mouth now? 'You need to leave,' I tell her. I want to just curl up inside my own hopelessness for a while.

'This can't go on,' she insists.

'No, probably not, especially as he's escalating things. He wants me to move in with him. He wants to be her father.'

'But he's a rapist.'

'Only if I keep saying no. If I say yes, he's something different.'

'You can't place yourself and Millie in that position.' Lucy gazes at me with a complex mix of emotions: horror and compassion, frustration and fire.

'I know,' I admit.

'Then what are you going to do, Daisy?'

'Run. I'm going to run.'

46

Simon

Sunday, 7th July 2019

That very next night Simon received a delivery. He had not expected things to move so fast, but thinking about it, he supposed the cell searches meant things were floating about and needed new homes, quickly. Vagabond contraband. Or maybe the Dales just needed him to know they owned him now, there was no getting away. He was stood in the supper queue. He'd been hoping for a small carton of orange juice, because he was thinking he could stash it and maybe risk making his own hooch. Even as the thought half-formed in his mind, he acknowledged doing so would be stupidly risky and wondered at himself for even contemplating the idea. Still, he couldn't shake it. His addiction was creeping over him, choking him. Leaving him vulnerable, helpless and hopeless *again*. However, as soon as the con on hatch duty slid the small cardboard carton on to Simon's plastic tray, he knew that he wasn't getting orange juice. The con was making too much of an effort to look casual; he was actually whistling. There was something about the weight of the drink carton

— which he could estimate as it was slid onto the tray — that was wrong, it was too light. He walked straight back to his cell, sat on his bunk, carefully tore open the carton. It was weed.

Fuck.

Simon wasn't interested in weed, and even if he had been, he instinctually knew that this wasn't his to consume. This wasn't a treat or a gift. This was his to hide, to hold. To pass on. It was the beginning of a line of favours. A payback for something he'd never even enjoyed. Despite all Simon had done for, and because of, alcohol he remained scared of drugs. He viewed them as wicked, torrid and destructive. He had seen paranoia, violence, total Armageddon flood into the veins, hearts and minds of druggies; he'd seen men turn into liars, thieves and thugs. He knew that drink could do that to a person too. But he'd never seen or heard of anyone murder because of a drink cartel, that was a very real possibility with drugs.

The difference mattered to him.

The difference terrified him.

So, this was just weed, but this was just the beginning. He knew that much for certain. He didn't know what to do. The room was always over-warm or freezing, he never got used to that. He hid the weed in one of his socks, slipped it under his mattress. He didn't mention it to Leon. Safest not to. When it was Purposeful Activity time, he went to a meeting. He felt that was the only place he might be anywhere near safe.

Billy seemed genuinely pleased to see Simon;

relieved, hopeful. The Chaplain smiled and waved at him as he walked into the room but didn't say anything because another prisoner was mid-flow. The prisoner was talking about the fact that alcoholism was self-diagnostic, that you had to take responsibility for the fact that you were an alcoholic before you could hope to take responsibility for getting dry.

'You can take a dozen online tests, see a doctor, but in the end it's in your gut, you know if you are or you are not. If you've stepped over the line.'

On another occasion Simon might have engaged. It was a sensible enough comment, an interesting thought. Simon craved any sort of intellectual stimulation but not this evening. This evening, all he could think about was the weed stowed under his mattress. He imagined it not as a small mound that was unlikely to draw attention, but as a screaming siren or a neon sign. He thought of it as having heat. Literally smouldering and then setting fire to the bedclothes, burning the whole place down. How long would he be expected to hold on to it for? Who would he have to pass it to? What would he be given next? Because unquestionably there would be a next. If he stayed quiet and did a good job for the Dales, they'd want more from him. If he snitched, or fucked up in any way, they'd hurt him. By mixing himself up with the Dales he'd basically doused himself in petrol and lit a match.

He was just days away from getting out, but he knew their all-powerful, evil tentacles reached through bars and over walls; they had influence on the outside too. The wrong people would find him, curl their grasp around his neck and his possibilities. They'd get him to deliver things, do things, hide things. He'd be an employee. It wasn't an optional post, one for which you were offered a contract with an expense account, health insurance and a car. Although, he could imagine he would be given expenses of sorts; a few quid to tide him over. Maybe he'd be given a place to stay, a skinny bed in some other thug's flat. The health insurance would be such that if he did what they asked, he wouldn't be beaten to a pulp. Maybe he'd get a car if they needed him to drive anyone or anything. It was a sentence. He'd be on the outside, but it was another sentence. Time he would have to serve. Simon wanted to punch himself. He could not believe he'd walked into this. Just for a drink.

Oh, a drink. What he wouldn't do for a drink.

Daisy wanted a divorce.

The Dales wanted their pound of flesh.

He wanted a drink.

The room had fallen silent, the man banging on about self-diagnosing had shut up. He was now leaning back in his chair staring at the ceiling. Looking for answers or a way out, as they all did, all the time. 'So, Simon. You're on the home stretch,' commented Billy, cheerfully. Simon nodded. 'And how are you feeling?'

'Scared,' he replied. 'Shit scared.'

47
Daisy

People think rape is a masked stranger, finding you late at night, grabbing you from behind, then dragging you to a side street. Forcing his way into you, up against recycling bins, at knife point. It is.

Or, it is the unlicensed cab driver who locks the doors and drives you somewhere far away, not to your specified address. To a place where no one can hear you scream. Even if you dared.

Or, it might be the man you spotted across the floor in the night club, the one you quite liked the look of, the one you danced with, flirted with, and gave your number to. Then, you said you wanted to call it a night and go home with your friends. He didn't want that.

Or, it might be your boyfriend, your husband, a relative. It might be in a street, in a car, a nightclub, a tent, a stockroom, a park, a train, an office, a hotel. Your bed. You might have been wearing a short skirt, a long one, a work overall, sexy underwear, dungarees, a burqa, pyjamas, nothing at all. It can be a myriad of things. The only consistency is, you didn't want it. He did.

I was first raped at one of Connie's glorious, celebrated, much-anticipated parties. I was wearing a new, prettily patterned, floral dress. I'd had my hair blow-dried and had made more of an effort than usual with my makeup. Do you want to know why? They would want to in a court of law. If this rape had gone to trial, they might very well have asked me why I'd waxed my legs. If I'd waxed elsewhere. Why I'd chosen a scarlet colour to paint my toenails and fingernails. They might have believed I'd picked out the wraparound dress because it was a forgiving, flattering style for my body shape, or a defence lawyer might have argued I'd deliberately chosen something with easy access.

And the makeup? They'd want to know why I'd made 'more of an effort than usual'. Something could be read into that. Well, Simon had got a bit drunk at lunchtime and spent the afternoon in bed sleeping it off, so I took more care over my makeup because I had time on my hands.

Or, maybe I did so because all my friends are prettier than I am and I've always felt a need to present myself as best I can.

Or, because my husband and I were going through a difficult patch, well more than a patch, a stretch. We longed for a baby and there wasn't one. It was destroying us. I was possibly hoping to reignite something.

Or, had I simply made an effort with my makeup because it cheered me up.

All of the above.

In a court, it might have been argued that I'd taken care with my appearance because I knew Daryll Lainbridge was going to be at the party and I used to fancy him a long, long time ago. He'd overlooked me back in university days but seemed to be starting to notice me now, which was flattering, wasn't it?

We're trained to want to be physically appreciated, aren't we? Women. We're told over and over again that how we look matters.

It's a sickness.

Am I on trial here? If so, I might as well admit, I also wore high heels. Silver, open-toed ones. They were new and frivolous, and I enjoyed seeing my scarlet nails peek through.

That night, when Simon did finally emerge from his drunken slumber, he showered and came downstairs fresh, expectant. Most probably excited about having a drink, but I told myself it was the thought of going to a party with me that made him so eager. Indeed, there was a moment when I almost believed as much. When his gaze pulled the entire length of my body, and he muttered huskily, 'You look nice. Good.'

'Good enough to eat?' I asked with a wink. It was one of our old jokes. His mother's innocent phrase, a compliment that she often threw about. We'd made it rude and suggestive, years back, when we were very young.

'Yeah,' he smiled. 'Good enough to eat.'

We left our house holding hands, we walked up Connie's pathway with our fingers still interlocked, but then we had to knock on the door and once it was open, Simon headed straight for the kitchen, the drinks. He left me behind. I was disappointed. I helped myself to a G&T too. Then a second one. I wandered about, talking to various guests about this and that. Connie had, as usual, made a huge effort. There was a magician doing tricks with balloons and playing cards. There were two waiters carrying trays of posh little nibbles and another one constantly proffering drinks. Even so, I wasn't having an especially good time. That sometimes happens to me. I find anticipating a party and getting ready for it far more fun than the actual event. It's probably because I'm fundamentally shy and therefore happier in smaller groups. Don't get me wrong, I wasn't having an awful time. It was just OK, good enough.

But then Daryll arrived.

And the night went up a gear.

Daryll had been nudging his way into our social crowd for some months by that point. I didn't like it. I was quite protective of our close-knit gang and wary of newcomers because they could upset the balance. I worried that the group wouldn't expand to absorb someone new, but instead operate a one-in-one-out policy. What if Simon or I were ousted? I know, I know, I have self-esteem issues, but Simon was being a pain around that time. His drinking was annoying people. Anyway, Daryll was determined. He seemed to have an 'Access All Areas' badge when it came to infiltrating our group, just because we'd all studied together at university. He turned up at parties and dinners, trips to the cinema or bowling.

I didn't fancy Daryll by that point. Yes, I'd lusted after him at university, but those days were well behind me. I had Simon. I loved

Simon, despite everything we were going through. If anything, being around Daryll was a bit awkward because he clearly believed I still had the hots for him. He seemed to interpret everything I said to him a little oddly and not as I intended. For example, if I made a flip comment about men being — oh I don't know — untidy, or something innocuous like that, he'd catch my eye and insist, 'We're not *all* slovenly, you know, Daisy. I really wish you wouldn't tar us all with the same brush.' I did wonder why he was bothering to recommend himself to me. Was it simply that he couldn't stand the thought I'd once wanted him and no longer did? Was that the challenge? I don't know. All I do know is, at the time, even the most innocent of remarks made by me were interpreted by him as flirty, or regretful, or wistful. It was complicated, and it shouldn't have been. I resented him for muddying things. I found I was always trying a bit too hard to make things normal between us, which never works. So, when I say the night went up a gear, I don't mean I was thrilled to see him. I mean there was an extra layer to manage. Just something.

Surprisingly, he didn't have a girlfriend with him, which was a pity because he was a bit bored and therefore headed straight towards me. A girlfriend would have meant he was unlikely to notice me; he'd have been distracted.

'I've been watching you dance,' he informed me.

'Oh,' I replied. Stumped. I'd been thrashing about the dancefloor with Rose, we'd been acting up, miming to the words of the songs, and not just YMCA. The crazy abandonment was something I only ever really managed with my sister. His comment made me feel self-conscious, uncomfortable with the thought of being watched.

'You're pretty good,' he added.

'Don't sound so surprised.'

'Shall we dance?' He looked at me, over his glass, right in the eyes. I knew the look. It didn't often get beamed my way but I'm not a nun, I have dated in my lifetime. The look was more than friendly. It had suggestion, intent. It didn't have the desired effect on me though, as it seemed so practiced, glib, almost too charming. It made me want to laugh more than melt. Anyway, I'm a married woman.

'You know what, I need some water. I've danced for the last half an hour, I'm all hot and sweaty,' I stated bluntly hoping to repel him a bit, douse him.

'Tell as it is, Daisy.'

'What? Does my talking about sweat offend you?'

'Far from it. It excites me.'

It was such a full-on bizarre thing to say, I gasped. I didn't know how to respond so I just chose to pretend I hadn't heard him. 'Where's the obligatory beauty tonight?' I asked instead. I was just trying to turn the conversation away from me but later — when I went over and over what was said — I wondered whether I sounded flirty, interested. I jokingly made a thing of searching about, looking for the stunning woman that usually hung on his arm, an accessory.

He suddenly looked sad or, to be exact, he looked a badly acted, close-approximation of sadness. 'I think I'm destined to be a bachelor for ever,' he said, shaking his head. 'I just don't get women.'

I wanted to show him I wasn't taken in. 'Oh, come on, Daryll. You've had too many women to claim that.'

'I probably just haven't met the right one then. Or if I have, I let her slip through my fingers.' He held my gaze as he said this. It was odd, embarrassing. Because if I'd been talking to anyone else I'd have thought that line was laden with something intangible: a hint of regret, nostalgia. But it wasn't real, it couldn't be. He was a player. Why was he even bothering to play with me? I wondered if he was drunk. His behaviour was so strangely full-on. 'Can I talk to you, Daisy?'

Before I was able to reply and point out that I thought that's what we were doing, he grabbed my hand and led me out of the busy kitchen and into the family room. There were far fewer people in there. Those that were, were stood in chattering clusters, no one was sat on either sofa but Daryll flopped into one and pulled me down next to him. I landed close by him. Thigh to thigh. I edged away, placing a little distance between us. It would have seemed strangely rude, unfriendly, if I'd stood up and left him. And honestly? It wasn't the worst thing in the world to spend the evening talking to him. On balance I thought it was a bit better than having to force my way into established conversations with crowds of strangers. He started to tell me about his latest break up.

'I had thought she was the One,' he confided. But before I could feel sorry for him, he called her a bitch. This yo-yoing appraisal of an ex is not new. Many people do the same, but it's never appealed to me. How can you love someone one moment and then hate them the next? It seems immature and unconvincing. I accepted a glass of wine from the tray of a nearby waiter and let Daryll's words drift over me. He didn't really seem to require much input from me, anyway. It was obvious he just needed to vent. He talked about the horrors of online dating. It surprised me that dating sites were his modus operandi. I don't know why but I'd assumed he was still working his way through acquaintances and friends of friends in the old-fashioned way. He was handsome, clever, he had a good job. I could see people wanting to set him up with their single women friends. I suppose it highlighted to me how out of touch I was. When Simon and I had met, no one found love online. Barely anyone found their washing machine that way. Daryll seemed to have very exacting standards when it came to dating. He complained that the women he met were all 'gold-diggers', 'cold' or 'calculating'. He argued that they were all 'boring', 'teasers' or 'liars'. I started to feel uneasy as he was emanating so much fury and frustration. Then he mentioned that his latest lover had been married.

'Married?' I know I didn't hide my shock at all well.

‘I didn’t know in the beginning,’ he hurried to assure me. Then admitted, ‘By the time I discovered the truth I was halfway in love with her.’

I shifted uncomfortably. I’d heard this story a dozen times with the genders reversed but I wasn’t quite sure what to say to a man who was in love with a married woman. ‘Well, you must have known that could never have worked in the long run.’

‘Why not?’ He looked confused. ‘People leave their partners you know, Daisy. People do have affairs,’ he said with a smile that I thought was a little bit patronising.

‘Yeah, they do, but how could you ever trust anyone like that?’

We’d been talking for at least an hour by then. I wanted to go and find Simon, or Rose or Connie or Luke. Daryll’s account of the dating world was depressing me but also it had the effect of making me feel grateful for my own relationship. Simon and I were struggling, we had our problems, but we were loyal to one another. Daryll was clearly thinking along similar lines because he added, ‘Simon is so lucky. I hope he knows how lucky he is.’

‘We both are,’ I pointed out.

‘What you have is just perfect,’ he added, longingly.

‘Well, nothing is perfect,’ I commented, partially to cheer him up, partially because it’s true. I looked around the room for an escape route out of the conversation. I’d heard enough. Been polite. It would have seemed tactless to say

I wanted to find Simon after Daryll had just lain himself open, telling me how hard it is to find a soulmate. 'Will you excuse me? I need the loo.'

It was in the bathroom that he did it.

I walked to the top of the house. The previous year, Connie and Luke had converted their attic into a big bedroom with an en suite. There was a queue for the downstairs cloakroom and for the loo in the family bathroom. I knew few people would be aware of the spare at the top, and besides the house was hot, noisy, Daryll's conversation had been draining. I just wanted a few moments alone to collect myself, so I climbed the stairs. Took myself away from the crowds.

I peed, then washed my hands, checked my make-up. Not surprisingly, my mascara had started to smudge around my eyes. How come other women never seemed to melt? I splashed some water under my eyes and rubbed at my skin. I'd do. Then I unlocked the bathroom door, planning to return to the party, find Simon, maybe persuade him to dance with me.

Daryll was waiting for me. He was big, his bulk blocked the doorway. He walked into the bathroom. Kicked the door shut behind him and locked it. 'Daryll, what are you — '

He roughly put his hand over my mouth and then pushed me backwards. I banged my back on the basin. Pain shot through my spine. As I registered that, he turned me around and bent me over. He kept my mouth covered as he undid his flies, hitched up my dress. I did struggle. I think I did. I was so shocked. I didn't know how to react. You think you'll know. You think you'll shout and kick and fight. You don't know what you'll do. I couldn't believe what he was doing. It was when I felt his hand in my pants that I bit a finger of the hand that was covering my mouth. I was about to yell out. Say no. But he smashed my head against the mirror that hung above the basin. I started to cry. I must have been making a noise, telling him to stop. Begging him to stop. Something, because he said, 'Shut up, Daisy. Someone will hear us. You don't want that.'

It was so efficient. In. Out. Violent, painful thrust after thrust. I could feel the anger and hate throb through him, into me. Deadly. It took for ever. It was over in a flash. I don't know which. He finally withdrew, and my knees crumpled beneath me. I knelt on the floor. I don't know if I was still crying. I was certainly shaking. He tucked himself away. He didn't look at me, he looked in the mirror, swept his hand through his hair and then said, 'Thank you, Daisy. I know we've both been wanting that for a while. Don't worry, I'm the soul of discretion. Simon will never have to know what you've just done.'

48
Simon

Thursday, 11th July 2019

Simon had arrived in prison an alcoholic, not a criminal. He'd tried hard to keep his head down, to keep clean and clear of trouble. A survival instinct. But now he'd invited trouble in, created it. He was awash with regret and frustration. He wished Daisy had never visited him. He wished that he'd listened to Leon and never approached the Dales. But most of all, to his utter shame and horror, he wished they had given him the whisky and that he'd drunk it because he longed for the underwater, you-can't-touch-me feeling that came with being drunk.

We wished for that more than anything.

Whilst the blackouts he used to suffer were horrible, scary, he now realised taking responsibility for your own mess was worse. It would be better if he was, once again, a dead-eyed drunk; at least then the Dales would not be able to see the horror in his mind that shone through his eyes. But wishing did no good, this was his life. He'd made it this way, no one else.

It was as he imagined. He was being asked to do things for the Dales. He'd had to deliver the weed to another prisoner. He hadn't been told how to go about this. 'You're a clever man, be inventive,' the Dales' messenger had instructed. In the end, Simon decided to take a book to the dopehead's cell. He handed both things over. He'd need to get the book back soon though. It belonged to the library, he had to return it, but he was afraid of going back to the dopehead's cell. He didn't want to tighten their association. He was also instructed to put a sock down a loo, take a crap and then call a screw and tell him the loo was blocked. It was obviously a diversion, Simon didn't ask what from. He wasn't told and that suited him. The less he knew, the better.

Both jobs had been excruciatingly nerve-wracking. Blocking the loo could lose him privileges, yard time or Association Time; being caught with weed would mean he'd kiss goodbye to his release. Although, he had started to wonder whether that was such a dreadful thing. What did he have to look forward to on the outside anyway, if Daisy didn't want him? If the Dales did? Maybe he was safer here. The thought, skimming across his mind, sickened him, as he realised that if he preferred to be in than out, he was on the road to being institutionalised. He'd heard about lifers; old blokes that re-offended the moment they got released because they couldn't cope with being anywhere else than prison. When he'd first been told about these men, he'd thought it was the most depressing thing in the world, a monumental defeat, a waste so catastrophic that he couldn't compute it. The fact the concept now seemed attractive to him, even fleetingly so, was sickening. Simon used every moment of his yard allowance to try to fight his drift towards wanting to stay inside. He felt the weak sun on his skin, he watched birds swoop in the sky and insects scuttle on the tarmac. He remembered to envy their freedom.

Simon was given things in return for his help. People didn't jostle him in queues with the indifference he'd encountered up until then. They gave him space. His status as a Dale man earned him respect, or maybe fear. Simon preferred it when the cons had thought he was a nobody. Then, a bar of chocolate turned up on his bunk. It was Dairy Milk Wholenut. Daisy's favourite. The coincidence unsettled him. He stared at it as though he'd been confronted with a live snake. How had they got it in his pad? Who were they anyhow? Another one of the Dales' men, or a not-completely-legit screw? If the screws knew he was one of the Dales' gang he was no longer under their radar either. That was dangerous. He didn't want to eat the chocolate.

'What you got there?'

Simon jumped as he heard Leon's voice. He was just back from showering; his hair was wet, dripping on his shoulders. Shower days were treasured by not only the person taking the shower but their cellmate too. Small things were valued. Slightly less stinky pits or feet were just that.

'Chocolate.' Simon waited for Leon to ask for some. Leon didn't.

Instead he asked, 'Where did it come from?'

'Not sure,' Simon admitted. 'It was here when I came back in. Just lying on my bunk.'

'Shit.' Leon's eyes, grew round, panicked. He understood, as Simon had, the implications of finding such a gift. 'I don't want to know what you are being thanked for,' he muttered darkly.

'I'm not sure about that yet, either.'

'Come again?'

'Well, maybe this is a thank you for services rendered thus far but what if I'm looking after something else that I'm not aware of?' Simon nervously glanced around the cell. It was conceivable that whoever brought the chocolate had left something else behind too. The chocolate was a flag. They could be harbouring contraband without knowing it. Not just chocolate or even weed, maybe a mobile or cocaine. Leon absorbed this, unsurprised. He'd spent his entire life expecting the worst. Bad luck, compromising situations, cul-de-sacs and violence. He'd spent his entire life eating it up. Sharing his cell with Simon had, up until recently, seemed too lucky, too good to be true.

'Shit, mate. What have you got us into?'

'Not you, Leon, I promise. If there's anything here, and if we get caught, I wouldn't involve you.'

'What should we do?' asked Leon, demonstrating that, despite the evidence, he thought Simon was the one who might solve this.

'For now, nothing. We need to act normal. Just carry on. Let me think.'

They got through roll call and when the cell doors were locked it felt like something close to a reprieve that they were locked in for the night. Everything else locked out.

'Should we start looking or is it wisest to stay ignorant? It probably is. Then if there is a cell-spin and they find something, we'll be genuinely surprised,' Simon suggested. Leon groaned, climbed up on to his bunk. 'Mate, I won't land you in this,' promised Simon. It was clear Leon didn't believe him. People had made promises to Leon all his life. And broken them.

There were risks to being padded-up with someone involved with any stashing. Besides their cell being ransacked top to bottom, there was the chance of a thorough strip-search of both cons. It was hassle Leon could have done without. Silently and simultaneously both men ran through the scenarios that Simon's involvement with the Dales could result in. Searches and sniffer dogs may or may not turn something up. If anything was found, then both cell inhabitants were liable to be charged and would have to face an adjudication hearing in front of the governor. A range of penalties could ensue. A loss of privileges, or wages, time in the isolation unit. Worst case scenarios, depending on what they found, were that time might be added to Leon's prison sentence, and Simon would lose his chance to serve the rest of his time on-licence. He'd be in here for another three years.

'We should search,' said Simon, suddenly.

'Why the change of heart?'

'Well, if the contraband is found in my locker or hidden under my mattress, then only I'd take the wrap but if they've concealed anything in a communal area we're both liable to be charged.'

Leon dropped down from his bunk and glared at Simon. Simon hurried on, 'I said I'd own up but sometimes they can be bastards. Decide to make an example. We can't risk it. We should check around the loo, under the basin. Is there any room for anything inside the window-frame?'

Leon rolled his eyes. 'And if we search and we find something, what then? You gonna take it to the Dales and say, 'Thanks but no thanks. I won't do this for you'? Don't be a dick.'

The men knew that a few nights in the isolation unit was a holiday camp compared to what the Dales could dish out. They'd seen men scalded, beaten and cut as punishments. They'd heard stories about ex-junkies being forcefully injected with heroine to 'teach them a lesson'. They lived in a place where, worst case scenario, people were murdered for breaking the complex, unforgiving internal codes. 'You're a Dale man, now. We can't do anything but wait.' Leon said with a weary, defeated air.

'I'm sorry,' whispered Simon into the darkness.

49

Daisy

Lucy works long hours and although she offers to take holiday, I can see it wouldn't be an easy thing for her to swing. Besides, how would I explain that? Lucy and I suddenly bonding? Surely a flag for the apocalypse, the end of the world, when all will be revealed. Connie would be suspicious, she'd want to know what was going on. I tell Lucy I'd be fine, as Daryll is busy through the day at work too, he never visits then. She's clearly far from comfortable with my plan. 'We should go to the police. If you run, he has won,' she argues.

'No, he hasn't, because I have Millie.'

'At what cost? You both have to give everyone else up; your family, your friends. You have to give up your job, Millie's school, your home. Daisy, you shouldn't be made to do that. You've done nothing wrong. He's the one that needs punishing.'

'It's not your business, Lucy.'

'It is. Now you've told me, it is.'

'No, it isn't. You can't boss and barge your way into my life.'

'That's not what I'm trying to do,' she replies, patiently.

'I'm trying to protect you.'

'I'm not yours to protect.'

'You sort of are. That's what friends do, they protect each other.'

My heart moves into my mouth. She thinks of herself as my friend. After all the years of me sniping at her, being rude to her, it's quite something. But Lucy thinks she can sort this out because she's pretty and has a great life; she can't really imagine how awful someone else's life might ever turn out to be. What it is to be trapped, choiceless. This isn't something you can charm or talk your way out of.

'If you want to be on my side, then listen to me, please. Don't bully me as he does,' I tell her. She looks shocked but clamps her mouth closed, prepared to listen. 'Think what will happen if we go to the police. He'll just deny it. And he can be very convincing. Even if they believe me and we get a case to court, he'll deny it there and in court I'll have to convince *more* people, an entire jury. It will be a horror,' I sigh, 'I just can't face anything more. I just can't. I've been through too much already. So has Millie. Please, Lucy, if you can't keep quiet for me, then do it for Millie. Imagine the impact on her. She'll grow up knowing her father was a rapist. In which case, an alcoholic who nearly killed you looks like a relatively good bet by comparison.'

Lucy falls silent and considers. 'I do understand but you said he's still hurting you. How can you think of living with that? *I* can't live with that.'

'I'm not even sure he sees it as rape. He thinks

we are in some sort of a relationship.'

'What sort of relationship? I don't believe that for a moment,' argues Lucy hotly.

'A dysfunctional relationship, maybe, but there are plenty of those. He implies the way he has sex with me is some sort of game.'

'A rough game by the look of your bruises.'

'Yes, but some people do play rough games. He twists things, somehow makes out that I want this but I'm just not that into sex, that I'm a bit shy so I won't say that I want it.'

'That's sick.'

'He's clever.'

Lucy looks furious. 'Don't build him up to be something bigger and better than he is, Daisy. He's a rapist. Have you ever told him you don't want sex?'

'Yes. Every time.'

'Then he knows what this is, Daisy. And so do you.'

'I've asked him to stop. I've told him I don't want to see him. I don't want him to come to my house. But he says he'll take Millie. He says he'll have a DNA test, prove she's his and then sue for custody. He keeps going on about what a life he could give her in comparison to the one I give her. He has a great job, he's buying a big flash house, he wants to send her to private school. He could offer quite a different narrative. A court might look favourably on all that.'

He is an animal. And Lucy is right, he does know what this is. It's not any sort of relationship. We have never kissed. He sometimes has to tie me up. It often hurts. I always cry. My body doesn't want him, my mind doesn't want him. My soul hates him.

50

Simon

Simon and Leon didn't have to wait long. At around about 11 p.m. an alarm went off. It was the alarm that a guard sets off if he was calling for backup. It could mean a fight had broken out or that someone (usually a guard) was being attacked. Both scenarios were unlikely at this time of night because everyone was locked up in their cells. They'd found something.

It was an unsettled night. Footsteps clanged up and down the metal staircases, along corridors. Voices could be heard but it was impossible to make out specific words. The voices seemed irritated and forceful, not angry or violent. Not a riot but something.

The next day, the routine for breakfast was not as usual. Very small groups of men were taken to the hatch, given cereal and juice, returned to their cells, locked up and then another group of half a dozen men were brought forward for food. It took a long time and the cons started to get impatient. They complained about everything all the time anyway, it gave them something to do. Complaining about being hungry and issuing threats about reporting the screws to the relevant bodies bounced about abundantly and with increasing aggression.

Despite the tight controls the rumours started up, because the only thing prisoners liked to do more than complain was gossip. Someone was in intensive care. Had been found in his cell last night. Cocaine. Might not make it. It wasn't clear how the screws had missed this at roll call. Apparently, he was in bed under the covers. The screw checking had been in a hurry, thought he was asleep already. Who was it? Different names were knocked about. No one was certain.

They would probably spend the day in their cells. Possibly for as long as twenty-three hours. There were always staff shortages and that situation was currently exasperated because it was the summer and even screws had to take holidays. It was hard to imagine them at the beach with their families, building sandcastles with their kids, drinking wine with their wives, but it happened. The consequence was the prisoners were left in their cells for longer and longer periods of time. This combined with a crisis was unlikely to spell Association Time or even Purposeful Activity. Simon wished he had his library book. He re-read Leon's tabloid paper, even though it was four days old now. There wasn't much else to do, and he doubted Leon was in a chatty mood. They took turns in pacing about the cell, sitting at the small desk and then, defeated, simply lying back on their beds again. Leon played solitaire. Usually they played cards together but neither man suggested as much. Simon was taken by surprise when Leon suddenly broke the silence and asked,

'That thing you told me about your wife, is it true?'

'That she was driving? Yeah, it's true.'

Leon sighed, shook his head. 'You must really love her to have come here.' Simon didn't say anything. He had never been the sort of man who was especially comfortable talking about love and now, considering everything, Millie's parentage, the request for a divorce, he felt like a fool. The air sagged. Stale and hopeless.

'I can't get my head around it. You gave it all up for her. Your freedom, your reputation, your ability to walk down the street and nip into a shop and buy a packet of chewing gum. Why would you do that?' Leon asked.

'It was just better if she was the one on the outside. You know: better for Millie, my mother, for everyone. She had a job and responsibilities. People depend on her. Whereas me — ' Simon broke off. He didn't need to detail how much of a screw up he was, Leon knew. As if to underline the fact, at that moment, two guards banged open their cell door. They dragged Simon to his feet, turned him towards the wall and put restraining cuffs on him. 'You step over there,' one yelled at Leon. 'Put your hands on your head and keep your mouth shut, if you know what's good for you.' The guards started to turn over their cell. Within a minute they found it tucked beneath Simon's mattress. It was the first place he would have looked if he'd followed through on his intention of searching. He was glad now that he had not.

He was able to say, 'I've never seen that before

in my fife,' and mean it.

The guard put the cocaine in his pocket. 'That's what they all say, my friend. This place is chock-a-block full of people who are innocent. But we found a library book in Carter's cell.'

'Carter?' Simon asked, faking innocence, although he had already guessed. The dopehead he's visited with the weed was Carter. He imagined he was the man who caused the middle of the night commotion, too.

The screw rolled his eyes. 'We traced the book back to you and unluckily for you, your man Carter pulled through. We asked him if he knew you and he was quick to confirm that he did. You're the main man for this stuff, he tells us.' The guard eyed Simon with something like surprise. He didn't look like a main man, not in any sense of the word. He looked tired, weary. The guard roughly led Simon out of the cell. 'Solitary and then a chat with the governor for you, my friend. You can forget any chance of getting out on-licence. This little game has cost you.'

'Wait. Carter actually fingered him?' Leon asked.

'Yeah.' The guard nodded, shrugged. It was unusual. Most dealings inside were swallowed in a cloak of secrecy but Carter had readily grabbed at Simon Barnes' name when it was suggested. 'For the avoidance of doubt, pointed him out when we showed him some mugshots.'

'Yeah, well, he's a liar because that stuff isn't Simon's, it's mine. And he didn't give any to Carter. I did.'

'Really?' The guards exchanged sceptical looks.

'No, that's not true,' said Simon.

'I did it,' repeated Leon firmly. 'You can't blame him if I'm confessing.'

The guards were exhausted. It had been a long night. There would be an enquiry. A stink. How did the stuff get inside in the first place? The guard made a quick calculation. If the alkie, with days left on his prison sentence, just about to be released on-licence, had handled the drugs, there would be questions. A time-consuming enquiry. Maybe an external body would have to be involved. Man-hours they could ill afford would be swallowed up. If it was this other guy, they could put him in solitary. Give him some hard duties when he got out. Maybe fine him or stop his visiting rights for a while. It could all be sorted quietly.

The guard released Simon and put the cuffs on Leon.

'No, no mate,' Simon objected. He tried to push himself between the guard and Leon.

Leon shook his head. 'Just sort yourself out, right? Now you're the one who is better on the outside. You understand that, right? You believe it?'

51

Daisy

Friday, 12th July 2019

I thought Lucy would continue to push hard for me to go to the police. I didn't imagine that her promise, or even the fact she'd sworn on her daughter's life, would hold. However, so far, she is respecting my wishes, albeit reluctantly. She has concentrated on making me safe. On Saturday night she insisted on staying with me and she hung about all the next day too. It was awkward. I've resented and avoided her for so long that it was overwhelming to have so much of her company. She wanted us to go out and kept suggesting we shop or go to an art gallery, but Millie was reluctant to leave Eric. I wonder if that was something else Daryll thought of. Planned. He's made me more housebound for weeks until the cat has had his injections and been neutered. A clever way to clip my wings this summer or, as Lucy puts it, turn me into a sitting duck. Because we wouldn't go out, Lucy was left with no alternative but to mooch around my house making coffee and smoking cigarettes.

Now it seems she has organised some sort of rota, to provide me with company, protection, without telling the participants that's what they are doing exactly. I'm still at work, although this is the last week of term and so I'm only vulnerable in the evenings. On Monday, Peter came around to look at a leak under the kitchen sink. He seemed as perplexed as I was by his wife's request that he did so. 'I'm not really a handyman sort,' he said to me apologetically, when he confessed he couldn't find the cause. 'I could call you a plumber and maybe, since I'm here, we could order pizza?'

On Tuesday, the plumber came. On Wednesday, Connie and her girls suggested we went to Westfield shopping, again Millie demurred about leaving Eric, so they all came to us instead. The girls stayed inside with the kitten but Connie and I sat in the garden, reading books, watching the sun go down, chatting about whatever drifted in and out of our heads — the name of an insect, the neighbour's noisy dogs, how lucky she is to be self-employed and therefore have flexitime and how lucky I am to be a teacher and therefore have a long summer holiday to look forward to. We have been quietly reading together over many years. Some people shop or go to fancy restaurants, others debate politics or go to the theatre. We've done all those things together at some point or other too but reading quietly is our thing. It was peaceful. I felt content, loved, and yet sad too because I won't be able to do that again. I have to leave it all behind.

On Thursday, after work, Luke popped by. Sophie was with him again, as the kitten is a magnet for her too. He brought me some colour charts and material swatches. 'I wasn't aware you were planning on doing any decorating,' he said, obviously a bit bemused. 'But Lucy said you were, and she was pretty insistent that you needed these, right now, tonight.' I don't need colour charts, I am not planning on decorating the house in the short time I have left here. I'm sure Lucy knows this, she's just scheming to make sure I am not alone. Each night, late, after she's finished a long day at the office she calls me. She talks about her workload, the weather, her irritating boss, and which sunglasses style suits which face shapes. She just keeps talking, sometimes for two, or three, or four hours. When I tell her I really need to sleep, she asks me if the chains are across the door.

This rota puts me in mind of when Millie was in hospital and my friends rallied. I have glorious friends. True, sometimes they irritate me or disagree with me. I guess I do the same to them. But they are loyal, reliable. I realise now, too late maybe, that Lucy is a good friend to me. She fell in love inconveniently, yes, but I should not have hung onto that resentment for as long as I have. I'm not sure why I did, especially as Rose didn't. I guess I wanted the world to be black and white, fair and simple. Goodies and baddies. I guess it was easier to resent the things that Rose had to deal with, than admit to how many grey areas I was dealing with. Or perhaps not dealing with. I suppose I might have been deflecting. It was easier to focus on Peter's infidelity, Lucy's betrayal, Rose's hurt, rather than trying to understand Simon's drinking or accept how I had conceived. Truthfully, I've always been a little wary of Lucy, a little jealous. Maybe it was comforting to find something wrong with her. After all, she's beautiful, clever, wealthy, confident, it was easier for me if I could tell myself she wasn't a very nice person.

By sending my friends to watch over me, Lucy has — perhaps intentionally, perhaps inadvertently — not only protected me from Daryll but also given me the space to do what I must do. The chance to say goodbye. They don't know that it's the last time I'll see them, but every time I've closed the front door this week, I've known that is exactly what it is. I think Lucy is beginning to accept my idea of running. It's a relief not to be fighting her on this issue, but it's also depressing that even the irrepressible Lucy can't see any other way out of this.

Simon is to be released on Saturday. Connie told me. Knowing Simon's release is imminent, I'd like to have left sooner, but I need to see my sister one last time. Rose and Craig are home from their holidays on Saturday too. Millie and I are going to theirs for lunch. The boys and Craig will be there as well. I'll get to hug them all, leave them with happy memories. We fly to Hamburg that evening. I studied German at A Level and whilst I'm not sure that's where we'll settle for ever, it's my first bolthole. Most likely, we'll move about a bit for a while, in case anyone tries to find us: Daryll or Simon.

It is the last day of term. I stumble home under the weight of chocolate oranges, bottles of cava and thank you cards from my pupils. The last day of term is always an emotional one; it's never easy saying goodbye to a class after spending a year with them, day in, day. out. This year I know I'm also saying goodbye to Newfield. Primary for good. As it's Friday, Lucy assumes Millie and I are heading off to Connie's. However, tonight they're visiting Luke's parents. Connie was very apologetic about skipping our usual Friday get-together, but Luke's father has been in hospital for an operation on his knee, he was discharged today and Luke's mother can't manage him on her own at home. Besides leaving me, the other reason she's concerned about having to visit Luke's parents is that she wanted to be here for Simon's release. But Luke put his foot down, he said she had to put their family first. I don't ask where Simon is going to be living. I don't ask anything about him, which I know bothers Connie.

'So you are going ahead with this divorce?' she asks tentatively.

'Yes.'

'Well, we can talk about that more when I get back,' she says, clearly convinced she can persuade me to do differently. 'We've the whole summer holidays stretching out in front of us.' I can hear the optimism in her voice. Connie is still hopeful for a happy ending. Ignorance truly is bliss. 'We'll be back in a couple of days. Pick up as usual next Friday, yes?'

'Right,' I hope she can't hear the lie. This time next week, I don't even know where we will be living.

I haven't drawn Lucy's attention to the fact

I'm on my own tonight, because if she thinks I'm alone, she's bound to come around and I want to spend some time reading the thank you cards that I've received before I pack our suitcases and put everything in place. I haven't heard from Daryll all week. Each day that he doesn't turn up at my door is a blessing, and yet it's like being stretched on a rack, torture. The longer he is away, the more likely it is that he'll reappear.

I pack one medium and one small sized pull-along suitcase, plus two backpacks. Millie and I should be able to manage those between us. I've told Millie we are going on holiday, which she isn't happy about.

'But what about Eric?'

'I thought we'd take him to Rose's and ask her to look after him whilst we are away.'

Millie is, as usual, holding the kitten. He's nestled into her chest and she's stroking his back. He's a sweet and placid thing, quite accepting of her constant handling.

'Oh, look at this, what a scene. The absolute epitome of cute.' I jolt as I hear Daryll's voice, so close. 'I let myself in the back door,' he explains. 'It was unlocked. You ought to be more security conscious, Daisy.'

Is he tormenting me? He must know the only person I really need to keep out is him. It is only 6 p.m. on a summer evening, Millie and I are always popping out to our small garden; it hadn't crossed my mind to lock the door yet. Now I'm furious with myself.

Daryll walks towards Millie and strokes the kitten she's holding. 'So, Millie, how are you and

Eric getting along?'

'I love him,' she gushes, with no reserve.

'Did I get you the best present ever?' Daryll asks, fishing.

'Absolutely,' Millie beams.

'Can I hold him for a bit?' Daryll holds out his hands.

Millie relinquishes her pet even though I can see she'd rather not; she's extremely polite. She gets that from me and I worry what it will cost her in the future. Do we still live in a world where being polite keeps order, or does it just leave you vulnerable? Daryll sits down in the armchair with the tiny kitten on his lap. He's tickling the cat behind his ears. Eric is only about seven weeks old and looks small enough in Millie's hands; in Daryll's he looks like a toy.

'Fix me a drink, will you, Daisy?' It's not really a question. I prepare Daryll a gin and tonic and present it to him like a 1950s housewife. Millie is sat at his feet, looking longingly at Eric, but Daryll seems oblivious to her desire and continues to pet the kitten himself. I don't like her being in the same room as Daryll. Although, so far, her presence has meant I'm safer, I feel she is not.

'Haven't you got something you need to be getting on with?' I say to Millie. It's a pretty useless comment as she's too young to understand the hint and needs me to give her a specific instruction. As it's the end of term I can't suggest homework and as Daryll's holding the kitten, I can't imagine she'll want to leave the room. I'm not thinking carefully.

She replies, 'I thought you'd done all the packing.'

I freeze; how stupid of me! I should have told her that our going away was a secret. Daryll keeps caressing the cat, seemingly unperturbed, unconcerned. But then he asks, 'Why are you packing, Millie?' His voice is calm but sends a splinter of ice through me.

'We're going on holiday,' she replies.

'Really, where?'

'Hamburger. No, Hamburg. I just remember its name because I think of burgers,' she says innocently. Oh no, why did I tell her where we were going? Now he will have a lead once he discovers we've migrated. I'd only revealed our destination because she kept picking out bikinis and sparkly tops, insisting I put those in the case. I told her it wasn't necessarily going to be hot where we were going. Of course she was curious.

'And what's in Hamburg?' Daryll asks, this time he stares directly at me.

'Churches and art galleries,' replies Millie, rolling her eyes. 'I don't know why we can't go somewhere sunny with a beach, like Spain or California. That's where India is going. Cal. I. Forn. I. A. That's how she says it.' As Millie prattles, Daryll continues to glare at me.

'You never mentioned you were going on holiday.'

'Just for a few days, we'll be back before you know it.' His eyes drift towards the suitcases that I've stored near the table. Why did I bring them downstairs? I should have hidden them. There was always a risk he'd appear, but I'd been hoping he wouldn't.

'You seem to have packed a lot for just a few days. I don't like you making decisions without consulting me, Daisy,' he snaps. 'I have plans for us this weekend. We're a family now. We should go on a family holiday.'

Millie looks from Daryll to me. He is not family and she knows it. He isn't making sense to her. She senses the tension, his anger and maybe the threat of him. She sees I am speechless and so, adorable girl that she is, she tries to fill in the gap, say something that pleases him.

'I didn't really want to go. I was worried about what we should do with Eric'

It happens in a flash. I hear it before I understand or even see it. The kitten smashes against the wall. A thud and then a yelp. He slides down the wall and drops to the floor, leaving a heartbreaking trail of blood smeared from where he made impact all the way to where he dropped. Millie screams.

'Run, Millie!' I yell. But Daryll is already on his feet. He leapt up to fling the kitten. He heads for the back door and locks it, pockets the key. He grins at me. Cold. The front door is locked and has a chain on; we'd never get out. 'Upstairs bathroom. Lock the door,' I yell. Millie charges out of the room, sobbing, casting a quick disbelieving look at Eric, who is lying broken and still, 'Run!' I scream again, Daryll lunges at us. I throw myself between him and her. She lumbers up the stairs, with all the speed her limp allows. His fingers grab at the ends of her hair but with me acting as a barrier, she gets away. He turns to me and punches me in the face. The pain of the impact is excruciating; hurt and fright invade my mind. He then shoves me backwards with such violence that I can't control my limbs. I crumple on the floor.

'You are going to have a black eye on all your holiday photos. Shame,' he sneers, grasping my hair and pulling me towards the sofa.

52
Simon

Saturday, 13th July 2019

He was released at eight in the morning. It seemed unnecessarily early, the entire day stretched out in front of him, taunting him. Shouldn't he just be delighted? He took a deep breath, took in the damp air, the traffic fumes. This was what his freedom smelt like. It was raining. In his mind he'd imagined the sun would be shining the day he was released. It had been hot all week. The men inside had smelt worse than usual. He knew that Daisy and Millie had broken up from school yesterday, he imagined her making wry jokes about it being typical that the weather had broken now the kids were on holiday. She had made the same observation over many years.

He stood outside the prison, hands in his pockets. Not carrying a cardboard box. There was nothing he wanted to bring with him. The few, meagre possessions he had collected over the years he had left for Leon. Some writing paper, some stamps, a couple of books, it wasn't much but it was all he had. Simon had not been able to say goodbye to Leon, who had another two days to endure in solitary. He wouldn't be able to visit him either, it was a condition of his licence. He would write. He would send money orders so that Leon could buy newspapers and chocolate, it was the least he could do.

Lucy tooted her horn and waved at him. Gratefully he ran towards her car. Lucy had always had nice things, impressive cars with smart interiors, he remembered that, but as he slipped into the leather seat he felt overwhelmed by the luxury, the cleanliness. He felt grubby, inadequate and judged. He pulled on his seatbelt. It caught, jarred. It was embarrassing. He wanted things to go smoothly. He repeatedly tugged at the belt.

'Hello, long time no see,' Lucy said with a grin.

Simon tried to smile back. The seatbelt finally cooperated. It was a relief. Something. Lucy started the engine. Initially he'd been disappointed to hear that Connie couldn't pick him up, although not surprised when she also revealed that Luke had vetoed her idea about him staying with them. He hadn't imagined Lucy would come forward and provide not only the lift, but also an offer of a home, an address he could have approved by the authorities. He hadn't imagined anyone would. He was grateful, he just didn't know how to show it. For three years he'd been careful to suppress all emotions: gratitude, fear, happiness, hope — they all just left you vulnerable inside. Anywhere really, he thought grimly.

'It's very kind of you to do this,' he muttered.

An understatement. He was awash with appreciation and embarrassment. He didn't want to feel the ignominy of being beholden but feared he would for a long time, if he was lucky enough that kindness came his way. And if it didn't? Then he'd feel livid, disappointed. He couldn't win. He was doomed to a life of shame or anger. Was that the truth of coming out of prison? Was it now impossible to win at life?

'It's not a problem,' replied Lucy lightly, and he wanted to believe her. 'Connie told me you needed a safe and permanent address before they'd let you out. Peter and I are model citizens,' she added dryly.

'I won't impose for long, I'll be on my way soon.'

Lucy raised a beautifully manicured eyebrow, sceptically. Where was he going to go? She didn't ask that, instead she said, 'You can stay as long as you need. We have a spare room.'

'Connie has a spare room,' he pointed out, sulkily.

'Yeah but we have three.'

'I only needed one.'

Lucy flicked her eyes over him. 'Hey, I could be offended. Why aren't you happy to be staying at ours? Ours is way cooler than the Bakers'. Is it the minimalist thing? It's not to everyone's taste,' she joked.

Simon smiled obligingly. 'I'm sorry. Of course, I'm grateful.'

'I don't need you to be grateful.'

'Honestly, it doesn't matter where I stay.'

'It just made sense, they have three kids, we

have one. Luke's father has just had an operation. They've a lot on.'

'Yeah, right.'

'What does that mean? 'Yeah, right'.'

Simon stared out of the window throughout the conversation. There was so much to see. The streets were already teeming with life. The traffic was heavy, people dashing to work or maybe on day trips. Delivery vans causing bottlenecks which led to horn-honking and rude hand gestures. Shopkeepers were rolling back their shutters and café managers were stood in the doorways of their premises, smoking a cigarette or vaping, assessing the weather, wondering if it would clear up later and they'd get to unstack the metal bistro chairs. The streets were full of pedestrians walking their dogs and hurrying their children, scooters, people on skates, boards, bikes. Everyone was in a hurry. They'd all been dashing about for three years. Simon sighed and replied, 'It's just that Connie has been visiting me and she offered first, so that's what I was expecting, but I know why I can't stay with her and, obviously, that pisses me off.'

'You've lost me.'

Simon couldn't be bothered to dissemble, not even to protect Connie. He didn't have the energy. 'It's because Luke had an affair with Daisy. Luke is Millie's father. Luke is no friend to me. He doesn't want me staying. He doesn't want that to come out.'

'What?' Anyone else might have hit the brakes, hard. Lucy didn't say another word until she spotted a car parking spot which she neatly pulled into. She turned to him. 'What are you talking about?'

'Oh, I know, it's hard to believe. St Luke and Daisy, Mother Teresa's more devout sister, having an affair, but they did. I know they did.'

'You know nothing, Simon.'

'I knew before I went inside. I'm not Millie's dad. I've accepted it for what it is. What pisses me off is that Luke has got away with his treachery. Connie hasn't a clue, which is galling.' Lucy stared at him, astonished. 'Oh, don't worry, I've no intention of telling her. I don't want to hurt her. I've had long enough to think about it.'

'And yet this is what you've come up with?' Lucy looked frustrated. 'Luke is besotted with Connie. He'd never have an affair. And he was your best friend.'

'He never visited me in prison once.'

'You did run over his goddaughter. He's pissed off with you. But before then, he found you work, he was forever bailing you out of trouble. He was your best friend.'

'But was he, though? You had an affair with Rose's husband. People do. You should know that more than anyone.'

'That was entirely different.'

'How?'

Lucy looked as though she wanted to scream at Simon.

'Because Peter and I are nothing like Luke and Daisy. We're morally fluid.' Simon looked confused. 'We're selfish, OK? I've said it. Do you even know your wife at all? Have you forgotten that as a result of our affair she gave me the cold shoulder for over *fifteen* years? If she could, she would have me branded with a scarlet letter 'A'. There is no way that woman had an affair. She's not the type.'

'Clever cover,' replied Simon confidently. 'Playing the part of the one amongst us with the strong moral compass. Such a hypocrite.'

'I've known her forever. She's a lot of things: judgy, passive-aggressive, sometimes boring, but she's not a hypocrite. Think, Simon. Think!'

Lucy started up the engine and continued with their journey. They sat in silence until after half an hour Simon realised she was not following the route back to Notting Hill.

'Where are you taking me?' he asked.

'Home.'

53
Simon

Lucy pulled up outside Daisy's small two-up, two-down, unprepossessing house. 'Where are we?' Simon asked.

'This is where Daisy and Millie live.'

'What are we doing here?'

'Well, that's up to you.'

Simon looked at the front door and wondered if it would ever open to him if he knocked. He'd like to see Millie. No, he longed to see her. He understood that the biology meant she wasn't his, but she was. With his heart and soul, he'd thought of her every day. He'd thought of both of them. That's why Daisy asking for a divorce was such a blow.

'Your license conditions don't ban you from visiting them, do they?' Lucy challenged.

'No.'

'I'll pick you up later in the day. You have to check in with your probation officer at 4 p.m. right?'

'Yes, that's right.' He felt like a school boy.

'Or do you want to get a tube?' Simon coloured. Even if he wanted to, he couldn't. Lucy reached for her handbag and opened her purse. She handed him twenty pounds. 'Here, you can pay me back when you get a job.' He didn't want to take the money, but the alternative was Lucy driving all the way back across London to pick him up. He didn't have any choice. He took the note. 'Good luck.'

He watched her drive off. He wished he still smoked. This would be the moment to have a fag. Or a drink. A drink would really help right about now. He looked at the twenty quid and then pushed it into his back pocket. Sighed. He stood outside and stared up at the windows. The curtains were still drawn. Was it too early to knock? It was half past nine on a Saturday morning. When he'd last lived at home, Millie would have been up for three hours by now, but there was no sign of life throbbing from the little house. He couldn't hear the TV blaring out cartoons, or breakfast pots being clanked together, he couldn't smell bacon sizzling under the grill. He put his ear to the door. He couldn't hear them chatter, or the radio playing songs. The place was still. Dead.

He reasoned that they must be out or maybe still sleeping. He thought that option was the most likely because Daisy would never leave the house without opening the curtains. Had things changed so much? Could it be that Daisy no longer cared about things like what the neighbours thought? Or was it that Millie was no longer an excitable child, but a pre-teen who liked to lie-in? Did that happen at nine years old? He didn't know, and he was abashed that he didn't know. He wanted to know. He wondered what it looked like inside their house, their life.

He'd missed so much, and suddenly it became unbearable to think he'd miss so much as a moment more. He decided to go around the back, perhaps the curtains would be open there and he could sneak a peek. As he walked down the side alley, around to the back of the house, he thought to himself that they ought to have a gate on this thin path. One that locked. Now he'd been in prison, he knew what the world was, who inhabited it. Daisy and Millie clearly weren't overly focused on security and in a way that was lovely, still he'd suggest a gate. A lock.

The back door was wide open, swinging on its hinges. The rain was falling into the kitchen. He knew at once that something was wrong because he still couldn't hear anything other than silence. This was not a door that had been flung open to allow the smell of burning toast to escape. It was a wet, cool morning; this door wasn't open to let in a refreshing breeze. He rushed inside. Two, three big strides and he was through the empty kitchen and in to the sitting room. What was he looking at? He didn't understand. Furniture was upended, a suitcase was open, and clothes were strewn all over the room, ornaments were broken, smashed to pieces and there was blood. Blood on the wall. On the door and floor. His own blood slowed. His body was seized with a dry, tight dread.

'Daisy! Millie!'

54

Daisy

When we first heard our names being called we tightened our grips on one another. We thought it was Daryll returning for more. Millie was shaking, and tears were streaming down her face although she wasn't making any sound. Her silent weeping was distressing, eerie.

'Daisy, Millie!'

'It's Daddy,' she says turning to me, her face suddenly full of glee. For a moment, I don't understand her. My head is sore and fuzzy from where he pounded me, threw me, slammed me against the wall. 'Daddy, Daddy!' She's jumping to her feet, calling to Simon. She starts to push at the chest of drawers that we've dragged across the doorway. 'Help me, Mum, it's Daddy,' she insists.

Simon is banging on the door. Throwing his entire weight at it by the sounds of it. I jump up and help Millie push the furniture out of the way. The door falls open and she flings herself into his arms.

'It's OK, it's OK. I'm here now,' he says. It's another lie. We're not OK.

* * *

I'm surprised that Simon doesn't immediately insist we call the police. Instead he carries Millie downstairs, holds her tight whilst he rights an armchair, which is an awkward manoeuvre, but it seems he's not prepared to put her down until he can make it cosy. When he eases her onto the chair, he looks about and finds a throw, which he tucks around her legs, like he sometimes used to when she was ill with some childhood bug or other. Then he starts to make pancakes. I follow behind, silently. I don't know what to do. Should I call the police now? So much evidence, such clear brutality, this wouldn't be a case of he said/she said. This would be clear-cut, surely. But I don't have a phone. Last night, Daryll ran my phone under a tap and then smashed it against the wall for good measure. This was after he had demanded I show him the flight booking to Hamburg, after he'd discovered that the tickets were one-way. He held my head under the water too, then smashed me against the wall too. I dived for the landline, but he yanked it out of the wall and then cut the lead. He threw the phone at me. It's a repro 1970s one, so big, chunky. I tried to dodge it and was successful insomuch as it hit my shoulder. I think my face had been the target. 'Do you have a phone?' I ask Simon.

'Sorry, no. I didn't have one on me when I was arrested so . . . ' he breaks off and glances at Millie.

I nod, I understand. He has nothing other than the clothes he's stood up in.

If I want to call the police, I need to go to a neighbour and ask to use their phone, but I don't know my neighbours. I couldn't pick them out in a lineup. Next door is a rental property and there's been a series of young couples living there since we moved here. I'm not sure I've even said hello to the present occupants. I can sometimes hear them listening to Radio 1, or even singing in the shower. If they were in last night, I assume they heard everything. Heard everything, did nothing. Or if they were out, and maybe it's better to think they were — a more generous view on humanity — if they were out, then they don't know anything and I'm not sure I'm ready to face their sympathy, their shock. Not yet. I need a coffee first. I don't right any of the furniture though, because it's a crime scene. We sit amongst the chaos and destruction. Millie keeps glancing at the wall. Oh god, Eric. 'Don't look,' I instruct.

'Look at me, keep your eyes on the pancakes,' murmurs Simon. She does as she's asked. As Simon makes her pancakes in the shape of Mickey Mouse, I hunt about for an old shoe box and scoop up the tiny kitten, place him carefully inside, put the lid on. I then wash my hands because his blood is on them. I'm guess I'm lucky it's just his blood. What if Daryll had hurt Millie? In silence, we eat the pancakes, drink orange juice and coffee, and although I didn't think I'd manage a bite, I find I am hungry and that eating helps. Somehow the pretence of normality eases things. Millie wolfs hers down and the moment she finishes I notice that her eyelids begin to droop. Neither of us have slept all night. After Daryll finished with me and left in the early hours, I crawled upstairs and persuaded Millie to unlock the bathroom door. We then ran to my bedroom and barricaded that door, just in case he returned, in case it was a trick to get to her. We've sat bolt upright, too terrified, too sickened to consider sleep. I still feel the same, I can't imagine sleeping ever again, but Millie is a child and it's a blessing that her body is shutting down, taking charge of her mind. She's in shock and needs to sleep. Simon carries her upstairs and lays her in her own bed.

'Don't leave me,' she begs.

'Never,' he lies. He sits on the bed and strokes her hair until sleep overwhelms her. I stand in the doorway, hurting, hating.

When she is sleeping soundly, we slip out of her room and head downstairs.

55

Simon

Simon wanted to scream. He'd caused this. It was the Dales, there was no doubt in his mind. They had sent someone to his house, beaten his wife, terrified his child, apparently killed their pet, all to teach him a lesson just so he knew that he couldn't brook their plans. If they wanted him to take the blame for supplying cocaine, that's what was supposed to happen. He didn't understand why he meant so much to them, but he must do, it was the only explanation. They obviously wanted him on the inside not on the outside. They were showing him that Leon taking the fall was not acceptable to them. Daisy must know all this, they must have 'explained' it to her, otherwise she would have called the police by now.

'I'm sorry,' he said, the moment they were alone together. He started to weep. Pain, regret, shame sliding out of him as tears. The bruise on Daisy's face was purple and tender. Her lip and cheek were cut, her eye blackened. It made him sick to look at her. And Millie, what had she seen? What had she heard? The way she clung to him stole his breath. It was heart-rending and yet such a privilege at the same time. He couldn't believe it, she'd ran into his arms, no hesitation, the same little girl. Obviously taller and somehow more angular, different physically but the same little girl. When he looked at her he could see the baby she had once been, overlaid with all the other versions of her. He remembered laying her in her crib, he remembered walking her around the furniture, he remembered her practicing at the barre. He'd thought he might have lost sight of those earlier Millies, that he wouldn't recognise her, that she wouldn't recognise him, but memory was sturdier than he had dared to hope. When he'd carried her downstairs, he'd remembered she always liked to sit hitched on his right hip. She was far too big to be carried under normal circumstances and yet today it had not been a struggle, it did not feel awkward. She fitted. He recalled how she would coil her arm around his neck, planting it there like a vine, or a root. He'd remembered the smell of her. Not her shampoo, not the washing detergent on her clothes, her. Her skin, her breath. His baby. None of that had changed. She stared at him with such hope and confidence, she believed he could save her and protect her. He'd made her pancakes, he'd tucked her in, he'd kissed her forehead.

But he'd caused this. He'd put them in terrible danger.

'I'm so sorry,' he sobbed, again.

'This one isn't on you,' replied Daisy with a sigh.

He sat down heavily on the sofa and allowed his head to drop into his hands. 'You have to believe me when I say this is exactly what I was trying to protect you from. I never wanted this sort of violence or brutality to be in your world.'

Daisy remained standing, facing him. She shook her head. He couldn't read her expression. She looked despairing, disgusted. Disbelieving? 'You've never been able to protect me from anything,' she muttered, misery and grief emitting from every pore.

'But I tried.'

'When? When have you ever tried? You were always too drunk to take care of me and then you were in prison. How could you protect me from there?' She sounded bitter and angry, of course she did. He deserved that. He didn't know what to do. He wanted to hold her, as he'd held Millie, but he knew that wasn't right. He couldn't think clearly, he could smell the blood on the wall, on the floor. The room was too hot, they should open a window. It was all too much. Too heavy a burden. He couldn't carry it any longer. He had to set it down.

'I tried when I said I was driving,' he blurted.

Daisy looked at him, narrowed her eyes. 'What?'

'I tried to protect you. I took the blame then, but I wasn't driving. You were.'

56

Daisy

I have heard many of Simon's lies over the years. Lies about whether he stopped off for a drink after work, lies about how many he'd had, lies about whether he's spent our savings in pubs and bars. But this doesn't feel like a lie.

I have had dreams. So many and so vivid, especially since Millie's birthday, and with increasing frequency since I visited Simon in prison. I've been telling myself that my sleep is unsettled because of what Daryll is doing to me. My subconscious is dealing with the fact I'm under constant threat; of course I'm not sleeping well. I wake up and remind myself, it's not real. I tell myself that repeatedly. But it feels real. And I want to throw up. I want to bite my arms and pound my head. If I hurt her. If Simon was punished unfairly. After these dreams I get up and I do everything I usually do. I walk into the bathroom and turn on the shower. I pick up the toothbrush and somehow I do not jab the handle into my eyes but, if the dream was a memory, I would want to do that. I walk down the stairs. I do not throw myself down them as I should if the dream was real. I do not hurl plate after plate at the wall to hear them smash satisfyingly.

Because I was not driving. He was.

Simon instantly stands up, moves towards me. 'Forget what I've just said. Forget it. Of course I was driving.'

'No, you weren't,' I whisper. His face collapses.

'I just said that to hurt you,' he insists.

'No, you were finally telling the truth. I remember.'

He reached forward and put on the radio. He turned up the volume. The car was practically shaking. I leaned forward to turn it off, but he lunged at me and pushed my hands out of the way. I am in the driver's seat. I realised it was safest not to struggle with him. I needed to keep my two hands on the wheel. The mindless, pointless, clubbing tune hurt my head, it was hard to concentrate. He was making accusations. Crazy, insulting accusations. He said I'd had an affair with Luke. Because Luke is blonde. My head was full of Daryll. Him grabbing my wrist, pulling me out of Sophie's room, into Fran's. What would he have done if Luke hadn't interrupted us? What might he still do to me? I was so scared. So lost. The weather was horrendous. The windscreen wipers swished backwards and forwards, backwards and forwards. Simon screamed at me.

Millie? She shouldn't have been in the street at that time of night. She just stepped out.

The world stopped.

'I did it.'

Simon looks horrified. 'You're wrong, Daisy. You feel sad, full of grief and guilt because you let *me* drive. Your mind is playing tricks on you. You're making false memories, mixing up dream and fears with reality.'

'I'm not wrong,' I say with determination. He's right, my mind has been playing tricks on me for three years. I have mixed up dreams and fears with reality. But now the void is filling. 'I remember the thud, her body against the car.'

'When *I* hit her,' he insists.

'You pulled me into the passenger seat. I remember you pulling at my shoulders. I never understood that, until now, I thought it was people pulling me away from her that I remembered.'

'No,' he mutters, but he doesn't sound convincing.

'Stop lying to me,' I whisper hoarsely. 'I need to know Simon, is it a dream? Or — ' I wait on the cliff edge. Part of me wants him to give me an alternative. To take the burden from me. But I know he can't. Not again. It would be another lie, he can't lie anymore. He doesn't say anything. He looks at the table between us. 'Or is it a memory?' I whisper, closing my eyes. To stop the tears, so as not to have to see him.

'What do you believe?' he asks.

I open my eyes. My lungs are burning. 'I was driving,' I admit quietly. 'You didn't hurt Millie. I did.' The confession sits between us. Heavy and staggering but determined and vitally important. I wait to see what he will do with it.

'I'm sorry. I'm sorry. I never meant to tell you. I hadn't planned on doing so. Now it's all for nothing. The time I served because you will still — '

'Feel guilty.' I finish his sentence for him. 'Hate myself.'

He shakes his head slowly. It's a forlorn movement and it fills me with pity and admiration. It's been so long since I felt anything other than anger or disappointment for Simon. It almost floors me. He looks horrified, stumped. 'But Daisy, you shouldn't. You mustn't. You have to understand, *I'm* the one who deserved to be in prison. Who needed to be there. I dried out, you see, Daisy. And out here, people needed you. No one needed me here. Ever.'

But he's wrong about that.

I'm shaking, my knees buckle. He lowers me into a seat. I try not to wince, not to draw attention to the fact it hurts to sit down. Simon kneels at my feet.

'I couldn't let you go in there, Daisy. Because of people like the Dales. Or whoever the female equivalent might have been. It was my choice. It was my decision. I don't want you to feel bad about it, not for a moment. I don't regret it. At least, I didn't until now. Now, it means I led them to your door.'

'Who are the Dales?' I ask. I can't follow him.

'The men who did this to you. I wouldn't do something they wanted me to. They think I owe them. Look, it doesn't matter. I'm just so, so sorry. You do believe that, don't you?'

I take a deep breath. 'I don't know who the Dales are, Simon. They sound like trouble. But Daryll Lainbridge did this to me. Not your prison people.'

Simon looks stunned. 'Daryll Lainbridge? The

Daryll you went to university with?'
I nod and then whisper, 'He's hurt me before.'
'But why?' I lift my head. I watch as realisation dawns on him. He sees it in my eyes. All of it. He sees through the lies I had to tell and finds the truth. 'Where does he live? I need an address? Do you have a car? Give me the keys.'

57

Simon

He had never felt such cold white fury in his entire life. His rage was such that he felt transformed. No longer a man but now an animal, a hunter. He had no barriers, no walls. He was going to find Daryll Lainbridge and he was going to kill him. He imagined knocking on the man's door, him opening it and then whoosh, Simon would beat him, and he would keep beating him until he lay on the floor, lifeless, the sack of shit he no doubt was. He wished he had a gun, he would shoot him point blank. It would be quick and Lainbridge didn't deserve quick, but Simon would at least feel certain that the job was done. He didn't have a gun, however. Then a knife. He could stop and buy a knife. He wanted to plunge it, time after time, into the man. He wanted his blood to splatter up walls, on to ceilings.

It didn't matter that this man was Millie's biological father. That mattered not a jot to Simon. He wasn't jealous or insulted. This wasn't about his pride or his place. This was about Daisy, one hundred percent Daisy. What she had endured. It was unthinkable. That could not go unpunished. It would not.

Lainbridge lived on a quiet, leafy, street, just a mile or so from where Daisy lived. On either side of the road, the street was lined with parked cars: posh, wide cars, that were parked confidently, inconsiderately, leaving too much space between each one. There was no room for him to park. Lainbridge lived at number 32. Simon stared at the door; it was shiny, painted navy. There were bay trees either side of the entrance. It didn't look like the home of a rapist. No doubt, Lainbridge had depended upon how respectable and charming people found him. He depended on his shiny door and his bay trees to draw a cloak over the vileness, the cruelty, arrogance and entitlement in his heart, in his fists, in his head and body. Simon watched the door and thought about just leaving his car in the middle of the street, blocking the road entirely. He didn't care if he caused a traffic jam, he just wanted to confront Lainbridge. Simon was just about to turn off the engine when the shiny door swung open.

Lainbridge emerged. Simon recognised him, not so much from that fateful night but from before then. Things had come back to him since he became sober. He noted the man's height, his blondness. He looked rested, serene, a horrible contrast to Daisy and Millie. He was whistling. It was insulting. Simon watched as he crossed the road, walked to the corner shop. Simon waited and only a couple of minutes later, Lainbridge emerged with a newspaper tucked under his arm, a broadsheet, he was carrying a protein drink. Lainbridge crossed the road, headed back towards his house, no doubt anticipating a lazy Saturday morning. He glanced at Simon's car. Probably wondering why someone was sat in the middle of the road, running his engine. Simon liked to think that they made eye contact, that Lainbridge recognised him in that last moment.

Before he put his foot down on the accelerator.

58

Daisy

When Simon returns, he knocks on the back door. I quickly unlock it and let him in. He appears wired, alert, purposeful. He doesn't tell me what has occurred but starts to ask questions instead.

'Is Millie still asleep?'

'Yes,' I whisper back. I'm still struggling to find my voice.

'What were your plans for today? If I hadn't turned up?'

'I was supposed to be going to Rose's for lunch and then . . . ' I break off but decide I might as well tell him. There is no room for any more lies between us. I don't want there to be. 'Millie and I have tickets to fly to Hamburg this evening.'

'A holiday?'

'One-way tickets,' I confess. I watch as he takes this in, understands.

He nods, looks to his feet. 'OK, well you need to repack those cases.' He points to the clothes that are strewn all over the floor. Daryll threw them there in a frenzy. 'We must tidy the house and then you need to go to Rose's as planned. 'Here,' he hands me the car keys. 'I popped your car through the wash. It's all shiny now.'

We work quietly and efficiently together. I repack, and Simon washes the walls and floor, tries to remove any traces of blood. I watch as he dips the soiled cloth into a bucket of water and the water turns pink. The more he scrubs, dips, wrings and scrubs again, the deeper pink the water turns. 'We'll need to paint over this,' he mumbles. 'I'll bury the cat, you sweep up the broken ornaments. There can't be any sign of a disturbance. Then I'll go and buy paint and do the painting whilst you are at Rose's. Does that sound OK to you?'

'Yes.' I'm grateful to him for his focus, his clarity. I'm also grateful that he asked my opinion, it feels a long time since I've been consulted on anything. It feels respectful, equal.

'I have to get back to Lucy's by 4 p.m. The probation officer will be calling by then.'

I nod and start to sweep up the broken china. I watch as he carefully picks up the shoebox, inside which lies the poor kitten. He turns to me. 'What was his name?' he asks tenderly.

'Eric. Eric Cloud.'

I wake Millie and tell her to get showered and dressed. When the house looks close to normal, Simon lets Millie come downstairs. He hugs her tightly and then kisses the top of her head. I can see he doesn't want to let her go, but he checks his watch and says, 'You two need to get going. Go upstairs and check your room one last time, Millie, see if there's anything you might need to take with you on holiday.' As soon as she's out of the room he says, 'Take the car to Rose's.'

'I always take the tube,' I point out.

'Always or usually?'

I think about it. 'Usually.'

'OK, well if it's not unprecedented, take the car and then leave it at hers.'

'Why?'

'It's just better that it's not seen around here, or at least not straightaway. Leave it at Rose's and get the tube to the airport from hers. Tell her you want to leave it in her street, so she can keep an eye on it while you are away. If you don't come back, she'll think you were gifting it to her.'

'And what if I do come back?'

Something flickers across Simon's face. Hope, possibly. 'You should stay away until all your bruising has healed, at least.'

'How should I explain the bruises to Rose?'

'You can tell her whatever you want, whatever you need to. She's your sister, but we can't risk others seeing you like this.' I nod, beginning to understand how much he is trusting me. 'Is there a way I can reach you?' he asks.

'I don't have a phone anymore.'

'OK, well call Rose and I'll find a way of letting you know if it's safe to come back.'

I gasp. 'Can he still hurt me?' I ask, hating myself for trembling.

Simon shakes his head. 'No, never again.'

'You mean . . . ?'

'I think you should come back to England, Daisy. It might look suspicious if you disappear permanently, just after what's happened.'

I want to ask him if that's the only reason he

wants me to come back, but I don't have to because, very carefully, he leans towards me and kisses me on the forehead.

'If you come home, Daisy, I'll be waiting for both of you.'

59

Simon

'You cut that fine,' said Lucy, as she opened the door to Simon. 'Fifteen fifty-nine. The probation officer is due at four. Why have you got paint on your hands?'

Simon quickly walked to the kitchen and ran his hands under the tap, scrubbed them with a brillo pad. Lucy stood by, watching. She only left him when the doorbell rang.

The probation officer was accompanied by a policeman. Simon hadn't been expecting that. He didn't think it was usual. Luckily, Lucy had no idea what to expect under these circumstances, and so behaved with her usual imperturbable poise. The policeman was stern-faced and silent, the probation officer was chippy; he didn't like Lucy's beautiful house and beautiful neighbourhood. He did not believe this was a fair place for a man to serve his on-licence sentence. He would have preferred to see people banged up for the duration of their sentences, but if they had to be released into the community, he didn't like to think of them dwelling in such luxury. He also found Lucy attractive and he was the sort of man who thought being attracted to anyone was a weakness, being attracted to someone in this situation was unprofessional, so he covered it up with a blunt, terse tone.

'Of course, I won't be trekking out here every day. From now on, you will have to go to the police station. I'm just here to see everything's in order,' he told Simon. He did, after some persuasion, accept a cup of tea. 'Just usual tea. Builders,' he said gruffly, in a tone that suggested he believed fruit teas to be morally reprehensible. The police officer still hadn't said anything, other than 'yes' to milk and 'no' to sugar. Neither man accepted a slice of cake, although the police officer did ask, 'Make it yourself, did you?'

'Me? No, I'm not the baking type. I got it from local patisserie,' replied Lucy.

The probation officer wanted to see Simon's bedroom. He opened a few drawers, looked inside the wardrobe. Simon had no idea what he was searching for. He asked if Simon understood the rules of his curfew. Simon assured him he did.

As the men were about to leave, the policeman turned to Simon and said, 'Just one thing, Mr Barnes. Are you acquainted with a man called Daryll Lainbridge?' His tone was neutral but obviously calculated.

Simon tried to keep his breathing steady, to look as though he was wracking his brains. He understood now why the policeman had accompanied the probation officer. They were on to him. His hands felt clammy. He put them on his hips so he could furtively wipe the sweat away. He might have to shake hands in a moment. 'The name does ring a bell.'

'I know a Daryll Lainbridge,' piped up Lucy.

'A friend of yours, is he?'

Simon noticed that Lucy didn't answer the question, not exactly. 'We went to university together.'

'I understand he's a friend of Mrs Barnes too,' said the police officer checking his notes.

'We all went to the same university.'

'She's down as his next of kin.'

Lucy didn't look too surprised by this, but Simon knew she was a cool customer. She matter-of-factly pointed out, 'They're not related.'

'Well, next of kin isn't a legal term here in the UK, Miss.'

'I'm married,' said Lucy.

'Sorry?'

'I'm not a Miss.'

'Oh, Madam, sorry.' Simon could see that it took every ounce of Lucy's self-control not to roll her eyes at the casual condescension. 'Next of kin doesn't even need to be a relative. Just a person you consider important. We are trying to get hold of Mrs Barnes, but her phone is ringing out, we've had no luck.'

'I know she was going on holiday today, I'm not sure of timings. She might be on a plane right now,' Lucy explained.

'Oh, I see.' The policeman tapped his pen against his notepad. 'But you say you are a friend of Daryll Lainbridge too?'

'I said we went to university together. Why?'

'You might want to take a seat.'

'I'm perfectly fine standing.'

'Well, I'm sorry, Madam, but I have some distressing news. Mr Lainbridge is dead.'

Lucy gasped. Rubbed her forehead, slowly. 'I don't understand. When? How?'

'I'm afraid I'm not at liberty to share any details at this point.' The policeman turned to Simon. 'Where you have been today, Barnes?'

The question was brusque, designed to catch him off-guard and most certainly the only question the officer had ever wanted to ask from the moment he walked in the door. 'Here,' said Simon, with a casual shrug.

'All day?'

Simon almost hesitated. He wasn't sure what he was going to say or do. He had wanted to eradicate Daryll, that he was certain of. He hadn't thought beyond that. Did he want to get away with it, or did he want to be punished? What sort of punishment would be fair? He opened his mouth to answer but Lucy jumped in, 'I picked him up from prison this morning and I brought him straight home with me. Neither of us have left the house all day.'

'Not even to visit the local patisserie?' the police officer asked.

'I bought the cake yesterday,' replied Lucy.

Epilogue

The death of Mr Daryll Lainbridge, as a result of a hit and run, was reported in the local north London papers and in a small paragraph, on the seventh page of the *Evening Standard*. The case was investigated and it was agreed that it was a horrific accident involving a driver with no moral compass, someone who panicked, decided to save his own skin. There was one police officer, Sergeant Heidi Kent, who continued to think there was more to it than that. She did not believe in coincidences and was unsettled by the fact that Mr Lainbridge had been knocked down the very day Mr Simon Barnes was released from prison. Mrs Daisy Barnes was named as Lainbridge's next of kin, so clearly they were in a relationship of some kind, Sergeant Kent reasoned. Her daughter was set to inherit his entire estate, following a DNA test, so an ongoing, long term relationship. That was a motive for murder.

Unfortunately for Kent, there were no witnesses to the incident. Only one woman came forward with anything. She said she saw a dark car leave the road at high speed at approximately the right time. She wasn't much help in the end, her baby grandson had been crying and so she was mostly concentrating on him. She had only glanced up for a second.

'He's not normally a fussy baby,' she explained.

'Can you confirm the gender of the driver?'

'Yes, a man,' she nodded, confidently.

'And can you give us a description of the man?'

The witness's assurance immediately vanished. 'My eyes are not as good as they once were. I keep meaning to get my prescription updated. I think he had a beard, but perhaps not. I suppose he must have, they all do nowadays, don't they? The young men. They all like a beard.'

'So, a beard?'

'Probably. Not certainly.'

'You say a young man?'

The grandma chuckled. 'Well everyone seems young to me, love. I'm seventy-two. The grandchild I was looking after, he's my ninth.'

'Could you give an approximate age?'

'Well, less than fifty.'

The police officers conducting the interview had shared a look, and the grandmother wished she hadn't bothered coming forward. It was a waste of her time and they didn't seem grateful. 'Hair colour?'

'Brown, or black. It was only a glance,' she said huffily, punishing them for the side-eyeing.

'Skin colour?'

'I'm not sure. I don't really notice skin colour,' she replied, looking affronted that they might consider her racist, the sort of person who *noticed* skin colour. 'He might have been white, or brown. Or white with a tan. I suppose. I don't think he was black.' She looked uncomfortable.

'The colour of the car then? Do you notice the colour of cars?'

'It was dark. Maybe black, or navy, possibly a deep purple.'

'And a make?' It didn't seem too hopeful.

'I'm not very good with car makes. You know, it could possibly have been dark grey.'

It wasn't much to go on. Practically nothing. The road wasn't covered by CCTV, the police found it infuriating that half the world was protesting that their privacy was under threat, complaining that there were cameras everywhere, but law enforcers usually ran a blank when hoping to depend on footage for a case.

Sergeant Kent thoroughly pursued her hunch that Simon Barnes was the most likely suspect, but he had a rock-steady alibi in Mrs Lucy Hewitt-Jones, which was ratified by her husband Mr Peter Hewitt-Jones. Kent checked out Daisy Barnes too, but she had been at her sister's home at the time of the incident, in Holland Park, miles away. The sister corroborated her story, as did the brother-in-law and nephews. The boys couldn't give an exact time as to when Daisy arrived for lunch but agreed, 'Mum will know for sure, whatever she says will be spot on. She's a stickler for detail.'

Anyway, the case for the hit and run being premeditated, and something more than a tragic accident, was weakened when the seriousness of the relationship between Mrs Barnes and Mr Lainbridge came under question. The DNA test, that was a condition of inheritance, proved that Millie Barnes was not Daryll Lainbridge's child. Sergeant Kent had received this information from Lainbridge's solicitor and requested that she attend the meeting where Daisy Barnes was given this news. At this point, her Inspector had told her to give it up, let this one go, move onto something more pressing. But she was a good reader of people and she wanted to be there to see for herself how this Daisy Barnes might react to the news.

But the Barnes woman was hard to read. Cool. Collected. Sergeant Kent thought there was something in the eyes, a widening, that suggested surprise, and then a lift. She looked relieved. Pleased. But Sergeant Kent could have been imagining it. It wasn't anything to go on. The matter was dropped. The case closed.

Daisy

I didn't want to check Millie's DNA. Not at all. The last thing I wanted was for her to be forever connected to Daryll Lainbridge, even if it did mean she could inherit hundreds of thousands of pounds. I didn't want a penny of his money. Lucy, not unsurprisingly, had a very different view. She badgered me. She pointed out that the money was no use to him now, that he'd written a will and this was what he wanted.

'I don't care what he wanted.'

'No, I don't suppose you do,' she admitted. 'I'm just saying that Simon and you are never going to be able to give Millie that sort of cash, so why shouldn't she have it?'

'But she doesn't need that sort of cash,' I argued. 'She has everything she needs: a mum and dad, a home.'

'You are a very romantic person, Daisy, but people do need money. When she grows up, this sort of money would make a huge difference to her life.'

'She can earn it, like everyone else. I don't want anything from him. I don't want to have to tell her she came from that monster, and I will have to tell her if she inherits his estate.'

Lucy paused and considered. 'You don't have to tell her he's her father, just make something up.'

'No, never again,' I said firmly. 'If there's one thing I've learnt from all of this, it's that lies and cover-ups only muddy already murky waters.'

I don't want there to be any more lies in our home. Only truths.

Simon and I are doing so well. One day at a time. He's still dry and we're both still honest. I want our home to stay honest.

But then, the months passed and I started to wonder, was I being honest? Which is why I told Simon the whole truth. As hard as it was for me to do so, as hard as it was for him to hear.

We sat in the kitchen, a large jug of iced tea on the breakfast bar between us and I began. It was hard to find the words, harder even than speaking to Lucy about it. The words caught like splinters in my mouth. But then he took my hand, ran his fingers over mine.

'Take your time,' he murmured. 'We have all the time you need.' So I reminded him that Connie and Luke once threw a circus-themed party. 'There was a magician and clowns. Right?'

'Yes,' I confirm. It's surprises me that he remembers that detail. I tell him everything I told Lucy, about Daryll cornering me, insisting on talking to me about his love life. 'There was a queue for the downstairs cloakroom and for the loo in the family bathroom, you know how it is at their parties, so many people. But do you remember Connie and Luke had only just converted their attic into a big bedroom with an en suite? I knew few people would be aware of the spare bathroom at the top and so I took myself away from the crowds. As I climbed up to the third floor, I passed Connie and Luke on the stairway, coming out of their bedroom.'

'Up to their usual, were they?' Simon asked, with a knowing grin.

They are rarely together at a party, normally such great hosts, always looking after their guests, except they have a tradition.

'They were grinning at one another, giddy. So yes, I guessed they were just returning to the throng after secreting themselves away for party sex.'

It was their thing. Always has been. A quickie in the middle of the celebrations. Originally, when they first met, they did this because they couldn't keep their hands off one another, then as time went by, they did it for thrills, because it's daring and sexy, because it's a way to put two fingers up to the conventions expected of parents. I briefly considered pausing to chat, take the opportunity to tease them. We were good enough friends that I could have done that.

'I always wonder how differently everything would have turned out if I had stopped to chat to them. To tease them. But I was hot, the place was noisy, Daryll's conversation had been draining. I just wanted a few moments alone to collect myself. So I just apologised to Connie for using her private loo, explained I couldn't be bothered with the queue. Of course, she urged me to go ahead. Luke barely looked at me, he was kissing her neck.

'I peed, and that's when I saw it. The condom full of sperm, neatly knotted, just lying on the sink unit. Obviously, it was destined for the bin but somehow Luke had just left it lying about. My first thought was yuk, icky, eye roll. I gingerly picked up the condom, ready to throw it in the bin so that no one else would encounter it. But then I thought about our situation.' The failed IVF. The heartbreaking, relentless longing. Simon's drinking. 'And I thought this could be the answer. This is all we need. Just something someone threw away.'

I dared to look at Simon at this point and he nodded, he understood. He squeezed my fingers gently. 'The answer to our prayers.'

'The answer to everything. So, I inseminated myself.' I didn't think it would work. Not really. But I hoped it might. I lay on the cold bathroom floor with my feet in the air for five minutes. 'Then washed my hands, checked my make-up. I unlocked the bathroom door, planning to return to the party to find you, maybe persuade you to dance with me. And there was Daryll, waiting for me.'

Simon stood up, walked around the breakfast bar and took me into his arms. He tenderly kissed my head and then, without any malice, any pain, just as a matter of observation, he murmured, 'So she's Luke's, after all. I was right.'

'No, Simon, you're wrong. She's yours. She's ours.'

Acknowledgements

I have so many incredible people to thank.

Firstly, thank you Jonny Geller, the dream-maker, for twenty stupendous years of continual support, advice and true friendship. I couldn't have had the career I've had without you, and you know what? I just wouldn't have wanted to. I love it that we've been together every step of the way.

Thank you, Kate Mills, you are everything I could have ever hoped for in an editor and publisher: you are simply brilliant. Thank you for being a unique combination of determination, dedication, honesty and creativity. I'm so incredibly lucky to have you. The same goes for Lisa Milton: you tremendous women! You are the lynchpin of the powerhouse that is HQ, HarperCollins. I have such respect for you both.

Thank you to Charlie Redmayne for being an involved, supportive and astute CEO.

I'm so delighted to be working with such fantastic teams in the UK and across the globe. I am thoroughly grateful for, and appreciative of, the talent and commitment of every single person involved in this book's existence. I've always believed that if a book is lucky enough to be successful, then that's because there's an enormous team of people doing their jobs incredibly well. That's so true of Sophie Calder, Anna Derkacz, Georgina Green, Eleanor Goymer, Darren Shoffren, Claire

Brett, Victoria Moynes, Jack Chalmers and Louise McGrory. Thank you all very much for your supreme professionalism and commitment.

I want to send another massive thank you across the seas to the amazing James Kellow, Loriana Sacilotto, Margaret Marbury, Leo McDonald, Carina Nunstedt, Celine Hamilton, Pauline Riccius, Anna Hoffmann, Birgit Salzmann, Eugene Ashton, Olinka Nell and Rahul Dixit. There are many others who I have yet to meet, but I know I'm so lucky that incredible professionals worldwide are giving my books their love and attention. It's so ridiculously exciting. Thank you.

Thank you to all my readers, bloggers, reviewers, retailers, librarians and fellow authors who have supported this book. I'm so glad you continue to get passionate about reading because, without you, there would be little point in me sitting in my office every day making stuff up!

Thank you to my mum, dad, sister, nieces and nephew, who are continually supportive of everything I do, who love me and my books whether the sales are good, bad or indifferent!

Thank you, Jimmy and Conrad, no woman could ever hope for more support from a husband or son. I am utterly and completely grateful for you both.

Finally, I'd like to warmly thank all the people who gave me an understanding of police procedure and prison life. Clare Henson, Adam Gale, Louise Daniels and Zoe, the prison librarian known to me as ZoeFruitcake. You were so incredibly generous with your time and knowledge. I'm in awe of the incredible work you do and am so grateful that you found the space to help me. If I've made any mistakes in presenting or recording the reality of what you do, I apologise in advance. They are entirely mine! Thank you to Michelle Harries, Leigh Fleeman, and Michelle Ratcliffe who also offered advice, or their spouse's time! I couldn't have written this book without you.

Other titles published by Ulverscroft:

I INVITED HER IN

Adele Parks

When Mel hears from a long-lost friend in need of help, she doesn't hesitate to invite her to stay. Mel and Abi were best friends back in the day, sharing the highs and lows of student life, until Mel's unplanned pregnancy caused her to drop out of her studies. Now, seventeen years later, Mel and Abi's lives couldn't be more different. Mel is happily married and has a chaotic but happy family home with three children. Abi, meanwhile, followed her lover to LA for a glamorous life of parties, celebrity and indulgence. Everything was perfect — until she discovered her partner had been cheating on her. What Abi needs now is a true friend to lean on. And what better place than Mel's house, with her lovely kids, and supportive husband . . .

IF YOU GO AWAY

Adele Parks

1914: Young Vivian is hurried into a pedestrian marriage to hush a scandal — and war breaks out on her wedding day. Quick to escape the disappointment of matrimony, her husband Aubrey immediately enlists, and Vivian has no alternative but to take up the running of his estate . . . Howard, a brilliant young playwright, rushes to the front in an attempt to understand his fellow man's eagerness to fight a faceless enemy — and finds he wants no part of it. In 1916, when conscription becomes law, he refuses to enlist, becoming one of the most notorious conscientious objectors of the time — and a threat to the government. Narrowly escaping a death sentence by agreeing to take on essential work on Vivian's farm, it is only then that Howard understands what is really worth fighting for . . .

GONE

Leona Deakin

When sixteen-year-old Jane's mother goes missing, the only thing she leaves behind is a card saying 'Happy 1st Birthday' with the message inside: 'YOUR GIFT IS THE GAME. DARE TO PLAY?' Frustrated by the lack of interest from the police, Jane goes online and makes a chilling discovery: the same card has been discovered in four other missing persons cases. She turns to a family friend for help, former MI6 agent Marcus Jameson, and soon he and his partner, psychologist and private detective Dr Augusta Bloom, are on the case. As Bloom delves into the lives of the missing people, she finds something that binds them all. And that something makes them very dangerous indeed. What if, this time, they are the ones she should fear?